Drummer's
BEAT
SATAN'S DEVILS #2

COPYRIGHT

AUTHOR'S NOTE

Drummer's Beat is the second in the Satan's Devils MC Series, but can be read as a standalone.

I've been overwhelmed by the reception given to the first in the series, *Turning Wheels*, and the support and encouragement to continue with the Satan's Devils series. *Turning Wheels* was meant to be a sole spin-off novel form the Blood Brothers series, but those bikers all kept screaming at me to have their own stories told. Already there are more books in the pipeline.

If you're new to MC books, you may find there are terms that you haven't heard before, so I've included a glossary to help along the way. I hope you get drawn into this mysterious and dark world in the same way I have done–there will be further books in the Satan's Devils series which I hope you'll want to follow.

If you've picked this book up because, like me, you read anything MC, I hope you'll enjoy it for what it is, a fictional insight into the underground culture of alpha men and their bikes.

CAST OF CHARACTERS

Officers

Drummer – President
Wraith – Vice President
Heart – Secretary
Dollar – Treasurer
Peg – Sergeant-at-arms
Blade – Enforcer
Mouse – Computer Expert

Patched Members

Beef
Bullet
Buster
Dart
Joker
Lady
Rock
Slick
Shooter
Tongue

Viper

Prospects
Marsh
Roadrunner

Old Ladies & Children
Carmen (Bullet's)
Sandy (Viper's)
Crystal (Heart's): Amy
Sophie (Wraith's)

Sweet Butts
Allie
Jill
Pussy

Deceased Members
Adam
Buster
Hank

CHAPTER ONE

*D*rummer...

"What d'ya reckon, Wraith?" As I cock my head to one side, I nod to indicate I'd appreciate my VP's input on this discussion. After all, it was his old lady who bore the brunt of our mistake last time we allowed someone to transfer to the Satan's Devils' Tucson Chapter. She almost ended up being raped. When Wraith stays silent, I glance over at him, raising my eyebrow as I see him tapping his fingers against his chin.

I've always known Red to be straight with us, but Wraith's friendship with the president of the Vegas Chapter goes back much further than mine. They prospected together until Red moved on and up the ranks. If anyone can spot he's pulling a fast one, using us as a dumping ground for members he wants to get rid of, it's my VP who'll be able to.

Right now, both men are staring at each other. "How did he get that fuckin' handle?" Wraith's eyes narrow.

Red grins as he takes a swig of his beer. "Well, he can be a bit of a joker, but he's serious enough when he needs to be."

"He better be," I growl. "And what kind of idiocy does he get up to?" Putting sugar in a brother's gas tank would not go down well back at the compound.

Now Red shrugs. "He's not into practical jokes, or anything that would cause any damage, but he can keep us on our toes. It's all verbal. Just give him a slap down occasionally to pull him back into line." As the grin fades from his face, I see he's being serious now. "Drum, I wouldn't pass my rejects on to you. Joker's a good man. Yeah, he comes across a bit shallow, but he'll have your six. He's had mine often enough."

"He wants to move to Tucson, why?" Wraith is still being cautious.

Red shrugs. "No mystery there. He's got a sister down that way and her old man's getting a bit handsy. Joker wants to be close so he can keep an eye on it."

That sounds reasonable, and if we patch him over, he'll have the backing of the brothers if he needs it. That's the way we work. "He's your road captain?" That's the bit that interests me the most. At the mother chapter we haven't had anyone in that position for a while. When Red nods to confirm it, I ask the other important question, "And losing him won't leave you undermanned?"

The Vegas prez shakes his head. "Nah, I've got someone else in mind for that position. It won't leave me short, Drum."

I tap my fingers on the table, thinking. We lost a member and a prospect in our recent and still raw battle with the now non-existent Rock Demons out of Phoenix. Oh, we managed to get the better of them that time, but it made me appreciate just how much we needed to build up the mother chapter, again. Hence our recruitment drive and our offer to let brothers from other charters patch over, as long as they are going to be a good fit. This Joker fucker sounds like he might be just what we're looking for.

"Wraith?" I prompt, waiting on my VP's opinion.

He thinks for a moment, then lifts his chin toward me.

That's all the answer I need. "Okay then. Joker's in as well as Lady." Saying the name of the man we've just discussed I can't help but shake my head. Who the fuck would go by that handle?

Oh, the name Lady suits him down to the fucking ground. He's a pretty boy, tall, slim and lithe, looks like a breath of wind would blow him over. But Red had arranged for us to see him in the ring where I'd watched him take down men twice his size, impressing even me.

"You're absolutely sure you can manage without them?" Wraith questions his old friend.

Red waves his hand in dismissal. "Yeah man, I've got two prospects ready to patch in. They've proved themselves and we'll soon be up to speed. And a couple of hangarounds waiting in the wings ready to take their places."

I'm not surprised—Vegas is a draw for many with its bright lights and opportunities. Red just has a hard job keeping the men in line and spotting the ones with a likely gambling addiction.

"Right, that's fuckin' it then." I'm happy. We've picked up two, hopefully useful, members today.

Reaching behind him, Red opens a mini-fridge and pulls out three fresh beers. After handing them over, we break off the tops and all take a drink. Pointing his bottle in my direction, Red asks, "You heading off now? You're welcome to stay another night."

"Yeah, it's nearly a seven-hour ride so if we head out now, we'll be back by evening." We'd partied Vegas style last night. I'd taken advantage of the sweet butts, though Wraith had declined. Christ, he handed over his balls when he hooked up with Soph, his old lady. A trap I'm never going to fall into. It makes me shudder just thinking about it. Why would you commit to one woman when as a biker you've got all the pussy you could wish for? Especially, as in my case, I'm wearing the president patch.

Beers drained and dispensed with, cuts rolled up in our packs and exchanged for anonymous sweatshirts, well, anonymous except for the discreet Satan's Devils' Tucson Chapter logo on the back. With the SDTC badge warning those in the know not to mess with us, we take our leave of Red and the brothers in the Vegas Chapter. Joker and Lady will be following on in a couple of days once they've got their shit organised.

Our journey back to Tucson is uneventful, allowing me to indulge in the satisfaction of a long ride with the wind in my hair blowing away the last vestiges of my over-indulgence last night and the freedom of the black asphalt beneath my wheels. It's been a while since I've been able to get out on a road trip. Being prez means I'm normally stuck resolving problems from behind my desk, so with a feeling of liberation, I sit back and enjoy the open road. When we enter the borders of our territory, we stop at one of our new locations we've settled on to put on our cuts. It's only recently we started rotating our stopping off points. We had learned the lesson of the risks we ran having a regular place when the Rock Demons had caught us out and Hank, one of our prospects, had lost his life as a result.

Getting back on my bike, I see Wraith's got his phone to his ear. Delaying switching on my engine, I can hear his side of the conversation. Not that it's much.

"Shit, Peg, just what we fuckin' need."

"Yeah, I'll meet you there."

"Yeah, an hour should do it."

I raise a quizzical eyebrow as he ends the call. "Problems?"

"One of the strippers has had an altercation with the new fuckin' bouncer. He laid his fuckin' hands on her. I'll meet Peg and go see what damage has been done."

I draw in a breath and look around before I say something I shouldn't. We might own a strip club, but we treat the women well. None of us like it if a stripper's manhandled, especially by one of our employees. Unfortunately, we've just had to replace a bouncer as Roadrunner, as he's become known, now only works part-time since he's come to prospect for us. "Peg and you gonna sort it?"

"That's the plan. I'll meet him at the end of the road."

The road Wraith's referring to is the half-mile asphalt track that leads up to our unusual compound, a burned-out vacation resort we bought dirt cheap many years ago and have since done up to make it a biker's dream home. *Can't I get one moment of peace around here?* There's always seems to be something or other to get to grips with, but at least I've got good men behind me to handle that shit. So, I wave my hand, giving Wraith the signal we should mount up and continue on home. As we get to the turnoff, the VP peels off and heads out in the direction of Tucson. I continue along alone, slowing my speed now. Half of me is anxious to get back to the compound, while the other half is reluctant to give up the freedom of the road and pick up the onerous burden of being prez of the mother chapter. I've only been gone a couple of days, but there'll probably be forty-eight hours' worth of trouble waiting for me to resolve.

Knocking it down a gear, I breathe in the air which I swear smells sweeter around here. Apart from the rumbling of my engine and the chirping of the cicadas, there's no other sound disturbing the peace and quiet here in the foothills rising above Tucson. The air's still warm, but cooling now that we're getting into the evening, and it won't be long until full darkness falls. A drink or two... or three in the clubhouse, and then I'll take one of the sweet butts to bed with me. Allie or Pussy, or both maybe. Hmm. My cock starts to harden in anticipation.

Wait! What the fuck is that?

Halfway up the track there's a strange bike by the side of the road, and a man standing beside it. Someone I don't know. All my senses now on high alert and easing my gun from its holster, I slow my speed to a crawl, watching for any sign of a threat or weapon. As I draw closer, I let out a slow whistle, my eyes transfixed on the bike. It's only a fucking Vincent Black Shadow! Dating from the 1950s, one of the most iconic bikes ever built. It's in a fairly good state of restoration too, and probably worth something approaching a hundred thousand dollars. A bitch to ride though, and I take my hat off to the biker who's able to handle it.

All thoughts of who, why, and what the unknown biker is doing halfway up to my fucking compound disappear as she turns to face me and I get a look at her features. Yes, *her*. It's a fucking broad!

Pulling my Harley to a halt a few yards behind, my gun still in my hand, I'm wary in case of danger. *Could this be a set up? Have the fucking Demons sent a bitch to kill me?* Oh, yeah, we got most of them when we blew up their clubhouse, but I still feel twitches in my back when I remember the couple we let escape. There's no way I'm going to let long brown locks framing a face which can only be described as fucking gorgeous knock me off my guard.

The girl is staring at me, returning my scrutiny. Then, as she takes a step toward me, I draw up my gun and point it at her.

Bravely, she ignores the weapon. "Oh, thank Christ! I thought this place was deserted." Her arm airily waves around, indicating the desert surrounding us. "I've been here for over an hour."

It crosses my mind that Peg should have passed her, but then I remember he'd come up from the city to wait for Wraith and not down from the compound. But the thought doesn't make me feel any easier. Had she been waiting for *me*? Glancing around, I can't see anyone else and apart from a few sprawling prickly pears and an ancient saguaro, there's nothing but open desert and nowhere for someone to hide.

While an ambush this close to the compound is unlikely, my gun remains steadily on target, my aim unwavering. Glaring, I instruct, "I don't know what the fuck you're doing here, girl, but you better start talking. And you'd better have a good fuckin' story."

Her eyes widen and focus on my hand as if just now noticing my weapon for the first time. She swallows a couple of times, and I can see her throat working, but no words come out.

"Think you might have taken a wrong turn, darlin'," I start, hoping the fuck that's all it is. "This road only leads to one place. The Satan's Devils' compound."

Now, she's looking at my cut, and then she nods and a tentative smile spreads over her face. It only serves to make her look even more attractive, and my dick twitches in appreciation. "That's good. I'm in the right place then."

The right place?

"You looking to be a sweet butt?" I sneer. It might not be anything I'd take objection to, and the brothers would love her, but it seems unlikely. The bike, her appearance—oh, she's showing she's got the right equipment—her leather jeans hugging her in all the right places, highlighting a nice tight ass. She's removed her jacket probably due to the heat, which allows me to see her tight t-shirt hugging some very attractive looking curves. But there's something about the way that she carries herself that makes my suggestion seem doubtful. Something she immediately confirms.

"No way. I'm no whore." She almost spits out the denial.

Well I can cross that explanation off, but that still leaves the question—she's heading for my compound, but why? "Think you better start talking," I tell her, impatiently. Though the light's starting to fail, I can see her well enough in the beam from my running lights. I'm anxious to get back to that beer and that warm wet pussy I've been looking forward to, but I don't want to leave any stranger out here, not so close to our club.

She looks down and indicates her bike. "I've run out of gas."

Well if that's all it is, it's easy enough to solve. "I'll get some brought down to you." Running an auto-shop out of the compound, we've always got gas on hand, and one of the brothers wouldn't mind bringing it down. Especially when they catch sight of her. A low unintentional growl escapes me as I suddenly know I don't want any of those fuckers near her. No, I'll go get the gas myself and then she can be on her way—in the opposite fucking direction.

Her eyes light up. "That would be great!" And then her face falls. "But I can't pay for it."

Now we might be getting somewhere. "If you're looking for work darlin', you've come to the wrong fuckin' place. Unless you want to earn on your back."

Retreating a step, she places her hand almost lovingly on the seat of the Black Shadow, as though seeking its support. As she strokes the plastic again, I find my cock swelling, wondering what it would feel like if her hand was touching me in such a familiar way. The idea of taking her up to the compound myself and throwing her down on my bed enters my mind. It wouldn't be any hardship having someone like her under me tonight.

But why is she here? The incongruity of the situation strikes me like a slap around the head. *You don't find an attractive woman halfway up to your clubhouse with an expensive bike for no fucking reason.* And until I find out what's going on, she's going nowhere near my club.

CHAPTER TWO

$\mathcal{S}$am...

If my bike wasn't my baby, I'd have walked up to the compound myself. It couldn't be that far away, but I wasn't going to leave my most precious possession unattended by the side of the road. I'd tried pushing it, but on the slight uphill incline it proved an impossible task, at least for me. I'm not a big woman, and this time the bike beat me. Shit, why did I have to run out of gas here, so close to my goal?

It should have been easy; I was going to fill up when I got to Tucson, but wouldn't you know it? This road trip keeps getting better and better, giving me one problem after another, and the bitch who stole my wallet from me last night was the final straw. I'm now penniless and unable to pay for anything until I get replacement cards from my bank. At least I keep my license and identity cards separate, that's one blessing, I guess.

Right now, the only option I seem to have is to persuade this rough biker to let me up to the compound. *Not that things are going to become any simpler when I get there.* And I can't begin to predict the reception I'll receive when I break my news.

The biker has removed his helmet, allowing me to see he's probably somewhere toward the latter end of his thirties, as there are signs of greying at his temple and white speckles peppering his short beard. He's got the most beautiful steely grey eyes, but his face seems fixed in a permanent scowl. Or maybe that's just the outward sign that he doesn't trust me. Then my eye's fall on the patch on his cut which tells me he's the freaking president of the club. Oh shit. Why hadn't someone else come along? Someone who might have been easier to convince.

He's training his eyes on me, and it takes all that I have to meet his gaze and not to reel away from the intensity of his hardened stare. "I think you better start talking, darlin'." He's still holding that gun, although at least he's relaxed it down by his side. But were I to make just one wrong move...

I sigh, and this time I do look down before making my decision. Had it been anyone else, I might have concocted something just to get me inside the gates, but this man's the top of the food chain. I understand nothing but the truth will do, instinctively knowing he would quickly sniff out any fabrication. Returning my eyes to him, I wonder if he's even going to believe me. My reality sounds fanciful enough after all.

Leaning back on the Vincent, idly noticing the plastic of the seat is still warm despite the cooling of the air around me, I take a deep breath and begin, "My name's Samantha," correcting quickly, "Sam." No one's ever called me anything else. Samantha's too much of a mouthful and far too girly for me.

"I go by Drummer," he growls. "I'm the president of the Satan's Devils. So now the fuckin' introductions are out of the way, why are you here? And why are you heading for my clubhouse?"

It's hard not to notice the ownership he gives to it, and a shivery feeling inside me makes me wonder what it would be like to be owned by such a man. *Owned? For goodness' sake!* But I can't deny that deep controlling voice makes parts of me tingle, parts which really shouldn't be making themselves felt in this situation, and that are far too distracting. Swallowing a couple of times, as much to get my thoughts back on the right track as to try and elicit his help, I start once again to explain, I don't understand the effect he's having on me. *If I get to the compound, I'll make sure to stay well out of his way!* "I'm looking for a man going by the name of Viper."

His face stays blank, not giving away that Viper's one of his members. *He's protective and loyal.* "Not sure as I know any dude with that handle."

I know he's staying just this side of lying, but I've done my research. I'm positive as I insist, "Viper is a member of the Satan's Devils, and as far as I know, he's still with the Tucson Chapter."

"Is he now?" His eyes feel like laser beams burning into me. "Say, if this Viper was at my compound, what would you be wanting with him?"

Again, I drop my head, shaking it a little before raising it and meeting his steely stare once more. He's not going to believe me. Fuck, when I found out, I had enough difficulty accepting it was true, myself. I take a deep breath, and then state the bizarre fact, "He's my father." I can't bring myself to call him Dad—in reality, he was just the sperm donor. In all fairness, he never got the chance to be anything more.

The president of the Satan's Devils looks back in amazement and then bursts out laughing. He wraps his arms over his belly as the chuckles come forth. *At least the gun's no longer pointing at me.* "The fuck you talking about, girl?" He gives me another of his probing looks, examining me from head to toe. "Viper doesn't have any kids. Never wanted any. And you, you're what, twenty-five, twenty-six?"

He's obviously astute; he's hit the nail on the head. "Twenty-six," I confirm. I don't try to be coy; I couldn't pull it off if I wanted to.

Another bark of laughter. "I don't know where you got your information from, or what game you're trying to play, but it isn't possible. Viper's just turned forty." He shakes his head. "Whatever stunt you're pulling, you picked the wrong fuckin' person there." Jerking his chin toward my bike, he adds, "I'll get you some gas and then you can get back on your bike."

Not when I've come this far I won't! Meeting him stare for stare, I keep my voice level. "I want to see Viper, to speak to him myself. When I do, he'll know I'm telling the truth."

Gradually he stops laughing, and his scowl returns. He keeps silent for a moment as though considering whether it could actually be possible. "You got fuckin' proof?"

Putting my hand on the Vincent, hoping it will be enough to convince the man who doesn't know either it or I exist, I reply firmly, "Yes."

That gives him pause for thought. Wiping his hand across his face, his fingers lingering on his short beard, he starts to put it together. "Christ, so what you're saying is he fucked your mom when he was no more than fourteen?"

Just that mention of my mother brings tears to my eyes, and angry with myself, I swipe them away. Something tells me it would be wrong to reveal any weakness in front of this man. "That's exactly what I'm telling you," I throw back at him.

Now his eyes narrow, and again he's thinking about it. He's quiet for a few moments before he says, "Viper's never said nothing about any kid."

"He never knew." And until only recently, I didn't either.

It's completely dark now, and as he moves to the side, I can see him only as a silhouette backlit by his headlight. But it's enough to show his arm is pointing to the sandy bank at the side of the road. "Even if you are who you say, he isn't gonna like it; I can tell you that for a start. You're either fuckin' lying or there's a story here. How's about we take a load off and you can tell me exactly what your game is?"

With relief, I see him holster his gun, and I warily eye up the bank. There are no snakes here that I can see, but coming as I do from Washington, I'm cautious about what wildlife there is in the desert. He sits himself down, obviously not affected by similar worries, so folding my legs, I sit beside him.

"Tell me everything, and then I'll decide whether or not I'll let you see Viper." His voice has gentled a little.

I look up at the stars, *God, it's pretty here!* I feel him shift impatiently; the stars are nothing new to him. After taking a deep breath, I begin. It's easier now that his eyes are no longer blazing into me. "My mom died a couple of months ago."

"Sorry to hear that, darlin'." There's real sympathy in his tone.

Her loss still too raw, empathy is hard for me to deal with. Shaking off the unwelcome blast of grief, I carry on, keeping the tremor out of my voice, "Yeah, well, she had cancer. Lung cancer. She always smoked, and it took her pretty damn quick." My voice falters as I put into such simple cold words the months of shock, horror, and misery I have dealt with; and for her, pain and regret. Another deep breath, and blinking rapidly to stave off the threatening tears, I carry on, "She'd always evaded the question of who my dad was. She'd been upfront that he didn't know about me so I wouldn't feel abandoned, but however much I asked, she'd never admit his identity." I break off, hesitating. "She only let on just before she died."

He fills the silence, "And she told you it was Viper?"

I nod. "It was the last day she was able to speak coherently before the morphine blurred her senses, and it was quite the story." It's dark, but I feel him grab my hand and give it a little squeeze before letting it go again. It wasn't what I expected from such a man, but it gives me the strength to carry on with my tale.

"Viper, or Matt Knowles as he was known then, was quite the teenager. He was tall, handsome, and well-built, even at fourteen." I'm repeating the words Mom had told me, in exactly the same way—as a justification, or excuse, I'm still not sure. "He was young but looked a lot older. Mom thought he was closer to her age. She was almost twenty." He'd been a virgin, but I don't think his prez needs all the information.

"They were only together that one time—in a barn of all places. The next day she saw him getting on the freaking school

13

bus and asking around, found out how old he was. They'd planned to meet up again, but once she knew his age, she stayed well away."

There's silence, broken only when he surmises, "And you were the result?" Again, I just nod for my answer. In a harsher voice he questions, "Why didn't she go to Viper? Why didn't she tell him? Surely he deserved to know?"

"That's freaking obvious, isn't it? She was nineteen; he was fourteen. By the time she found out she was pregnant, she knew there was no way she could admit to anyone who the father was."

"Shit!"

I can almost hear the penny dropping, but I spell it out for him anyway. "I don't know what would have happened, but it was statutory rape, and in Arizona, there's no statute of limitations."

"Fuck! Never considered it that way around." A laugh barks out of him. "A woman being accused of technically raping a man? What a situation! So, what did she do?"

I resume my sad narrative, "Her parents disowned her, there was nothing for her here. She worked her way up north hitchhiking, doing waitressing jobs and anything that would give her a few dollars. Finally, she ended up in Washington. She had me, worked her butt off to support us…" My voice falters, there's no point going into the rest—how she ended up doing the paperwork for a garage, working her way up to managing it, spending almost every waking hour there, taking me along with her as she couldn't afford childcare—by the time she could, I didn't need it.

He's filling in the gaps for himself. "So she died penniless and left you nothing. So you thought you'd hit up your long lost pop." Before I have the chance to contradict him, he continues, "How the fuck did she know he was here?"

"She kept in touch with friends in Tucson. Viper didn't go far. And no," I put more strength into my voice, and point at my baby, "look at the bike. That's mine. I restored it myself, been working on it since I was sixteen. I'd hardly call myself penniless." I pause, considering how much to say, and how I can put it into words. Holding out my hands to the light of the headlamp so he can see they're calloused with short unfeminine nails, I explain, "I'm a mechanic, and a good one. Never have trouble finding work, well, when I can get over the barrier of being a woman that is.

"Mom ended up managing a garage." Succinctly I sum up her working life. "But it suffered when she was ill. Most of our money got taken up paying for her treatments, but I've got a little behind me as well as the Vincent. I was mugged on the way here. Freaking yesterday. I'd been on the road for weeks, taking my time, enjoying the trip and having the space to let it sink in that I'm now all alone. I suppose I always knew I was headed this way, something was driving me here. After all my time on the road, I got to Arizona and then that happened."

"Not having much luck, are ya, darlin'?" Again, his tone is sympathetic.

Silence descends. In the still air, the sound of a motorcycle revving in the distance reaches us, reminding me I'm so close to my journey's end, yet, so far. The man sitting beside me rules the club to which I'm heading. And if he decides to turn me away, I don't know if I'd have any recourse. I give him the space to digest what I've told him and hope he believes me... and introduces me to the man who sired me.

"You come looking for your pop as you've lost your mom." He turns my head to face him. "Darlin' you're wasting your time. Viper's no family man. He's got an ol' lady, but they've never had children."

"I don't expect anything from him. I just want to meet him, that's all." I roll back my head and gaze at the stars again. "I needed to get away. Needed to clear my head and just ride. This seemed as good a destination as any."

He looks at me sharply. "It's a fuckin' long ride from Washington."

I give a little proud smile. "Fifteen hundred miles give or take."

A glance toward the Vincent and then back at me, and I see a new look of respect in his eyes. "If I let you meet Viper, and he wants nothing to do with you, what are your plans then? Have you thought further than that?"

Not really, is the answer, and I point to my bike. "Then I get back on her and go wherever the wind takes me."

My response seems to satisfy him. Giving me a nod, he takes out his phone and places a call. "Slick? Can you bring some gas? I'm halfway down the clubhouse road." He listens to something that makes him snarl. "No, I fuckin' haven't. What kind of fuckin' idiot do you take me for?"

He ends the call, presumably having assured the person on the other end that the gas isn't for him, then he stands and holds out his hand to help me to my feet. In the light of the headlamp, he frowns at me. "Viper's my brother. I'll let you meet him, but his word goes. If he wants nothing to do with you, then you're out. Understood?" Again, he leaves me in no doubt of my unpredictable welcome here.

I'd left Washington just wanting to be on the road with my bike, wanting to leave the memories of the last few months behind. As I'd ridden aimlessly, the idea of finding out what kind of man had sired me wouldn't get out of my mind and seeking him out had given me purpose. But I'm twenty-six years old. I've survived long enough without him, and if he doesn't want to know me, then fine. It makes no difference to me. I have no hesitation in agreeing. "If Viper doesn't want anything to do with me, I'm gone."

That that's the plain truth of it must be written on my face as again he nods slowly, showing he's content with my response. Then the sound of a motorbike drawing closer reaches us, a headlight coming into view.

My stomach rolls as I realise I'll soon reach my journey's end. Will I immediately be sent back on my way? Despite my brave words, I'm not sure how I'll handle rejection. Knowing it might only be minutes before I'm meeting the man who's technically my father causes butterflies to start flapping inside. *Will he believe me? What will he think of me? And will he want me to be part of his life?*

CHAPTER THREE

*D*rummer...

Slick's eyes look like they're going to pop out of his head when he pulls up, but it's hard to see whether it's the rare and valuable bike that's caught his eye, or the girl standing beside it. As his attention flicks from one to the other, I'm starting to regret calling him when his gaze lingers a little too long on the woman, and my fists tighten at my sides. Luckily for him, he turns his head toward me before he starts drooling.

"Only you, Drum," he laughs, shaking his head. "Only fuckin' you. Where'd you pick her up? On your run? In Vegas?"

I'm not going to get into it and waste time explaining how I came across her stranded, so I just wave toward the Vincent. "Just fill her up, Slick."

It must have been my tone. Without further discussion, Slick pours gas from the gallon can into her tank.

Once done, I indicate he should take position at the rear and turn to her. "You gonna follow me, darlin'?" It wasn't really a question, and her nod of agreement shows she knows it.

Throwing my leg over my Harley, I push on my electric start, and the engine comes to life with a roar. I watch as she puts her jacket back on and steps astride her bike, expertly taking it off the prop stand—the Vincent was built with stands on both sides making it convenient to park on either side of the road—and kicks down hard on the kick-start to fire her up. It's a practised move, and on the second attempt, it rewards her with a throaty growl. I can't help but be impressed, knowing the Vincent's reputation as being a devil to start, its kickback being known to break bones in its time. That she's got both the knack and the strength that's required is impressive. Getting that sixty-year-old engine to turn over wouldn't be easy.

As I drive ahead, I throw a quick glance over my shoulder, noticing she's handling the beast with ease, and not for the first time, I wonder why she's riding such an unusual bike and how she got a hold of it. Not many bitches ride, and even fewer would tackle what even the best of bikers would call a death trap. And she's ridden here from Washington? Well, fuck me! I might be harbouring doubts about the credibility of her story, but I'm full of admiration for the way she handles that bike.

Roadrunner, the new prospect, is manning the gate, and we're only held up for a few seconds as he rolls them open. Once we're inside, I continue past our auto-shop and up through the compound to the clubhouse itself. Slick and I back our Harleys into the row in a choreographed move. To my surprise, she does the same, taking a vacant spot between two bikes and making it look easy, as though she's been doing it all her life. I exchange a look with Slick, knowing he has to be wondering who the fuck she is, and where she's come from.

Kicking down her stand, she steps off, taking a hefty chain from her saddlebag.

"No need to lock it up here, darlin'," I butt in when I realise what she's going to do. "No one's gonna steal it here."

She glances at me and looks uneasy.

"The boys might want to take a look, but I give you my word they won't touch."

"Yeah, they'll be all over that!" Slick's own eyes are open in amazement as he gets his first proper look at the gleaming machine in the light bleeding out from the clubhouse. "It's fuckin' beautiful. Where'd you get it?"

I want her inside, meeting the man she thinks is her father, not discussing her history with the likes of him. "Time for that later, Slick." *If her incredible story is even true!*

Suddenly it hits me how remiss I've been. *I've let a stranger into the compound. Fuck! Are my brains in my cock today?* My brow creases as I take a step toward her. "Got to pat you down, darlin'. Make sure you're not carrying or nothing."

Her eyes flicker with something that could well be fear or just nervousness that a strange man intends to touch her, but she shrugs off her jacket and stands with her arms outstretched, and it only takes me seconds to discover she's unarmed, not wearing an obvious wire, and has a soft body that I'd like to take the time to explore further. My hands burn as I pull them away, and my cock is at full mast by the time I've smoothed my hands between her small, but perfectly ample breasts. And her little shiver and muffled moan as I inadvertently tease over her nipples? Fuck, that only sends more blood rushing straight down south. Stepping away, I try to bring myself under control.

I'm as satisfied as I can be—she's no physical threat to the Satan's Devils, but to me? I wonder if there's a chance I can persuade her to stay the night and give my cock some relief inside what I expect would be a very sweet pussy. Obviously, I wouldn't be able to go there if Viper really is her old man. I couldn't do that to a brother if her story is true. In which case, I'll definitely need the services of both Pussy and Allie, and maybe even Jill as well.

When I'm able to walk without embarrassing myself, I invite her into the clubhouse. "Come on then, come inside."

Now I know I might know next to nothing about her, but when she goes stiff and tense as she hears the rowdy noise spilling out of the doors, and for the first time I see a flicker of uncertainty in her eyes, I wouldn't be at all surprised if she hasn't thought through what coming to a biker clubhouse might actually entail. I take her arm, not to be friendly, but to encourage her in. If what she's told me is fact, well, who knows how the fuck it's going to play out? If Viper denies all knowledge, then she's out on her ass, and fucking fast. Never mind how much my cock would like it to play out another way.

It's not one of our official party nights, but there's still enough of the boys here. And fuck me if the first thing that greets us isn't Viper getting a fucking blow job from Pussy. Raising my eyes to the ceiling, I shake my head. If she's told me the truth, this is about as far from the best fucking way I'd have wanted to her to see her father for the first time. Making a split-second decision, I pull her toward the bar, purposefully ignoring what's going on behind me.

Marsh runs up, a beer already in his hand, and falters when he sees the strange woman by my side. He recovers fast, his eyes registering my quick nod before he asks, "What can I get for you, sweetheart?"

She points at my beer. "One of those will do me."

Good, she's not demanding a girly drink. She turns as if to survey the clubroom, but I quickly get her attention back to me. "So, your bike. You really restored that yourself?"

A fleeting smile and a glimmer of pride shines in her eyes before she says, "Sure did."

"I'm betting there's a story behind that."

She looks down at her beer. "Sure is," she mumbles, and then changes the subject. "So, is Viper here?"

My eyes go to the mirror behind the bar; Viper's still otherwise engaged. Whoever she is and wherever she's come from, this is categorically not a good moment to introduce her to the man she's come to find. I doubt Viper would want the interruption either. "So how did you come across it?" I ask to distract her.

There's a hesitation before she answers, and when I think I'm going to have to prompt her again, she starts to open up. "When

Mom and Viper, er..." Her face is going a delightful shade of pink, and I guess what she's alluding to.

"When your mom and Viper fucked?" I suggest, helpfully.

She's bright red now, as she confirms my assumption. "Yeah. I told you they did it in a barn. Well, the Vincent was there, buried under some junk. An unrecognisable heap of metal as far as Mom was concerned, but Matt, *Viper*, well, he knew what it was. She said she'd thought he had more of a hard-on for the bike than for her." She laughs. It's not a feminine laugh, more of a masculine chuckle which rumbles as though making the air vibrate and going straight to my dick.

"When I was born, we were living hand to mouth. When I grew older, Mom got the manager's job, but we'd gotten so used to not having money to spare that she'd managed to get quite a bit saved up. For my sixteenth birthday she wanted to give me something special." Her eyes seem to glaze over as she gets lost in the past. "I'd been hanging around the garage for years, ever since I could remember. The guys let me help around the cars from the time I could walk, and the bikes. Especially the bikes." She pauses to smile at what is clearly a pleasant memory for her. "So, when she asked what I wanted for my birthday, I said a motorcycle."

It's obvious where this is going, but I have to confirm it. "She got you the Vincent."

"Yeah," another smile. "she didn't want me to have something I was going to kill myself on, well, not immediately."

"So, she gave you something you could kill yourself on after you restored it?"

She shakes her head and that chuckle rumbles through me again. "I don't think she believed I'd be able to do much with it. I didn't know why at the time, but she got in touch with the owner of the barn and bought it fairly cheaply. The man who owned it knew he had something special by the emblem, but thought it was beyond repair. She offered five hundred for it, he wanted another zero on the end. After a bit of bartering she got it for two grand."

As I'm thinking she got it for a bargain, Sam's looking distant, and I believe she's only just putting it all together—why that particular bike had been purchased for her. It makes me wonder. "Your mom. There ever been anyone else for her? She hook up with another man? You got a stepdad, darlin'?"

An adamant dismissive movement. "Never. And no, it was always just her and me."

She held a torch all those years for the boy who'd left her pregnant? Well, fuck me. I take a long drink. If this story's right, and there's one fuck of a lot of detail here for it not to be, would Viper remember? Would he recognise the bike? What's he going to think of his daughter who restored it, presumably by her own hands? Starting to get a grudging admiration for her, I want her to clarify who actually did the work.

"You get much help fixing it up?"

"The guys were good, I got one hell of a lot of advice and a hand here and there when a nut or bolt was too tight for me to turn, but I did it all. It took a while to source the replacement parts I needed—most are original, but I had a few machined for me. I finished it while Mom was in the hospital." Her eyes grow watery. "She never saw it."

I can't stop myself. I reach out and put my arm around her, pulling her to me briefly, and then letting her go after giving her a manly pat on the back while reminding myself she could be here for a totally different reason and the whole account could be a fabrication, just like those spares for her bike.

No tears fall, and she's had enough distraction. Pulling herself up straight, she looks me directly in the eyes. It's a fair way up from her five foot eight or so as I stand more than a head taller. "Is Viper here?" she asks again, this time forcefully, and I know I won't be able to delay any longer.

Neither can I stop her swinging around, and as I turn at the same time, it's to see Viper pulling out and pushing his cock back into his pants, a well-satisfied look on his face. Her sharp inhale can only be interpreted as disgust at the scene playing out in front of her eyes, and she looks smartly away, her gaze flicking around the clubhouse, settling on the other members as though trying to find the man she's hoping to see. Well, it's too late, what she's seen can't be unseen. I don't suppose there is ever going to be a good time to make this introduction.

"Viper!" I call out, beckoning him over, hearing her gasp beside me as she notices just exactly whose attention I've caught with my shout. Without looking to see her reaction, I take her arm again. "Grab your beer. Let's take this to my office. Viper!" I call out to him again and wave my bottle indicating I want him to follow us.

CHAPTER FOUR

*S*am...

Oh shit! The president, Drummer, is beckoning me to follow him. And the man who's just been enjoying a blow job by a whore—I'm assuming it's not his old lady as she looked like a real slut—right in plain view of everyone answered to the name Viper. *That's my dad?*

Right now I want to get back on my bike and ride. Miles away. I don't care where. Of course, I didn't know what kind of man I expected to find, but it certainly wasn't someone I'd catch doing *that*. To be fair, my mom had warned me about biker clubs, trying to put me off going to find the man who'd caused my existence, but knowing when she'd gone I'd have nobody left, she had given me all the details that would enable me to find him if it turned out I wanted to.

But shit, it's clear now that biker clubs aren't going to be like anything I've ever experienced before, even though I've led a life mainly surrounded by members of the opposite sex. In my naivete, I had thought the men I would find would be more like the mechanics I worked with, maybe a bit rougher around the edges. What I've seen so far is enough to show me they're an entirely different breed.

Pulling back my shoulders, I give myself a pep talk. I've come a heck of a long way to reach the end of my journey. Perhaps I shouldn't rush to condemn him without letting him even speak, maybe I should take the time and meet him properly and then leave.

As my feet stay glued to the spot, Drummer turns back and pauses his step, waiting for me to start moving toward him. One last moment of indecision, then, having seen Viper putting himself back in his pants and zipping up, wishing his prez had given him time to at least wash his hands, I follow the two men into an office.

There's a big flag behind a desk, a full-scale version of the picture they have on the back of their cuts. As Lucifer looms large holding a scythe over the three demons crouched below him, I suppress a shudder at the image. Hanging as it is over the president's desk, it's intimidating, just as it's probably meant to be.

Seating himself behind a desk large enough to emphasise his position in the club, Drummer waves Viper and I to two seats conveniently placed in front. Viper's staring at me, his features pulled into an expression which is half-sneer, half look of confusion. After examining me from head to toe in a way that makes me shift very uncomfortably, his lips curl into an outright evaluating leer, and he turns to Drummer.

"New sweet butt, Drum?"

Drummer snorts. Taken by surprise, it seems even he didn't expect that my father's first reaction would be to reveal he has the hots for me. I open my mouth to cut that shit out fast, but Drummer beats me to it.

"No fuckin' way, Brother. She's off-limits, particularly to you. Seems she might be a relative of yours and she wants to talk to you about it." As Viper looks even more confused, Drummer continues, "It's a personal matter. Want that I should go?"

No! My eyes plead with him. Drum might have been surly and mistrustful from the moment I met him, but there have been

26

a couple of times he's shown some sympathy. Something about him draws me to him, something that makes me hope he'd be on my side. The other man, what do I know of him? Nothing except he sees nothing wrong in getting a blow job in the middle of a crowded room and that I carry part of his DNA. The vibes coming from him don't make me at all comfortable. I start to think I might have been stupid coming here. Mom warned me to steer clear for a reason.

Viper's looking at me with distaste, and while his eyes watch me, he directs his words to his president. "Well, she isn't my sister or mother, and I don't have no fuckin' other female relatives, so I think you better stay, Drum. Don't know what this is about, but it has to be a fuckin' con."

Drummer rubs his hand over his beard. "Think you better listen up, Viper. Hear her out, okay?" Having made his suggestion, he leans back in his chair and folds his arms, but his piercing eyes aren't missing a thing, and the fractional turning up of one side of his mouth suggests it's a source of amusement to him to see how this all plays out.

I've had hours and hours of the open road to plan what I'm going to say, but now that I'm here, words fail me. Viper shifts in his chair, crossing one leg over the other knee, then clasps his hands behind his neck. As he stares at me vacantly, I see he's showing me there's nothing I've got to say that will faze him.

If I address it head on, he'll deny it. He doesn't want to listen to me. He doesn't even seem to like me, particularly. While I gather my thoughts, I glance down at my motorcycle boots, scuffed, well worn, and covered with the dust of the road. Soon, very soon it seems, I'm going to be on my way again.

"Well fuckin' spit it out girl, I've got better things to do."

I can't help my face twisting as I think about what he could be referring too. Unless one woman a night is enough for him, that is. Clearing my throat, I start. "Do you remember a girl called Sylvie May Redkin?"

Viper starts to deny it, then creases his brow, and his fingers pinch the bridge of his nose. His eyes flit toward Drummer, back to me, then back to his prez again. For a second, I think he's going to deny it, but Drummer raises an eyebrow and gives a slight nod of encouragement.

"Sylvie. Sylvie May." As Viper repeats the name, his hands come to his front and he cups one elbow, his fingers sweeping over his brow. Just as I think he's going to admit it, he shrugs. "Can't say that I do."

I didn't expect him to outright forget. Maybe it's not the same for a man as a woman, but I'd have expected him to remember his first time. Now it's my turn to look at the prez, who's quietly drumming his fingers against the table as though playing along to some unheard music. *Is that how he got his name?* He's looking carefully at us both, poised like a snake waiting to strike. *Is he going to dismiss me as a liar?*

Then he surprises me, gesturing for me to continue. "Why don't you remind him, Sam?"

Blinking fast, I do. "A barn," I start softly. "A heap of junk you identified as a Vincent Black Shadow…" I pause, waiting for him to remember. A tensing of his body suggests he does.

"Nope." Another shrug and a chin jerk toward Drummer.

"Oh, for fuck's sake!" I lose my temper. "It was your first freaking time! Not just with Sylvie May, but ever."

Drummer chuckles at that piece of information and prompts, "Is it true, Viper?"

Viper looks between both of us; he doesn't seem quite sure what to say. Then, at last, he draws in a deep breath. "Yeah, I think I remember fuckin' a girl in the barn. Didn't remember the name Sylvie May."

"Well, your poor memory might explain things," I snap. As both heads swing around to face me, I carry on in the same tone, "You forgot a condom that night, too. Let me introduce myself; I'm Samantha Redkin. The daughter of Sylvie May, and the result of your bad freaking memory."

Well, I suppose there are better ways to introduce yourself to your father. Viper's reaction isn't at all how I imagined it might be. Oh, I'm not so stupid as to think he'd welcome me with open arms, I'd expected some suspicion and disbelief, but what I hadn't expected was outright denial and hatred. He stands so fast his chair smashes to the ground behind him, making Drummer jump to his feet. Feeling in a vulnerable position, I get up as well.

Viper's face has gone red; his hands are clenched into tight fists as he looks from me to his prez. Grateful that Drummer stayed, fearful Viper might have even hit me if we'd been alone, my eyes go to him for some moral support. But there's nothing there, Drummer's face is shuttered.

"Get her out of here, Prez. This is some fuckin' joke."

"I've told you the truth." My anger matches his.

"No fuckin' way. I don't know what plan you cooked up with your bitch of a mother, but you're not fooling me. You aren't nothing to do with me."

Wiping a speck of spit off my brow, I do the only thing I can —defend my one proper parent. "My bitch of a mother, as you call her, is dead, you motherfucking bastard! She told me what happened on her fucking death bed."

"Why didn't she tell me, then, eh? When she was still fuckin' alive, and I could have told her face to face what I thought of her lies?" His meaty palm crashes down on the desk causing it to shudder, but it's a fine piece of furniture, sturdily made and doesn't even dent. I cringe thinking how badly I riled him. Drummer moves to stand behind me, and I get the strange notion that he's being protective.

I try to calm my voice, though I can do nothing to stop my body shaking. "Because she didn't want to go to prison." At his surprised look, I continue, "She was nineteen years old, Viper. You were fourteen."

His stance not quite so bullish, Viper seems perplexed. "But she was a woman, and it wasn't rape."

"Statutory rape," Drum drops it in. "You were a minor."

Viper actually winks at his prez. "Yeah, well I had it even then." He puffs out his chest and then seems to remember what I've told him was the outcome of that coupling.

He's a tall man, almost as tall as Drummer, but broader too. His stomach is just starting to show that middle age spread that affects many men of his age. Suddenly he turns away, walking to the wall and facing it, resting his weight on both palms. Neither his prez or I say anything; we give him time to process the bombshell that I've just dropped.

When he turns back, all his anger has gone. For a split second I start to think he's going to give me a chance to get to know him. However much I've acknowledged this isn't the hearts and flowers man I'd been hoping to find, however much I doubt I'll ever have a proper father/daughter relationship with him, he is my dad after all. Now that Mom's gone, he is the only relative I know of in this world. Having the chance to know him, even if he won't be able to live up to my ideal, is something I'd jump at. But I'm to be disappointed.

"Look," he comes over, his hand coming up as though to touch me, then quickly dropping to his side again, "Samantha? Is that what you said your name is?" At my nod he continues, "You may be telling the truth. But for all that, Sylvie May could have been with someone else after me. Before me, even. How the fuck am I to know? What I do know is, I don't want no kid. Not even one all grown up like you. I'm sorry, but I need you to go."

I'd thought through all his possible objections, knowing he probably wouldn't believe there'd been no one else for my mother since him. It seems unbelievable, but she had no doubt I was his. I'm prepared for his rebuttal. "We could do a DNA test," I offer.

The anger comes back in full force. "I'm not taking no fuckin' DNA test. It doesn't matter what it proves. I'm not gonna be a daddy for you. Got it? Now get the fuck out and leave me alone!"

I don't move. Despite all my preparation, I hadn't expected

such a forceful rejection—I thought he'd at least speak to me. We stand there, the three of us, frozen like a tableau.

Then it's Viper who throws his hands up in the air, mumbling, "I'm fuckin' out of here!" and exits the office, slamming the door behind him.

All the air has been stolen from my lungs. I've been stupid; I should never have come here. Sinking into the chair behind me, I lean forward putting my head in my hands, trying hard not to cry when all I want at the moment is a hug from my mom. Suddenly it all crashes down—how alone in the world I am— and I recognise just how much hope I'd stupidly been pinning on finding my one remaining parent. *So now I have,* I scoff at myself, *and he's made it clear he wants nothing at all to do with me.* It would have been better never to have known who he was.

The sound of a throat clearing reminds me I'm not alone, and I glance up to Drummer. I don't know what I imagined his reaction to be, but what I didn't anticipate was for his face to have gone dark, his thin lips pursed in a scowl. His expression makes it feel like all the warmth has disappeared from the room.

"It's late. You can stay tonight. I'll show you to a room in the clubhouse, but tomorrow you need to leave." His voice sounds cold, his words spoken almost in a monotone.

"I've got no money, nowhere to go until my replacement cards come through," I remind him.

He shakes his head. "Not my problem." He paces over and I'm forced to look up at him. "Viper's my brother." With just those simple words he reminds me exactly where his loyalty lies. Why would I even think he'd give a second thought to me? Bleakly, I nod, knowing I'll have to go to the bank tomorrow and try to get out some emergency cash, but until my cards arrive, I'm stuck. But that, as he so plainly stated, is nothing that's going to cause him to lose any sleep.

Realising the offer of a room for the night is, under the circumstances, probably more than I could have hoped for, I nod. "Thank you. I'll stay the night, then I'll get back on my bike."

CHAPTER FIVE

*D*rummer…

Viper's my brother. If he doesn't want to know his daughter, then he's the one I'll be backing all the fucking way, even though it's obvious they don't need a DNA test to prove their relationship. During the exchange between father and daughter, it was as plain as the nose on your face that they swam in the same gene pool. Certain mannerisms—the red spot on the cheeks when they became angry, the wave of the hand in dismissal, and their eyes—they're a perfect match. Their chins mirror each other, slightly pointed, giving both their faces a heart shape. Yeah, though I'll admit to having had some before, once I'd seen them side by side, there was no doubt in my mind. Sam is telling the truth.

His reaction wasn't what surprised me—fuck, what man wants to find out years later that he's fathered a child? But the vehemence of his rejection did. As I show her to a room, I mull it over in my mind, wondering how I would have behaved in the same position. Part of my offer to give her somewhere to stay for the night isn't just out of the kindness of my heart, but to allow him some time to get over the shock. Once he's slept on it, Viper might feel differently, and at the very least, want to talk to her.

Even in the short time I'd known her, it's clear Sam's a fucking treasure wrapped up in a beautiful package and a great bike mechanic to boot. What man wouldn't be proud to have produced someone like her? No, I will give him some space to think on it. He might just come to regret his hasty dismissal.

Pointing the way, I lead her down a corridor, stopping at an open door and putting my head inside quickly to check it's relatively clean. Then I leave her, her palatable sadness damping down the arousal I felt for her earlier. Whatever my earlier intentions to sink my cock into her tonight were, there's no way I'll try to take advantage of her now. I can't even consider it; I'll back a member of my club against a stranger any day.

Leaving her to get settled, I return to the clubroom, my eyes flitting around, seeking out my brother. I'm not surprised to find Viper sitting alone in the corner, a bottle of Jack beside him. Collecting a glass from Marsh, I go to join him.

As I approach, he looks up with an unexpected look of utter desolation on his face. He pours himself another shot, downs it, pours another, and only then deigns to speak. "She fuckin' gone?"

"It's late, Brother. I've given her a room out back. I'll make sure she's out of here come morning." I don't understand why, but Viper looks like Sam's revelations have completely destroyed him. Okay, it was an incredible piece of news to receive out of the blue, but the intensity of the effect it's having confuses me.

The Jack doesn't even seem to be taking the edge off; he's showing no sign he's feeling it. His head moves side to side in dismissal. "It can't be true, Prez. And even if it is, I want nothing to do with her. She's got to get gone. Fuck!" Wiping his hand across his face, he repeats it, "It can't be true."

He turns back to the bottle, remembers his manners sufficiently to fill my glass, then puts his head in his hands. Fuck me; I suppose it must be a lot for a man to take on board. Maybe he just needs some time to let the news sink in. Hearing something like that would likely blow a man's mind. Having an adult daughter turn up out of the blue? Well, at least she's long past the age when she requires support.

Viper's wallowing in his misery, and I want to do something, anything, to pull him out of his stupor. "Fourteen, eh?"

I'm not sure I'm going to get a response, but I give him a moment, raising my glass and downing the contents, then replenishing it from the bottle. When I give up on any rejoinder, he looks up, one side of his mouth twisted up.

"I was a mature teenager."

"You must have been," I chuckle.

"I told her I was nineteen and she believed it."

So now he's admitting it. "You do remember then?"

"Doesn't everyone's first time stick in their mind?" Now he smirks.

Yeah, he's right about that. But I have no fond recollections of mine; I'd barely lasted a minute, something I'd rather forget. Eyeing him, I wonder what else he'll admit. "You know that Vincent she was talking about? Well her mom, Sylvie May, bought it for her, for her sixteenth birthday. Sam restored it herself."

That makes his eyes widen. "That slip of a girl rebuilt it? No way. It was a fuckin' piece of shit. Little more than a rusty frame and a smattering of broken parts."

Jerking my chin up and down, I confirm it, "So she says, yeah. Well, that's her story. It's outside. She rode it here from Washington." He gives me a look of utter disbelief, but I can see I've sparked his interest, which has got to be better than seeing him wallowing in despair. It gives me an idea. "Wanna come see it?"

I can almost see the wheels working in his head as he considers my question, probably wondering whether looking at the bike might get him more involved than he wants to be. But finally, curiosity gets the better of him. He gives a nod, and a "Yeah, why not?"

As if in an orchestrated move, we both drain our glasses

and stand. Viper leads the way out to the front of the club-house and looks along the line of motorcycles backed up against the wall. When his eyes light on the gleaming machine, he moves quickly forward until he's standing right in front of it. Then he just stares. A few seconds later, he can't help himself and his hand reaches out and starts lovingly stroking along its lines.

"Fuckin' beautiful," he whispers reverently.

Like its owner. The thought goes through my mind, surprisingly not just in a sexual way. If I had a daughter, I think I would feel blessed to have one like Sam, so attractive it almost hurts to look at her, and capable of restoring and riding such a beast? Fuck, if Viper thought differently, he might think he'd won the fucking lottery.

"She rode it all the way from Washington." I reiterate what I already told him. Having my brother's back includes making sure he doesn't make a mistake, one that he might regret if he thinks more about it. If she disappears from his life tomorrow, fuck knows if he'll ever be able to trace her again. Something tells me she'll get back on that bike and just keep riding. It's what I'd do if I were in her place.

"A little girl like that? Christ, these take some starting! Let alone riding."

Which reminds me of the way she stamped down on that kick-start earlier, her whole body weight behind that practised move.

"It's a good bike for long distance riding." Viper's walking around it. "But the brakes and steering take some handling." He knows his bikes, and apparently, has been lusting after this particular Vincent since he was in his teens. Now he crouches down, examining it more carefully. "It's a C model. Well ahead of its time. It had a top speed of one hundred twenty miles per hour. I wonder if it still does that?"

"I reckon it would." Sam had restored it with so much love I'd bet money it was very well tuned.

His hand now traces the V-Twin engine. "It's only nine nine eight cc, but it's fuckin' beautiful, isn't it?"

It's a rhetorical question, so I don't bother to answer.

Then he stands up again, his face falling as his thoughts return to his dilemma. "Means fuck all. Her mom got muddled is all. There's no fuckin' way I could be her father." He brushes his hand down over his face, and I swear I see moisture glimmering in his eyes.

"Do you want me to call Sandy? Have her come collect you?" Viper won't be riding tonight; now that the Jack's caught up with him, he's not steady on his feet. It makes sense to offer to get his ol' lady to come and fetch him home. They've got a house down Tucson way, though there's always a room for him to crash here if he wants it. My thought is that he'd like to be gone so he doesn't bump into Sam in the morning.

His vehement reaction, as he turns and snarls, startles me. "Keep Sandy out of it."

I pull myself to my full height, I'm the prez after all, and however he's feeling, he needs to remember and respect that. But something's eating at him. Instead of toning it down, he grabs my cut with both his hands, something I'd normally never allow, but one look at the desperation in his eyes stays my immediate, and what was going to be a very violent objection.

"Sandy must never know. Keep this between us, please, Prez?" he pleads. "Don't tell the others. Please. Make up some story, anything. But don't let anyone know what relationship she's claimin' with me."

Wondering how I'm going to explain a lone woman when she emerges from her bed and not mine in the morning, one look at his facial muscles, taut with tension, I comprehend just how much the right answer means to my brother, even if I don't understand why. He's shaking, his eyes wide. Fuck me; he's absolutely terrified someone's going to find out.

Doing the only thing I can, I give him the reassurance he

needs, "It's your story to tell, Viper. If you don't want it shared, no one's gonna fuckin' hear it from me."

At last, he removes his hands from my cut and backs away. With one last lingering look at the Vincent, he slips back into the clubhouse.

I stand outside, listening to the cicadas and the voices coming out from the building behind me. What a fuck of a day this has turned out to be. I can't stop myself wondering just why Viper's so adamant his old lady doesn't find out. Christ, she knows he lets the whores swallow his cum, even if he doesn't take it further than that. How could one indiscretion, way back when he wasn't old enough to know any better, be any worse than that?

As I ponder the puzzle, the quiet of the night is broken by a couple of bikes approaching. Head tilted to one side, I listen until I recognise the engine sounds as they draw close. It's Wraith and Peg, back from Tucson.

I watch as they park and when the throaty roar is replaced by the sounds of cooling engines ticking, I walk up to them, exchanging chin lifts with the pair as they dismount. "Sorted?" I have confidence in my VP and sergeant-at-arms, and know that if there was any problem, they would have found a resolution to it.

"Sorted," Wraith confirms.

"But we'll have to get a new bouncer." Peg's glare shows me he hadn't been particularly pleased with what he'd found at the strip club.

"The girl, she okay?"

"Yeah. Shaken but she'll heal, Prez. Split lip and a black eye. Bastard backhanded her when she wouldn't put out for him. Seemed to think it was his fuckin' right to sample the goods."

Emitting a low growl, I turn away. Women should be under our protection. I already know many of the strippers would prefer to do anything but take their clothes off for money, but we pay well, and most of them haven't got any other option. The bouncers are there to make sure the customers don't get their hands on them, not to pressure the girls themselves. Of course, some of them are exhibitionists and enjoy what they do, but for the majority, we make their work as easy as we can. And in return, they give all they've got. The club makes good money for us, but if we don't protect the girls, we'll lose them. Wraith and Peg will know how angry I am; I don't have to say the words.

"What the fuck?" Swinging back around, I see just what has caught Wraith's attention. It's the Vincent. Seems I've run out of time. Now I've got to think fast and come up with some account of why it's here and who it belongs to. Both he and Peg are walking over to it, their eyes gleaming with envy. While it's not something any of us would want to swap our modern Harleys for, it's a thing of beauty in its own right, and there's probably not a biker alive who wouldn't take a moment to drool over it. Completely absorbed in eyeing up its sleek lines, I'm given a moment to concoct my explanation. In the end, I decide to go for a short version of the truth.

"It's a woman who owns it. Came across her stranded, run out of gas."

"Wow," Peg breathes. "A bitch?"

Wraith thumps me lightly on the arm. "Only you could do that, Prez. A fuckin' bitch with a Vincent. Gonna add to your collection?" He's referring, I hope, to my stable of vintage bikes. "What you doing out here if you've got her warming your bed?"

I might have guessed they'd jump to the obvious conclusion, so I give them a bit more. Once again, I'm not veering far from the truth. "Nah, she's not a club whore or after biker cock." *Though I wish she were.* "She'd had her wallet stolen and had no money. Got her topped up with gas and brought her here as it was late. She's bunked down in one of the back rooms for the night."

My VP's not stupid, and he quirks a brow at me as if asking for the rest of the story, but I stay silent. Saying too much is worse than saying too little. I'm the prez. If I want to do something out of character, I should be able to do so without anyone questioning me.

After one more piercing look and huffing a laugh, Wraith slaps my back. "Well I'm off to my bed which actually has a woman in it." He bids us both goodnight then marches off up the track.

His words resonate with me and I start wishing there really was a bitch in mine. But when the sweet butts come to mind, despite my earlier intention, I know it's not one of them I want between my sheets tonight.

Peg only lingers a moment longer, and from his expression I know he's puzzled too. But he's a patient man and will be content to wait for me to enlighten him at the appropriate time.

CHAPTER SIX

*S*am…

The room Drummer has put me in is to the rear of the clubroom and is obviously a crash place when people don't want to go home. Or, I realise as I wrinkle my nose in disgust on entering, where they fuck. It's not particularly clean, but it has a bed, and in all honesty, tonight I'm just grateful to have somewhere to lay my head.

Sliding under the sheets fully clothed, as I don't feel comfortable getting undressed in a clubhouse full of rowdy bikers even if I have turned the flimsy lock on the door, I rest my head on the lumpy pillow, throwing my arm up over my eyes and hoping I'll be able to sleep despite the thumping music still playing outside. And if I don't? Well, it's just for the one night. Hopefully tomorrow I'll get to the bank and get my money situation settled and be able to get on my way.

But on my way where? Since my mom died, my goal had been coming here and finding my father. Now I've found him and discovered he wants nothing to do with me; I've no real purpose in mind. Thinking practically, soon I'm going to need to find a job as my dwindling savings won't support me for long, and the only thing I own of any value is the bike that I ride. For the first time since the funeral, I'm at a complete loss as to what to do. Undriven, which isn't like me at all. *I'm close to California; maybe I could settle there?* The thought that I could go anywhere should be freeing. Instead, it causes a churning in my gut. *I feel adrift.* Fighting back tears, I'm conscious I'd been hoping my father would at least have provided an anchor, if not an actual home.

After tossing and turning all night, a loud knocking is a welcome warning that morning has arrived and soon I'll be back on the road. It doesn't do anyone any good to stay where it's so obvious they're not wanted. As I unlock and open the door, my eyes widen as they settle on the last person I expected to see. The president of the Satan's Devils himself, who's entering carrying a cup of coffee.

Spying the cup, my hands reach for it eagerly. "Thank you. I didn't expect room service."

He stares at me for a moment, and his scrutiny makes me wish that I'd at least had a chance to brush my hair. It must look like a bird's nest after my restless night. A feminine wile that's totally alien makes me try to go smooth it down as I steadily return his gaze.

His eyes break away first. He glances over at the steaming cup and nods toward it. "There's a reason for that. I needed to speak to you." As he indicates the end of the bed and I see there's nowhere else to sit in the room, I incline my head, and he sits. He leans forward, his elbows on his knees. "I spoke with Viper last night."

Curious and eager to learn whether he'd made Viper change his mind, I place my butt on the bed beside him and tilt my head, this time to encourage him to continue.

"I think it's safe to say he's in shock."

I'd seen that, and it wasn't an extraordinary reaction. But how else could I have broken the news? Viper didn't want to believe it, and part of me can understand why. I add my observation, "And in denial."

Drummer nods. "Yeah, there's that as well. But at the moment there's no proof." As I go to speak, he holds up his hand. "For the record, I think it's true. You are his daughter. You look like him, you know?"

I do? I think back to the burly biker I'd met, his hair shaggy and needing a trim, his brown eyes reddened from riding in the wind and drinking. I hadn't thought I'd been looking in a mirror, but maybe I'd been looking for the wrong things. I tilt my head to one side and shrug.

Drum chuckles and points at me. "That right there, that shrug. It's all him." Then his face grows serious. "It's too much for him to handle right now, and he certainly doesn't want his ol' lady to know." He rubs the top of his slightly crooked nose, drawing my attention to it. It must have been broken at some time, but it doesn't make him ugly, far from it. "Here's the thing, he doesn't want *anyone* to know who you are... Who you might be."

I came to find my father, to discover who and what type of man he is, I didn't come to cause trouble. Having been dismissed, there's no point leaving any problems for him in my wake. It had never been his fault that he hadn't had any involvement in my upbringing. It had been a stupid mistake by a boy too young to know better. A boy taken advantage of, albeit unwittingly, by a girl five years older. Though the rejection hurts me to some extent, I understand it. "I'm okay with that. I don't want to cause problems, Drummer. I'll just get on my bike and make myself scarce."

The president gives me what I interpret as a smile, and a nod of appreciation. "Thank you. Glad you understand, darlin'."

"So, what is my story? If I meet anyone?" I suspect he's already had to explain my presence away.

"You ran out of gas, it was late, I let you stay here." It's a succinct explanation.

I'm curious. "Do you normally rescue damsels in distress?" Unlike his, mine's a full smile.

42

His thin lips purse together, and then one corner turns up. "You're the first."

Somehow I can believe that, and I can only be grateful. There's a moment of silence before he reaches into his pocket and comes out with a handful of bills. "Here, to tide you over until you get your money situation sorted."

I push his hand away, even while my eyes notice there must be a couple of hundred dollars there. "No, I don't need it. I'll go to the bank. I'm sure they'll be able to help me out by giving me cash to tide me over until I get replacement cards." I sigh. "Though I will probably have to stay in Tucson for a while. I've no address, so they'll probably want me to pick them up from the bank."

"It's a big enough city," he replies. "That won't be a problem, unless you come back here." The last is added as a warning, but it's one I don't need.

I shake my head adamantly. "I won't be coming here again, I promise you that." The rejection from Viper had been final, but there's a flicker of disappointment inside me, telling me I'd have liked to have gotten to know this enigmatic man who's brought me coffee a little better. But why would he be interested in me? He's a biker, he's probably got hundreds of women just begging for him. Women who know how to attract such a man, what his needs are, and how to fulfil them.

"Where will you go?" He's just making conversation, there can't be any reason he'd want to know. It seems he's in no hurry to leave.

Again I shrug, the gesture now making me feel self-conscious. *Did I really inherit that from my father?* "I've no idea. I'll maybe try California."

All at once he seems to come to a decision. "Let me know where you end up. You never know, once he's had a chance to think about it, Viper might change his mind."

It seems unlikely, but as it wouldn't be any hardship to give him a call and let him know, I agree.

At last, Drummer stands, indicating a door that I already know leads to a bathroom. A filthy, smelly, bathroom. "You can shower in there and then I'll be waiting for you out front."

"To escort me off the premises?" I grin.

He almost grins back, but it seems smiling doesn't come easily to him. "No, to run interference if any of those fuckers out there try to hit on you."

I'm a bit taken aback he'd think any of them would. I mean, I'd seen the women who were around last night, and they're far more glamorous than me, but I thank him anyway.

Once he's gone, I drink my coffee and get ready fast, not wanting to keep the president waiting, doubting he'd appreciate being kept hanging around. Feeling only slightly refreshed by the weak trickle of the shower, I leave my room and retrace the steps I'd taken the night before. As I walk through the clubroom, I notice it's fairly empty, just a man wiping down the bar who throws me a nod. I think nothing of it, it is still early and the men partied hard last night after all.

When I get outside, I find the real reason why there was no one around. Here are the bikers, Drummer in their midst, in various poses around my bike. A couple of them are even kneeling on the ground giving it an up-close-and-personal scrutiny. Viper, I notice, with a pang of regret, isn't amongst them. Fleetingly, I wish I'd had the chance to show him what I'd done with it.

Seeing me approach, Drummer stands and tells me with a grimace, "I think you ought to see this."

Having been convinced they'd only been admiring it; his words give me pause. Curious, I look where he's pointing. *Oh, shit!*

I often feel the Vincent's a living creature—there have been times on the road when she certainly seemed to know her own mind and wanted to argue with me. Right now, if she had been a live animate object, I'd have scolded her for peeing all over the ground. But it isn't pee or water, or gas. It's oil. Lots and lots of freaking oil. Without examining it closer, I already know in my gut, I'll be going nowhere today.

"Hey, I'm Blade." A tall man—but aren't they all?—calls out.

"Sam." I introduce myself and nod across at the biker who's picking at dirt in his nails with a knife.

He points the blade toward my bike. "I'll take it down to the garage and have a look at it for you if you like?"

"No." It comes out more forcefully than I intended, so I add, trying to sound a little more reasonable, "No one touches her but me."

A hand cups my elbow, and I swing around to find it's Drummer. "Marsh here will run you down to Tucson in the truck. You can get your stuff worked out with the bank, find a hotel or something, and Blade will sort your bike out." He uses a tone that suggests he will take no argument.

But he knows nothing about me. I'm like a mama bear with the Vincent, and I won't have anyone else working on her. I remember the auto-shop we passed at the entrance to the compound. "I presume you've got all the tools and stuff at your shop? Let me use them. I'll get her fixed and out of here in no time." I have to stop myself snarling at the thought of someone else getting their hands on her. No one knows her like I do. Normally a reliable bike, why the fuck has she chosen to embarrass me like this right now when all I want to do is to escape?

The shuffling of feet and the attention the men are paying to me lets me know not many people refuse an instruction from Drummer. As he glares at me, his steely eyes go cold. I think fast. I'm a woman, and these men surrounding me could easily use force to get me to do whatever they want.

"Drummer," I use a more conciliatory and feminine tone which I manage to summon up from somewhere, "I know you don't want to extend your hospitality." I remember the story he's probably told everyone by now. "And I'm grateful for you getting me out of a jam yesterday, but really, I know what I'm doing, and the fastest way for me to get going is for me to work on her myself. And I'll be down at the shop, out of sight."

He doesn't seem to know how to respond. If I were a man and here for another reason, he'd probably allow me to follow through on my suggestion. While his brain ticks over, another one of the bikers butts in, "Why not give her a couple of hours, Prez? See what she can do? If she can't fix it, we can take her downtown then."

I won't be leaving my bike. Under any circumstances. My hands clench at my sides, getting ready to fight. Not physically, I wouldn't have a chance, but verbally at least. My Vincent's my baby, and all I have of my past. It's not the value; it's the one thing I've got left to remind me of my mom. Holding my breath, I wait for Drummer's answer while pondering what on earth could have caused the oil spill. With luck, it will be something simple I'll be able to quickly repair.

The scrutiny of the men surrounding me is making me nervous, but I refuse to let that show on my face. Instead, I tilt my head to one side, watching Drummer as he deliberates. At last, he comes to a decision and steps back, waving in the direction of the shop. "You've got two hours," he tells me, his set features showing he's not comfortable with the situation at all.

I could hug him, but I resist. Instead, I give a business-like nod, then, kicking the bike off the stand, I balance the weight and start pushing. None of them help me, it's as if they're testing me. I slip slightly on the oil but righting myself regain my footing. She's a heavy beast, but one I've manhandled many times before. Like an old friend, I limp her down toward the garage, the incline this time in my favour. Out of the corner of my eye I see the bikers are following me. *Great, now I'm going to have a freaking audience!* I hear what they're saying, they're freaking making bets on whether I'm going to be able to make her right or not. Well, fuck them. I rebuilt this baby from scratch, and she's not going to beat me now.

It's not a long distance, but by the time I reach the shop, my arms are aching. At nearly five hundred pounds she's almost four times my body weight, but I've learned the trick is in the balance. When I come to the ramp, I look up in despair, but at least the biker called Blade steps forward and helps me push her up.

Standing back, I can't help but admire my sick but beautiful baby. Drummer taps me on the arm. "Two hours," he reminds me before he marches away.

Knowing I have no time to waste, I nod toward one of the bikers. "Tools?"

"Here, you can use mine." The bald-headed man who'd brought the gas yesterday brings over a large, heavy metal box. Slick, I think Drummer had said his name was. Eyeing the ground, which like in any garage, is filthy with dirt, tyre residue, and of course, oil. I ruefully wish I had my overalls with me, suspecting my leathers are going to get ruined.

It can't hurt to ask. "Any spare overalls?"

"Here!" Another man chucks me some. They're certainly not clean and about ten times too big, but better than nothing. Shrugging off my jacket—God, it's hot in Arizona—I pull them on, roll the sleeves and legs up as best I can, and then get down to work, ignoring the men watching me as I get lost in my task.

First, I clean off the engine to try to see where the oil is coming from so I can start to identify the fault. That's a messy job in itself, and quickly my hands are greasy and black. After a while my audience seems to get bored, and they wander off, thankfully leaving me to get on with it. The shop becomes filled with the sounds of engines revving, bangs and clattering of the tools, and the odd swear word as someone struggles to win the battle between a tight bolt and a wrench. The sounds comfort me, reminding me of home.

Concentrating, I zone out, not even hearing the conversations going on around me. It takes me longer than it should to find it, mainly because I'm trying to prove the bad feeling I have at the back of my mind wrong. But however hard I try to look for another explanation, I've identified the cause of the leak. Just before my allotted time is up, I stand, stretch, and bow my head. Of all the freaking things that could have gone right now.

Blade noticed I've stopped working and comes over.

"Found the problem?" He sneers as if I'm going to have to admit I'm flummoxed.

But I'm too upset to take it to heart. "Sure have," I tell him, tonelessly, and point to the offending part lying sadly on the ground. "Crankshaft oil seal is fucked."

His eyes narrow and he glances at my face, correctly reading the consternation there. "You sure?"

"Yeah." I wipe off my hands as best I can and look around for somewhere to throw the oily rag, then seeing a bin, chuck it in.

"Mind if I take a look?"

Well, he asked nicely, and if he could show me I'm mistaken for once, I'd be grateful. Otherwise, there's no alternative but for me to try to source an original replacement part, and for that, I'll need access to a computer and have the money to pay for it. Then, assuming I find one available, wait for it to be delivered.

"Be my guest."

Quicker than I did, because I was hoping to prove my original diagnosis wrong and find instead something that would have been simple to fix, Blade goes over the Vincent. When he stands again, he's shaking his head. "Sorry, darlin', you're right." There's a flare of admiration in his eyes. "Smart bitch, aren't cha?"

His compliment washes over me; I'm just trying to work out what to do now.

There's a clock on the wall, a Harley clock. Now, why doesn't that surprise me? And at the two-hour mark exactly, Drummer returns. I'm still staring at the Vincent as if it could miraculously regenerate the broken part.

"Well?" I hear his gruff voice behind me. I fill him in, Blade confirming my assessment. Drummer lifts back his head and lets out a sigh.

"Your bike isn't going anywhere, darlin'."

Yeah, tell me something I don't know.

"Okay, so the prospect will make sure you get to town—"

I interrupt him, "No."

"No?" he growls, and the sound resonates through me. *This is not the time to get aroused. Focus.* I feel my face flush, but I stand my ground.

"No," I insist. "I'm not leaving my bike."

"Can't have you staying at the clubhouse. Remember our agreement?"

I know he's reminding me that Viper wants me out of sight. Quickly considering my options, not that I've got many to choose from, I look around. "I'll stay here." It wouldn't be the first time I've pulled an all-nighter in a garage, but normally I'm working there, not sleeping. My eyes fall on the Harleys waiting to be serviced or repaired, and I point to them. "I can help out. You seem to have a lot of work."

"I'm not having no bitch touching my bike!" Slick growls.

I see there are cars here too. "What about them?" I point in the other direction.

Drummer and Blade exchange looks. "If she's any fuckin' good, we could use an extra pair of hands," Blade tells his prez. "We've got a lot of work, and if she knows her way around cars like she seems to do bikes, she could come in handy."

After looking around him, and then looking at me, Drummer sighs. I must look a sight, standing here, my hair pulled roughly back in a bun, overalls shrugged down to my hips, my skin gleaming with sweat and probably oil smudges on my face. I hope he's seeing a mechanic and not simply my sex. He stares at Blade.

"You," he points to him. "You watch her like a hawk. Don't let her near the bikes, get her going on an oil change or some-thing. And," now he raises his voice so everyone can hear, "I don't want any slacking just because you've got a fuckin' bitch working here."

Then he turns to me. "You can use the computer to search for your part. You find it, Blade will give you the shop's card and you can put it on that. You work your fuckin' little ass off as repayment. And you stay here—right here. You don't come back to the clubhouse. I'll get one of the bitches to bring you some food. Got it? And as soon as your fuckin' bike's fixed, you're out of here, and we'll never see you again."

I feel like high-fiving someone. It's no hardship to me at all. And working my butt off around cars and bikes? That's all I've ever done and all I've ever wanted to do. After weeks on the road, I can't wait to get my hands dirty again. Unable to restrain myself, I do the most stupid thing I can, I leap toward him and pulling his head down to mine, give him a smacker on his cheek. Well, that's what I meant to do. At the last second, he turns his head and I catch him right on the mouth.

Big mistake! As my lips touch his, it's as though an electric current has passed between us. Time stands still and I breathe in his masculine scent, a perfume that goes straight to my head. My stomach clenches, and I feel a tingling between my thighs.

He steps back quickly and sneers before throwing one last glare toward his brothers, as though daring them to comment. Turning on his heels, he leaves as though the hounds of hell were after him.

Shit!

"Come here, Sam." Blade's laughing.

"Wrench," I tell him as I go toward him. When he raises his eyebrows I continue, "Where I last worked, that was what they called me."

Slowly a face splitting grin crosses his face. "Come here, then, *Wench.*"

Oh God, I suppose I walked right into that. But as they're letting me stay on to fix my bike *and* letting me work on my beloved engines, I'm not going to cause a fuss. I can only hope it doesn't catch on. But that hope is short lived as he leads me into the small but fairly organised office, and introduces me to a man who must at least partly be of Native American descent. He's got striking features and long dark hair reaching down to the middle of his back. I'm green with envy—his hair is sleek and straight, unlike mine with curls and waves unless I attack it with straighteners.

"Mouse, this is Wench. Wench, meet our computer guru. He can set you up with your own account and password so you can surf to your heart's content."

Clearly having overheard Drummer's instructions, Mouse makes no protest and simply gets on with his task. Blade stands behind him as he indicates a chair for me, and then his fingers fly across the keyboard. In no time at all, he writes down an account name and password for me, then with a nod waits while I log in. I see the access he's given me only lets me onto the internet and doesn't let me into anything else—no accounts or general order screens for the garage. Not surprising, I suppose. The Satan's Devils would be wary of anyone poking around in their business.

"You any good with computers?" Mouse asks, his eyes watching me carefully.

"I can use them to order parts, know my way around some accounting software, but that's my limit." Oh, and to go on bike forums, but I don't think he needs to know that. My answer seems to satisfy him when, after a moment of consideration, he jerks his chin toward Blade and they both leave the office.

Wishing I had access to my notes where I'd stored the details of all the decent scrap dealers I'd normally use, I begin my search. One hour and several phone calls later and I've found exactly what I'm looking for, and hopefully they'll be able to FedEx it to me in a couple of days. Going to the office door, I call out to Blade, and he's soon handing me the shop's credit card so I can complete my purchase. That done, I offer to get down to work.

"You gonna show us what you can do?" Blade asks, a smirk on his face.

"Rather she shows us her tits!" another man calls out.

"Shut it, Bullet!" Blade shakes his head, but he's chuckling too.

I cut my teeth on oil changes, I could do them in my sleep. I work on the first couple of cars that Blade points out, having them done in no time. I work quickly and efficiently, and Blade watches me for a while and then checks up on me periodically, but he soon seems happy enough that I know what I'm doing— as he should be. He's getting a good mechanic for the price of an oil seal.

Various men wander into the area I'm working, treating me as though I'm a curiosity. I ignore comments about my ass and suggestions what they could do to me as I'm bending over an engine. I've worked with men all my life and am well used to such repartee and just let it roll off me. Soon, they'll get over the fact I'm a woman, they always do. Soon they'll be treating me just like one of the boys. If I'm here long enough, that is.

I don't want Drummer to see me like that.

Stopping my mind thinking about the enigmatic president who I've no business lusting after, I'm polite when Blade introduces me to Dollar, who's apparently the treasurer—who knew that motorcycle clubs even had positions like that?—and another good-looking man called Dart as well as a biker strangely called Tongue, who seems transfixed on my unremarkably-sized chest. After Tongue stuck out that organ and waggled it at me, his stud glinting in the overhead light, I'm not left in any doubt how he'd gotten his name. *Ew.*

I think they try to flirt with me, but I'm used to the banter of this type in such an environment, and while I wouldn't know how to respond to it, I do know how to ignore it and focus instead on my task.

As the afternoon draws on, the men start to disappear. Blade pulls something out of the back and attempts to dust it off. When he unfolds it, it's an old camp bed, and I appreciate him thinking of it. After the camaraderie of the afternoon, I feel a bit lonely as they all drift away but remember my strict instructions not to go to the clubhouse. I don't much mind as I recollect the types of things I saw there yesterday evening. I have no wish to see any more dicks being openly sucked in full view. Drummer needn't have worried. I have no intention to invade their privacy again. My memories mean my own company doesn't seem so bad.

I dig my e-reader out of my bag ready to amuse myself with a book. Just before the men close up the shop, the prospect appears with a plate of food, some water, beer, and other snacks. As I remove the cover on the plate to find a tasteful dish of what's obviously homemade fried chicken, I wonder who does the cooking here. I don't think about it too long, the food's calling to me, and I realise I'm starving.

By the time I've finished eating, I'm entirely alone.

CHAPTER SEVEN

*D*rummer...
Leaving the garage, shaking my head, I'm wondering how the fuck Sam had managed to outmanoeuvre me and had me agreeing to her staying here. I should have shipped her off to the city and refused to have her back on the compound. We could have taken the bike down to her when it was fixed, but instead she's got me twisted around her little finger, and now she's going to be sleeping in the shop. *Maybe after an uncomfortable night she'll be happy to move to town.* Knowing my brothers, she's got to be less than pleased with them as company. *What if one of them hits on her?* Oh for fuck's sake, get a grip on yourself man. She's a bitch, and you've got those aplenty. There's nothing special about *her*.

But she kissed me.

Why the fuck had I turned at that precise second? I knew she had planned only to graze my cheek, but our lips had met. The softness of hers as they touched mine, well, just that gentle momentary caress had my cock swelling. I'd inhaled her perfume and it was almost enough to make me bend her over the nearest workbench, yank her jeans down and thrust into her warm tight hole to get some relief, and without having a care if any of the brothers were watching me stake my claim. Oh no, I'm not shy when it comes to things like that. How does she get me so aroused so fast? Vroom, it's like zero to fucking sixty in one second flat. I'd had to get out of there fast before I disgraced myself or had done something I might regret. Her reaction to me that she'd been unable to hide? Well, I wasn't blind to that either. It would be an attraction that I might like to explore if there weren't other complications.

I'm reminded that there are other issues at stake as soon as I enter the clubroom. Viper's pacing, his face as black as a storm cloud, his legs kicking chairs out of the way. Most brothers are staying clear, but Peg's trying to calm him down and Wraith's swearing at him to knock it off and asking what the fuck is the matter. As I step through the door, Viper notices me immediately and approaches with his hands tightly balled.

"What the fuck d'ya think you're playing at?" he throws at me.

"My office! Now!" I barge around him giving him no option but to follow. As he enters behind me, he slams the door shut, so hard the walls rattle.

"I thought you were gonna get rid of the bitch?"

"Sit and calm the fuck down!" I lean over the desk, my weight on my hands, muscles bunched in my arms.

He doesn't. He stays standing, his arms swinging at his sides as though he wants to take a punch at me and is only just managing to hold himself back.

"SIT!" My loud snarl gets his attention and he does what I ask, but pulls the chair around the other way and straddles it. His position means he can lean over my desk and proceed to yell into my face.

"I want her gone, Prez. Today!"

"And I want you to calm the fuck down and listen to me." My hand thumps down on the desk making my laptop bounce. Curling my fingers into my palms, my knuckle duster rings glint in the light. He doesn't want to take me on, I've had enough already with his daughter pushing me around today.

It's at that point he sees just how angry I am and begins to come back to himself. He sits up a little straighter, which at least has the effect of moving his face out of range of my fists and runs his hands through his hair. "I don't want her here, Prez."

"I think you've made that fuckin' clear, and if you'll listen to me for a moment, you'll hear that she won't be coming anywhere near the fuckin' clubhouse. I've made sure of that. Okay?"

"She's down at the fuckin' shop. You can't fuckin' guarantee she'll stay there—"

"I fuckin' can!" I take a moment to push my temper back down. If there's one thing I don't like, it's being openly challenged. "Look, Viper, I understand this has been a fuckin' shock to you and that you don't want your ol' lady finding out. But Sam will keep her mouth shut, she's made that promise. No one else knows there's a reason she came here other than I helped her when she was stranded on the side of the road." I break off and wipe my hand over my beard, idly noting it's time for a trim. With so much grey coming through now I don't like it getting too long, it just seems to emphasise it. "Look, I accept I have no fuckin' idea how you're feeling. Christ, it would be a shock for any man, but she's here, and she's staying unless she puts one fuckin' foot out of line. Look at it this way, once you've thought about it, you might want to change your mind. At least talk to her, maybe get to know her—"

"I don't want to fuckin' get to know her!" Viper's shouting again now, just when I thought I'd managed to bring him down a bit. His head drops into his hands. When he looks up his eyes are full of hurt. "I just want her gone. I fuckin' can't have Sandy finding out."

I don't understand why. "But Viper, you were barely out of diapers at the time, long before you hooked up with Sandy. Surely, she'd understand? Heck, I can understand you not wanting her to be part of your family, you don't even know the girl, but when it's all sunk in, you might want to at least talk to her. Get to find out a bit about her?"

I can see I'm not getting through as he continues shaking his head sadly. "You don't know the whole story, Drum."

"Do you want to tell me?" I'm not totally sure I want to know. As president sometimes I feel I'm looked on as a life coach or confident to the members, and I've got enough on my plate as it is, thank you very fucking much.

He's considering it, but to my relief he answers in the negative. "No. Just know this. The sooner she fuckin' disappears, the better. I'm relying on you, Drum. The brothers and Sandy must never know who she is."

With that parting shot, he leaves my office. Which he did well to do. I'm not having any brother questioning my integrity. I've given him my word, he just has to accept it.

I need a drink. Wouldn't you just fucking believe it? Opening the mini-fridge behind me, I find it's empty. Shit. I rub my temples, trying to ease away the aching behind my eyeballs. Viper's got me all stressed out. A beer would really help right now. I go back into the clubroom and head toward the bar.

"Hey, don't slap me on my arse." The sight of Sophie, standing with her hands on her hips, glaring at Wraith, greets me, and the memory of just how much she's changed since she's been here makes me give an inward grin and lightens my mood. She was so timid when she first arrived. She's certainly taken to her position as the senior old lady, belonging as she does to the VP.

"Ass, darlin', ass. How many times do we need to tell you?" Peg, who contributed one hell of a lot to getting her up on her feet and out of the darn wheelchair raises his beer toward her.

Her attention switches to him, and her glower now encompasses Dart, Slick, and Bullet too, who are sitting with the sergeant-at-arms all wearing wide grins. "And I keep telling you bloody heathens, it's my arse, so I'll keep the extra R in it."

Wraith's trying to keep a straight face as he puts his arm around Sophie. "And I'd prefer you to keep putting two letters in it, my love."

Loud guffawing bursts from the table and I bark a laugh myself. "Good on you, Vee Pee," shouts Dart, drawing out his title. "Way to go, man."

Sophie turns bright red and playfully slaps Wraith on his arm. "Bloody hell! Do you want everyone to know what we do?"

"Think you've just confirmed it, darlin'."

I grab a beer and walk away, shaking my head. Soph's good for Wraith, anyone can see that, but there isn't a woman in the world that I'd tie myself to.

For the next couple of hours, it's business as usual. I remember, at last, to send a prospect down with some food for Sam. Just when I start to think I've made inroads into the heap of work that piled up while I was in Vegas, the phone rings.

"Speak to me."

"Drummer?"

"Yeah."

"It's Ben Carter here. We met at Emir Kadar's wedding."

Well fuck me, I remember him and the occasion. Just thinking of it makes me smile. What a mixed bag of people were there. I'd never thought my boys would fit in alongside politicians, film and pop stars and all the hoity-toity, but they sure did. Mouse even beat the desert sheikhs in the bareback riding competition. Getting back to the man on the other end of the phone, I recall he's the senior partner of a security firm in London. We'd exchanged business cards, well, he'd given me his. A president of an outlaw motorcycle club doesn't exactly carry advertising around, but I'd given him my number.

"Yeah, I remember you, Carter."

"Got something you might be able to help us with. The pay's good."

"Talk to me." We don't turn dollars down.

"I'd like to set a meet up with Jason Deville. He's my other partner."

"He wasn't at the wedding?" I recall there was a fair contingent there of what is it now Grade A Security—some as guests, others beefing up the protection.

"No, he likes to stay under the radar. He's got something going on that your guys might be able to help with. We'd like to explore it anyway."

I think for a moment. "I'd need to know more."

"Not something we want to discuss on the phone."

Although he can't see me, I nod. I understand business like that. "Give him my number and we'll set up a meet. I'll listen to what he has to say." In the meantime, I'll get Mouse to dig further into Grade A. I believe they're a reputable company, so it's strange why they want help from us. Hopefully they're not working for the feds and planning to set us up, but I don't waste my breath asking. If that were the case, I wouldn't be given an honest answer.

"Thanks, Drummer. He'll be in touch in the next few days."

I end the call and lean back in my chair. This day is turning out to be decidedly odd.

Having spent the weekend in Vegas, we're making up for the missed church, and it's fast approaching the time when I need to make my way to the meeting room. Tunnelling my hands through my hair, I expect people think the life of an MC president is about riding bikes all day and having fun. In reality, it's quite the opposite; more like being the CEO of a small business as well as house mother to a fuckload of unruly boys. This being the mother chapter, there are always issues and problems to resolve or discuss with my fellow presidents. Wraith, as my VP, has often said he wouldn't want to walk in my shoes, and I don't blame him.

Entering church, I walk to my seat at the head of the table, the vision in my head, as it unfortunately too often is, of the body of Chrissy bleeding out, her blood soaking into the wood.

It hangs heavy on my conscience that it was in this very room that I took the life of a sweet butt who'd betrayed the club. Still too fresh in my mind, I can only hope those memories will fade with time. While I had no other choice, it's in my mind as I take the chair. It goes against the grain for any of us to harm a woman, that was the reason why I did the deed myself, not wanting to put that burden on any of my brothers. It's a heavy responsibility leading the club like this.

Remembering Chrissy's betrayal for some reason makes me wonder about the woman working in our garage. Can I trust her? Is she who she says she is? Oh, I'm certain she's Viper's daughter, but was finding her father the only reason that brought her here? Is it right for me to go with my gut feeling that she's not out to cause us trouble? Fuck, I don't normally take things at face value, so why do it with her?

Sitting down, I let the rowdy conversations going on wash over me. As normal, Blade, our enforcer and head mechanic, is trying to get a smoke from Dart, who's complaining it's time for him to either finally quit or start buying his own again. Wraith is sitting on my left and Dollar our treasurer next to him. Peg is on my right, then Heart, our secretary, completes our officer complement. They are currently trying to keep order as the rest of the members discuss the very thing that I've just been thinking about, the woman I've brought into the compound. Halfway down the table sits Viper, looking as though he's wishing he could be anywhere else, his face dark and glowering, his eyes staring at nothing.

Rapping on the table with the gavel, I get everyone's attention. "Shut the fuck up!" As voices start to quiet, I ask, "Wraith?"

There's still a murmuring at the end of the table, but Wraith's glare is almost as effective as mine, and soon there's silence.

Wraith clears his throat and then starts to give his report. "We've got two new members coming in at the weekend from the Vegas Chapter. Joker and Lady."

I knew it was coming. There's a roar of laughter, and it's Dart who slaps his hands down on the table. "What kind of fuckin' handle is Lady?"

"Someone you wouldn't want to fuckin' take on in a fight." Wraith verbally knocks him down. "And in the looks department, he might give you a run for your money, Dart."

Dart is very much our own lady's man with long curly dark hair, an aquiline face, and dark eyes. Casting a glance his way, I see his face fall when he grasps he might have competition.

"Joker?" Beef calls out. "He better not fuckin' joke around with me."

"Joker," continues the VP, ignoring the interruption, "will be our road captain."

Nodding to show my agreement, I think they'd all accept it's about time we had that position filled. A road captain's job is to plan routes and ride at the end of the column to make sure all riders on a run get to their destination and back again safely. It's a role Peg's been partially filling up to now, so it will take some of the load off of him; something he's just realising.

"About fuckin' time," the sergeant-at-arms pronounces, showing he's on the same page.

"Now we all know Roadrunner has started prospecting for us. Any complaints about him, come to me." Wraith continues his report.

"I've got a fuckin' complaint! He brought his fuckin' rice rocket in for a service," Tongue growls from the end of the room.

The VP glares at him. "He's got a Harley now too. He rides his pocket rocket in competition. Nothing against the man for owning one."

There are still comments thrown around showing the brothers' dislike for the plastic rice burner Roadrunner prefers, but the VP and I have seen the man race, and he impressed us with his riding skills. I reckon he'll be a good man to have in the club. If he survives the next twelve months, that is.

"We still on the lookout for more members?" Now it's Bullet who speaks up.

Wraith nods toward me. "We've got the room, so yeah. After what happened with the fuckin' Rock Demons I'd like to boost the numbers here. The right people, of course."

"Don't want no more fuckin' Busters," Tongue snarls, and there are snarls of agreement from all around as we all remember the man who tried to rape the VP's old lady, and who is now rotting in the ground.

"Right." I have to bang the gavel again to get their attention, wanting to get down to the main business. "Dollar, what's the money looking like?"

Dollar, always serious, consults some paperwork in front of him. "We're bringing it in just fine. In fact, we're turning away work at the garage as we just don't have enough mechanics."

Now that's interesting. What if Sam proves she's as good as she says? *What the fuck am I thinking?* Having a bitch fix our bikes? *That's never going to happen.* But whatever the fuck is wrong with my head, I can't prevent my hand moving to my mouth and smoothing my lips where she kissed me. My cock starts lengthening. *In church.*

Forcing myself back to the task at hand, I make myself listen and hopefully make intelligent contributions to the rest of the reports from the officers. No one starts looking at me strangely, so I assume I'm acting normal enough. For once, it's hard to keep my mind on the business of the club when I can't help my mind wandering to pretty brown hair scrunched up in a bun, which I'd love to undo to see it cascade over her naked body, or wrap around my hand while I'm pounding into her from behind...

"Yeah, Shooter. What was that again?" When he repeats his question again, somehow, I manage to find an answer which seems to be the right one as he looks satisfied.

Then that's the end of the standard business. "Okay, any other business?"

"Yeah." Slick waves his hand. "What's this with the bitch in the garage? How long she gonna be there?"

"I can answer that." Blade jerks his chin at Slick. "Wench will be there until Friday. She managed to get hold of the part and is waiting on the delivery."

"Wench?" Wraith asks before I can.

Blade laughs and leans back in his chair. "Apparently, her handle was Wrench at her last place of work. I reckoned Wench was more fitting."

Wraith is shaking his head. Fuckers always seem to come up with handles for the bitches that are amusing to us, but which they tend to hate. He's only just managed to stop them calling his old lady Wheels, and that was only when she got rid of the wheelchair for good. But I don't like anyone giving Sam a fucking handle. If anyone should, it should be me, and that thought makes me frown.

"We having a party for Joker and Lady?" Beef asks.

"Goes without fuckin' saying." Peg grins.

"If Wench is gonna be staying here, why not bring her up to the clubhouse? She might wanna join in. Could do me some of that." Pushing back his chair, Beef cups his meaty hand around his junk and thrusts his hips so we all can see.

My leg starts bouncing under the table, and it takes all my effort to control myself and to keep anger out of my voice. "And that's the fuckin' reason she's coming nowhere near the clubhouse. She's not a whore or a hangaround."

"We're feeding her, giving her the run of the shop. Fuck, we paid for the part for her fuckin' bike. What's she giving us?" Slick looks confused. In our world, a woman's only good for one thing. Fucking.

Viper's face is red. He's said nothing throughout the meeting. In addition to my own strange desire to protect Sam from the likes of my brothers seated around the table, I've a lot of sympathy for him. He might not want to accept it, but it's his fucking daughter they're discussing like some fresh meat.

I bang the gavel loudly. "She's under my fuckin' protection and that means from you motherfuckers too."

Wraith is giving me a strange look, Peg's grinning widely.

Fuck, I've got to rescue this before they all get the wrong idea. *Or the right one.*

"For fuck's sake. She isn't from our world, but she's a biker who needed help. As long as she keeps herself out of trouble, she can stay until next week. But she isn't coming to the clubhouse and she isn't coming to no fuckin' party. And you douchebags," I pause and let my steely gaze roam around the table, "are going to leave her the fuck alone!"

Heart speaks up. "We've got spare rooms, why make her sleep in the garage? Surely, she'd be more comfortable somewhere else?"

I shrug. "She refused to be put up at a hotel as she wanted to stay near her bike. So, that's what she's doing. Staying with her fuckin' Vincent."

Now there are appreciative laughs. Thank fuck. They think I'm teaching her a lesson when my overriding intention is to keep her away from Viper... and from them.

I bang the gavel for the final time. "Church fuckin' over! Officers, can you stay for a minute?"

"You need me, Prez?"

Heart's our secretary and doesn't need to be involved in this. "Nah, you and Dollar can go."

As they follow the other members out, I'm left with the VP, sergeant-at-arms, and enforcer. Blade's spinning his knife on the table in front of him.

"I've had a strange phone call." I start to fill them in with my conversation with Carter, quickly bringing them up to speed.

When I've finished, no one speaks for a minute; then I'm not surprised Wraith's the first to voice his concerns. "What do we know about Grade A Security? Could they be working for the feds? Setting out to trap us?"

"That was my first thought, VP."

"I was talking to some of them when we were out in Arab land. Seemed fairly straight." Peg pauses, then emphasises, "Very straight."

Blade's nodding. "So, what would people on the right side of the law be wanting with us?"

I jerk my chin toward the enforcer. "Precisely my fuckin' concern. They work with the law, not outside it like us."

Tapping the table with his fingertips, Wraith chimes in, "Prez, we gave protection to Sophie. Could it be another job like that? Keeping someone safe and out of harm's way?"

"Like we did a good job with that," Blade answers him.

I don't want a rerun of everything we went through with Buster, or when we'd left ourselves exposed and the man who wanted to kill Wraith's old lady walked straight in—after he killed Adam, of course. "We did okay in the end." Then I remember to give credit where credit's due. "Thanks to Shooter."

"Yeah, the kid did well."

"It can't hurt to meet him, Prez. See what he's after." Wraith gets us back on track.

"That's my thinking, VP. Somewhere off-site would be best. I'll get Mouse to see what he can dig up about Grade A. We don't want to let in a Trojan horse."

There are nods and chin jerks now.

"Okay, when he gets in touch, I'll arrange something. We'll use the Wheel Inn for the meet." I'm referring to the restaurant we own, and which Sandy manages.

Wraith points his hand toward an empty seat. "What is it with Viper today? He looks like someone's stolen his ride."

Knowing I can't say anything without giving everything away, I shake my head. "No idea, Wraith. Probably just having a bad day."

"Perhaps he's had an argument with Sandy. I'll have a chat with him."

"Nah, Peg, I'd leave him alone." That's one conversation that wouldn't go down well at all.

CHAPTER EIGHT

*S*am...

After the guys all disappear, I settle down, catching up with my reading. I'd downloaded an MC romance series a few weeks back but never had the chance to start it. Tonight, this seems just the right location to have a read of this particular subject matter.

The prospect had dropped off a couple of blankets and a pillow. Pumping up the latter and setting it behind me, I lean back to make myself as comfortable as possible on the cot and start turning the pages. Pretty soon, I have my eyes opened to a completely different world, one I'd never dreamed of before. Sweet butts, old ladies... and here I am, right in the middle of a real-life biker club. Reading on, I wonder how close to reality the fiction I'm absorbing is, and whether they run this club along the same lines? If so, no wonder the men are treating me with suspicion. Putting my e-reader down for a second, I lean my head back and close my eyes. They *do* come over as misogynistic pricks, so the book has gotten that right. But can they also be as protective and loving toward their women? And just what is it about how they use that male piece of their anatomy that gets women desperate to give them a try?

Weary, through stress and the lack of sleep last night, my eyes are so tired, it's an effort to open them again, so I put my book away and settle down, breathing in the comforting scents of oil and grease. To me, it's the familiar smells of home. I think back— I could only have been about two when Mom first took me to the garage. She'd landed a job doing their books but couldn't afford to have anyone look after me. For the next couple of years of my life, and then every day after school and every school holiday, I spent my time surrounded by cars and bikes in various stages of repair. I was a quiet, unassuming child, wary, even then, of getting under anyone's feet. Slowly I became a fixture, accepted by everyone.

It started when I was old enough to be asked to get bottles of water out of the fridge or to take an empty cup back to the small kitchen. Gradually, my chores progressed to being asked to pass tools. Before I could read, I could identify one socket wrench from another. I was ten when I did my first oil change by myself.

The sound of engines was the main music I heard. And, as it turned out, for which I had a particular ear, often telling the mechanics when something wasn't right before they'd even noticed. When my mom bought me my bike, they put an area aside for me to work on my Vincent. I didn't go to my prom; while my friends danced, I was attempting to install a new alternator. While my contemporaries dated, I was connecting the throttle cable or fixing the brakes.

Having been brought up alongside, the men treated me like one of them. From time to time a new mechanic would come in and would flirt with me, but I was more interested in the workings of a carburetor than in anything a man might have under his clothes, and before long they too treated me just the same as everyone else.

Oh, I was asked out, often by customers, but my mom had impressed on me the importance of choosing wisely. Time and time again, she'd explain that while she never regretted me being born, being pregnant and alone had rewritten her life. Her lesson learned, she became wary of the opposite sex until the day she died. A lesson she'd passed on to me.

These bikers don't frighten me, not when I've been surrounded by their kind all my life. No, if I can believe the book I've been reading, it's the sweet butts and old lady's who'd worry me more. I'm not sure how to hold a conversation with a woman, unless she's got a good knowledge of bikes or how to strip down an engine.

I don't much mind having to stay in the shop. I just wish it wasn't quite so damn hot! I'm dog-tired, but the heat is keeping me awake. I throw off the sheet and turn over, doing so, I spot something over my head. It's a freaking air conditioning unit! But they didn't even use them during the day. Why not? Is it broken? Hmm, I'll have to take a look at that in the morning.

Eventually I fall into a fitful sleep, but wake at dawn, sweat sticking to me, my tank and shorts fused to my skin. Oh freaking hell, I can't take another night like this. The first thing on my agenda has to be checking out the dust and cobweb-covered unit hanging on the wall.

It takes a few moments to get the rusty screws to turn, but once I've got the cover off, I study it for a moment, tracing the wires, imaging the circuit in my head. It's old and mechanical... Ah, yes, there's the problem. I find what I need by rummaging around in the metal cabinets, and there we go. I've even found the remote that works it and switch it on. Blissful cool air sweeps over me. Great!

Looking around, I spy, as I'd suspected, another unit on the opposite wall. Repeating everything I did with the first, I soon have that one fixed and working again too.

Once I'm down from the ladder with my feet back on the floor, I turn to see a beautiful woman with a slight limp coming in carrying a tray. After looking around to find a surface to place it on, she stands back and looks at me. At first I think her expression's critical, but then her face splits into a welcoming smile.

"So, you're Wench," she says with a grin.

"The name's Sam," I correct her. I brush the dirt off my hands and then reach one out for her to shake.

"If they've named you, you're stuck with it." She laughs, and glancing across to a bench, leans herself up against it, her arms folded across her chest. Her eyes seem to be assessing me. "I was called Wheels for months. All because I was in a wheelchair when I got here."

My mouth opens. "That's cruel." Then I comprehend what she's said and that it might explain the limp. "You okay now? Must have been serious if you couldn't walk."

"Oh, I'll never be better as such." She pauses and rolls up one leg of her jeans, allowing me to see her leg ends below her knee, and that she's wearing a prosthesis. "It's thanks to Peg and the rest of them that I'm walking again. The buggers' have got a rough side, but underneath, they're the kindest men you'd want to meet."

Hmm, I think I need to be convinced of that. "So, what's your name?"

"Sophie. Wraith, the VP, is my old man."

Oh, so this is a real-life old lady.

She pushes away from the bench and points at the tray she's brought. "Hey, you might want to get that down you. It will get cold otherwise."

As I thank her, something about her strikes me. "Are you English?" I ask, suddenly picking up on her accent.

"Yes. I've only been here since February. It's a long story, but perhaps I'll tell you one day."

It sounds intriguing. "Sure."

"Well, better be getting on. See you around, Wench." She giggles as she mentions my new name and goes off. This time I'm watching how she walks, she carefully chooses how she places each foot. Yeah, perhaps I'd like to hear her story, though I doubt I'll be sticking around long enough to get to know her better. Which is a shame, despite my concerns about being able to talk to the women here, she seemed easy enough to get along with.

It's a workday, but the guys don't seem to be hurrying in to start work. One of the first to arrive is wearing a cut with the word "Prospect" on it. He comes over to inspect a dirt bike that has been relegated to a back corner of the garage. He wheels it out front and fires it up, I grimace, not able to help myself. Try as I might, the words just start spilling out, even though I suspect he might not welcome what I'm going to say.

Stepping outside, I point to it. "That has a problem."

"It's why it's here." The obvious comment is said without malice. "I'm supposed to race next weekend, but I'm not happy with it. I took it out the other day and it just wasn't right. I'm Roadrunner by the way."

"Sam." Once again I brush off my hand and reach out to shake his.

He throws me a grin. "Wench," he corrects. "I've already heard about you." He ignores my scowl and continues, "What d'you reckon is wrong with it?"

"The timing's off. You can hear it."

He revs the engine.

"Sounds alright to me."

Sounds freaking dreadful to me. "Hang on a minute." I go back into the garage, grabbing the tool I need. When I return, he's staring at me in horror, but ignoring him, I crouch down and make the tiniest of adjustments. "There, try it now."

This time it purrs, and I give a satisfied smile. Even he can tell the difference.

"May I?" I walk around the bike, examining all the wires and pipes, checking the fittings. I find something a bit slack and tighten it. His throttle's sticking, so I loosen it a fraction. "Want to give it a test run?"

By this time, we've drawn an audience; Blade's standing watching me with Slick. Slick laughs at the prospect. Coming over, he slaps him on the back. "Rather you than me letting a fuckin' bitch near my bike. Fuckin' thing might fall apart."

Blade, however, has a different expression on his face—he's not laughing, he's looking thoughtful. Nodding toward the prospect he suggests, "Why don't you take it for a spin?"

Slick chuckles, "Just watch yourself. Wench could have fucked it up good and proper. You didn't let her near the brakes, did you?"

Roadrunner's pulling on his brain bucket and getting ready to roll. "I'll let you know when I come back," he grins at them. "Assuming I come back, that is."

I shoot him the finger, well, I've been around mechanics a long time. Then he's zooming off out of the compound. That engine sounds sweet to me.

Taking the couple of steps which closes the distance between us, Blade puts his arms around my shoulder and starts steering me into the garage. As we enter through the doorway, he stops, looks around, and holds his hand up in the air. Finally, his eyes settle on first one, then the other of the fully functioning air conditioning units making the inside of the garage at least tolerable.

"Fuck me!" He walks over and stands underneath it, staring up with disbelieving eyes.

"How the fuck?" Slick comes in and stands next to him.

Tongue appears and comes across to see what the other two are looking at. Like Blade, he holds his hand up to test the now cool airflow.

Finally, all three turn to me. I shrug. "A fuse had gone, and I replaced a corroded wire and cleaned up the terminals. The other needed much the same treatment."

"Thought that thing was a complete goner." Blade approaches me. "Fuck, you're a useful bitch to have around, Wench!" He pulls me into his arms and swings me around.

"Put her the fuck down! What did I tell you fuckers?" The roaring voice can only belong to one person, and Blade almost drops me in his rush to obey. As I stagger to get my balance, only slightly more quietly, Drummer yells out, "What the fuck is going on here?"

Slick points upwards. "Fuckin' bitch fixed it."

"Fixed what?" Drummer presumably doesn't spend enough time in the shop to immediately notice the difference.

"The fuckin' air conditioner," Blade enlightens him.

Now Drummer's looking up, noticing the vent on the units moving slowly up and down in the way they're supposed to do. Slowly, his eyes seem to widen. "That right?" He's moved closer now, and the tone of his voice sends tingles zapping through me. That my nipples are hardening and poking at the material of my t-shirt is down to the cold air, right? But as I turn around, I catch his eyes on me, there, on my breasts. His steely gaze is almost caressing me, causing the nubs to peak even more. I'm not sure I'm fooling anyone.

Covering myself with my overalls before answering and giving an exaggerated shiver as though the cool air's making me cold, I respond, "Yeah, it was simple enough to do."

He's smirking as if recognising the effect he has on me, and for the life of me, I don't know what it is about this man that magnetises me. No one's ever made me embarrass myself like this before.

"Where did you learn that?"

Shrugging, I tell him, "We had a similar unit often going wrong at the shop back home. I've got smaller fingers than the men, so they were always getting me to fix it."

There's a tinge of admiration in his eyes, and then he spoils it, leaning forward to whisper into my ear and asking with a leer, "And just what else are you good at with your hands?"

His intentionally crude comment, delivered in a tone that leaves me in no doubt I'm not mistaken, stumps me, and I don't know how to respond. Am I expected to flirt? Or say something to try to shut down further suggestive comments? While I understand engines, I have no clue where to start with a man. In the end, I pretend to misunderstand. "I can show you my certificates if you want. I'm a qualified mechanic."

Stepping back, he shakes his head and gives me a curious look. *Did he expect me to hit on him or something?*

We stand, in an awkward silence. Blade and the others have wandered away and have started getting on with their jobs for the day. I shift uncomfortably, not knowing what to say, not used to having any man's attention focused on me. Part of me wants to encourage his interest, but I don't have the first clue how to do that. Another part of me wants to run. Fast. As far away from him as I can. He seems to sense my conflicting emotions, raising an eyebrow, as though expecting me to say more. Then, to my immense relief, I'm saved by a roar.

Roadrunner pulls up, dismounts and shouts through the doorway, "Fuckin' ace! Now I might have a chance in the race on Sunday. She's running fuckin' sweet!"

He runs in and, not noticing his prez standing in the shadows, pulls me in for a hug. "Fuck, girl. You know what you're doing, don't cha? Never known her to go so smoothly before."

Then he's on the ground, his hand nursing his cheek as he looks up in surprise at Drummer standing over him. "Hands fuckin' off the woman! How many fuckin' times do I have to tell you fuckers?"

His eyes rolling, still stunned from the blow, Roadrunner tries to explain, stammering out, "Sorry, Prez, but she fixed my bike—"

"She isn't supposed to be fixing bikes!" Drummer roars. "And you!" He turns to me. "You keep your hands off anything until I give you precise instructions that you can touch it. Are we understood?"

I was just trying to help. But for once in my life, I have the sense to know when it's best not to speak. I jerk my head to show I understand. Drummer lets out a snort of disgust, turns on his heel and leaves.

As soon as he's out of sight, Slick calls out, "What the fuck's all that about?"

Blade throws me a knowing look. "Reckon I've got a good idea. Just remember Brothers, Drummer wants us to keep our hands off his woman."

Now they're all laughing, and I'm standing there with my mouth hanging open. What Blade's just said makes no sense at all. I'm not Drummer's woman. No way. Hang on, he can't be insinuating that Drummer's attracted to me? Just no freaking way. *It's not possible.* No, it's just that the president knows my relationship to Viper, even if the man himself doesn't want to acknowledge it. Getting tangled up with any of his fellow members would be a complication he'd want to avoid.

I crush the bubble of excitement rising inside me, putting it down to a touch of indigestion, and get on with my work.

CHAPTER NINE

*D*rummer...

    I think it's safe to say I have never, ever, met another woman like her. Not only does she know her way around bikes and cars *and* can fix a fucking air conditioning unit, but she's a beautiful woman and doesn't seem to know it. She doesn't doll herself up like the sweet butts do. No, she doesn't dress for attention nor adorn herself with makeup. But somehow, in those oversized overalls and grubby t-shirt with oil smears on her face, she's as gorgeous as any woman I've ever seen, and I'm unable to deny she's captured my interest. Well, if my cock being at least at half-mast every time I'm around her is anything to go by.

I hadn't missed the way her nipples had hardened when she was speaking to me, and I know for damn sure it wasn't the cold air causing them to peak. No, whatever attraction I feel for her is reciprocated, even if only in a small way, but she's got more sense than me. I couldn't resist giving her an opportunity to show it, a few suggestive words which would have had any other woman fluttering her eyelids and responding, but she ignored me entirely, though that betraying red flush to her cheeks showed me she wasn't unaffected. Her refusal to flirt hadn't been any deterrent to my throbbing dick.

Isn't that a fuckup of a situation? Whether Viper wants to admit it or not, she's the daughter of one of my brothers. And that, there alone, is a more than sufficient reason for me to keep away, but the swelling against my thigh tries to argue it doesn't matter. She's a grown woman and knows her own mind. We're both adults. We should be able to fuck who we want. *I can't go there.* I wish I could. What would it be like, thrusting into her warm wet hole? *Oh, for fuck's sake!*

I pause before walking into the clubhouse, again needing to adjust myself before seeing any of my brothers. Once under control, I pop my head around the door to Mouse's cave. Waving away the inevitable smoke wafting toward me, I see him hunched over his computer as normal, his eyes flicking from screen to screen.

"Hey, Mouse!" The fucker's so intent on what he's doing, it takes a moment before he looks up and acknowledges me. At last, he notices he's no longer alone. "You managed to find anything out about Grade A Security yet?"

"I've looked. They're one of the most respected security companies in the UK. Squeaky clean, they often work with the government. They have satellite offices in a few other countries —none in the US, though—and provide bodyguard services for the sheikhs of Amahad, as we already know."

I hope Mouse isn't going to use the mention of the Arab state as an opportunity to boast of his prowess in showing the said sheikhs exactly how to ride a horse again. It's a story he retells at every opportunity. "What about Jason Deville?" I ask, partly to distract him.

Sitting back, he picks up his joint and lights it. After a long drag, he glances at the glowing tip. "Now he's a strange one." He puts the blunt to his mouth, his cheeks hollow and then he exhales, causing the scented smoke to drift my way again. "He seems to be a silent partner. For the past few years, he hasn't even been back to the UK, and I can't find any cases he's been assigned to. I presume he works for them, as he draws down a salary, but as to what he does?" He shrugs.

Leaning against the doorjamb, I fold my arms. "Could he be working with the feds?"

"If he is, I can't find any mention of it. He's like a ghost. Can't find him anywhere. If it wasn't for his name as a partner of Grade A in their official papers, he almost doesn't exist."

Hmm. Well, that's fuck all use to me. A ping shows Mouse has got some info coming in. As he turns back to his screens, I leave him to it. My attempt at distracting myself from thinking about Sam hasn't helped one bit, except to give me one more headache and puzzle to solve. *Should we take the chance and meet with the man?* But if Mouse is right, and he's rarely wrong, and if Grade A has such a stellar reputation, and is completely above board, they're far more likely to be working with law enforcement than with us on the other side of the tracks. Hmm.

For the rest of that day and the next I successfully avoid going down to the shop, hoping keeping Sam out of sight is putting her out of mind as I try to occupy myself with other matters, including the elusive Jason Deville, who I've yet to hear from. I start to wonder whether he's actually going to get in contact. Maybe the delay's because he's putting his final touches to the sting before arranging to meet us. Fuck, we can't be too careful.

I sit through meetings with Dollar and Wraith, concentrating hard on processing what they're saying, with thoughts of a certain woman distracting me. I haven't seen her for two days, but it doesn't stop me thinking about her. As I busy myself in my work, I congratulate myself—I've only thought of Sam twice in this past hour. *And doesn't she have nice tits?* Not too big, my hands would cover them easily. *Christ, get out of my head, woman!*

That's it, I need something to take my mind off her. Heading out to the clubroom, I find Blade tunelessly whistling as he waits for Marsh to serve him a beer. When the prospect glances over toward me, I shake my head. It's only just past noon, and I want to keep a clear head.

Blade jerks his chin toward me. "Wench's parts arrived."

The words make me go cold, especially when he continues, "She's gonna be stripping down the engine and putting on the new gasket later. She could be gone tomorrow." He looks morosely down at his beer. He doesn't seem to be much happier about it than I am.

I force myself to be distant. "Good."

"Good?" He raises an eyebrow. "She's one of the best fuckin' mechanics I've worked with. I'd like her to stay on for a while. She's been pulling her weight; we're almost on top of the back-log. It'll be a fuckin' loss when she goes."

A loss for me, too. But how can you miss something you've never had? "That was the arrangement, Blade." How could I allow her to stay knowing how she's got Viper twisted up in knots? I've given him time, but he's still as determined to steer clear of her as he was the day she arrived. I hate seeing a brother suffering the way he is, but he's on tenterhooks the whole time, worried sick in case Sandy finds out. I still haven't a clue as to why.

"Can we give her at least another week? Got some stuff I'd like her help with."

"I'm sorry, Blade, but no. When her bike's fixed, she's fuckin' gone. Got it?" Glaring, I wait until my words get through and he understands I'm not going to be moved on this one. *He has no fucking idea how much I wish I could.*

The thought of never seeing her again causes my heart to skip a beat. The thought of never making her mine... Fuck it! Maybe I'll come back to my senses once she's gone. For now, I want her out of here. If she stays much longer, I might give in to temptation. The thought of her being so close...

I've got to do something, *anything* to get my mind off of her. "Hey, Wraith!" I shout at the VP who's just entered the room. "You busy?"

As he lifts his chin in question, I walk over and put my hand on his shoulder. "Wanna go for a ride?" What's the point in being the prez if you can't just take off when you feel the need?

His face lights up. "Yeah, why the fuck not? I'll be your wingman."

Since the problems we had with the Rock Demons, none of us much like riding alone. That wound is still too raw, and we're letting more dust settle before we start taking any risks. Although we don't expect the few Demons who managed to escape after their Phoenix clubhouse exploded to come after us, there's always a risk. And risks, when they're avoidable, are something we don't choose to take.

"You got a full tank, brother?" I know I have.

"Yeah. Where you thinking of?"

I make my suggestion and Wraith agrees, his face splitting into a wide grin. The fresh air and the challenge of the ride might just clear my head.

We take the Catalina Highway to the top of Mount Lemmon, the road twisting and turning as we weave our way round the hairpin bends and alarming drop-offs, and make our way to the top, rising through the forest of pine, fir, and spruce. When we reach the summit, we dismount just a short way away from the chairlifts where the tourists tend to congregate. The temperature's twenty degrees lower here, just forty miles from the city of Tucson, but even the cooler air does nothing to chill the heat in my blood. The image of Sam writhing beneath me as I hammer my cock into her slender frame just won't get out of my head.

Wraith's hand goes to his back pocket, and then he turns to me with a wry smile. "Still miss having a smoke at a time like this."

"I feel you, man. Fuckin' feel you." I gave up cigarettes about the same time as he did. After the ride, and here, relaxing on the summit, looking out over the Santa Catalina Mountains, it's an itch I'd love to scratch.

"You got something on your mind, Brother?" The VP cocks his head to one side, waiting for me to speak.

Am I that easy to read? Planting my backside on the seat of my bike, I hoist one foot up onto the foot peg and rest my arms on my thighs. I've known Wraith for ten years; he's been my VP for three. Maybe it would do me some good to admit to my strange feelings, to talk it out. "Fuck knows, Brother. It's that woman. Sam, Wench, whatever you want to call her. There's just something about her. She seems to have parked herself in my head, and I can't get her fuckin' out of it."

"Thought it might be something like that. She's got you all twisted up." He's grinning, the bastard. "Seen the way you look at her. Reminds me of me when I first saw Soph."

"It's nothing like that!" I spit out. "But I wouldn't mind takin' her for a test drive, I have to admit."

"If she's willing there's nothing stopping you."

Oh, if only he knew. I couldn't do that to Viper. "We don't know anything about her." I try to justify why I have to keep away without telling him the real reason.

He shrugs. "You brought her here doing your Good Samaritan act." He shakes his head and laughs. Yeah, it's unlike me to be anyone's knight in shining armour, I'm not surprised he finds it amusing.

"She's only here another day. Spare part came in today." Then she'll be out of my hair. Out of sight, out of mind. I hope.

"Hmm, about that. Wench is a bloody good mechanic. Roadrunner's singing her praises. Blade too."

Frowning, I glance up at him wondering where he's going with this.

"We've got more work in the shop than we can handle. Why not keep her around for longer? See how she gets on?"

Immediately, I search for justifiable reasons why not. "The brothers wouldn't go for it. No one wants a bitch working on their bike."

"Bitch or brother, if they can do a good job it shouldn't

matter. Bit out of the ordinary, but she could work on the citizens' cars if they'd prefer. Give her time, and she just might prove herself."

"Would *you* let her touch your ride?"

Another shrug. "If she's as good as she seems, I don't see why not."

Fuck me! Sophie's changed my VP. And sometimes, like now, I have to wonder whether it is for the better. "You going soft in your old age, Brother?"

"Seems like I am." He chuckles but doesn't take offence. He bends down and puts his hand to the grass. Finding it dry, he sits himself down, drawing up his knees and cupping his hands around them. "Don't want it broadcast yet, but Sophie's pregnant." Glancing at him quickly, I see he's grinning like a fucking loon.

Well, fuck me! "Hey, Brother, that's great!" While congratulating him, it goes through my mind that being saddled with an old lady and a kid on the way in no way appeals to me. Why limit yourself to one woman when you're surrounded by pussy just begging for your cock? I can't understand how much he's changed. Before Wheels, *Sophie, I remind myself*, came along, he was up for variety, the same way as me.

"When's it due?" I ask to be polite; it seems the right thing to ask.

"March next year," he says, proudly.

Thumping him on his back, I tell him, "Well, that's just fuckin' great!"

"See, I've been thinking, Wench got my mind focused in that direction. Whether the baby's a boy or a girl, I'd like it to be whatever it wants to be. Shouldn't be any restrictions if it's a girl. She wants to be a fuckin' mechanic? Then that's what she'll be."

"And if she wants to join the club? Be patched in?"

The look of shock on his face is comical. "Fuckin' no way. Never. Not gonna have bitches as members."

I laugh out loud. "So at least you've got some fuckin' boundaries you aren't gonna cross."

"Too fuckin' right man."

Taking out my phone, I check the time. "We better get back for church." Though I'm reluctant to return and pick up the reins of being a president again. This afternoon's been great, a good ride out with a friend. Despite having an old lady waiting for him, Wraith seems as reluctant as me to go back. He takes his time stretching while taking in one last look at the view.

"Fuckin' love this place," he confides.

I nod, being able to see so far in all directions holds a magic to me too. Regardless of my hopes, the ride and the fresh air have done nothing to make things easier in my mind. Going to my bike, I sit astride it, waiting for Wraith to come up alongside. Then we make our way back down. Leaning into the bends, speeding up and braking for the curves, I try to concentrate on enjoying the ride. *But that hair, wrapped around my fist…*

All too soon we're back at the compound and backing into our regular parking spaces outside the clubhouse. Immediately I notice the two new bikes, and I'm not the only one.

Wraith points over to them. "I see our new patches have arrived."

"Good. We can get to know them at church."

Inside the clubhouse, it's as if the brothers have forgotten our meeting tonight; it also seems like the patching over celebration has already gotten started. We like to party, any excuse. Friday nights after church, the weekend as it's simply that, or, on this occasion, the opportunity to welcome our new brothers. For now, it's a fairly family-friendly affair, and the old ladies are busying themselves setting out the food. Crystal and Heart's little daughter, Amy, is getting under everyone's feet, but the brothers are used to her and tolerant of her antics. As I watch, Bullet swings the kid up into his arms making her giggle and laugh. His old lady, Carmen, is chuckling up at her man. Rough, tough bikers we are, pandering to a small child.

As soon as she sees Wraith, Sophie makes her way over, falling into his arms as if he'd been gone for days rather than a few hours. Their kiss is long and sensuous, then, when they break off, they share a secret smile. Their obvious affection for each other scares the shit out of me. No, no way am I ever going to be handing my balls over to a bitch. No fucking way.

Seeing our new recruits up by the bar, I make my way over, holding out my hand as I approach. It's grasped first by Joker, and we slap each other on the back. Then I offer the same gesture of welcome to Lady. Fuck me; he *is* a pretty-looking man. Pulling away, making sure they've got beers to hand, I notice Peg eyeing Lady suspiciously. But when I see Lady's eyes firmly fixed on the sweet butts, I don't think we need to have any concerns about him.

Beckoning Peg over, I introduce him.

He's still looking wary. "So, Lady. That's one fuck of a handle."

The man he's addressing raises and lowers his shoulders. "Started off as Lady's Man, got shortened," he explains. "I've gotten used to it now."

The unusual moniker clarified, Peg seems to relax, and getting onto a safer subject, starts quizzing both new members about their rides.

Feeling I've done my part in being sociable, I move away, my eyes surveying the room. *Ah, there's Viper,* and Sandy's with him. Viper's being abnormally quiet, and Sandy looks like she's trying to engage him in conversation. She's got a worried look on her face, as if she knows something's up, but I doubt he's enlightened her. So far, he's remained adamant that she must never know about Sam.

A gentle tap on my arm makes me turn. "Hey, Soph." I lean closer so no one else can hear me. "I hear congratulations are in order?"

She's already glowing. "Yeah, but we want to keep it quiet

for now. It's early days, so just in case... Wraith wanted you to know, though."

I nod. "I won't let your secret out." Seems I'm carrying far too many of those lately—another one won't hurt.

"Drum," she starts, hesitantly, "can Sam come to the party later? It seems such a bloody shame that she's stuck down in the garage. She seems a nice girl."

Yeah, too nice for this unruly crowd. Even if Viper weren't glowering over in the corner, I wouldn't want her anywhere near this rowdy lot of fuckers. As she doesn't belong to anyone, she'd be fair game. "No. The deal was she'd stay out of the clubhouse."

"But—"

"No," I repeat firmly, using the tone that even while I'm not raising my voice would let anyone know not to press the matter further.

Sophie's no exception, but her eyes narrow and her lips press together, leaving me in no doubt she doesn't agree but isn't going to push her case any further. Wraith's arm snakes around her shoulder and he leads her away.

"Alright! Church!" I shout to make myself heard over the crowd and wave my arm over my head, pointing the way to our meeting room. The brothers start following me in, animated conversations continuing while they arrange places for our new members, and I have to bang the gavel a few times to get their attention.

It's a fairly short meeting, as we've had one already this week, and the main topic is about how our new road captain's going to fit in. That doesn't take much time, so barely an hour later we're done, and soon the party gets going in earnest.

Drinks flow freely; voices are getting loud. The old ladies slip away, either trusting their menfolk to behave or turning a blind eye if they can't. Standing by the bar, there's a fair number of hangarounds up from Tucson, local girls gagging for biker cock. Our resident sweet butts, to whom we provide food and lodging in return for their services, are seated together on a couch eyeing up the newcomers warily. It's a normal Friday night.

When Pussy gets sight of me watching them, she gets up and comes over, placing her hand proprietarily on my arm. "Wanna have some fun, Prez?"

Pussy's pretty enough, if a little loud once you get her going. Usually I enjoy the release she offers to me, but she's just another hole to be filled, and one who's been shared by all my brothers. Nonetheless, at any other time I'd have been up for that, but for some reason, right now, I'm just not feeling it.

I pat the hand she has on me. "Not tonight, sweetheart." I've a soft spot for the sweet butts who quite literally do anything for us, so I let her down gently.

She looks disappointed, and I'm not surprised, knowing how much she likes my kind of fucking. Not wanting to give up easily, she waves toward Jill. "What about a threesome, big boy?" Her hand comes around and touches my cock. But instead of hardening, the residual arousal I'd been sporting from the thought of the woman in the auto-shop disappears.

Gently I remove her fingers. "Not tonight," I repeat. At last, she gets the message and moves away.

Wraith comes up and stands beside me, a beer in his hand. I've an empty bottle in mine. Turning, I glare at Roadrunner who's minding the bar. He still doesn't notice me, too engaged in listening to a conversation between Mouse and Dart.

"Prospect!" I yell.

He jumps about a foot in the air and strides down the back of the bar, and an opened bottle appears within seconds. He better start paying better attention, or else it will be a fucking long time before he patches in.

My VP's smirking. He tips his bottle toward the prospect. "Got a lot to learn."

Turning away so the man in question can't see my face, I say, "It's a fuckin' laugh breaking them in." We share a laugh; then Wraith taps my arm. "What is it with Viper? He's still not right."

Now normally on a party night or any night for that matter, Viper's getting a blow job in full view of everyone in the club-room. Tonight, he's sitting on his own, staring miserably into his beer.

"D'you reckon Sandy's found out what he gets up to and put a stop to it?" Wraith continues.

"I think she's known all along." Sandy and Viper seem to have an understanding; they must, the length of time they've stayed together. Perhaps he doesn't get blow jobs at home? It's true he never disappears with one of the whores into the back rooms as the rest of the unattached brothers do. Maybe it's his strange way of being faithful to her.

"Viper's dealing with something," I mumble, knowing the secret isn't mine to share.

"Want me to have a word?"

"Truth, Brother, leave it alone." Now I tip my bottle toward him. "Word of warning. Do not poke the angry bear."

He nods, his empty bottle bangs down on the bar. "Well, I'm done for tonight. I've got a warm and willing woman waiting on me."

"You've got women here." I can't understand how any man can be content with just one pussy.

"Yeah, but when you've got the best meal to be had at home, eating out doesn't hold the same attraction anymore. See you later, Brother."

I don't, *can't* understand. I've never found any woman who'd make me give up all others. Still, to each their own. "Yeah, later," I respond and nod as he walks away.

Roadrunner is quicker this time and, furnished with a new beer, I push away from the bar. The word 'Prez' on my cut makes me a target for the local talent, and usually that doesn't bother me and I'll partake once, twice, sometimes three times in one night. But tall, short, skinny, or with a nice cushion to their asses; blond, dark, or brunette, none of the hangarounds are doing anything for me tonight. I walk between the tables, skirting around the couches where brothers are already getting some action, hoping someone will make my cock twitch, but it does nothing at all. Fuck, I know I'm getting older—I'll be forty next birthday—but surely, I'm not in the market for Viagra just yet? Fuck, wouldn't that be the motherfucker of all motherfuckers?

Maybe I'm overworked, been too busy. *But there's someone who can get your cock hard.*

Shit, whatever, I'm out of here. With everyone occupied, no one will notice if I slip away.

CHAPTER TEN

*D*rummer...

Leaving the party, I'm not consciously aware that I'm taking the road down to the shop; my feet just seem to take me there. *Oh for fuck's sake, admit it. You want her.* Yeah, I want her. And if she's leaving tomorrow, this is the last chance I'll get. That's why I wasn't interested in the whores or hangarounds; there's only one woman I want tonight. Suddenly I'm unable to resist taking the only opportunity I'll have to relieve my cock, which has been hard for her for days.

I know I shouldn't be doing this, should be steering the hell away. What I'm planning on doing will certainly lead to disaster. Particularly if Viper finds out.

Maybe I'll just talk to her? *Yeah, fuck, right. Like that's all I want to do.* Or perhaps she'll turn me away? She'll know it can only be one go-around, and from what I've seen of her, I don't think she's that kind of woman. She's given no indication that she's a biker groupie, so what could I offer her beyond tonight? In my head, I see Viper returning to his usual jovial self as he hears her engine fade away into the distance. I can't do anything to distress him further; he's put himself through enough. Yeah, I'll just talk, thank her for the work she's done in the shop, which was over and above what I'd expected, and wish her well on her way…

Oh fuck, no. She's sitting on the picnic bench outside the shop, clearly enjoying the lingering warmth of the summer evening. She's holding a cold bottle up to her face, resting it against her cheek as if to cool herself. Hidden by the shadows, I watch as she takes a sip of beer, wiping away moisture from her lips. Now divested of her overalls, she's wearing a pair of shorts, her long sleek legs on display. As usual, her t-shirt is hugging her breasts, which admittedly aren't large, but perfectly adequate to fit in my hands.

Her hair, for once freed from its confines, cascades around her shoulders. She's the most beautiful woman I've ever seen, and the fact she's totally unaware of it is just another thing to entice me. That she can be so alluring without even trying draws me in.

All my good intentions fly out of the window. Stepping forward into the light, I take the few last steps and approach her, seeing her startle as she wasn't expecting anyone to appear.

I hold out my hands, palms facing her. "It's just me."

Her eyes widen. "Drummer? I thought everyone was at the party."

Resting one leg on the seat, I lean over my knee. "I wanted some space." *I wanted to see you.*

She doesn't know why I'm here, but she's not alone there. Neither do I. *What the fuck am I doing?* She's staring at me, and by the light spilling out of the shop, I can see her chest rise and fall, and then rise and fall more rapidly. *I'm affecting her.* My cock swelling in my jeans tells me she's affecting me too. But that's not surprising; I've been half hard since I first saw her. Let her give me this. Just once, just one time. Then I might be able to break this strange spell she's cast over me.

Without warning, I stand and take hold off her arms, pulling her up and to me. Even through the barriers of material, I can feel her nipples are peaking. In a move full of innocence, she pushes against me, her mouth opening, and she gulps as she feels my hardness against her.

A little tug, a vain effort to get away. "Drummer, I don't think this is a good idea." She's looking around as if someone might save her. But there's no one else here. No one else will be leaving the party for a very long time.

"Darlin', I think this is about the best fuckin' idea I've ever had." My voice sounds husky, even to myself.

I give her no more time to think, my mouth crashing down on hers, my tongue forcing its way in between her lips. She's shocked by the intrusion and gasps, but I don't give her any choice, forcing her to join in the dance. Cautiously she begins to mimic my movements, her uncertainty showing me she's never been kissed like this before, never had a real man's mouth on hers. Her arms come up, her fingers holding onto my biceps, her nails biting in and then retreating as if she doesn't know whether to hold me closer or push me away.

She tastes of beer and sunshine, a unique, fresh flavour all her own. A delicious smell of coconut oil, presumably from the residue of suntan lotion, mingling with the strawberry smell of her shampoo seduces me like never before. And underlying it all, the undeniably sweet perfume of her arousal.

I continue my assault on her mouth, kissing her like the rough biker I am, sweeping away the thoughts of any boys she might have had prior, showing her what a man can do to her. Almost punishing her unfairly for my part in denying myself this for so long.

Becoming used to the sensation, she starts pushing up against me, little murmurs of appreciation rumbling past her lips, vibrating on mine. Fuck, the thought of her mouth doing that when it's around my cock makes it throb so uncomfortably, I know I'm going to have to get a release soon.

Like a cat in heat, she's rubbing herself against me; her thighs pushed tight together. *She's as turned on as me.*

We don't need words; I don't want conversation. Swinging

her up in my arms, I take her into the shop, closing and locking the door behind me.

Letting her feet drop to the floor, I walk her backward until she's pushed up against the wall. Her eyes are wide open and staring, and her pupils have dilated. There's a glow on her cheeks, a flush spreading down her neck. Following it down, I know I have to see more.

Placing my hands on the top of her t-shirt, I rip it from neck to hem and push it apart, too impatient to wait for her to take it off. Quickly I dispense with her front fastening bra, and her gorgeous breasts fall free. I pause for a moment, letting the sight enthrall me. They're just what I expected, will easily fit into my hands, and tipped with pink aureoles and hard erect buds. I can wait no longer to touch them.

Taking both her hands in mine, I hold them over her head, then lower my mouth to those glorious orbs, sucking first one, and then the other teat into my mouth. Her skin tastes a little salty, a tang which inflames me. Laving attention on the first nipple again, I lick and suck, then nip with my teeth. Her sharply inhaled breath and the way she pushes her groin against mine lets me know that she likes it. Encouraged, I repeat the same actions on the second.

Now I entrap her slender wrists with just one hand, leaving my other one free to explore. Trailing my fingers down her slightly concave stomach, I appreciate her curves—she's not all skin and bones like some of the clubhouse sluts, and I love her womanly softness. Her sighs encourage me on, and my fingers sneak lower, pausing for a moment at the waistband of her shorts, then, *oh fuck it*, I flick open the button and undo the zip and push all her remaining clothing to the ground.

My hand's there, my fingers swiping along her slit, gathering up her copious wetness. Making a small gap between us, just enough so I can sneak up and suck my fingers into my mouth, I taste her arousal for the first time. A smile is forced from me at her stunned look, her disbelief at my enjoyment of her taste that is so fresh, so clean, so uniquely her. My hips thrust automatically, and I know I'm losing control.

As my hand travels downward once again, I touch her clit, circling my fingers, then pinching and rubbing that small nub. My eyes fixed on hers, watching for the point when I've hit just the right spot. She's panting now, her body straining against my hold, pushing up against me, closing the space between us, her breasts squash up against my chest, her nipples so hard I can feel them through my shirt.

I push two fingers inside her, contorting my hand so it's now my thumb that presses on her clit. She sucks in air, then stops breathing. Her legs start to shake, her muscles suddenly lock, and a scream comes from her as she quickly reaches her climax, her body shuddering and jerking in my arms.

All the time I've been watching her face, and I can't remember ever having seen such a look of amazement and wonder before. *Yeah, baby. This is what a biker can give you.*

Now it's my turn. I swing her around so she's facing the wall, pulling up her ass to line her up with my cock. Not bothering to dispense with my clothes, I unzip in a flash, and freeing myself, have a condom on in seconds, and then pause at her entrance.

"Tell me you want this." My voice sounds shaky; I'm proud I can speak.

There's no hesitation at all. "I want you," she cries out, almost desperate in her pleading. "God, I want you!"

That's all the permission I need. I've been on edge for days, long hours when I've had no release. Now, she's ready and willing and begging for me; I've no strength to hold back, and I'm not going to wait for a second more. With one quick parry, I thrust hard inside her tight channel.

She screams, but the sound's not wrought from her in pleasure, I've hurt her.

What. The. Fuck?

I hold myself still, already as deep as I can go. She starts to struggle.

"Hold still, darlin', wait." Perhaps it's been a long time for her, or maybe she's just not used to being fucked the way I like to fuck.

I hear a strangled sob.

"Hush, darlin', I was too rough. Just hold still a moment and get used to me. I'll slow it down."

My cock should deflate at the clear distress of the woman it's resting in, but her muscles are squeezing me involuntarily, and it's keeping me hard. I've no desire to pull out. If I stop now, it will leave us both unsatisfied. I'm sure I can rescue this.

Another small squeeze. "Fuck, you're killing me here, darlin'. You ready to go now?"

She makes a panicked sound and shakes her head.

"It's alright, darlin'. I'll wait until you're ready." She'll be the death of me if I don't move soon. I'm trembling with the effort to keep still.

Then she says the words I've started to fear I'm going to hear, "I've never..."

"Never?" *Never had a biker cock, or...* I feel myself go cold as realisation dawns. "You're a virgin?"

"Not now." In a husky voice, she huffs out a mirthless laugh.

For once in my life, I'm at a loss for what to say, what to do. Fuck, but I'm a bastard. I never even dreamed she'd never been fucked before. I'd swept her away, consciously deciding not to give her a chance to protest, and now I've taken away the one thing I can never give back.

But she's pushing back a little against me, her movements making me grow harder. Her fingers are reaching back around me, gripping my cut, pulling me to her.

"It doesn't hurt so much, now." Her voice is quiet and nervous, as if she's not sure what she's asking for. *How would she know?*

I'm not going to make another mistake. "You want me to keeping going?" *Fuck, the devil in me hopes she says yes.*

"Can you be gentle?"

I've never done gentle, but for her? "I'll try, darlin', I'll try."

Experimentally, I ease out a little and then push back in. She doesn't react, so I do it again, holding myself back, unable to remember a time when I'd had to exercise this much restraint over my desire to simply drive in. I find a slow pace, fighting my natural instinct to hammer into her until we both come.

I reach around, one hand toying with her clit, the other tweaking her nipple. The combined sensations eliciting her muscles to tighten around my cock. I'm unable to suppress a groan as I ask, "How you feeling, now?"

"Good," she breathes out. "Good, Drummer. Oh please, don't stop."

Having no intention of stopping, I allow myself to quicken my pace, all my senses aware of every slightest reaction of her body while knowing I've never concentrated so hard on pleasing a woman before. The next sounds I hear are music to my ears.

"Drum, fuck, Drummer. Oh, oh…"

She squeezes her cunt again, trapping my cock as tightly as a garrote as she screams once more, this time, thank fuck, with pleasure.

It triggers the cum to rise. I can feel it starting as a tingling in my spine, initiating a boiling in my balls that causes an eruption shooting up through my dick and into her sweet, oh so sweet depths. But again, I curb my instinct and pump gently. It feels like my orgasm has drained me entirely. Never, ever before has it felt this intense.

Finally exhausted, I rest my forehead against her back, my fingers gently stroking her soft skin, delaying pulling away, unsure how I should finish this. I don't cuddle and say sweet nothings after sex. Normally, once my balls are empty, I lose interest in the woman I'm with, sending them on their way and only sleeping with them if I'm too drunk to be able to get out the words.

She was a virgin. I didn't particularly give her much option to stay that way. Oh, I asked her permission, but only after using all my skills to make sure her body wanted me as much as mine did her, but whether her head was into it as much... Guilt washes over me, an emotion I don't normally feel. I wait, still connected to her, desperately searching for something to say. She seems as speechless as I am.

My softening cock slips out of her, breaking our connection. I pull out, reaching down to do up my zip. Fuck, I didn't even take my clothes off! She was probably expecting hearts and flowers when she eventually gave her virginity to the man she was saving herself for, and I just took it, without even bothering to get undressed.

Shit! There's blood. A *lot* of blood. *Well, I did take her roughly.* Self-reproach slams into me with a force that almost makes me stagger, but it does spark me to speak. "You're bleeding darlin'. Wait here a moment while I find something to clean you up."

"No." Still facing the wall, again, she reaches back her arms and grabs mine, stopping me from moving away. "No, Drum. Drummer, what do you normally do after having sex?"

It's a direct question, and without thinking about it, I answer honestly, "I usually fuck one of the club whores or hangarounds, darlin', so I just send them away."

"Well, just go then."

"Not going to happen. You aren't a club whore."

"I want you to go, Drum." There's a tremor in her voice that makes me die a little inside. "Please go."

I'm out of my depth. I don't fuck civilian women or the ones who don't make themselves available at the club, and I've never fucked a virgin before in my life. She's got no experience with this, and neither do I. Deep down, I know I should stay. Surely, there are words I can use to help her come to terms with what's just happened between us? But I don't know where to fucking start. She'll be gone tomorrow, we both know that. What is there to say? There are no promises I can make. There's no way I can take what's just happened back. Nothing I can do to make this right.

Placing my hand on her shoulder, I try gently to turn her around to face me, but she's stiff and keeps her body turned toward the wall. *She can't look me in the face.* Suddenly I realise, I don't want to see what's written on hers. Recrimination? Hate? Christ, I've fucked this up good.

"Drummer, don't make more of this than it was. I'm leaving tomorrow." There's the strong Sam I've come to know. I hate that she's right. I have nothing to offer her. Whatever I said would just be empty words, and she's well aware of that.

"I'll go." As I make my decision, I wonder if I'm just taking the easy way out that she's offered. "I'll leave my number by the phone if you need me... If you want to talk about what's just happened... Give me a call."

I see her head nodding but feel certain she won't be ringing me.

Knowing it's probably the worst thing I can do, I turn and walk away.

CHAPTER ELEVEN

*S*am...

Waiting until I'm sure he's gone, I listen for any sound to suggest he's lingered and then carefully look around before I finally push my aching and sore body away from the wall. Feeling something sticky between my legs, I look down to see with horror that he was right. There *is* a lot of blood. But he's a big man to have been my first, and he wasn't particularly careful. Well, at least, not initially.

Going to the small bathroom, grateful it's got a shower, I turn on the water, having it as hot as I can stand, and begin to wash away all evidence of what just transpired. My mind at first completely numb. Then the tears start, disappearing down the drain with the water as my body heaves with great gulping sobs. Bending double with remorse, I slowly sink on to the tiled floor and put my head in my hands. *I've completely messed this up.*

From the moment I saw Drummer, I'd known he was someone different, a man who touched me on a level no man ever had before. At first, it was his presence, his bearing, the confidence he had in himself. The way he seemed the absolute ruler over his domain, his club. The power he extruded drawing me in. Then it was the man underneath the leather, his face rugged and weathered from riding under the unforgiving Arizona sun, his piercing steely grey eyes that seem to miss nothing. It's not a pretty-boy face, but handsome nevertheless, one that's worn and lived in, the face of a man who's seen more than most.

The way he walks, his self-assurance, and the manner in which the others look up to him. I've seen enough interaction to know they have not only respect and admiration for him, but affection too. He's so different from the men I'd known before; he's a natural born leader with charisma to match.

Of course, he didn't want to make love to a virgin. *Make love?* Angrily swiping away my tears, I correct myself—we hadn't made love. We'd fucked. In just the way a man like him would have wanted it. Or that's how he'd intended it to be. Christ, I must have been such a big disappointment, the frightened, scared innocent who hadn't had a clue what to do.

But he'd swept me away. His mouth had touched mine, and from that point on I hadn't a choice. Electricity had sparked between us, a switch thrown that was impossible to turn back off. His touch had caused my every nerve ending to sing, and I hadn't had a chance in hell of hiding my reaction to him. Every part of my body had come alive in ways it never had before. Like a runaway train, I couldn't have stopped myself if I'd tried, let alone him.

The water's running cooler now; gingerly I stand, wincing as muscles I didn't even know I had start to protest and turn the shower off. I reach for the worn towel and wrap it around me. I'd felt so ready, so turned on. I'd had no idea that his first thrust into me would hurt so much. Maybe if I'd warned him, he'd have taken it easier.

Or maybe he wouldn't have wanted me at all.

No, a man like Drummer would want a woman who knew the score. That's why I'd sent him away. Now I've got to pretend it meant nothing to me, when in fact it means everything, but when, *if* I see him again, I'll have to behave as nonchalantly as any club whore.

Throwing down the towel, I pull on my shorts, panties, and bra, and grab a fresh t-shirt out of my bag. I pick up my torn and ruined shirt, debating what to do. It could go in the rag bin; the shop could always use more. *Great idea, and everyone would know what had gone down.* At last, I stuff it into my pack along with the rest of my clothes. Then take it out again and put it at the bottom of the trash. I'm not going to want to be faced with a reminder when I leave here in the morning.

Now I'm dressed, but about as far from wanting to go to sleep as I could be, half tempted to get on my bike and leave now. But I need to give it a test drive first; it would be stupid to go now and get stranded again. I give a strangled laugh. Who'd rescue me next time? Certainly not the president of an outlaw MC.

I move to stand by the side of my treasured Vincent, knowing I'll do what I always do when I need something to comfort me. Picking up a tube of Autosol, I allow myself the luxury of polishing up already gleaming chrome, something I can't do too often or else I'll rub all the chrome away. I burnish it until I see my face mirrored back at me. Shit, I look a mess. My eyes are red and puffy. Hopefully they won't look so bad come the morning, or I'll have to plead a sleepless night. Well, I doubt that will prove to be far from the truth. Moving on to the next part, I apply more Autosol and then wipe it off. Slowly I work around the bike, polishing every bit I can. It's a labour of love, and gradually, as always, it calms me.

The night my mom had died, I had done the same thing, finding solace in something routine. So what if I've blown my chances with the president of the Satan's Devils? There was never any chance of me being more than a one-night stand whatever happened; he'd said nothing to suggest he'd changed his mind and wanted me to stay. At least I've lost my V-card now, and in a rather amazing way. *I'll never forget my first time.*

Like a cat, I stretch, bowing my back to remove all the kinks. When he'd started moving so gently, so carefully, stimulating my clit and nipples, God, how he'd made me come. I'd never dreamed it could be anything like that. I'd thought I was going to pass out.

As my memory goes over how he'd made me feel, my nipples grow hard once more, and I give myself a mental slap. If I ever see him again, which seems unlikely, I've got to be cool and collected and can't have my lady parts signalling I want another round. Just no way. It's going to be embarrassing enough as it is.

I don't regret sending him away. What could we have said? In the morning, I'll be on my Vincent and away in the wind. There's no future for us. Even if I was staying, I'm hardly old lady material for the president of the Satan's Devils.

CHAPTER TWELVE

*D*rummer...

As soon as I left the shop, I knew I'd made a huge fucking mistake. Sam isn't a club whore or one of the girls from Tucson. She wasn't even experienced, and yet she'd given me, or allowed me to take, the greatest gift that she could. Like an awkward teenager who didn't know any different, I'd jumped at the paltry excuse she'd given me afterward and had left her alone.

I should be there for her, caring for her. Helping her come to terms with what transpired between us. *Looking forward to round two.* Oh, for fuck's sake! When will my cock ever learn? I adjust myself in my pants as memories of just how tight she'd been return to me. *Yeah, she was tight because no one had ever taken her before.*

Mine. All mine. Fuck me if that thought doesn't make me glow.

She'll be gone in the morning.

"Where the fuck you been?" Viper's sharp eyes are staring at my groin and he couldn't have failed to miss seeing my hands making myself comfortable.

My eyes narrow at the pitch of his voice. Normally, he'd

know better than to use that tone with me. "None of your fuckin' business," I reply, while a voice at the back of my head reminds me it was his daughter I'd just deflowered.

Maybe it's the guilt of that thought that shows in my eyes, but something makes him suspicious. He comes up close, invading my personal space. As his hand points down toward the gates of the compound, I grasp he'd seen me walking up the track. *Smart man, he's put two and two together.* "You been with Sam?" Spit loaded with beer lands on my face.

I wipe it away. "So what if I fuckin' have? You want nothing to do with her!" If it weren't for him, she wouldn't have to leave.

"That's not the fuckin' point," he yells, but this time I've taken a step backward. We're right outside the clubhouse. If he wants to keep his relationship with her quiet, he needs to tone it down.

I give a pointed look to where Dart and Slick are standing having a cigarette. "Viper," I start with a bit of bite, "unless you've changed your mind about everyone knowing, I'd keep it quiet if I were you."

I don't know whether it's the drink talking or whether he's been rethinking the situation, but he keeps coming for me. I take another step back.

The muscles on his arms are bulging, and I start to get a bad feeling. I watch his hands, curled into fists, tapping against his thighs. His face is as dark as I've ever seen it, his mouth twisted into a scowl. Another step back, he takes one more in my direction, and then another, bringing him up close.

"You fucked my fuckin' daughter!" Suddenly he screeches and lurches forward at the same time, bringing up his fist.

He's right, that's exactly what I have done. I make no move to defend myself as he throws the first punch, understanding he deserves at least one. My head rocks back with the force of it. Ruefully, my hand rubs my jaw, and my tongue counts my teeth. All seem in place.

"Someone get Peg!" Dart's voice shouts from behind me.

Momentarily distracted, I turn to tell him not to bother and doing so, I miss the fist that knocks the air out of my stomach and puts me on the ground.

Dart and Slick, their cigarettes quickly discarded, move forward and each takes hold of one of Viper's arms. He tries to shake them off, but they've got him in a tight grip.

I'm rolling on the ground, clearly lit by the lights on the outside of the clubhouse. Suddenly Viper's eyes open wide, his mouth works and again he tries to get free, almost managing to shake off his captors with his rage-fuelled strength. Unable to escape, he makes do with a gesture from his head. This time when he speaks, his voice has gone up an octave. "What the fuck have you done to her?" A look of fright crosses his face. "If you've fuckin' hurt her, I'll kill you."

Why would he think I'd hurt her? I look down at myself and see... *Oh, fuck!*

I rush to put his mind at ease, my hands fluttering up in supplication. "Viper, no, Brother. I didn't hurt her. I promise you. Fuck, you know me better than that."

"Then whose blood is that on your jeans?" In his surprise, Dart has let go of one of Viper's arms, and his shaking hand is pointing at my groin, which had gotten smeared in her blood as I'd tucked myself away. "Is it yours?"

Oh fuck, how am I going to get out of this? "It's hers," I admit, "but it's not what you think."

Thankfully Dart's fast, reacting to Viper's first movement and having him back in his hold before he can come at me again. Once again restrained, all Viper can do is screech, "Then you did fuckin' hurt her. I'm gonna fuckin' end you!"

I roll and get to my feet. "No," I shout back, the unjust accusation making my tongue loose and words coming out before I can think what I'm saying. "She was a virgin!"

I hadn't noticed the music had been turned down, nor that at some point during the exchange all my brothers had come outside. Yes, every single one of them, including the two newly patched over.

Peg pushes his way through. "What the fuck's going on here?" He looks from me to Viper. That there's blood on my chin becomes clear when the sergeant-at-arms grimaces and peers at my injury. "You okay, Prez?"

"I'm fine." I push his arm away.

"I'm gonna kill him! Let me go!" Viper's struggling, trying to get away from his captors. If they release him, I think he'll have a fucking good try.

"What the fuck's got into you, Viper?" Peg snarls at him. "What's the prez done to hurt you?"

It all comes out. Viper screams at the top of his voice, and while I'm sure it isn't intentional, it's loud enough that everyone hears. "He fuckin' raped my fuckin' daughter. Not only that, she was a fuckin' virgin!"

Jesus! It wasn't rape. There's part of me that wants to say there's no such thing as a fucking virgin, but I hold my tongue, knowing levity wouldn't be welcomed at this precise time. In fact, in the stunned silence that follows his announcement, I'm not sure what would be the right thing to say. Great, so everyone now knows what a bastard I am.

But Viper isn't going to leave it there. Now that everyone knows, he seems to relax. At a signal from Peg, Dart and Slick release him. Viper steps forward. "You fucked her and walked away from her. Just like you treat the club whores."

I've got to put a stop to that right now. "I did not rape her! I have never taken a woman by force." I look around checking everyone heard my denial, and to show he's making it into something it isn't, add, "It wasn't like that."

"Well tell me what the fuck it is like then? You fucked her, now you're here? Why aren't you with her? Or why isn't she here with you." I can see tears in his eyes. "You took advantage of her, you fuckin' sorry excuse for a man. Her first time and you walk out and leave her."

"Viper." Peg's calm voice seems to get through to him. Viper turns wet eyes on him. "Never knew you had a daughter. Who and where is she?"

I realise that's what everyone else wants to know and feel some compassion for Viper. There's no way he can keep this secret now.

As Viper's gaze turns to me and he seems to slump in defeat, I know this is the very last way he would ever have wanted it to come out. Or in any way. As if hoping I'll be able to come up with some explanation, he allows a few seconds to pass before responding to Peg. He says simply, but loud enough for everyone to hear, "It's Sam. Sam's my daughter."

As everyone starts talking at once, all manner of questions he won't want to answer coming at him from all directions, I know it's time for me to take control. Even though they'll have little respect for me right now, I use my most authoritative voice. "Quiet! That Sam is Viper's daughter is his business, not ours. He'll tell you what he wants you to know when he's ready."

There are murmurs of discontent, the brothers can be nosy busybodies at times, and I let that die down before I continue, "And what's gone down between Sam and myself is equally nothing to do with any of you."

"It is," Viper says quietly, "if it was rape."

What? I thought I'd already made it clear it was consensual. *But you didn't give her much say in the matter.*

"You've got her blood on your clothes."

I lift my head to the heavens and back down again. "Viper, you've known me years. Have you ever known me to take a woman who didn't want to be taken? Come on, man, think about it. Would I do that to her? To you?"

"Then why didn't you stay with her?"

It's the question I'd been asking myself. "You're right, I shouldn't have fuckin' left her," I tell him. "I'll go back and see her now."

"No, no you fuckin' won't. *I* will."

"Viper, think about it. She's upset—"

"So, you admit that? You motherfucker!"

I seem to be digging a deeper and deeper hole. I take in a sharp breath, trying to keep hold of my temper. "Listen the fuck to me! She's upset because it was overwhelming." Fuck, it was like that for both of us, and I have to admit it. "For me too. What happened wasn't planned, it took us both by surprise. I had no idea..." Well, reminding them right now that I'd taken her virginity was probably not the best thing, so I just break off and shake my head. "Last time you spoke to her, you disowned her completely. Let her have some peace tonight, think it through. Speak to her tomorrow."

He spits on the ground, it narrowly misses my boot. "I'm gonna go speak to *my* fuckin' *daughter* now. Get her side of the story. This is me stepping up, like I should have done all along. Then, perhaps," he pauses and points a finger at me, "you wouldn't have had a chance to shame her. She'd have been under my protection." He's right, as a club member's daughter, none of us would have been able to touch her. Not even me.

"What d'you want us to do, Viper?" Peg's not even looking at me now and instead looks to his brother for direction.

"Watch this prick while I go get to the fuckin' truth." With that parting shot, Viper spins on his heel and walks off down to see Sam.

As Peg goes to take my arm, I brush him off. Looking at the others, I see them averting their eyes as if they can't look at me. *I shouldn't have left her.* But it's too late to recognise that now.

With my head held high, I walk into the clubhouse and go straight to my office, shutting the door, and shutting all of them out. I pull a bottle of Jack out of my drawer and declining to search for a glass, take a swig. It's going to be a long night.

CHAPTER THIRTEEN

*S*am…

Still engrossed polishing the Vincent, the sound of the door to the shop opening makes me jump. *Has he come back?* But it's not Drummer's voice I hear calling out.

"Looking good, darlin'." The compliment is thrown out in a tentative manner.

My body tenses as I recognise who's speaking. Last time I heard him, he was shouting at me to get gone and to stay away. *What does he want?* Perhaps he's making sure I really will be back on my bike and out of his life tomorrow.

I stand, rubbing my hands on a cloth to remove the Autosol, hesitant to turn around and see the sneering expression on his face. Tonight's been enough of an emotional roller coaster, and I'm not sure I can take much more. My back stiff, I respond over my shoulder, "Look, Viper, I'm going to be out of here in the morning. You don't need to tell me again." I don't want to face him. Not now.

"That's not why I'm here." There's still that touch of hesitation in his voice.

What else could it possibly be? It's unlikely he's had a last-minute change of heart. "Then why?" I'm tired and drained.

Footsteps approach, and he's standing at my side. "She's beautiful. I can't believe it's the same heap of junk that was in that barn. You really do all the work on it yourself?"

"Every last bit." I can't keep the pride out of my voice. I still don't turn toward him. He sounds conciliatory, but is he? But if I have the chance to exchange a few words with my father without shouting involved, shouldn't I take it? If not, I might always regret it. Now could be the time to explain why I made the journey. "When Mom told me about you, I wanted you to see it." My voice breaks off.

"You're showing me what I could never have."

"No, no." I stop him; it's not like that at all. "I wanted to show you what I'd done with it." Oh, to hell with it, I might as well admit it. "I think I wanted you to be proud of me. Stupid, huh? I knew nothing about you, why should I have thought for a moment you'd be interested in me? I should never have come here." I toss the rag I'd used to clean my hands into the bin.

"Oh, Sam." His voice hitches. "We need to talk."

Now I do turn around. I see him clenching his jaw. For a moment there I thought things had changed, but obviously he's still angry with me. "I don't think there's much more to say. Not tonight, Viper. I've had enough tonight."

"That right there! It's Drummer, isn't it? What the fuck did he do to you?" His eyes blaze into mine, but this time it's not me he's angry at.

An inappropriate urge to giggle comes over me. Viper sounds like a concerned father about to berate his teenage daughter. His eyes narrow as I delay giving him a reply. *Is he worried on my behalf?* "Nothing." It's such an awkward position to be in.

He reaches out his hand, and after a slight hesitation rests it on my cheek, his thumb gently stroking away an errant tear escaping from my eye. It's an odd sensation. I don't know this man, but the genetic link between us seems to fool my brain into thinking I do. I lean into the touch, welcoming the comfort.

"Did he force you?" The words come out through gritted teeth. Has Drummer told him what happened? Why the fuck would he do that? Suddenly I'm angry. Did he return to the club-house and boast about taking me? Boast to *Viper*?

I step away. "No." The word manages to convey my astonish-ment that he's asked such a question. "Of course, he didn't. And how the fuck do you know? What's he been saying?"

"He said nothing," he reassures me. "Until I beat it out of him."

"What?" *He hit Drummer? His president?*

"Knew something had happened, girl. But you have to tell me. Did he hurt you?"

"No," I tell him again, watching as the lines on his brow start to smooth out, but he still seems to need more of a confirmation.

"Are you sure, Sam? What did he do to you?"

This time I shake my head adamantly. "It's none of your busi-ness, Viper. What happened, happened between two adults. It was fully consensual, and I don't want to talk about it."

"He did hurt you."

"No." Why won't he let it drop? I'm not going into details. "Look, Viper, I'm twenty-six years old. I think that's more than old enough to know my mind and who I want to go to bed with." But there was no bed involved, only a wall.

He has the grace to look embarrassed for a moment, then the anger returns. "If you're not telling me the truth, if you're protecting him for some reason, I'll kill him. Prez or not."

I heave a sigh. "He didn't hurt me, and I'm not protecting him. There, have we got that straight, now?"

"He didn't treat you right. Leaving you like he'd leave a whore."

I correct him. "I sent him away."

We stare at each other, neither backing down. Him trying to get me to tell him what happened, me trying to convey that it's none of his business. At last, he shakes his head. "Stubborn." There's a hint of a smile as he says it. "Just like your ol' man."

Thankfully, at last, he's dropping the subject, turning away and starting to examine the Vincent instead. "I owe you a fuckin' apology, girl. And an explanation."

Tonight might be the first and last time I get to speak with my father. If he wants to talk, and as long as he avoids the subject of Drummer, I'm ready to listen. There's beer in the fridge in the kitchen—I've learned beer and bikers are never far apart—so I go and collect a couple of bottles and returning, hand one to him. He breaks off the top and gulps some down. Then he props himself up against a work bench.

"You," he points at me, "are a fuckin' surprise." I nod, knowing my appearance must have shocked the hell out of him. He huffs a short laugh and shakes his head.

"I'm sorry." When I came to find him, I hadn't considered the possible consequences. Losing my mom had probably warped my thinking. I'd given no thought to the implications for him. Suddenly I feel guilty. "It must have been one heck of a surprise, especially when you never wanted kids."

"That's where you're fuckin' wrong." When I cock my eyebrow, he continues, "When I was twenty, I had mumps. Fuckin' childhood illness took me late. Affected me badly." As my eyes widen with horror with the idea of where this is going, he gives a slow nod. "Left me sterile."

"Oh, Viper, I'm so sorry."

A little shrug, one hand comes up to rub the back of his head. "Me, I'm used to it. But Sandy?" He laughs softly. "Sandy's my ol' lady. My wife. We've been together years. Met and married when I was eighteen. She's a year older than me." He pauses. "She always wanted kids. We'd planned a big family, fuck; I didn't care. Would have agreed to anything to keep her happy. But before we could start on it, the chance got taken away. She's a good woman, but she's never gotten over it."

Oh no. Now I'm filled with sympathy for her as well as him. Up to now I've never considered having children, but hearing his story, know I'd at least want to have the choice. "Did you think about adopting?"

His head flicks left then right. "We weren't exactly the types who they'd give a fuckin' kid too. I was in the MC by then." He rolls his head on his shoulders. "Sandy always wanted a rug rat or two of her own. As did I. But we came to accept it just wasn't gonna be. Sam, I just don't know how she's gonna take it, knowing you were out there all this time. My child, my blood. Fuck, I don't want to hurt her."

"You wanted me out of the way so she didn't have to know." It all becomes clear.

"Fuck, Sam. I'm so mixed up. *I* wanna get to know you. You can't imagine how it feels seeing someone that came from me; you're a fuckin' miracle in that way. I accepted I would never father a child a long time ago. But I love Sandy; she's my whole world. Always has been and always will be. I wanted to protect her. I don't know what this will do to her, and I'm scared it will go the wrong way. I can't have her hurt."

"You love her so much, yet you fuck the whores." I sneer, I can't help myself. The vision of the first time I saw him is set firmly in my head.

"I don't fuck 'em," he disputes.

"Viper, I saw you with my own eyes—"

"I don't *fuck* them," he repeats, emphatically. "They give me blow jobs, that's all. Sandy knows all about that."

She does? And she doesn't mind?

He looks embarrassed as he explains, "She doesn't like to, er…"

"I get the picture." I wave dismissively to stop him saying any more about the subject. He is my father after all, and what he does or doesn't get up to with his wife should remain their own business. It dawns on me how much she must love him, having stayed with him all these years even though he can't give her the thing she wants most, and having to put up with his extracurricular activities.

With a deep sigh he informs me, "I can't keep it quiet, not after this. I'm gonna tell her about you when I get home. See where we go from there. How she takes to it and all that."

"We could stick to the original plan, I'll go, and she'll never need to know. Hell, Viper, we should get the DNA test done first."

Another short, barked laugh. "I remember your mom, Sam. It was my first time; I remember it, every fuckin' thing about it. She was a beauty; never thought I'd fool her and get into her pants. And we talked, about the Vincent and about her hopes and dreams. Stupid things. Like what we'd call our children. She had foolish fuckin' ideas about fancy names, so I shut her up saying let's make it simple. We'd call it Sam. Boy or girl." He throws a twisted smile over at me. "Soon as you told me your name, I knew you were hers."

A strange feeling of elation comes over me, any lingering doubts now gone. But that doesn't address the immediate problem. "I don't want to upset your life. I don't want to hurt your wife. Don't tell her, Viper. If you want to stay in touch, we can, but don't say anything. There's no point." He's accepted me, that has to be enough.

"Couple of things wrong with that, sweetheart." His face looks sheepish. "'Fraid I lost it when I saw Drum and realised what he'd done. I lost it in front of all the brothers. While they might keep it quiet, the whores heard too. Sandy will hear all about it the moment she steps foot in the club whether you go or stay." He takes a step toward me, and for a second time his hand comes up and carefully touches my face. "I'd like you to stay. 'Cos the other thing is, I'd like to fuckin' get to know you."

He does?

"We still ought to get a DNA test done." I try to be practical.

Another nod. "We do if it's only to prove it to everyone else. But I already know. I don't remember much about your mom, but she wasn't one to sleep around. And if that's the story she told you, and your name being what it is? I'd put money on it being true. But we'll get the proof if that's what you want." He studies me for a moment, his hand reaching out and brushing a strand of hair off of my face. "Doubt you were too thrilled having a biker as an ol' man."

"You're kidding me, right?" I wave toward the Vincent. "It's in my blood. I'd be freaking thrilled to be in your life."

"Roadrunner reckons you're an engine whisperer." A hint of a smile appears on his face.

I burst out laughing, appreciating the term. "They speak to me," I joke back, but I'm telling the truth. In some ways they do.

"You ever gonna let me have a ride on the Vincent?"

My dad? Riding the bike I restored? The bike that my mom had bought for me? That had so many memories for them both? For the first time since she died, I feel a lightness come over me. "Of course, you can. Whenever you like."

It's at that point I yawn. Loudly.

"Best you get some rest." His brow furrows. "You should come up to the clubhouse, use one of the spare rooms. Everyone knows who you are now, no point making you stay down here."

I can just imagine how that would go. "I don't want an inquisition tonight, Viper. It's been a lot for me to take in. If I go to the clubhouse, they'll be staring, talking, asking questions. I can't handle that now." Especially as it seems everyone knows what Drummer and I have been up to. Just the thought makes my cheeks go red. I walk over to the Vincent. "And, I don't like leaving her alone."

"No one's gonna touch her here."

"No," I say again. "Anyway, I'm leaving in the morning. Makes no sense to change things now." I don't want to face Drummer again.

"No girl, you aren't going nowhere. I told you. I want to get to know you."

"But Drum—"

"Drum nothing. The prez only wanted you gone because of what I said. The brothers here?" He waves his hand around the shop, "They want you to stay. Even heard Slick saying he'd like you to look at his bike. Drummer will agree." His mouth narrows. "Specially after what went down tonight. I'll make him."

After tonight, I wish I had the confidence that he did. I'm not sure what I want to do either. Staying close to Drummer, watching him go off with the whores? That would hurt and that's how it would be. He's a one-time man, I know that. And being an inexperienced virgin, I hadn't been what he expected. Go or stay, I've already blown my chances with him. I feel my cheeks burn as I remember the details again, how unwanted my reaction must have been. Christ, I'd made a fool of myself.

Luckily, Viper has no idea of the thoughts going through my mind. He raises his arms in the air and stretches, then lowers his head, his eyes fixing on me. "Come here, girl. Give your…" He falters and stumbling out the words offers them hesitantly. "Give your dad a hug?"

I take a step forward. He's a little uncertain as he lifts his hands and places them on my arms, bringing me gently toward him. I lean into him, my fingers on the back of his cut, breathing in the combined scents of leather, motor oil, and a tang of masculine sweat.

It's awkward and short lived, and quickly we move apart, but it's the first hurdle crossed. He strokes his hand down my face and then walks across to the door. As he opens it and the night air wafts in, I call out, "Viper, I, er, I hope it goes okay with Sandy."

He pauses before leaving, pulling his back up straight. "So do I, Sam. So do I." Then he's gone.

CHAPTER FOURTEEN

rummer…

    "Prez?"

The uncertain voice makes me lift my head from where it's been resting on my arms on my desk. I look up to see Roadrunner standing in front of me. He's got a cup of coffee in his hands, the welcome aroma helping bring me to my senses. "What time is it?"

"Ten."

I groan. Christ, I didn't plan on spending the night in my office. Rolling my head around, I try to get the stiffness out of my neck.

"The VP and Peg asked that you join them in church."

Did they now? I glance down at myself, realising I'm still wearing the clothing from last night, dried blood still on my crotch. Fuck, I need to change before seeing anyone. "Tell them I'll be there in half an hour."

"Er, I think they meant…"

"Who the fuck is the prez? Get out of here."

Roadrunner lives up to his name, escaping my office, fast. I down the scalding drink, then make my way out the back of the clubhouse, going to my house that's up at the top of the compound. When we were restoring the old vacation resort, making the guest suites habitable for the brothers, I'd had this place built to my personal specifications. I take a quick shower and throw my stained jeans into the wash, hardly wanting to look at them. *I hurt her.* I hadn't meant to. Fuck, I'd had no idea she'd been a virgin. Looking at myself in the mirror, I see a stranger looking back at me. *What the fuck do I do, now?*

Getting some Advil out of a drawer, I swallow them dry. I'm ready to face the music.

Twenty-nine minutes later, I walk into church. Wraith and Peg are sitting in their normal places and fall silent as I enter. Striding confidently, I go to my seat at the head of the table.

Wraith's staring at me as though he's never seen me before.

"You got something on your mind, VP?"

"Yeah. We," he nods across to Peg, "want to know what the fuck that was all about last night. What's going on with Viper?"

"Is Wench really Viper's daughter?" Peg throws in.

Pushing back my still damp hair, I sigh. "Yeah, it looks that way." I hate that name they've coined for her.

"Tell us you didn't hurt her."

"I didn't hurt her, Wraith."

I wait for their reaction. Out of all the brothers, these two men have been my closest friends for a very long time. It takes a few seconds, but then their faces relax, and I can see they believe me. I let out the breath I'd been holding.

"Look…" I decide to fill them in. "Sam only found out when her mom died that Viper was her father." I continue to explain the whole sordid story, and why Sylvie May kept her secret until her death.

"Fuck me!" Peg's looking at me with a look of disbelief. "He was only fourteen? Fuck!"

Wraith's grinning. "Hell, it could happen to anyone I suppose. Shit! What a story." He shakes his head as if remembering his own teenage misdemeanours and wondering whether an adult child might turn up for him one day. "And he wanted to keep it from Sandy?"

"Yeah."

"So, some latent paternal instinct got him riled up last night when he'd thought you had hurt her?"

I pinch the bridge of my nose. "Well, I guess it wasn't my finest fuckin' moment. I fuck whores; you know that." I point at Peg. "Same as you and the rest of the brothers. I'm not like you, Wraith, I don't, well I've never wanted to hug and canoodle after sex."

"So, you just left her and walked away?" Peg asks. "Same as you always do? Prez, I love you, you know that, but you treated her like any of the sluts. And that she's not."

"Actually, she told me to go," I correct him.

Wraith shakes his head. "That might have been her words, but she probably didn't mean them."

He's got that spot-on. I decide to lay it on the line. "I wish I'd stayed."

"So, what you gonna do to make this right?"

Now isn't that a fucking million-dollar question?

Leaning back in my chair, I rest one foot up against the edge of the table. Whether or not Viper has had a change of heart, *I* don't want her to leave. But women in the clubhouse are either old ladies or sweet butts. She's certainly not the latter, and I'm not going to make her my bitch. But I can't leave things how we left them last night. Somehow, if it's possible, I've got to make it up to her. If Viper still wants her to go, I don't want her leaving on such a sour note. If she stays, I don't want her hating me. I can't restore her virginity, but perhaps we can clear the air. A seed of an idea starts to grow in the back of my mind.

Got it! I slam my hands on the table. "I'm going for a ride!" Decision made, I stand and walk around the table to the door, leaving them staring at me with open mouths.

After exchanging glances, not party to what's on my mind,

Peg rasps out, "You going alone?" As sergeant-at-arms, he's responsible for the safety of the club.

"No." My back is still turned toward them so they can't see my grin. "No, I'm not."

Realising I could have left them in some confusion about what exactly I had in mind, I huff a laugh, leave the clubhouse, and walk on down to the shop.

It's Saturday. Dollar and Tongue are fiddling with their bikes and give me wary nods as I walk inside just in time to see Joker hunkering down examining the Vincent.

"She's beautiful." He's speaking to Sam. "Just like her owner." That he's even daring to talk to her annoys me, that he compliments her makes me see red.

I'm close enough to give him a slap round the back of his head. "Enough of that, fucker," I snarl.

Throwing a knowing grin at me, he stands up, his hands held up in submission. "Didn't know you were there, Prez."

Sam's shifting on her feet and biting her lip. After what transpired between us last night, I suspect she'd prefer to have any discussion without an audience. I'm a man with an aversion to talking things through... well... when it comes to emotions that is.

"She fixed?" I point at the Vincent.

I hate the defeat I see on her face before she bows her head, and then she looks up bravely, a challenge in her eyes. "Yes, just going to take it for a test ride and then I'll be on my way."

"Want some company?"

Her eyes narrow.

"On your test ride."

"Oh."

She's going to refuse so I say the words that will make Peg proud. "We ride in pairs. Safer that way."

Now her head cocks to the side. "Okay." She draws out the word. "But it won't make any difference, I'll be heading out alone after."

"No, you won't. You're going nowhere, Sam. You'll be staying here."

Her eyes widen. "Has Viper spoken to you?"

I roll my head back, knowing we've got busybodies hanging on to our every word, but right at the moment not giving one fucking damn. It wasn't until now that I realised that I've made the decision. I'll go against my brother if I have to. Something I'd never seen myself doing. "No. And I don't care what he wants. *I* want you to stay." I'm not sure whether I've gone out of my mind or come to my senses, but the idea of watching her ride away fills me with dismay.

"Thank fuck for that! Wench, my bike's waiting—"

"Shut the fuck up, Slick!" Roaring, I swing around, wisely he takes a step out of reach. Blade starts clapping and there are hoots and hollers all around us.

"Don't say anything. Don't overthink it," I warn her, my hands going up to my hair as I link my fingers at the back of my head. "I've no idea what the fuck I'm doing, but let's just take a ride. Together. See where we go."

That it's a euphemism for a relationship, I'm certain she understands.

Then I have an idea. "Come with me? There's something I want to show you." I ignore the shouts of 'I'm sure you do, Prez,' and focus my attention on her.

After glancing around, noticing all eyes on us, she gives a tentative nod. She follows me to the door and then out into the sun.

Once we're away from prying eyes and out of earshot, I pause my steps. "I'm sorry I left you last night. I should have stayed." Now I can see her in the light; I can see her eyes look red as though she'd been crying.

"Drum, it's alright. *I'm* alright."

I don't think she is, not really. I'm feeling my way here, not having any experience in these matters, and wary of saying something that will make it worse. With no knowledge of what to do otherwise, I accept her words at face value. "Okay then. Here, come with me."

She hesitates. "Drum, I—"

"I'm not asking for a repeat of last night."

She shakes her head too quickly. "No, I didn't expect that."

Of course she fucking didn't, she believes I used her like I'd use a club whore, and there's no truth at all to that.

"Look," I start, then stop. Whatever I say, I don't think she would believe me. I don't know what I'm thinking myself, so I change what I was going to say. "I do want you to come and see something."

"Okay." She seems uncertain, and I wish I could see the return of the confident woman she was before.

I stride ahead, only looking back to make sure she's following. We make our way to the top of the compound. When we arrive at our destination, I wait for her to catch up. She's looking at the building ahead.

"My house," I explain.

"Drum—"

"No, wait. Don't say anything yet. Come and see." She's nervous. But I haven't brought her here to ravish her in my bedroom, even though I'd be well up for that. Instead of walking in through the main entrance, I take her round to the side. Pressing the button on the remote, the large garage door slowly glides up on its rails.

"Oh my God!" she exclaims, stepping eagerly inside. Far more animated than she had been so far today. She looks round at my stable and turns back, her eyes wide with delight. "Are these yours?"

"All mine," I confirm, seeing what she sees—four vintage bikes in various stages of restoration, and in pride of place, my war era Knucklehead, now completely road ready. I've also got a Triumph Bonneville, a 1940 Indian Chief in a glorious light blue with the original fringes on the seat, and a Norton Commando, which is in need of a loving hand.

As she walks around, peering at this and that, crouching down to examine something closer, she looks like a kid let loose in a candy store. I give her a few minutes to take everything in, propping my backside on a workbench as she absorbs it all.

"Might need your help with these. Your advice."

She smiles. "Help from a woman? You'd let me touch your bikes?"

"Babe, I'd let you touch anything of mine." My hand goes to my crotch; she won't miss I'm already hard.

"I…" Her face is glowing red.

I'm feeling like an oaf, after last night she'll probably still be sore. "Look, I promised you a ride. That we'll take our bikes out. You ready for that?"

"You riding one of these beauties?"

Only the Knucklehead's ready for the road, but today is more for her than me. "Not today, I'll take the Harley." Then there'll only be the likelihood of one of us breaking down.

Her eyes start to glow at the thought of a ride out, and some of my tension leaves me when she finally agrees. "Okay, Drum."

We meander our way back down to the gates. "Wait for me here. I'll get my bike from the clubhouse."

A nod and I leave her, returning within minutes. She's already got her old girl started, and I'm looking forward to watching her ride. I motion to her to go ahead, and follow her until we reach the main road, then I come up alongside her.

I've never wanted to have a bitch on the back of my bike, and never in my wildest dreams expected to be riding alongside one. But as we head out into the heat of the summer's day, I know right at this moment there's no place I'd rather be. She glances across at me, smiling widely. Placing her left hand on the gas tank of the Vincent, she gives it an exaggerated pat. I laugh into the air and give her a thumbs up, realising she's pleased with the way it's running. We increase our speed; I take my lead from her, knowing she'll want to put her repaired bike through its paces.

Sunlight sparkles off the gleaming chrome—hers polished

with love, mine by the prospects. I feel about as free as I've ever been in my life, able right at this moment to throw off the shackles of being a president and just allowing myself to enjoy the open road. We ride a few miles, each lost in our own contentment. She's handling the Vincent like a pro, the old girl drawing out all of Sam's riding skills, while my better handling Harley needs far less concentration. Her competent demonstration makes me go hard, the vibration of my Harley throbbing through my loins.

Once more, I laugh into the air, the asphalt under our tyres, the warm air rushing past, and the company I'm in so liberating. I'm enjoying myself, driving on automatic, periodic glances into my rearview, most of my concentration on the road ahead, but looks sneaked at the woman riding so adeptly by my side.

The next glance in my mirror shows there's a semi coming up behind us, moving fast as it hasn't got a trailer attached. Automatically estimating the distance, I can see he's closing on us and we'll need to go single file if he wants to pass. Or, we could see just what her Vincent can do.

The truck draws nearer. Positioning myself slightly ahead so she can see, I put my left arm out straight, palm up, and swing it. Her engine noise changes as she speeds up, and I have a moment of pride that she understands my language.

The driver of the truck must have slammed his foot on the gas; it's catching up quickly, not only matching our pace but closing the gap. I start to feel uneasy and open the throttle again. She keeps up, and so does the truck. Risking a glance behind, I see a flash of metal in the hand of the passenger. *Fuck, is that a gun?* I may be paranoid, but I'm taking no chances.

I might be able to outrun him, but her bike's sixty years old. If it can still reach its original top speed, the truck is likely to go as fast or faster. We're doing a hundred already. Glancing sideways, I note the hard shoulder is asphalt and I know what we need to do. A move practised with my brothers but it may be alien to her.

She's casting concerned looks toward me and worried ones behind. *She suspects we are in trouble.* Knowing we can't outrun them and hoping to hell she'll understand what I want her to do, I throw out my left arm, pointing to the left-hand side, then turn my palm down, and raise my arm up and down. Without hesitation, she leans to the left at the same time as I go to the right. We ease back on the throttles; the speeding truck zooms through between us. Now I signal her to stop.

To my fuckin' amazement, she reaches behind her, and when she pulls her hand back out, she's got a gun in it, Christ knows from where. I take mine from underneath my vest. Yes, as I'd feared and confirming this was no joyrider, the truck's stopping and doing a U-turn in the road.

As soon as it's within range, we both fire at the tyres, without me having to say a fuckin' word. One of the front ones explodes.

"Go!" I yell, pointing back the way we've come.

She wastes no time, expertly turning on the road and pushing that Vincent as fast as it will fucking go.

We don't stop until we reach the compound. I sound my horn and the gates slide open when we are only yards away. Then we're inside, the gates slamming shut behind us.

The first thing I do is yell out for Blade and warn him to keep an eye out for the truck, doubting they'll follow us here, but knowing we can't be too careful. Then I look at Sam, who's still sitting on her bike, taking off her helmet and shaking out her beautiful hair, which has come loose from its tie somewhere along the way.

I expect to see a scared and shaking woman. What I did not anticipate is for her to be sitting there grinning and smiling. When she catches my eye, she starts to laugh and continues laughing. Huge great guffaws that bend her double over the tanks. She's laughing so much she wipes tears from her eyes. Never, ever, have I seen anything so sexy in my life. Well, apart perhaps from that moment when she pulled a gun from her bike.

At last she recovers enough to speak, the words forced out

123

between giggles. "That was some freaking test ride," she manages to stammer out.

That sets me off too.

I can't wait any longer. I'm off my bike, pulling her off hers, holding her in my arms, tight. My brothers have gathered around us, some armed and manning the gate, others simply looking at us with their mouths wide open.

All I can fucking think is, *she'd make a great old lady!*

CHAPTER FIFTEEN

*S*am...

"Well, that's the second time you've given me a hard ride in less than twenty-four hours!"

It's not until everyone splits their sides laughing around us that I realise I'd said it aloud. Drummer hugs me even tighter and smooths his hand over my hair. "Fuck, woman. You fuckin' amaze me, you know?" He pulls away only a little so that he can touch his lips to mine. I open for him, and his tongue swirls inside. It's a reaffirmation of life, that we both got back alive.

"What the fuck happened? You two come tearing back like bats out of hell." Their sergeant-at-arms interrupts our kiss. "Wanna tell us what's going on?"

With one last caress, Drummer reluctantly pulls away from me, his hand smoothing the hair back from my face before he turns to Peg. But he doesn't let me go, putting his arm around me and holding me close to his side. "I'm still trying to work that out for myself. Nearly got rear-ended by a semi."

"They try to run you down?" Peg looks incredulous.

"Looked that way. They were armed, could see that. We went wide and let them go through, then shot out the tyres."

"I think that was my bullet." I look up at him and smirk.

As Peg raises an eyebrow, Drummer chuckles. "She's got a fuckin' gun hidden on that bike." He sounds proud of me. "Fuck knows why, but it came in useful today."

"That bike's worth money. I wasn't going to have some little punk stop me on the road and try to steal it from me. I adapted the toolbox and keep it in there."

"You learn how to shoot, darlin'?"

Duh, obviously. "Wouldn't have taken out the tyre if I hadn't."

Drum smirks. "That was my shot."

"When you're done arguing over who shot what, we gonna talk about this, Prez?"

"Yeah." He speaks to Peg while staring into my eyes. "Just give me a moment to sort my woman out, will you? Get the boys together, and I'll be there in a few."

"Are you alright, Sam?" A new voice enters the conversation. It's Viper. I don't know why, but at the sound of his voice the adrenaline rush fades and I start to shiver, even in the heat of the sun.

"I got you, babe." Drummer's arms come back around me, and I lean into his shoulder.

"I'm sorry—"

"Shush, nothing to be sorry for. Fuck, that was some shit we went through." Pulling me closer, he whispers into my ear, "I'm so fuckin' proud of you. The way you understood what I wanted you to do? The fact you know how to protect yourself? So fuckin' proud."

"Can I talk to my daughter now, Prez?" Viper's bouncing on the spot with impatience.

Drummer lets me go and swings around to look at Viper. It's then I remember that we haven't spoken about what went on last night. I touch his arm. "It's okay, Drum. Viper and I came to an understanding, and if you're really okay with me staying, we'd like to get to know each other better."

"If I'm okay with you staying? Fuck woman, I'm not letting

you leave!" Drum takes both my hands, his intense gaze pressing his sincerity onto me. "Prospect," he calls over his shoulder. "Take Sam's stuff up to the clubhouse and find her a clean room to stay in."

"I'll get right on it, Prez." Roadrunner snaps into action.

He kisses me again, a briefer one this time. "I'll come find you as soon as I can." Throwing a nod at Viper, he marches away.

I'm still reeling from the fact he genuinely doesn't want me to go, and I'm going to need some time to process what happened this morning. Why were we being chased? The club must have enemies, but Drum isn't letting on if he knows who they are. But someone was certainly gunning for us this morning. If I stay, are things like this going to happen all the time? Will I risk someone shooting at me every time I go for a ride? We got back safely this time, but only because Drummer knew what to do. *If I'd been on my own.* I shiver. But I'd driven fifteen hundred miles without having problems. It's only when I've been accompanied by a member of the Satan's Devils that my life was put at risk.

"Sam, you okay?"

As Viper's gentle words interrupt my thoughts, I shake my head. "Honestly, I don't know. Is it always like that here?"

His brow creases. "What are you talking about, Drum..."

"No, nothing to do with Drum, but the club. Going out for a ride, being chased, shot at?"

His eyes crinkle. "No, not usually. Or not for a while now. Had some trouble with another club a couple of months back but thought that was done and dusted." He waves in the direction of the clubhouse. "That's what we'll be discussing in church. For now, it's safest you stay here."

I'd already worked that out.

"Come." He puts his hand to the small of my back to encourage me along. "While we're in the meeting, there's someone who wants to talk to you."

I'd started moving, but now my steps falter. Touching his arm, I hold him back. "Sandy?" I whisper.

"Yeah."

It's hard to tell anything from his expression, so I ask, "You tell her?"

"Yeah." His bland expression gives nothing away as to how that conversation had gone. "She wants to meet you, to talk to you."

I swallow, feeling my eyes opening wide. "Do I need my gun?" I'm only half joking.

For a second, his eyes crease, and then he grows serious again. "Just have words with her, okay?"

Feeling slightly dubious about meeting the person who's technically my stepmother, I follow Viper up to the clubhouse. Entering, Sophie comes over to me and puts her arm around me.

"Wraith told me you were chased. Bloody hell, you kick arse, sister, don't you? Drum told him you coped with it like a pro. Shot the tyres out an' all." The way she speaks makes me smile— a combination of American and British English all wrapped up in one package and delivered in that delightful English accent— but I get the gist of what she's saying.

I shrug it off. "Just did what he told me to. Thank fuck he was there." That's what's been playing on my mind. I wouldn't have had a clue if his quick thinking hadn't got us behind the truck. *But if I hadn't been out riding with Drum, there would have been no reason for a truck to have been chasing me.*

The prospect, Marsh, is behind the bar. "Want a drink, Wrench?" he calls out, and I appreciate at least he remembered to add back in the 'r'. A drink would go down very well right now.

"Beer, thanks," I call back.

"I'm going to join the others now; I'll be back later." Viper stares at me for a second, before adding, "Fuck, but I'm proud of you, girl."

I may not know much about him, but his approval warms something inside of me. My eyes glisten as I nod back at him.

"Soph, can you introduce Sam to Sandy? I think she's out back."

"Sure, Viper. She's in the kitchen with the others; I'll take her through."

Sure enough, as soon as my drink's in my hand, Sophie leads the way through to the large industrial kitchen behind the bar area. "You haven't been in the clubhouse much, have you?"

"No, not since the first night, and then all I saw was this room, briefly." Very briefly, I remind myself, I hadn't wanted to look around after I'd seen Viper's cock disappearing down the slut's throat. "This and the room out back where I slept."

"Well," she explains as she leads me along, "we've got a big kitchen, the old ladies usually cook for the men, and we all eat there."

"Just the old ladies? What about the sweet butts? Don't they do their part?"

She laughs. "Old ladies and sweet butts don't mix, babe. Hey everyone, this is Wench. She's been allowed out of her cave." Ignoring the evil eye I throw at her, she waves at each of the women in turn. "This is Crystal, and that imp under the table there is Amy. Crystal's married to Heart. Heart so called—"

"Because he's got a great big heart. Pleased to meet you."

Pasting a smile on my face, I shake the hand Crystal offers to me, and then, to delay meeting the person I'm dreading to talk to, kneel down and give a little wave under the table. "Hi, Amy, how you doing?" As Amy looks on shyly, I look up to see Crystal beaming. It seems like I've done the right thing.

"And this is Carmen. She's a useful babe to have around; she's a hairdresser."

The introduction makes my hand automatically go to try and tame my windswept hair. She notices, and her eyes sharpen with interest. "I could do something with that if you like?"

I've never bothered to do much except having it occasionally trimmed, not having mixed with a lot of women before, but the idea of having a different style is intriguing, so I nod. "Maybe, but I'd still like to keep the length."

Crossing the kitchen, she reaches out her hand, her fingers touching my hair, her professional interest obviously piqued. "Maybe some layers? To bring out the curls?"

"As long as you don't take too much off." *Can this day get any more bizarre?* An hour ago, I was running for my life, now I'm getting advice on my hair?

"Come see me sometime, and I'll see what I can do. Anyway, nice to meet you, Sam. And if you're wondering, my ol' man's Bullet."

There's one woman left, a woman who's older than the rest, and who's staring down into a cup of coffee. Sophie is obviously at a loss as to how to introduce me, especially when the woman glances up and I see her red-rimmed eyes. Taking the initiative, I cross over to her, wondering for a moment whether to pull out a chair and sit beside her, then thinking maybe that might be too presumptuous.

"You must be Sandy."

She looks at me. Really looks at me, and I have to stop myself squirming under her examination. She nods and picks up her cup. "Let's take this next door."

Agreeing with her suggestion, I'd rather anything she has to say is said in private, I follow her back out into the clubroom and over to a corner table. As all the men are in church, and the sweet butts presumably know their services are not required, except for the prospect cleaning the bar, the room is otherwise empty.

Sitting down, Sandy waves me to the seat opposite her. She indicates the room with her hand. "You should have seen this place earlier. Ol' ladies stay well clear for a few hours after a party. Until the prospects have cleaned up." She shakes her head and gives a small smile. "At least Marsh remembered the air freshener this time."

Sniffing the air, I get a tang of some kind of perfume covering the odours of beer and sex. I smile and nod; she's being friendly enough.

Again, she looks down at her cup. "I know what Viper gets up to. I also know he's faithful to me in his own way." She huffs a mirthless laugh. "Probably was a shock seeing your father for the first time in a compromising position. Hardly a good introduction."

First off, I think it's strange she's started with that, but then it's got some of the awkwardness out of the way right from the start. I would have been wondering if she knew. It seems it's going to be full disclosure.

"I didn't come here to cause any trouble, Sandy." Rubbing my hand over my face, I understand I need to make an apology. "I wasn't thinking about the effect it would have on his life. I thought it would be simple, come here and introduce myself. If he didn't want anything to do with me, I'd have been gone." I lean slightly toward her. "And I would have been if I hadn't had trouble with my bike."

Her lips curl up. "God works in mysterious ways."

"He does that," I agree.

Now she's looking at me again; her eyes are grey, a similar colour to my mother's. "Viper and I couldn't have children."

"He told me." I can't meet her gaze, knowing how much they both wanted them.

"Your mom must have been a brave woman, going it alone like she did."

"She didn't have much choice." For something to do, I pick up the beer and drink. The memory of my mom is still too raw.

A hand comes out and covers mine. "I'm sorry you lost her, Sam."

I manage to choke out a thank you, a practised response for any sympathy shown.

"You look like him." She's noticed, like Drum did.

"I'm sorry."

"But it makes it easier, you know?"

I don't, so my brow furrows as I look at her.

"I love him. He wants to get to know you, and I'd like that too. I know you won't want a new mother, but perhaps we could be friends."

It's a gracious offer. I'd been thinking I'd remind her of everything she couldn't have, and here she is reaching out to me. That must have been the trigger, as all of a sudden, I have tears rolling down my eyes. Sandy gets up out of her chair and is wrapping her arms around me. Then she starts crying too, letting me know that while she might not be my mom, she's not going to stop me from getting to know my father. If she can overlook his extracurricular activities, then perhaps so can I.

I start to learn how this place works. Suddenly we're surrounded by the other women, a bottle of vodka appears, is opened, and poured into shot glasses, and two are pushed toward us. The women sit down and also take a glass, with the exception of Sophie.

When Wraith's woman sees me looking at her quizzically, she winks, then gives a little shake of her head. Ahh.

CHAPTER SIXTEEN

*D*rummer...

"Seems like we joined in time for the action." Our new brother, Joker, takes a chair at the end of the table. "It always this hot down here?"

I doubt he's talking about the Arizona climate. "Before we had trouble with the Rock Demons, we'd had it quiet for years." But he's right. We've certainly had more than our fair share of trouble lately.

Lady's clicking his fingers. "Looking forward to having some excitement."

Rock tugs his ear. "I'd rather it kept fuckin' quiet."

My brothers have said nothing with which I can't wholeheartedly agree.

"Drum, you've got one fine woman there. She did fuckin' okay, yeah?" Dart's looking impressed, I wonder whether I should voice my objection to the 'your woman' part. Sure, I'm interested in fucking her again, though certainly not thinking about making anything permanent, but Viper's glaring at me, and after what went down last night, I decide it would be smart to let it ride. For now.

Instead, I rap my fingers on the table. "She rode like a fuckin' pro. Understood every hand gesture." I shake my head at the memory. "None of you fuckers could have done much better."

"She done anything like that before?" Peg leans forward and cocks his eyebrow.

"I don't know. But she's obviously got some experience of riding in a pack."

"Not sure I like a bitch on a bike."

Dart throws a balled-up piece of paper at Tongue. "Get over it, man."

"Hey, Dart, throw a smoke over."

"When the fuck you going to start buying your own?" While complaining, Dart gets out his pack and rolls it over to Blade.

Blade smirks. "I've given up."

"No, you fuckin' haven't!" Dart throws him an incredulous look.

Well, he has in a way. He's given up buying them. But I can't let them get into that shit right now. I've got to bring it back to business. "Right, we've got to work out who the fuck came after us and damn near killed me and Sam." My voice is loud, drawing their focus.

Rock looks thoughtful. "You sure it was you, Prez?"

"That seems the most likely." Though obviously, I don't know for sure, but who the fuck would be after Sam? That doesn't make sense.

"She's used to riding at least two up, maybe she's been in with a club before?"

Now it's Viper who answers Bullet. "She doesn't know much about club life, so I doubt it. And she doesn't seem to be the type of girl who'd attract that kind of attention. I agree with the prez, they were after him."

"Rock Demons?"

I notice Wraith's bouncing in his seat, just the thought agitating him. It was the now defunct Rock Demons who'd taken up a contract to try and take Sophie from us. He certainly has no love for them.

I tap the table as I think aloud. "We saw, what, two, three get out when we destroyed their clubhouse? None of them were one of their officers. We took that club down good and fuckin' proper."

"Up," Slick corrects, shooting his hands in the air. "We blew it to fuckin' pieces." But even he's not smiling; we killed a lot of men that day. That's why, in the end, we'd let the ones who escaped the inferno go. *Was that a mistake that's coming back to bite me?*

"I've not gotten any intel they're gathering again. Mouse?"

"Heard nothing, Prez. The other chapters disowned them. If they're planning something, they're doing it rogue."

Hmm. "So if we don't think it's the Rock Demons, who else is fuckin' gunning for us?"

Head shakes and shrugs come from all around.

"You kept your dick where it should be, Prez?" Everyone except Viper laughs, and I treat the comment with the disdain it deserves, especially in light of the events of last night.

While all the brothers have to leave their phones outside church, as president I'm the exception and have mine with me. When I feel it vibrate in my pocket, I'm tempted to ignore it, but as the talk is going around in circles, I decide to at least have a look at the number that's calling. I don't recognise it.

Leaving them discussing who we could have picked up as an enemy, I discreetly glance at the number displayed, but it's reading 'No caller ID'. Intrigued, I decide to answer.

I bang the gavel and wave the phone. "I'm gonna take this." I wave my free hand and they lower their tones. Wraith's looking at me with interest, Peg's arms are folded as though he wants to get on with the debate. Hoping it's not someone trying to sell me life insurance, I answer.

"Speak to me."

"Drummer?" It's a low, gravelly voice that I don't recognise.

"Yeah. Who's this?"

"Jason Deville." He pauses while the information sinks in.

"I'm sorta in the middle of something right now." I'd rather take this phone call in my office and have the chance to consider whatever job he's going to offer us before bringing it to the table, but what he says next makes me reconsider that option fast.

"I expect you are... You're discussing who came after you this morning."

My eyes widen, and I gesture at the others for complete quiet. Putting my phone on speaker, I set it down on the table. I glance around at them, and nod at the phone. "Grade A's Jason Deville here knows someone was after me this morning." As various expressions of surprise come to their faces, I address myself to the man on the line. "Just what might you fuckin' know about that?"

"I'm close to your compound. It's probably best if we speak in person and not over the phone. I could be there in twenty minutes if you've got some time for me?"

Tilting my head, I look at Peg. He's shaking his head. *Not here,* he mouths.

I think quickly. "We own a restaurant in town, The Wheel Inn—"

"I can find it."

"We can meet you there in an hour if you want to talk."

"Works for me."

I end the call and sit forward, my hands steepled in front of me. I nod toward Mouse. "You know what you've gotta do?"

"On it, Prez." He gets up and leaves.

"Peg, Wraith, you're with me."

"You want me there, Prez?"

I think for a moment. "Rather have you here, Blade, watching the compound. We've no fuckin' idea what's going on or what this fucker from Grade A wants with us. I don't want to leave us light here."

"Could Grade A be behind what happened this morning?"

It seems unlikely, but... "We can't rule anything out right now, Wraith." I bang the gavel. "Church fuckin' dismissed. Peg,

Wraith, let's get going. I want to be there well before this fucker, Deville."

We reach the Wheel Inn and park in line outside. Entering, Marsha, the civilian assistant manager who works under Sandy, greets us and shows us to a table in the corner. It's that period between the lunchtime and evening rush, so the place is relatively empty. Enough tables filled to make us money, I'm pleased to note, but there's an area around us that Marsha's been able to keep clear. Wraith and I position ourselves with our backs to the wall. Peg, after having completed a round of the restaurant, joins us, sitting slightly off to one side.

"Anything?"

He's been looking for someone looking out of place. "Nah, and Marsha says no one's come in, in any particular hurry." We're wary that police or agents might have been planted inside, but Deville hadn't been left with much time to arrange anything.

"Mouse?" Coming up to the table, Mouse gives a negative shake of his head. "Clean." He's been sweeping for bugs. "Want me to stay, Prez?"

"Nah, you can get back to the compound." As he leaves, I discretely check the gun in my holster. I've one in my waistband as well, and one strapped to my ankle. Never hurts to be prepared.

"What d'ya reckon all this is about, Prez?"

Just as I'm about to say the obvious, that I have no fucking clue, a man walks through the door, my attention drawn immediately to the scar that crosses his face, pulling down on the corner of his eye, skirting the side of his mouth and ending just under his chin. He's dressed in jeans and a t-shirt and looks nothing like how I'd expect a partner of Grade A to look. That he's the man we've come to meet seems to be the case, when he scans the room. Checking the occupants, he notes us, then nods, then completes his assessment of the whole area. Apparently satisfied, he crosses to us.

His eyes read the patches on our cuts, and then he jerks his chin toward me. "Drummer." It's not a question, his powers of observation have shown who I am.

"Mr Deville." I nod in response. I don't offer my hand; I don't know why he's here. Even if he knows something about the attempt to kill me today, that doesn't immediately make him a friend of mine.

"Devil. Folks call me Devil," he states as he pulls out a chair to sit down. Instead of leaving it in position opposite me, he angles it to one side so with just a small turn of his head he can see most of his surroundings—a man used to watching his back.

"This place safe?"

"My man, Mouse, checked it before we got here." It had been for our benefit, but he seems to need the assurance for his.

Peg sits forward. "You wearing a wire?"

Obviously not an unexpected enquiry, Devil pulls up his shirt and shows us he's clean. His attitude, his concern that we won't be overheard and his obvious vigilance glancing across to the doorway every few seconds starts me believing he's kosher. But I'm still going to be careful with what I say.

"So, what's this all about, Devil? What exactly do you know about the incident this morning?"

Marsha's on her way over, so even though I asked a question, I hold up my hand to stay the reply and allow her to ask us if we want more drinks. When we're all fixed up, I cock my eyebrow.

He takes the hint. "First, I'll explain who I am. I am part owner of Grade A Security." He waits for me to nod my confirmation that I'm already well aware of that fact. "Ben Carter and Jon Tharpe run the business on a day-to-day basis. I'm, er, more of a sleeping partner in that side. The kind of work I do is off the radar."

I sit forward; it doesn't hurt to ask directly. "You working for the feds?" I'm watching carefully for any reaction.

"Sometimes," he admits. "And sometimes I do the ground-work before involving them. Things they wouldn't take on." He sneers. "Sometimes it's too much like hard work for them, or they plead a lack of manpower. That's where I come in, joining up the dots, picking up the pieces and putting them together. Then they come in for the kill and take all the glory."

I sit back, folding my arms. "What have we got to do with this?" Is he looking to take down the club?

"Doing what I do, I keep my head down and out of sight. As I said, I don't work for the FBI, but occasionally I do their work for them. Same as I do in other countries as well with their intelligence services. I don't often work in the states; most of my time I spend in Europe."

Peg clears his throat. "We're interested in what happened today and what you know about it, not your fuckin' life story."

Devil gives a twisted smile; he doesn't seem offended. "And so you should be. But to understand that, I need to take you back a little." He pauses while the three of us gesture he should continue. "I've been working with various authorities, going undercover to try and break human trafficking rings—it's the world's third largest crime, as you probably know."

"I didn't know it was so big a problem." Wraith is staring at him.

Devil nods. "Unfortunately, it is. It was when I was in France when I first picked something up that brought me to you... A girl."

Peg smirks. "You had to go to Europe for that?"

I wave at him to be quiet.

Devil continues, "She was hurt, pretty badly beaten up. It was just luck I came across her in a Parisian alleyway. She begged me for help and I couldn't refuse, especially when I heard her story." He breaks off, and his gaze encompasses all of us. "She was American, trafficked as a slave. A very particular and expensive slave, chosen for the way she looked and that she'd been a virgin."

So had Sam. Before last night. I shake my head, trying to get my mind back to the story Devil's spinning. I thought I already knew as much about the skin trade as I wanted to know, and that wasn't much. "I thought most trafficked people were girls picked off the street." I'm having problems trying to understand what this has to do with us.

"Often they are. That's why this ring's different. Anyway, I helped get this girl settled. She needed a new identity before she could return to the states, as she was afraid for her life, or of being picked up again. I got her into witness protection. Then I started to look into the information she'd given me about how she'd gotten to Europe." He picks up his beer, taking a gulp. "That's what I was saying before. The intel she had was sketchy, unbelievable. The person she'd been sold to untouchable. The FBI's Human Trafficking Task Force tried to investigate, but the ring was always one step ahead of them. That's where I came in."

I'm starting to get interested, even if I have no clue where this is going or why it would have anything to do with us. Satan's Devils would never be involved with trafficking. But a quick glance at Peg and Wraith show he's caught their interest too. Could he be suggesting there was a mole at the FBI?

"Who's paying you, Devil?" I want to know what's behind this. No one works for nothing.

He shrugs. "I'm contracted to the feds. But Drummer, you're going to have to suspend your suspicions and leave them aside for now, okay?"

I consider it and then give him the chin jerk he's waiting for.

He returns my gesture and continues, "I've been working underground. Found this particular group who kidnap women on demand. They have a bloody shopping list of what they're on the lookout for... Take their time fitting their precise require-ments. The buyers pay top dollar when they get the right girl. Once they've collected who they want, they ship them out to their various customers using a variety of routes. They might use the same one twice, but not very often." He pauses. "Sometimes they collect extra, and these go up for auction. Very exclusive auctions."

As he raises his glass again, I find I'm disgusted but intrigued. I know such things go on. Fuck, some of the MCs I'm aware of have a hand in such practices, but never the Satan's Devils. The very thought of taking a woman from her home and shipping her off to be used and abused fills me with utter horror. From the faces of my VP and sergeant-at-arms, it's clear they share my view.

"I've managed to find out the next route they're using is by way of Mexico, and they'll be coming down through Tucson."

Now I begin to get the drift of what he's saying, but I start hoping I'm wrong. "And you've told the feds?"

"They're aware, yes. But look, Drummer, I'll be straight with you. I've been speaking to Ben, and he remembered you were in these parts and your club might be called on to help me intercept the transport, to stop them getting the girls to the border. I think when you hear the rest, you'll agree to give your support."

"At how much risk to us?" Peg butts in. As sergeant-at-arms I'm not surprised that's his first thought.

Devil shrugs. "They're armed of course, and I don't currently have the detail about how many men will be with the transport. I'm hoping to find out more."

"You're suggesting someone infiltrates the group? Are you able to get in?"

"No, not unless I pose as a buyer. But that would need to be at the auction, and that's not happening here, so it would be too late. It's a tightly knit organisation and they'd be suspicious of anyone else coming in at this stage. Time's not on our side, the transport's already rolling." He pauses and leans forward. "I don't just want an interception and rescue, I want this slave ring smashed. That's where you can help."

I'm not sure how, but I'll play along for now. "Where's it coming from?"

"Washington." Now Devil breaks off and looks directly at me.

An unwelcome shiver runs down my spine. Coincidence?

"They mainly target women who won't be missed. One person they were looking for got away."

Now I start to feel very uneasy. A glance at Devil and my worst fears are confirmed. A cold hand grips at my heart. Sam. She's got no family and she gave up her job. Devil's looking at me, his eyes half-lidded, and slowly he nods.

"Sam Redkin. Her physical characteristics apparently fit the bill, and to add to that, it was widely speculated she was a virgin. She'd never shown an interest in men. But before they could pick her up, she left on her road trip."

Were they still trying to get her? Suddenly I know why Devil had said we'd want to be involved. And yes, I'd like to tear apart anyone who thinks they could just take a woman of ours. It starts to come together. "Was it them, this morning?"

Again, that slow nod. "Her picture's been given to a buyer, and he's committed to the purchase. They want her, Drummer, and they're not going to give up. They knew where she was headed, got in with one of the mechanics where she used to work and got all the intel from him." Again, he gives a dismissive gesture. "They decided to pick her up on the way to the border as coincidentally their route had already been planned and, very conveniently for them, Miss Redkin had come to Tucson. All they had to do was wait for an opportunity."

But until today, she'd never left the compound. They had to have been watching us. Or one of my men had turned traitor. No, it can't be that. I trust all my brothers with my life.

Wraith's kept silent. He now looks at me, his expression assuring me of his solidarity. "We'll keep her safe, Prez." Then he glances at Devil. "Presumably it's only until the transport goes through. They'll give up then, won't they?"

Devil's mouth twists again, the scar making it look like a scowl. "I'm afraid it's not as easy as that."

CHAPTER SEVENTEEN

*D*rummer…

"The fuck you mean it's not as easy as that?" My hand slaps down on the table. "She's under our protection. We'll keep those motherfuckers from going anywhere near her."

"You don't know what you're dealing with, Drummer. This ring is a multi-million-dollar operation. You think they care about your club? You might be able to stop one truck, but once they've got their sights on someone, they don't just give up." He wipes his hand over his forehead and looks up at the air conditioning unit as if it's too hot for him in here. I'm feeling heated too. "You have to understand, they've got a buyer set up, and she meets his tastes, exactly. The buyers have money to burn and the sellers have a reputation to lose. We're not dealing with your normal criminal types here."

"You suggesting they'll take out the club to get her?"

"They'll annihilate the Satan's Devils if that's what it takes. And don't doubt they can do it, Drummer."

Now I think Sam's amazing, but to have that much value for someone else? Could I ask my men to put their lives on the line and my whole club at risk to save her? I haven't claimed her and have no intention of doing so. But I don't need to step up, as she is Viper's daughter, that does put her under our protection. Thank fuck for that.

"We've got this, brother." Wraith's hand touches my arm. "We're all behind you."

As we were for him when Sophie was at risk, but from what Devil's saying we'll be up against something worse than destroying another biker club. I don't tell Wraith there's no comparison, that Sam isn't mine. Somehow the words don't make it out of my mouth.

"We could call in the other chapters," Peg suggests, showing he, too, is already on board.

Devil's face twists again, and again he leans forward, his palms flat on the table. "With sufficient manpower, you might beat them once. But make no mistake, they won't give up on taking Miss Redkin. The only way to keep her safe is to wipe out their whole operation."

"Which is your ultimate goal. Keeping Sam safe is a by-product, not your main fuckin' objective." It all becomes clear.

He doesn't try to deny it.

"So all that shit about Carter just happening to remember where we are based…"

"That wasn't crap." He leans forward, elbows on the table. "That's what made my plan fall into place. You've got the woman who eluded them, and Ben reckons you've got the nerve to go up against them. You keep Miss Redkin safe, and we smash this ring to smithereens."

I lean back in my chair giving him a long cold look. "So how do you see this playing out?"

His intense, challenging stare burns into mine. "We let them take the woman."

The woman. Put so coldly it doesn't sound bad. But the woman in question is Sam, and I'm not ready to let her go, or put her at any risk of ending up in a bastard's hands. "No." My one word of objection lets him know there'll be no debate.

Cocking an eyebrow, Devil ignores me. "This is the way

they'll probably do it. I expect an approach and an offer of an obscene amount of money to give her up."

Wraith scoffs—a million dollars hadn't been enough for us to betray Sophie. "They can't name an amount which would fuckin' tempt us."

"If that doesn't work, they'll take her by force." Devil takes no notice of the VP.

"Let them come," snarls Peg.

"Look, however much manpower you bring in; you run the risk they'll take her *and* take down one heck of a lot of your men. Do this my way and we can be prepared. This is our chance of tracking them. Of identifying the ringleaders. It's the drones who'll be transporting them; the leaders will be finalising the sale. You're close to the border here; we can make sure we get her back."

Something just doesn't add up. Drumming my fingers on the table I think over everything he's said. "Why us? Why aren't the feds here preparing to take them down?"

A sharp nod, a cursory look around the room, and then a deep sigh. "Because there's a leak somewhere, and we don't know how high up it goes. The kind of money we're talking about, Drummer, means it could go to the very top."

"You trust the agents you got contact with?"

"That they want to smash the ring? Yes. Absolutely." As his dark eyes meet mine, they seem to convey an unspoken message, but what the fuck he's trying to tell me I don't know. But it's Sam who's consuming my concern right now, and the fact he wants to use her as bait.

There's nothing about this that I like. "It's too risky. Sam could be hurt—"

Devil interrupts me, giving it to me straight. "She might be roughed up a little, to keep her in line, but they can't sell damaged goods, and the rumours of her virginity would stop them—"

I hold up my hand. I don't even want to think about her

being raped, and anyone laying their hands on her in any way is unacceptable to me. "Once they've got her, we could lose her for good. There's no way we can guarantee her safety." I'm definitely not onboard with the idea.

"Yes, there is." He brushes his hand over his face. "Look, Drummer, this is the way with the least risk. Whatever you think, the end result is one way or another they'll get hold of her, you've got to accept that. They'll call on all their resources to take her. My plan means we'll be the ones in control. We'll get a GPS tracker implanted as a failsafe. Use a spy microphone in an earpiece so we can hear everything going on. We'll know where she is and what's happening every step of the way."

Surely, what he's suggesting will just put her in more danger? "If they find anything on her, she'll be dead." He's not saying anything that makes me feel the slightest bit comfortable.

Devil carries on regardless. "I'll be bringing in the FBI's technical experts. You'll be amazed at some of their toys. An FM transmitter is undetectable, fuck, you can buy one on eBay for next to nothing. The ones I can get hold of are top of the range. Very new."

"Don't they have a very limited range?"

"No. The ones I'm considering are good for well over half a mile. We can stay out of sight but still know where she is and hear what's going on."

I still don't like the sound of it. Getting Sam involved in something so dangerous when I've only just found her doesn't appeal to me at all.

"You said the feds couldn't be trusted."

Now he grins, an expression that does nothing to soften his face, only making one side of his mouth turn up as the scar pulls down on the other. "Oh, I've got enough contacts I can rely on. Don't worry about that."

"You want us working with the fuckin' law?" Peg's shaking his head.

"I don't see that you've got much choice."

"Two hundred bikers would be enough to see them off." The sergeant-at-arms still wants to do this the old tried and tested way.

"You can house that many? On your compound? For months? If they don't get her this time, they'll just keep on coming."

Wraith's staring at me. "She's not as valuable now, not after last night. Maybe they won't want her anymore."

Devil barks a laugh and looks at me. I shrug and his raised brow shows he's had no trouble reading between the lines. "Then they may kill her. Out of spite. Or accept she's been devalued and take what they can get for her. One thing's for certain, that they think she's a virgin will stop her from getting raped. Any change in her, er, status, must be kept quiet."

Peg's got his eyes closed, then he slowly opens one and squints at me. "What do you reckon she'd say, Prez? Why not let her speak for herself? She's one of a kind, tough. She might do this."

If I got Viper's fist in my face last night, I'll probably find myself at the wrong end of it again if he gets a hint I'm considering letting her go into danger. "Viper won't go for it. Not now." Leaving Viper out of it, how could I possibly ask her? My greatest fear is that being the type of person she is, she'd agree. No, I don't want her to know anything about this. *I'll* keep her safe.

"Keep that part of it low-key," Devil suggests. "Bring your club in on stopping the transport, but the role Sam's playing can be kept to yourselves. When she gets abducted, no one will suspect you knew in advance."

That would be keeping the truth from my brothers. I don't like it at all. Devil looks down to check the time—he's got one of those fancy do-everything watches I notice. "I've got to go. I'll text you my number, Drummer. You'll need to discuss this. Your options are—prepare to be watching her and your backs for a very long time; or we get this ended quickly. You do need to ask her, I can't get the equipment on her otherwise. You can get back to me with your, and her, answer later today."

"And the feds? The ones you're working with. What's gonna happen if we don't play ball?" Peg's suspicions are on high alert, expecting retaliation if we don't offer our help.

"They've no interest in your club."

Those might have been the words that came out of Devil's mouth, but how far can we believe it? My fingers tap the table. "If, and it's a big *if.* If we go along with this, any idea when things will start moving?"

His mouth turns down, and the corner of his left eye sinks along with it. "We haven't got long. Early next week I'd guess. I'll get more intel later. Once you're on board, I'll give you everything I've got."

"Who are you getting your information from?" But he's not going to tell us that.

"Let me know your decision as soon as you can."

I guess there's not a lot of trust on either side.

Our three pairs of eyes follow him as he leaves the restaurant, and I wave Marsha away when she comes to see if she can get us anything else. I've such a bad feeling in my gut, I doubt I'd be able to stomach anything to eat right now, and looking at my brothers, they're feeling the same.

"What d'you want to do? Bring the others in or not?"

"I'm still not fuckin' certain what we're being asked to do." I frown. "He's playing his cards fuckin' close to his chest."

Peg puts his hands behind his head. "You need to speak to Sam. She needs warning whether we go along with it or not. We can't lock her down in the compound indefinitely without her knowing why. 'Specially not now her bike's fixed."

"I don't see how you can do anything else." Wraith's picked up a toothpick and is chewing it. "She's got a right to know."

Isn't that a discussion I'll be looking forward to? Not. But they've got a good point—it would be wrong to keep her in the dark, however distressing the news will be. For a start, she'll be wanting to go into Tucson soon to get her money situation sorted now she's mobile again. What valid reason could I give why she can't do that?

Slapping both palms down on the table I stand up. "Let's get the fuck out of here. Yeah, I'll speak to Sam. But if she doesn't want to do it, it's a dead fuckin' duck before it even gets to water. Even if she does, I'll need one hell of a lot of convincing that we can keep her from harm."

We make the trip back to the compound in record time. Unlike this morning's ride, there's no truck following us, and, although I keep an eye open, no one seems particularly interested in our little group of bikers. But somehow, someone had to know that Sam had left the compound this morning. Of course, she had been riding that exclusive Vincent Black Shadow; her bike would have stuck out like a sore thumb. Which means someone had to be keeping a watch on us. Again, I wonder about a traitor in our midst. For fuck's sake, don't let it be that.

The thought makes me look around suspiciously as I enter the clubhouse, unable to get the feeling of distrust out of my head. It's a bad fucking day when I harbour misgivings about any of the men I call brothers, but to dismiss even the possibility would be naïve.

I don't have to go and look for Sam. To my surprise, she and all the old ladies are sitting round the table, laughing, and fuck, they're knocking back shots. Not too many I would hope. Especially if I'm going to be asking Sam to make a decision with such dire ramifications. Viper's with the group, Sandy on his lap. Dart and Slick are hanging close by, and that fucker Joker is sitting too close to my woman again. *My woman?* My brothers have got me thinking that way and fuck me if I'm not feeling it too. It must be the situation, not the woman herself.

My eyes linger on her for a moment before I approach. It's not difficult to see why someone would want her. She's fucking beautiful, and clearly not just in my eyes.

"Ow!" Joker swings around and rubs the back of his head. When he sees who it is, he quickly vacates his seat. "Sorry, Prez."

I glare at him and take the now empty chair. Sam turns her head and smiles at me—it's like the sun coming out on a cloudy day. Just for a moment I allow myself to enjoy the normality of it all, putting to the back of my mind, if only for a short time, the devastating news I'm going to have to share.

Viper lifts his chin at me, I respond with a quick shake of my head. No one asks anything; we keep the old ladies in the dark for a good reason. What they don't know can't hurt them.

"Hi, Drummer, we're just talking about Sam's bike. It's the dog's bollocks, isn't it?"

Sam looks at Sophie as though she doesn't know whether her precious Vincent's just been insulted or praised.

Then she glances at me and I oblige with a translation. "I think she means she's impressed."

Looking mollified, Sam smiles. "She's rather special."

The club whores have decided to make an appearance. Sophie looks over to them in disgust and wrinkles her nose, she leans forward conspiratorially and stage-whispers, "Stay away from them, Sam, they're minging."

"She means disgusting," I translate automatically, then looking at Soph. "That's not quite fair, *Wheels*." I use the name she's always hated as my way of getting back at her. "They perform a function."

"They perform many *functions*, or so I've unfortunately seen." At Sam's statement, both she and Soph turn to glance at Viper, and while the rest of us laugh, he turns bright red and hides his face behind Sandy's head. There's a lot of chuckling at his discomfort.

I sling my arm over Sam's shoulder, getting her attention. "Can I talk to you, Sam?"

"Which translated means—"

A hand snakes around and over Sophie's mouth. "Think you've said enough, sweetheart."

Throwing a grateful look at Wraith, I stand, pulling Sam up with me. While the others laugh, thinking Sophie was on the right track, Wraith and Peg both look uneasy. They both know I'll be stepping into an extremely difficult conversation.

I lead her outside, into the sunlight, and then decide the best place to have a private discussion with her is at my house. She's giving me curious looks as I lead her up through the compound, and it guts me to think she's expecting a relationship talk, which at this point I believe would be far easier, even though that's something I normally run from. Avoiding the garage, I lead her to the living area.

As we enter, I turn her to face me, then, with my hand on her shoulder, push her back down on the black leather couch, which like the rest of my furniture is masculine and functional. Conveniently placed opposite is a wide screen TV, and my pride and joy, a top of the line audio system complete with turntable. But it's the woman in front of me, not my possessions, who captures my attention.

Kneeling in front of her, I take her hands. Oh, I've every intention of telling her what's going to be asked of her, but first, I can't resist just one taste. This time I'll go slow and give it to her the way I should have done the night before.

Curling my hand around the back of her head, I pull her to me. She offers no resistance, coming forward until her lips meet mine. Gently I move my mouth, encouraging her to open, and then slip my tongue inside, toying and dancing with hers. At first she's hesitant, then she responds, and it dawns on me that I've rarely kissed before, and even when I have it's something to get the formalities out of the way, to help escalate arousal so I can get down to the fucking part. Now I'm enjoying it for what it is, the closeness between two people, a sharing of affection as well as lust, and a celebration that we're both still alive. *I hope we'll both stay that way.*

She moves against me, silently asking for more. I deepen the kiss, her tongue curls around mine and my cock comes to life, rapidly thickening and lengthening. With anyone else at this point I'd usually open my zip and give my dick some relief, either in her mouth or elsewhere, it's not fussy. But this time, I'm going to do it right.

Strangely reluctant, I break our connection. Rocking back on my heels I take off my cut, folding it and placing it on a table to the side. Then, with more urgency, I rip off my t-shirt.

She inhales a breath; it's the first time she's seen me. Her eyes widen at the sight of my tattoos. She traces the mechanical design of a V-twin engine on my chest as if checking for accuracy, making me smile, and then twirls her fingers, so I turn around and show her the full Satan's Devils' tattoo on my back. Her gentle touch sends tingles down my spine. Her eyes shine in the light, and I take it she approves.

Reaching out unsteady hands I take hold of the bottom of her shirt. She leans toward me, her gesture the silent permission to continue. Reverently, I pull it over her head. She's wearing a plain white bra, practical and padded, as though she needs the extra lining to enhance what nature gave her. Before today is out, I'll make her understand that what she's got is more than enough for me. It fastens behind, so pressing my fingers to her shoulder I encourage her to come closer, and reaching around, undo it. It falls away. I run my hands down the smooth skin of her back as I gently slip the straps down, showing I appreciate every part of her, resisting the urge to simply tear her clothes from her body.

Then I sit back and just take a moment to admire her. I'd seen her but hadn't bothered to take much time letting my eyes soak her in last night. Her breasts are a perfect size. Not large, my palms can easily cover the milky white softness that's a stark contrast with the darker tanned skin that hasn't been hidden by a bikini, so unlike the whores who think nothing of sunbathing totally naked. The juxtaposition of pale and brown emphasise I'm seeing now what no man has ever before. I swear I feel faint as more blood rushes to my cock.

Under just my scrutiny, her nipples begin to protrude, just begging to be fondled. I don't disappoint. My mouth descends, and I hear a faint moan of delight as my tongue encourages them to become harder. I suck and lathe, tormenting both her and myself. Applying a little more pressure, I give a nip with my teeth. She throws her head back and her eyes roll as she squirms beneath my touch. I chuckle into her skin, and the vibration elicits an enchanting shudder. *Why have I never taken the time to do this with a woman before?* As I apply the same devotion to her other nipple, little tremors go through her, and she gives another moan as I again use my teeth.

Trailing my fingers down her skin, she flinches as I tickle her sensitive and aroused flesh. When I'm stopped by the waistband of her shorts, I place one hand on her stomach, pushing her back. Undoing the button and taking down the short zip, I speak for the first time.

"Lift your hips, babe." I'm surprised at the rasp of my voice, and hardly recognise it as my own.

With her eyes fixed on mine, she obeys. I take down her shorts and then remove her panties after noticing again they're white and plain. *She should wear silk and satin.* Beneath her underwear, her skin's almost as white as the material. A tremor shudders through me at the thought that she's all mine and only mine. Or at least for as long as it takes to get this obsession with her out of the way.

She's wet, her arousal glistening, the smell so enticing I have to put my mouth *there*. Replacing my hand on her soft skin, I keep her in place and at last allow myself to partake of her direct to my taste buds, rather than carelessly off my fingers like last night. Already my palate recognises her unique flavour, and I pause to savour it, knowing my beard will hold her unique perfume as it collects her copious juices. Again, I feel light-headed, relishing a task that I've only performed perfunctorily before, previously using a woman's arousal and release simply as a prelude to heighten my own. Now I want to give her pleasure, even if that means I'm delaying my own.

Wondrous little sighs and groans come to my ears as I lap up her essence, my tongue delving into that tight and until so recently, virgin hole. Using my fingers, I toy with her clit, circling around the tight bud. As her muscles tighten, I move my hand away, wanting to delay her gratification, to make it as good as possible for her.

Like a cat, I lap at her cream, the tang affecting me like nothing before. It's as though my mind is trying to analyse her particular pheromones, to categorise them as mine.

My cock throbs, almost painfully now. I exchange my tongue for my fingers, curling them up inside while sucking and biting at the bundle of nerves, determined to drive her wild.

She's murmuring, incapable of forming words, probably not even aware that she's even making a sound. She starts pleading, "Please, Drum, please. Oh please," as if she's not quite certain what she's asking for.

Her thighs press into me, trapping my head, her body goes back, and I can see her hands clenching, her fingers curled round into her palms. I tease and taunt her until all her muscles are tight, and then she comes with such a loud scream I think it's quite possible they'll hear her down at the clubhouse.

Her cries keep coming as I keep her there, sucking, massaging her inner walls, making it last as long as I can. Then she's pushing at me, and I pull away, resting my head on her pelvis. Turning slightly, I see when she slowly opens her eyes, peering through hooded lids into mine.

My hand clutches hers, a reassurance we seem to both need. As her breathing slows, I know my patience is at an end.

"I'm gonna do this right, this time." Throatily I make my promise to her, pulling her forward and to her feet at the same time as I rise, then sweeping her up into my arms, carry her through to my bedroom and tenderly lay her on my bed.

I stand back and watch her, realising how right she looks

there. Under my scrutiny she flushes, and her arms go over her body. "Don't hide yourself from me." I gently take her arms and move them back to her sides. "You're fuckin' beautiful." It's not hard to see why anyone would want to pay to own her, but no amount of money could ever be enough.

Straightening once again, I toe off my motorcycle boots and undo my jeans. As I slide them down my legs, my cock bobs free. She hadn't seen me last night, and now her eyes widen in appreciation. And fear. Yesterday I'd hurt her; now I've got to do what I can to make that right.

I can see her throat working as she swallows. Showing is better than telling, so I ease myself down beside her, then wrapping my strong arms around her, pull her on top, so she's straddling me. She gasps in surprise, and I grin. "You're going to control this, darlin'. You take it as fast or as slow as you want. Take what you want of me." Then I smirk. "I'm all yours."

Her head tilts to one side, and the corners of her mouth turn up in a beatific smile that reaches her eyes. "I can play with you?"

Fuck me! Yes, please! "Do what the fuck you want to do."

She looks down, again tracing the tattooed engine on my chest, her fingers following the V heading down. At the end of the tattoo, her fingers continue, pausing on my shortly trimmed pubes. "Can I touch you?" Her voice is tentative.

"Fuck yeah."

She takes hold of me in her small hands, the roughness of her calloused fingers makes me grow, not only from the stimulation but from the pride of all that she's accomplished and her dedication to hard work. She's one in a million. *Mine.*

Then I can't think anymore as she starts to explore, following the pulsing blue veins with her fingertips.

"Put your hands around me."

She can't hold me with one hand; her fingers don't meet around my girth. She flicks a worried look toward me.

"It's your show. You do what you want."

And fuck me, she does, lowering her head and tasting my pre-cum that's seeped from the tip, her tongue swirling around. And *oh yeah, baby*, her mouth's around me now. She tries to take more in; I resist taking hold of her hair, balling my hands so I keep them at my sides. She might not know what to do, but as her instinct takes over, I'd give her full marks. My balls feel so heavy I know I won't be able to...

"Stop." She looks up sharply at my strangled instruction. I shake my head. "It feels too fuckin' good, babe. Need you to fuck me now." I point to a condom I'd left on the table by the bed, and she passes it to me. Knowing she can't have sheaved a man before, in a quick well-rehearsed move I cover myself while wishing that I could take her bare.

"I don't know what to do." She speaks so quietly, I can hardly hear her.

"Lift up a little, put me where you want to."

A moment of uncertainty, and then she's easing herself up until she's positioned above me.

"Go slow, babe. Take as much time as you need. Just lower yourself down on my cock. You're in control."

She's killing me as she slowly sinks, her face twisting as she lets her weight take me inside. Her eyes crease in concentration, then close.

"That's it, baby. Fuck. That's it."

CHAPTER EIGHTEEN

*S*am...

Drummer's so big my eyes water just looking at him. Having been facing away from him, turned against the wall, I didn't see him last night, but now in the daylight and discovering all his glory I'm not sure how we're going to fit. And yesterday, it had hurt so much. Will it be as painful today? He's letting me take control; I just wish I knew what to do. I'm going to give it a damn good try. I'm desperate to feel him inside me.

Throwing back my head, I wince as I stretch to take him inside, somehow instinctively knowing if I rise and lower myself then my own lubrication will ease the way. I take a little more in, unable to still the trembling of my body. His large hands come out to cover my hips, a gentle touch of reassurance. Sinking lower, I straighten my neck and look into his eyes. His pupils dilate, his chest rises and falls as if he's struggling to take air into his lungs, causing the fins of the engine tattooed on his chest to vibrate with his actions, similar to the shuddering of a V-twin running. I focus on that, on what I know, and my mouth twists into a smile at the thought of tuning this engine up. Sitting forward, an action that pushes him deeper, I run my hands across the mechanical picture that seems to have come alive on his sweat-dampened skin.

He helps me lift off him, and I come back down. The feeling of him stretching my inner walls now transforms from pain to something else. As if he knows my body's accepting his, he takes one hand and toys with my clit. Oh my God, the feeling is so intense. His touch so light, it seems the only way I can get more friction is to fasten my pace, rising up and then down until suddenly he can go no further, his cock fully seated inside me.

My muscles clench, and he groans, and the feeling of power that sound gives makes me want to affect him more. The smell of our joined arousal fills the air, his masculine scent taunting me. I squeeze against him again.

"I'm not gonna last if you keep doing that, babe."

I start to ride him, using him. I'm so stretched as I pull up, then surge down, his cock incites nerve endings inside. At first I'm uncertain, experimental, and then I find a rhythm. Once again, he takes hold of my hips, his strong arms helping me, subtle hints to increase my pace.

"Touch yourself."

What? Where? Oh, there. Embarrassed, I move my hand to my clit as he pounds up into my cunt. I start to shake as sensations overwhelm me and my awkwardness disappears. My fingers strum against me faster and faster, and closing my eyes I concentrate on the feelings, striving to reach that elusive peak. I swear I feel him growing inside me, swelling as my muscles tauten around him. As my body goes stiff, he groans once again.

"Oh fuck, babe. That's it, that's it. Tell me you're fuckin' coming."

My scream is his answer, and then he's pumping, now in control of my satiated body. I'm weak as I work through my orgasm.

"Fuck, you're draining me completely! Fuck, so fuckin' good, babe."

Then his pace starts to slow, a few uncoordinated movements, and he too begins to relax. He pulls me down, his arms coming around me, his mouth nuzzling against my hair. "Fuck, babe, that was fuckin' amazing."

We're lying skin to skin, and I've never felt such a connection to anyone before. I have no idea what it means, just that if I'm not careful, I'm not going to want to let this man go.

We stay like that, our chests seeming to heave in unison, rising and falling together until the tempo slows to something approaching normal.

His hands caress my skin, his touch so gentle and light. Slowly his softened cock slips out of me. Lifting his head, he pulls me toward him. His kiss is deep and thorough, as if he's telling me something he can't put into words. *Had it meant something to him, too?*

"Let me get cleaned up." He shifts me so I'm no longer on top of him, and immediately I feel the loss of his warmth. My eyes follow him as he strides confidently toward the small attached bathroom, showing no embarrassment even though he must know I'm watching his tight ass. At the door he turns, a smirk showing he's well aware I'm staring at him. My face flushes red at being caught in the act.

"That right there," he laughs, pointing toward me, with a little shake of his head. As my eyes widen in confusion, he continues, "Gonna fuck that innocence right out of you, babe."

I hear water running, a toilet flush, and then he returns with a cloth in his hands. As mine go down to cover myself, he pulls them away, staring intently into my eyes. "This is what I should have done yesterday, darlin'." Then he proceeds to clean me. I squirm in embarrassment, so he tickles me, making me shout out for him to stop. And just like that, he takes any mortification away.

The cloth disposed of, he returns to the bed, sitting himself leaning back against the headboard, his legs slightly open, completely unashamed that his flaccid cock and balls are clearly on display. My eyes seem drawn there, and I'm transfixed as I watch it start to swell once again.

"See what you do to me?" he murmurs. "But we need to talk, darlin'. Come here."

Uh oh. The talk. I decide to get in first. "I know, Drummer, this is what it is and nothing more."

He easily pulls me up the bed and manoeuvres me until I'm sitting beside him, his arm around my shoulders holding me tight. "The fuck you say?" he begins, his voice almost harsh. "Darlin', I don't know what the fuck this is." He places a chaste kiss to my mouth. "I left you yesterday as I didn't know how to handle it, but one thing I do know, you aren't just a cheap fuck, okay?" His free hand runs through his hair and his mouth twists. "That's what makes it so hard to say what I've got to say. I've got feelings for you, darlin'. I'll be honest; I have no fuckin' clue what to do with that."

He's got feelings? Oh, my. Perhaps I can allow myself to feel for him too. Then I recall the rest of what he said. "What have you got to tell me, Drum?" Is it that he's still going to send me away?

He sighs. "I don't like this one bit, darlin'. And you aren't gonna like it either."

"You want me to go?" Let's get this out in the open now. No use prolonging the agony.

"Fuck, no. Though believe me, if I could, I would."

My eyes crease, not knowing what to make of this strange conversation. My lover isn't exactly whispering sweet nothings into my ear. His breathing has accelerated and his body feels tight. Suddenly, I feel his fingers take hold of my hair and gently twist it around them. He draws me closer.

"Just say it, Drum. Tell me." I'm imagining all manner of things. None of them good.

"I don't know where to start. Oh for fuck's sake. Sam, you

must have heard of people smuggling, of rings that kidnap women and sell them as slaves."

"You going to sell me?" I giggle, knowing it's the last thing he'd do.

But his fingers tighten around my hair, and his free hand takes mine, squeezing it so hard it almost hurts. "In a nutshell, darlin', that's exactly what it's been suggested I do."

What? A shiver of fear runs down my spine. *He doesn't mean it, does he?* However I'd expected this conversation to go, it certainly hadn't been down this road.

"Fuck this is hard for me, babe. I've never brought a chick into club business before, but you're at the centre of something, and I've gotta ask for your help." Letting go of my hand, he places his fingers on my chin and turns me to face him. "I can't see any way out of it, I've got to ask if you're prepared to put yourself in danger."

That shiver now turns into a shudder that he can feel. "Just tell me, Drummer. Tell me what you're talking about. Please."

Then he explains how I've apparently been targeted, how they want to shatter this slave ring for good, and the only way they can do that is if they allow me to be abducted. When he finishes his impossible, incredible story, I push away and get to my feet. The thought that I'm naked is the last thing on my mind.

"Why the hell would they want me? I'm nothing special."

A leer appears as his eyes rake up and down my body. "Take it from me, darlin', any number of men would want you. You're fuckin' gorgeous. And what makes it better? You have no fuckin' idea how attractive you are."

Shaking my head in dismissal, I continue to object. "You say they want me because they think I'm a virgin, what if you get the information out that I'm, er, not anymore?"

Now a grin of pride. "I made fuckin' sure of that." Heat goes through me as I remember just how. Not when he fucked me, when he hurt me without knowing, but when he slowed it all down and started making love. *Making love?* This is Drummer I'm thinking about!

"Devil thinks they'll still take you. The minute you're unprotected, darlin', they'll get you. There's a price on your head." Having mentioned the outlandish amount I'm apparently worth to some presumably flabby businessman somewhere who can't get his own woman the normal way, he shakes his head, his eyes half closed. "Believe me, I've fuckin' tried to think of another solution, but I can't find a way out. If they don't take you this time, you'll always be at risk. You'll be the one who got away."

I stare, unbelieving. "They were going to take me in Washington?"

"Devil says that was the plan, and when you rode off, it was easy enough for them to find out where you were gonna end up."

I hadn't thought it would have been a problem. "I didn't keep it a secret. I hadn't completely made up my mind then, but anyone who knew me would have known it was on the cards."

"How would you have known you should keep it quiet? Nah, you just got caught up in something that was none of your doing. Just like all the other women kidnapped on demand."

That statement is what gets me thinking. Since he'd told me, I'd only considered myself, reacting to the fear of what might happen to me. I pace the room, knowing his eyes must be on me, and at this moment not giving a damn.

"If I do this, the other women will be saved? If we smash the ring, we take out the people organising it?"

His eyes narrow. "One ring. There'll be others. But at least these particular motherfuckers won't be able to do it again."

More pacing, more thinking. I run through the options but come up short on finding an alternative.

"I'll have a GPS implant?" He's already told me, but I want to confirm. *Will that hurt?* "And some kind of superspy earpiece so you can listen to everything?"

"Yes, and it's FM, so undetectable, even if they're suspicious and put a wand over you."

He's sitting up now, his legs swung over the side of the bed. I go and stand between them. Taking a deep breath and the biggest leap of my life, I open my mouth and tell him firmly, "I'll do it."

CHAPTER NINETEEN

*D*rummer...
     She'll do it. With those three words, she's commit-
ting herself to a plan, which despite all of Devil's assurances
might not work. Regardless of the strategy we deploy, we might
not be able to keep her safe or protect her from being hurt. *I can't
allow her to put herself in danger, whatever honourable reason she
thinks she's doing it for.*

"No, Sam." My hands reach out for her, my fingers curling
around her biceps as though wanting to bind her to me. "I
shouldn't have told you. It's not going to work. I'm not gonna let
you put yourself at risk. We'll find another fuckin' way to protect
you. Get other charters to send more brothers here." I look up
into her face and make an earnest vow. "I promise you, Sam, I'll
keep you safe." *I can't let those bastards get hold of her.* I don't want
them near her, even for a minute.

"You're not letting me do anything, Drummer. I'm offering
myself." She's adamant.

She's too innocent. "No, darlin', I'm not gonna let you." *I just
can't.* To lose her after I've only just found her? When we'd
fucked just now, she'd owned me. Fucked? Who am I kidding? I
don't know another name for what it was, but for once it wasn't

just my body involved. When I'd come, it felt like her hand had reached inside and torn out my heart. Flowery thoughts for an MC president, but I can't ignore the truth. This woman affects me on a plane beyond the physical. I've no idea where it will take us, but I want longer to explore. For the first time in my life, I want to get to know a woman, and not just in bed.

"You don't have the final say, Drummer." Her hands touch either side of my face. "I don't want to spend my life looking over my shoulder. Who knows how long it will be before they give up? You can't interrupt other people's lives to watch over me, and if I left, where could I go where I'd know I'd be safe?" Releasing me, she takes a step away, her hands now clasped by her sides, her back rigid. "And those other women, who knows how many more they'll take in the future? If there's a chance that I can help to stop this, that's a chance I want to take." She looks away and then back, her face twisted with pain. "Torn from their homes, their loved ones and sold to be a rich man's plaything? I couldn't bear to think I had the chance to save them and walked away just to protect myself."

I stand and pull her to me, her back to my front. "If, and it's a big if. *If* we succeed, we'll only be takin' out one ring. There's a shitload more that will take its place."

"One woman, a dozen, however many are already being transported, and those this group has got their eye on. If we can save them, it will be worth it." Now her hands are on her hips and she's staring at me intently.

"Shit. You're a brave fuckin' woman." Running my hand over my face, it seems like I'm going to have to give in.

She gives a half-hearted laugh. "I'm not brave, Drummer. I'm scared, terrified. But I haven't a choice. I'm involved in this. If there's a chance they'll get me anyway, it's better for me to go in prepared."

But she's so innocent. My earlier thought returns to haunt me. When I'd disposed of the condom, I'd noticed a small amount of blood coating it, she's still bleeding from my savage assault the night before. Knowing that, and understanding how sore she must be, helps keep my cock at half-mast, but it reminds me how far away she is from my life. She's got no knowledge of the world.

But she carries a gun and isn't afraid to use it.

She can restore a vintage bike from nothing more than a mangled frame and a few parts.

She rode fifteen hundred miles alone to get here.

She's a mechanic and not afraid of hard work.

She's dealt with men all her life and gives as good as she gets.

Fuck, if there's any woman that can carry it off, it would be her. Any other woman would be screaming at me to protect her, but not Sam. And that alone makes me want to get to know her better. But I may have run out of time.

"I don't want to lose you. Not now." My gut clenches as it hits me. If the plan goes horribly wrong, I may never have the chance to learn what makes her tick.

She turns in my arms, her hands cupping my face, running down and toying with my beard. "I don't want to lose you either. But what else can we do? If we do it Devil's way, we're the ones in control. If we try to go on regardless, what if they take me when we've let our guard down and we're unprepared? That's got to be as big a risk as allowing me to be abducted now, when you'll be watching out for me."

Lifting my head back, I heave a big sigh. I know that she's right. Taking a deep breath, and a leap in a direction I really don't want to go but see no alternative, I say, "Okay." With that one word I dictate our fate, whatever that's going to be.

Reaching for my jeans I pull them back on. She's giving a wry smile. "Guess I better hunt down my clothes, then."

I try to hide my true feelings as we walk toward the club-house, my arm tight around her holding her close, unable to be apart from her for a second. The thoughts running through my head are dark. I hate what she's planning to do and despise myself for even telling her about it. But she's right, if she's such a wanted target, she won't be able to evade them forever.

One look at my face lets Wraith and Peg know what her answer is. They rise as we walk in, giving chin lifts in my direction and throwing pitying but almost admirable glances toward Sam. I jerk my head toward my office, and they follow me in. As Sam sits, Peg puts a supporting hand on her shoulder.

Before I can have any more second thoughts, I take out a burner phone and dial the number Devil had given me. It's answered after the first ring. "She's in." It's all I need to say. Those two innocent words that are possibly signing her death warrant or committing her to a life of slavery.

"What's the next step?" I ask, only for Devil to respond that he'll be in touch. It's an unsatisfactory answer; I want to know how much time we've got.

He hangs up before I can ask anymore.

"What happens now?" Her voice trembles a little. Now that I've committed her, she's become nervous.

I shrug. "We wait, Sam. That's all we can do."

"I feel like the sword of Damocles is hanging over my head."

Peg squeezes her shoulder. "Understand that, darlin'."

It's difficult for any of us to know quite what to say. Not having a sniff of any plan going forward means we're stuck in limbo.

We carry on as usual, eating a dinner which the old ladies have prepared that could be gourmet standard but tastes like cardboard to me. As the old ladies disappear and the sweet butts and hangarounds start to appear, I take Sam back to my house, not wanting to expose her at this stage as to what goes on at our parties. Although she's probably already well aware—the evening she'd arrived would have given her a very good idea.

I kick the door closed behind us, taking her into my arms, pulling her up against me. I'm hard as stone, desperate to have her one more time, not knowing whether it will be tomorrow, the next day or the day after that when I'll be losing her, if only, hopefully for a time.

She's rubbing up against me, her mouth meeting mine, her eagerness matching mine. I start to tear at her clothes, then I remember.

"Fuck, you must be sore, darlin'."

"It doesn't matter," she gasps.

But it does, to me, the last thing I want to do is to hurt her again. Bending, I whisper into her ear, "Think it's time for another lesson." I sweep her into my arms, loving how she fits so well in my hold, her arms encircling my neck. I take her into the bedroom.

"Strip." My head tilts to one side as I wait, smirking at the way she hesitates to obey, looking one way and then the other as though she can hide. "I've seen it all before, darlin'." She gives a weak smile and then proceeds to take off her clothes. It's not to the standards of the strippers at our club, but it will do for now, and my cock doesn't give a damn she's not teasing me like a whore.

As she gets down to her underwear, I make short work of getting naked too. Then, prowling toward her, I push her backward on the bed. Again, we start by the meeting of our mouths. Just what is it with her? I've never wanted to kiss a woman so much before, but her taste is addictive. Rather than just wanting to fuck, I want to draw this out, to enjoy *her*. All of her.

Now I'm fondling her breasts, squeezing them, smoothing my hands around them, loving the perfection of her satiny skin. My mouth wants to get in on the action, so I lave one with my tongue, and then the other, teasing her nipples until they peak. I move down her body, opening her legs until she's totally exposed to me. As my mouth touches her clit, she jolts in antici-pation. I breathe warm air over that bundle of nerves and then chuckle and raise my head.

"If you want this, you have to do something for me."

"Anything," she breathes.

I grin, turning my body so my cock dangles over her mouth. Lowering myself down, she eagerly opens and takes me inside.

She sucks me in, using her hands to control how much she takes. I pause for a moment, enjoying the sensations as she finds that sensitive spot below the head. She's reading my reactions, learning what I like. As she starts driving me wild, I reciprocate, sucking and nipping at her clit while inserting two of my fingers inside her. I groan against her, she moans against me, the vibrations making me swell.

As I love her, she loves me, the two of us rushing like unstoppable runaway trains toward our destination. She draws up her legs, pushing against me. As her movements become more frantic, I feel the tell-tale boiling in my balls. Lifting my head just a fraction, I rasp out to warn her, giving her the chance to pull away.

But she holds me in tight, and as her body goes taut as a bow, I'm unable to stop, my cum shooting into her mouth. I feel her swallowing around me, her orgasm fuelling her frenzy to drink it all down. As our bodies relax, she licks me clean.

I've fucked mouths before, but it's never left me feeling so drained and satisfied. Twisting my body back around, I crash my mouth down on hers, our essences combining so I can't tell whether I'm tasting myself or her. My beard is soaked but I don't give a damn, her odour will stay with me, all through the night. Suddenly I understand how Wraith's become addicted to just one pussy. That's how I'm starting to feel about Sam.

Curling her into my side, I hold her tight in my arms. As her breathing evens out, I know she's almost asleep when I tell her, "You're mine," and soon follow her down to the land of dreams, though mine are twisted and dark.

We wake at first light. I make her some breakfast in the small kitchen.

"Will it be today?"

There's no way of knowing, but I take her hand, placing a

kiss to her skin. "I don't know, darlin'. We won't know until Devil gets in touch."

"I'll go down to the shop then. I want to check out the Vincent after that ride yesterday."

Was it only yesterday we'd been riding for our lives? So much has happened in such a short time. "Okay, I've got work to do up at the clubhouse."

A simple kiss goodbye turns into more, and she leaves with a skip to her step and a grin on her face as she goes down to work on her beloved bike. With an unusual smile on my own face, I go to the clubhouse, stepping over the remains of the party the night before. Wraith hadn't partied, with his own old lady he's got no need to now, and Peg stayed sober in case of anything going down today. As I cross the littered room, the VP approaches, giving me a knowing grin. In return I scowl, then shrug. He slaps me on the back and I smirk. *Yeah, Wraith, I'm starting to understand it now.*

CHAPTER TWENTY

*S*am…

Me, a sunny day, a well-satisfied body, and my Vincent. What more could a girl want? I've spent time going over her, removing every speck of dust. Topping off the oil— well, she's over sixty years old, she's allowed to drink a little. Then the thought hits me, *what will happen to her if I disappear?* The practical side of my mind kicks in, *leave her to Viper.* The emotional side translates what it means if I never come back. Suddenly, despite the warmth of the day, it feels like the air conditioner has kicked into overdrive, and I get chills on my skin. *What have I agreed to?*

There was a party last night, which means apart from Road-runner tinkering with his bike in preparation for the race he's going to compete in later, none of the other members are around. Marsh is patrolling by the gates, which are closed and locked as citizens don't bring their cars around on Sundays. It's all so normal; everything Drummer told me yesterday seems like a bad dream. *It can't be real, can it?* Who on earth would want to pay an extortionate sum for me? Putting one hand on my bike, I brush the other up over my face. The whole situation is completely ridiculous. Someone's having a joke, they must be.

But Drummer left no room for doubt. It is going to happen. At least if, *when* something does, it's not going to take me by surprise.

My musings are interrupted by a shout from Marsh and the roar of several vehicles coming up fast to the gates. My natural impulse, probably stupid under the circumstances, is to rush outside. But as soon as I see who's arriving, I know it's not someone coming for me. Intuitively I understand it's much, much worse. Worse, that is, for the club.

There are five black SUVs, and as men wearing jackets descend from the first, it's just like a scene from a television programme. I can see they're heavily armed as one steps up to the gate. "ATF," he shouts loudly. "Open up!"

"Shit!" Roadrunner's got his phone out, presumably calling Drum.

Marsh is standing frozen with his mouth open.

Thinking fast and taking charge, I step forward. "You got a warrant?"

He waves a piece of paper at me. Knowing I need to buy Drummer some time, I indicate he should pass it through the gate. When he does, I waste a few seconds reading it. As I've no standing in the club, I pass it to Marsh. He scans it through, then, as the ATF agent growls at our delaying tactics, shrugs.

"Open up and let us through."

They'll simply bust the gates down if we don't. I nod at Marsh, and he slides them open. My heart's in my mouth as the five vehicles scream in, their engines over-revving loudly. The first four shoot on up to the clubhouse, one stops just inside the gate, and men jump out, waving guns and yelling at me, Marsh, and Roadrunner to lie on the ground. When we comply, our hands are cuffed behind our backs. Well, I suppose at least there's no sexual discrimination here; they're treating me the same as the men. Roughly they search us. My gun is back hidden on the Vincent, so they find nothing on me, but the prospects have their various weapons confiscated.

Pulling us to our feet, they lead us at gunpoint up to the clubhouse where pandemonium seems to have broken out. The ATF have cuffed everyone they've found; others are being brought down from their accommodations elsewhere on the site. As members and club whores are rounded up, we're all corralled outside. Inside, I can hear tables being overturned and bottles broken. *Fuck, it's going to be a mess in there.* For a second my mind pities the prospects who'll be doing the cleanup. *Or perhaps they won't. Not if we're all in prison.*

I grin to myself—well, if I'm locked up as being part of the club, maybe that will mean I won't be going on my suicide mission after all. Maybe it will be better to become some big dyke's bitch rather than a rich man's slave. An ATF officer catches me smiling and drags me away from the men, lumping me in with the sweet butts.

There're no old ladies, I notice, but then they went to their off-site homes last night. Being in female company, and in partic-ular, *this* bunch of females, doesn't comfort me; I'd rather be with the men. My point proven when the whores sneer at me.

"The prez will get tired of you soon," the one called Allie confides to me while looking me up and down. "You're nothing special. You've got no fuckin' experience."

Oh yeah, great. Drum had announced I was a virgin to one and all.

I just ignore her, instead my eyes search for Drum, and at last I see him being dragged out of the clubhouse. He's looking for me, an expression of relief spreading across his face as he sees me, but he doesn't have a chance to say anything as he's bundled away with his men.

The mood is sombre. I wonder what it is they will find, and what implications it will have for the club. Remembering what Drummer had explained to me, hoping this isn't all my fault, that the ATF are here has something to do with me. I try to find Drummer again but have lost him in the throng of brothers surrounding him.

The agent in charge steps forward. "Rick Felis," he calls out.

As Drummer shrugs and gives a jerk of his chin I realise that's his real name.

"Ronald Rinter." Well, that seems to be Peg's. Now that really doesn't suit him.

"Scott Remington." And that's Wraith.

"Jack Sharples." Blade swaggers as much as a man whose hands are cuffed behind his back can.

"Todd Bishop." That's apparently Dollar. He consults his list again.

"Dale Norman." Heart shakes his head and steps forward too.

"Bring them," the FBI agent instructs his men. "And her." He points to me. I turn my head, confused. So far he's called out the officers of the club, but why does he want me?

"Er, I'm nothing to do with…" But before I can finish my sentence one of his colleagues roughly grabs my arm. I can hear Drum's growl from here, but it doesn't deter the ATF agent, and he leads me inside.

The seven of us are taken into the room where they hold church. Drum doesn't waste any time. "Why the fuck are you here? We're a club for motorcycle enthusiasts, nothing that would attract a raid from the ATF."

The agent smirks. "Don't bother," he tells the president, "you can't say anything I haven't heard before." He indicates to his colleague, and then says words I didn't expect. "Uncuff them."

As soon as the men are free, each of them takes an aggressive stance. Immediately, two guns are pointing toward them. "Don't try anything. We've already searched in here. Your hidden weapons are gone." He pauses for a moment for that to sink in. "Right, *gentlemen*," another sneer as he labours the word as if it's a description he doesn't think fits, "let's all sit down."

Drummer moves to what I suspect is his normal seat at the end of the table; the agents don't stop him. I see Drum's hands move as though searching for something, but when he doesn't find it, he puts his hands flat on the table. The other members seat themselves around him, Wraith on his left with Dollar beside him, Peg on his right, and then Blade and Heart. The FBI agent moves to the other end of the table, taking up the alternative, but equally authoritative position as Drum.

At last they bother to notice me. "Sit, please, Miss Redkin." I plant my backside in the chair next to Heart.

"Agent Rutherford," he at last introduces himself, "and my colleague here is Agent North." He allows us a second to process that information. Drum stares at him without making a move to speak; his officers take his lead.

Rutherford shakes his head, and there's another smirk. I'm beginning to think it's his natural expression. Drum's scowling, his lips are pursed, and he seems a totally different man than the one who made love to me. But this is serious. The future of his club is on the line.

"Now, tell me where you don't want us to search." It's a strange question.

"That approach work for you?" Drummer's steely gaze stares down the table.

Rutherford shrugs. "Not tried it before, but then I haven't had to." He looks around the room as if there could be contraband hidden from sight. "But then, it's not a normal situation."

The door opens and another man steps in. He's got a cap pulled down over his face, which he now removes. As his features are revealed, Drum gets to his feet. "Devil," he breathes. "Might have fuckin' guessed you'd be behind this."

This is the man who wants to serve me up as a sacrificial lamb?

"What's all this about, Devil? You set up this raid?"

Devil's got a jagged scar running from the edge of his eye to the side of his mouth, giving his face a twisted expression. When he attempts to smile his face screws up even more. He's got a possibly unintended but definitely evil look about him as he answers the MC president, "Not a raid, Drummer. Well, not a real one at least."

Now Drum directs his glare at Rutherford. "You even ATF?"

The agent gets out his badge and flashes it. "Sure am. It's the real deal. But I meant it, you've got a one-time pass on this, Drum. Tell us where you don't want us to look and we'll steer clear. You helping the feds out with the slave trafficking ring? Well, in return for that we'll give you a chance to clean up whatever dirty acts you've got going on."

Drum flashes a look at Wraith, and they have some conversation using shrugs, grunts, and raised eyebrows. Eventually Drum turns back to the agent. "Don't have anything to hide."

I suppress a small smile as I translate their unspoken interaction. Whatever they have, they believe they've hidden it so well the feds won't find it.

Rutherford does bark a laugh. "Reckon if we checked those confiscated weapons, we'd find a fair few without serial numbers."

Drum raises and lowers his shoulders, shrugging off the remark, then leans forward. "Now why the fuck don't you get down to it? Devil, you've got some plan in mind. Wanna let us in on it?"

Devil moves to the table and pulls out a chair, he nods across at me, his gaze assessing as though he's wondering what all the fuss is about. "We're trying to accomplish three things here. First, we want to use your club to stop the transport."

"Already know that," Drum grumbles. But Dollar, Heart, and Blade look surprised. Drum nods toward them. "Sam's got herself noticed by a slave ring. The feds want to use her to infiltrate the group, and us to stop them." His succinct summing up leaves them with their mouths open, but his stare stops further comment.

Rutherford complains quietly, "It's unethical."

Devil looks at him sharply. "We've been through all that."

I wonder about Devil and the company he works for, and how he can seemingly direct the ATF, who in turn seem to be working for the FBI.

"Secondly, we want to make it easy, but not suspiciously so, for them to take the girl." Before I can protest at being referred to in that way, he points at me. "That's you, Sam."

"And lastly," he continues, "we want to surprise them."

Drum's tapping the table, an uneven rhythm. "Go on."

"The ATF will 'arrest' some of you." He puts the word 'arrest' in air quotes. "They'll 'impound' your bikes." He uses his fingers again for emphasis. "That gets a bulk of you out of the compound, and we can move you to where we need you."

"You're going to let us ride out of here? What we going to do, follow your SUVs?" Drummer shakes his head as if it's the craziest thing he's ever heard.

"No," Devil replies seriously. "We've got transporters coming to take the bikes. The word's out this is a RICO sting, and the ATF will be doing a thorough search."

"Word?"

"Somewhere the system's got a leak." It's Rutherford who answers this time, shifting uneasily in his seat. "Every time the feds think they're one step ahead of this gang, they end up trailing behind. That's why this part has got to look real. Whether they're getting into our systems or someone's talking…"

"All your men here today in the know? Can they be trusted?"

"No. At the moment they think it's the real thing. That's why we've got to put on a good show and make it believable."

Peg rubs his chin ruefully. "You want us to put up a fight."

Rutherford grins as though he's looking forward to it. "Certainly wouldn't hurt."

"Not you, perhaps," Wraith butts in. "You've got the guns."

Drummer taps on the table, his head tilting to one side. "Still don't understand why you need us. Surely you can get a trusted team together to stop the transport?"

Again, Rutherford looks uncomfortable and glances toward Devil who answers for him.

"This isn't the first time the Human Trafficking Task Force

has tried to take down this particular ring, and every time they've been tipped off. Changed their routes, or…" he pauses and throws me an apologetic look. "One time they abandoned the trip. Ditched the women first." He pauses and runs a hand over his face before continuing in a sombre tone, "Dead. We don't want to spook them again. So only a trusted few working within the feds are aware, keeping this low-key. That's why we're using the club, Drummer. We can't risk a sniff of what we're up to getting out."

Drum regards him, carefully processing what's been said. After a moment he responds, "Alright. I'll buy that, for now. We're in. And Sam's in. How's this gonna work?"

Devil lifts his chin toward Drum. "We've brought the GPS tracker with us. We can get that implanted now, and the earpiece. I'll show you how to activate and use that, Sam. Batteries good for thirty hours, so make sure you leave it until the last moment before activating it. Okay?"

It's getting serious now. Whatever's going to happen has already started rolling and I've lost my chance to back out. When he'd mentioned women ending up dead, I definitely had a few second thoughts. But now that he's back to practicalities, I manage to stop the protest escaping my lips. Although it might not show, I'm shaking inside. I manage to give him a small nod to let him know I'm still, if reluctantly, on board.

Devil continues to explain, "With your men gone, Drummer, the compound will be vulnerable. I reckon they'll come and take you then, Sam. We believe they've got eyes on this place, it's how they knew you were riding out yesterday. They'll seize the opportunity and make their move soon. Definitely before you can get people from other charters here."

Drum points at Rutherford. "They already know about the raid? Before they saw it happening, I mean."

Again, the agent looks uncomfortable. "If it's like the fed's previous stings, I think we can take it as a given."

"How do we know you're fuckin' clean, and that you're not working for them?" Drum's still suspicious.

"I'll vouch for him."

As Devil gives his assurance, Rutherford waves him away. "I saw the tapes of the interviews with the girl who escaped in Paris..." he pauses, and looks at me. "No woman should have to go through what she did. I might not like outlaw motorcycle clubs, but I like what those bastards are doing even less."

I lower my head, then, when I look back up, see all eyes are upon me.

"You can back out, Sam. It's not too late."

You could hear a pin drop in the silence. I know half the table would support me if I changed my mind and do all they could to keep me safe, the other half would throw me to the wolves. I look Devil straight in the eye and bite my lip. "What are the chances of success, Devil?"

He nods slowly. "Good, Sam. I won't pull wool over your eyes and say it's one hundred percent safe; things can go wrong. But I've looked at the plan this way and that, and not only do I think it's the surest way of putting a stop to this ring, but it's also the best, and the only route, to keeping you safe."

I can't see any other option. "I won't back out." My eyes leave the scarred man's face, and I turn to Drum.

His steely eyes blaze into mine as if he wanted me to say something different, but at last, his eyes crease and his face softens. "We'll be close. All the time, Sam. I promise you."

Peg growls. "You better bet we'll fuckin' be right behind you."

"We won't let you down, Sam." Wraith adds his assurance.

Blade and the others still seem to be in shock but have understood enough to give their own commitment to helping to keep me safe.

It should make me feel better. It doesn't.

CHAPTER TWENTY-ONE

*D*rummer…

I don't fucking like it. It doesn't feel right. We're a club of brothers for a reason, our women are there to be fucked and protected, and in some cases, cherished. We don't ask them to fight our battles or involve them in the business of the club. We are not misogynistic, though the title caveman might apply. Yet here's my woman, someone who rides as well as the best of us, who can take a bike apart and put it back together again, being sent out to do what I'd label under any circumstances as a man's job. And it fucking feels wrong.

Once she's given her final agreement, things start to move fast, leaving me with the impression we've cut the brake line on a runaway train. Devil gets out a pack, and within seconds and with only a muffled yelp, he implants the GPS tracker in Sam's neck, explaining it might form a small sore spot, which she can brush that off as a gnat bite if it's spotted. Next, he gets out the tiny earpiece device and demonstrates how it works.

He stares at her for a moment, checking to make sure she's comfortable with her instructions, then without further delay he looks up at Rutherford and gives him a nod. "Over to you, now."

I should have expected it, but when he starts cuffing my brothers' hands again, I realise all too quickly it's time to say goodbye. When he gets to me, I evade him, crossing to Sam and taking her into my arms, inhaling the scent of her hair, desperately hoping it isn't, but knowing there's a chance it could be for the last time, and wanting to store everything about her in my memory. Silently I vow I'll protect her with my life, and if I have to, I'll sacrifice mine to save hers. I stare into her eyes for a moment, and then my mouth plants on hers. She holds me as if she doesn't want to let me go. We kiss as though we're never going to get a chance to be close again.

"Time, Drummer."

Ignoring Devil's quiet but firmly spoken reminder, I put my mouth to her ear. "You're fuckin' mine, Sam. You don't take unnecessary risks, and you come back to me. I'm not finished with you yet."

A muffled sob, and there's a hitch in her voice as she replies, "I'm coming back, Drummer. I'm coming back. You take care too, you hear me?"

We're still standing close, our bodies touching as Rutherford cuffs my hands behind my back. Then he's pulling me away, and I'm leaving her, alone, unprotected, and ready to be stolen from me. It's against everything I am, everything I stand for, to leave her that way.

"No!" I suddenly roar and spin back around, knocking over a chair. "There must be something else we can do. How can I fuckin' trust you?" Peg and Wraith are looking at me for direction, we might not have our hands free, but we've head, legs, and feet as weapons.

"No." Sam repeats the word I'd spoken. "Drum, no." She's standing there, so brave, her head held so high even if I can see the tears glimmering in her eyes. "It's got to be this way, Drum."

I stare at her, wondering how she can be so fucking strong. Understanding if she can do this, then so must I. Rutherford walks me backward and out of the door. My gaze lingers, trying to imprint her face on my mind until she disappears from my view.

I'm dragged outside where my men lie cuffed on the ground. As I watch them get to their feet under the ATF agents' instructions, it's like all the oxygen has been sucked from the air and I'm finding it hard to breathe. *This isn't right.* I'm the fucking president of the club. I protect my men; *I protect my woman.* My hands uselessly try to escape the cuffs, metal biting into my wrists as I try to escape. How can I do this? How can I leave her to face fuck knows what fate? For the first time since I joined the MC I no longer think my brothers are mad for committing to an old lady, and they're stealing the one woman I might consider making that pledge to before I could even tell her how much she means to me.

"She's brave and resourceful, Prez."

I shake my head at Wraith's words. "But will it be enough? Fuck, what happens if we can't rescue her?"

"That's not an option. We'll get her back."

"Unharmed? What if those bastards…"

Peg growls, "They won't touch her. That would lessen her value."

He's talking about her as if she was a prize heifer. "She's priceless, to me," I snarl.

Under the unwavering stares of the agents, my brothers are getting to their feet, standing, complaining, and casting sideways glances at me. They all think this is real. And while it guts me and I hope they'll forgive me later, for now, in case anyone is watching the compound, it's what I have to let them believe. Watch their suffering as they think they're on a one-way trip to prison. I look down at my feet, hating that I can't give them solace. Prison isn't safe, not for the likes of us. Heart, Viper, and Bullet are looking bemused, clearly worried out of their minds. They're thinking about their women we're leaving behind…

"Agent Rutherford," I call out. When I get his attention, I jerk my head to the side. He takes the hint and leads me a distance away. When we're out of earshot I explain my concerns. "There are more women who'll be coming here. Three ol' ladies and the sweet butts too. Leave some of my men behind to protect them. Please." I've never begged in my life, but I'm begging now.

"This all your men here?"

Quickly I look round, they are. Every fuckin' one. "Joker and Lady are new, just arrived from Las Vegas. They shouldn't be caught up in our shit. And there are two prospects, leave them at least."

I look to the sky and heave in a deep breath; please let him listen to me. Rutherford turns to stare at the group of men, guarded by agents awaiting his next instruction. "Release the prospects," he calls out, "and the two we didn't have on our list."

I can't warn them; I can't tell them what's going down. I have to leave them here to fight a battle they've no chance of winning. *Am I leaving them here to die?* Even though I won't be here, I know they'll do what they can to protect the club, even if it means risking their lives.

Again, I plead, this time with just my eyes, but Rutherford jerks his chin and pushes me toward the group. But I can't keep my mouth shut. "Stay on lockdown," I call out. "All the women to stay in the clubhouse." Sam will know what she has to do, I have to rely on that, and the other women won't be going down to the shop. If I can keep my brothers up here, it might avoid blood being shed, or any of the other women being taken.

My shout causes the unnatural silence to shatter. As I watch my men being pushed toward the transport, suddenly mayhem breaks out as they struggle, shouting out their protests as the hard reality of what they think is happening hits them. Then a lowboy trailer pulls up, men jump out and start to load up the bikes. My brothers start pushing and shoving, complaining bitterly as they see their rides being impounded.

"What the fuck?" Beef calls out. "They're takin' the bikes, Prez?"

Rutherford waves his warrant in the air, as I respond, my anger, which isn't forced as I see strangers manhandling our rides, "They're searching everything."

And then it's our turn. Peg, Wraith, and I are pushed into the back of a truck and cuffed to the side. It doesn't take long after that, and soon we're leaving the compound, going out through the gates and leaving life as I know it behind.

Can I trust Devil? Casting a quick glance at my companions, seeing their faces set, their jaws clenched, I know they must be thinking the same. *Have we been fucked with? Could they have tricked us and this be for real?* It certainly feels like it is.

The only comfort I have is that all the ATF agents seem to have come with us. They hadn't left any to continue the search. We're an outlaw MC, of course there would have been something for them to find had they looked hard enough. But now that we're out of the way, what's to stop them going back? Have I just breathed my last breath of freedom?

Sharing worried glances with my VP and sergeant-at-arms, knowing we're all wondering whether we've been played, we sit in silence for about an hour before the vehicle comes to a halt. The doors are flung open.

Fuck, that man must move like a ghost. I hadn't even seen Devil leave the compound, but he's gotten here before us. He's the one climbing inside and uncuffing us. As soon as my hands are free, I rub my wrists to get the circulation back, noticing the blood from my earlier ineffectual struggles. *Damn ATF. They certainly made it feel real.*

Devil notices my action and his mouth twists. "Sorry about that, Drummer, but we had to make it authentic." He points behind him to where the agents have my men corralled. "You can speak to your men, but once the bikes are unloaded, make sure they know they're not to take off." I notice that the first lowboy trailer is pulling in with half a dozen bikes strapped onto it. I also get the chance to look around at where they've brought us to. We're in the middle of nowhere, outside a rundown barn.

It looks like the type of place where they might have kept cattle, but obviously has been disused for some time.

Seeing my brothers are still wearing their steel bracelets, I cock a suspicious eyebrow at Devil. "Not going to keep them like that, are you?"

"Let's see the mood once you explain." He nods toward Beef, who's looking particularly angry. "Punches might fly when they realise they've been set up." He points toward the building. "Let's get inside, out of the way."

Rutherford comes up as the agents start shepherding everyone inside, out of the heat of the sun. "We weren't followed," he tells Devil. "And everything including the bikes are clean. We've swept them for bugs or trackers."

My brothers are vocal, questioning our location. As they expected to find themselves locked in cells, I can understand their confusion.

"What the fuck is going on?" Rock yells out.

"Get inside and I'll explain," I shout back, and circle my hand over my head, a signal that they're all to follow me as I walk into the welcoming shade.

In the barn they gather around, expressions ranging from fear and worry to outright rage and indignation. They're looking to me to give them something that will make sense of the day. Knowing it's probably not going to go down well, I take a deep breath. "We're working with the FBI." Immediately there's a chorus of questions as well as defiant shouts and objections.

Slick spits on the ground. "We're fuckin' what?"

"Shut the fuck up and listen!" Peg barks, loudly. His expression, normally reserved for making our enemies cower, is now directed toward his brothers. "Give Prez a chance to speak."

As the murmurings and protests start to simmer down, I raise my voice. "The feds want our help to stop a slave ring." My opening words cause a few jaws to drop and eyes to open wide. Before they can comment I continue, "The motherfuckers are after Sam. We need to work with the feds to stop them."

Another round of 'what the fucks?' and I wave at them to settle.

Viper's looking around, his eyes wide and staring. "Then why the fuck isn't she here with us?"

This is the part that's going to go down very badly. "Because we're letting them take her."

As Viper steps toward me, I mentally thank Devil for having the foresight to leave his cuffs on, otherwise I think he'd try to kill me. "You fuckin' letting her be taken to be some bastard's slave? Are you out of your fuckin' mind?" Spittle flies as he speaks. "Prez, we can't do this. We gotta get back, protect her. There's fuck all of 'em left to save her at the compound. She'll be completely exposed." I don't respond, my face remains impassive, letting him continue until he runs out of steam. He pauses, but only to gather enough breath to shout in my face. *"What the fuck have you done?"*

He's only giving voice to my uncertainty that I've chosen the right path but acknowledging my own indecision won't help. I glare at him, my cold eyes narrowing, my mouth pursed. Tall enough that I can loom over him, I stare him down. "I've listened to Devil and the feds, Viper. I've taken into account what we're up against. If there was any other way, I'd have taken it. And Sam agreed, she knows exactly what's going on. I'm not fuckin' happy about it either, Viper. But this is our best way of protecting her."

Oh, there's huge fucking holes in the plan that I now explain to my men, while Rutherford goes around unlocking their cuffs. Much of what we're doing will be on the fly. We can only hope at the end of it we'll have saved the club and Sam.

After the agent has freed my brothers, he says something I can't hear to Devil, shakes his hand, then gathers up his men and leaves. I watch the black SUVs and the lowboy trailers trundle off down the track. It appears we're now on our own.

Devil's glancing at that watch of his, and then he tries to make an exit unnoticed. But I've seen him, I've had my fucking eyes on him the whole time. Pushing through my throng of brothers, I stop him with my hand on his shoulder. It's a bit like trying to stop the *Titanic*, but I'm a big man too.

"Where are you going?" I growl. His eyes flit sideways, and I can see he doesn't want to answer. "Something's happened, hasn't it? You got an alert." His watch, as I know, can do all manner of things as well as tell the time.

He looks at me darkly. I glare back. For a moment, we stare each other down. In the periphery of my vision, I see Peg and Wraith come up to flank me. Outnumbered, he gives in. "They're at the compound. About to take Sam."

"And we're still fuckin' standing here?" I remember my promise to Sam; I'd be behind her all the way. "Get the bikes," I snap out to my VP and sergeant-at-arms.

Holding up his hand, Devil stays me. "I'll let you know when and where, Drummer. You wait here for now."

I grab hold of his jacket. "You're fuckin' going nowhere without me. I'm coming with you. And so are…"

He gives me a hard look, then seeing I'll take no argument and that holding out against me is wasting time, relents. "You can come along, but your VP will stay here. He can bring the men when it's time. If you all go back to the club, it announces to everyone that today's raid was just a ploy."

I throw a look at Wraith, he doesn't look particularly happy about it but nods in response. "We got this, Prez."

"We're going to lose them if we don't hurry."

That's all Devil needs to say to spur me on. I follow him as he strides off toward a van with blacked-out windows. I slide into the passenger seat as he takes the driver's side. The dashboard is full of equipment. Devil waves an imperious hand. "Don't touch anything. It's tuned to her frequency." I presume he's talking about the radio gadget in front of me. Well, I'm hardly going to want to choose a music station when all I want to hear is what's happening to Sam.

Then he points to something else, a GPS tracking unit, but

more sophisticated than that found in a normal car. "She's on the move, about half a mile away from here. If we keep to that range, we should be able to hear everything."

But the compounds more than half a mile away, surely? "We were driving much longer."

"Took the roundabout route. Needed to be close but had to make sure we weren't followed."

I look around the van. "This vehicle wasn't part of the raid."

"No, we wanted to make sure they didn't clock it."

Reaching out his hand, Devil turns up the radio. There's nothing to hear but the rumbling engine sound of the vehicle they've used to abduct Sam.

CHAPTER TWENTY-TWO

*S*am...

I'd watched Drummer back out of the office, memorising every detail of his face until I couldn't see him anymore. I'd tried to sound brave in front of him, even while I was scared as hell inside. *Am I doing the right thing?* Well, there's a question mark hanging over me, but the plan to get the men away from the compound had to be the right one. I know Drummer would put his life on the line to save me, and if they tried to take me by force, he, and others, could have been killed.

I've never thought of myself as a coward, but I've never had to face anything like this before. *What if they can't save me?* Oh, that's alright, I'll just end up as a rich man's toy.

"We've got this, Sam." A comforting voice from a terrifying looking man tries to reassure me.

Dragging my eyes away from the empty doorway, I face Devil. "Have you, have you really? I know you'll do your best, but..."

"I wouldn't have asked you to put yourself at risk if there was any way around it, believe me on that. We'll get you back, Sam. Have faith in your man. He's not going to let anything happen to you."

It's the encouragement I wanted, but even I can see the flaws in the plan. I make myself remember they've already kidnapped other women, and if there's a chance I can do my part to break up the ring and save them, I've got to take it. Pulling my shoulders back I stand taller, pretending a confidence I don't feel. "How should I play this?"

Quickly he explains and then slips away, and I'm left alone.

Walking out into the eerily quiet clubhouse is disconcerting. There should be prospects behind the bar, bottles clinking, men laughing and joking. The old ladies should be around, or at least the sweet butts, but the place is empty. The unnatural stillness makes me shiver. But, hang on. There are voices outside, voices arguing. *Not everyone has gone.*

I step through the door and find Marsh and Roadrunner, the two prospects, and the two new members, Lady and Joker.

"What the fuck do we do now?"

Joker's pulling out his phone. "Well, I'm gonna call Red. Fuckin' unbelievable. We transfer to a club that's under a fuckin' RICO indictment."

Marsh's eyes open wide, and he exchanges worried glances with Roadrunner. "You gonna walk out on the club?"

Angrily, Lady kicks at a stone on the path. "There ain't no fuckin' club!" he shouts. "What the fuck d'ya expect us to do?"

"Hang around until Drummer and the others get back." Marsh is nearly pleading. "The feds didn't find anything, so they got nothing to hold them on."

Joker and Lady exchange glances. No one's noticed me yet.

"Oh, for fuck's sake. I'll ring the ol' ladies, tell them the news. There's no point them coming to the compound." Marsh seems to be taking responsibility as though he's a fully patched member. And if Lady and Joker bail, he and Roadrunner *will* be the only brothers left. Or so he thinks.

"The businesses?" Roadrunner asks. "I could cover the strip club. Fuck, once this gets out, who knows what panic there'll be or what staff we'll lose."

"Sandy manages the restaurant; I'll tell her to keep on with that and perhaps give you a hand with the strip club?" The two prospects nod in agreement with each other.

Making a mental note to tell Drummer later how impressed I am with how they're stepping up, I use the opening they've given me. "I'll keep the shop going. It'll be slow, but we want something for them to come back to." As they will do, and sooner than these men think, but I can't let on.

Joker's eyeing me up. "Of course, there is one benefit, there're three sweet butts and Sam. I like those odds."

I don't. "I'm Drummer's woman," I tell him firmly, even though I'm not quite certain of my status, wanting to knock those thoughts on the head right now.

Once again, he looks me up and down, a leer appearing on his face. "There are prison rights, you know?"

Giving a shake of my head, I rise to the bait. "And what the heck are they?"

Lady grins. "When an ol' man's inside, the other brothers can see to his ol' lady's needs if you get what I'm saying?"

"Oh no. You—"

"Messing with ya, darlin'," Joker interrupts me, his face twisting in an approximation of a smile. "Just fooling around trying to lighten the mood." Then he turns to the others, wavering. "Look, I'm not planning to jump ship, but I'm out of my depth here. I'm still going to speak to Red. See what he has to say. Fuck, this has been one motherfucker of a morning."

"Think we're lucky to be fuckin' breathing free air," Lady puts in. "Hate to think of our brothers chained up in cells."

"We need to get protection on them inside." Joker's all serious now. "They won't be safe without. Red can help get that shit organised."

I want to stay and talk with them, but I know that's not where I'm meant to be. I want to reassure them that everyone will be back in their right places soon, but I can't say a word. "I'm going down to the shop. There'll be a lot for me to manage, so I best make a start. There're customers expecting to pick up their cars after the weekend."

"I'll be down later, Sam. Help out until I have to go to the club." Roadrunner seems to have forgotten all about his planned race today.

I discourage him. I don't want anyone hurt. "You'll have enough on your plate. Let me work through the most urgent stuff, and I'll shout if I need a hand."

My legs are already shaking, my hands sweaty and it's getting harder to breathe. Not wanting them to suspect anything, I turn and make my way down to the shop feeling like a lamb going to the slaughter. If Devil is right, the slavers will have had eyes on the compound and will have seen the ATF leave. I reckon they won't waste any time, wanting to get me out before reinforcements can arrive.

I wheel my treasured bike to the rear of the shop and cover it with a tarp, not knowing when I'll be seeing it again. Then I make my way outside, noticing no one had locked the gates when the ATF had left. Feeling like it's too much of an invitation, I go across to close them, and see a van heading up the road. Oh, shit. Is it time already? Are they coming already? Quickly I activate my earpiece and replace it in my ear. Then, completely innocent, I do what anyone not connected to the MC would do, I stand in the gateway, the barrier half closed, and wait to see who wants to come in.

"Better get that gate closed, darlin'." Oh no, it's Roadrunner, and he's getting his gun out of his waistband while rushing to help me slide the heavy gates closed. I make a fuss of fumbling and not being able to shut my side, allowing the van just enough time to speed up and come through.

There's no doubt they've come for me. Roadrunner pushes me behind him, giving me hurried instructions to run to the shop, lock the door, and ring the clubhouse. But men have surrounded us before I can move.

One, who I recognise, steps forward. "Well, if it isn't Wrench. Fancy seeing you here."

He was a customer at the shop in Washington, a man who always had something going wrong with his car, and so incompetent at fixing it himself that he always seemed to be in the shop. A jovial man, or so he'd seemed; he was friendly with all of us mechanics. It dawns on me that he was only coming around over the last few months, but had gotten in tight with Jake, one of my fellow workers. *That must be where he got his information.*

I act surprised. "Hi, Mr Jackson. It's a small world, isn't it? We're closed on Sundays, so if you want your..." I peer around him, not seeing his car. "If you want your truck fixed, I can book you in for an appointment during the week."

He smiles. I'd never realised what a nasty smile he had before. Mind you, I saw more of his feet as I was more likely to be found sprawled out under the car. I should have taken more notice of his expensive Italian loafers, so at odds with the rest of his workday clothes. My apparent confusion must put him at ease.

Roadrunner's looking from the man to me in surprise. "You know this man, Sam?"

I shrug. "I don't *know* him as such, but he used to bring his car into the shop where I used to work." I pause and address myself to Jackson, still acting innocent and trying not to let my internal shaking show. "You had one heck of bad luck with that car. Did you sell it in the end?"

Stepping forward, Jackson waves at his men to move closer. Roadrunner shifts awkwardly.

"Luckily your brains, or lack of them, aren't a requirement for what we need you for," Jackson says with a sneer, his tone of voice causing Roadrunner to raise his gun. A wave of Jackson's hand and a shot rings out. As Roadrunner falls to the ground, I turn and look down in horror. Blood is pouring from a wound on his chest.

"What have you done?" I scream, falling to my knees to try and help the prospect, but not having a clue what to do. My basic first aid is no match for this.

"Take her."

I'm half lifted and half dragged screaming into the back of the van. "Let me go," I screech. "I've got to help him!" My panic is genuine, my fear off the scale. I'm fighting to get back to Road-runner, forgetting the danger to myself.

But they've got me inside, and the doors are locked. It's a panel van with no windows, and I'm thrown off my feet onto the floor as it makes a U-turn and tears away from the compound. They've taken me. I'm on my own.

Panic rises on a wave of nausea. Coldly discussing that someone was planning to kidnap me had nothing on the reality, and more than half of me hadn't believed it would really happen. But now that I'm taken, I don't have to pretend to be scared. My heart's beating wildly, making it hard to get air into my lungs. Making a conscious effort, I try to slow my breathing. I can't lose it now. As long as my earpiece works, maybe there is a way I can get help for Roadrunner. "Oh, Roadrunner," I cry out as though speaking to myself in case anyone in the front can hear. "Why did you try to protect me, and why did you have to be shot? Road, don't die there, in front of the gates."

Almost immediately there's the most wonderful sound in the world, a voice speaking in my ear. A voice I recognise, but one that's speaking more calmly than I've heard it before, and it immediately soothes me. "Doc is on his way to him," Drummer tells me. "And we're right behind you."

I don't know whether the vehicle is bugged, or whether the men driving can hear, so I don't say anything else. The earpiece is my lifeline; I don't want to give it away. Drummer must understand, as he speaks again, "Cough once if you're alright, Sam, twice if you're hurt."

Obediently I cough, just the once.

194

"Good girl. Is there anyone else with you? Are you with the other women? Cough again, once for yes, twice for no."

I cough twice.

"Okay, you'll probably be rendezvousing with the others at some point. We'll listen in for that," Devil adds in his gravelly tone. "We'll be with you all the way. Do nothing to put yourself at risk, Sam. Remember what I said, do everything they tell you without a fight."

I nod, even while knowing they can't see me, and then try to make myself as comfortable as I can. Who knows how long I'll be in here?

I lose all sense of time. It's dark, hot, and very stuffy, making me bite down my fear there's no air getting in. Of course there is, it's my mind playing tricks on me. Trying to focus on something other than my predicament, I think of Drummer, of the man, not the president. He's two different people—one hard and controlling, one gentle and kind, and that's the part of him that others don't get a chance to see. Perhaps he's allowed me an insight into the man he was before he became a hardened president of the MC. We didn't talk much about ourselves; he knows far more about me than I do about him. But there are so many things I want to ask him, things to find out about him. Will I get the chance to ask him? Will I get to hold him again, make love to him again? He told me he wasn't finished with me. What exactly does that mean?

A tear forms at the corner of my eye and I wipe it away, finding thinking about my lover isn't helping at all.

I've been kidnapped, abducted. By Jackson of all people. So, that's what he was doing constantly bringing his car to the shop, he was keeping a close eye on me. No wonder he'd found out about the lack of sexual activity in my past, it had been a standing joke where I'd worked, that I knew more about engines than I did about men. But I'd fooled him by disappearing.

Jake would have known where I was headed. I hadn't seen the need to hide what my mother had told me about my father, and I suppose I wouldn't have been human had I not decided to find him, to satisfy my curiosity about what kind of man brought me into existence. Jake wouldn't have seen any reason to keep it secret. No, he couldn't have dreamed his loose mouth might cause me harm and would be devastated if he ever found out. Jackson had seemed so plausible, giving no indication he was up to no good. His lack of knowledge about his car was a standing joke between us—one day he'd brought it in as the windshield wiper fluid had dried up. We'd charged an hour's rate to top them up again. Oh, how we'd chuckled at ripping him off, not knowing, of course, the tables would turn, and the last laugh would be on him.

The truck bumps over something, and then across rougher ground. As it starts to slow, I realise I haven't been thinking about the right things. Oh shit, what do I say when he opens the door? How do I play this? *Act naturally, don't give away that you were warned in advance.*

We stop, and the doors are pulled open.

"Out."

It's not Jackson; it's a stranger, an ugly brute of a man, his teeth yellowed and broken. His nose looks twisted as though broken in a fight, and one ear is ragged as if at some point it had been torn. He looks like a fighter, no stranger to violence. I think I'd rather see Jackson's face, someone familiar. This man's sneer, and the way his eyes roam up and down my body makes my skin crawl. *He's looking at me as though I'm a lump of meat.*

Looking round I finally see Jackson, he's flicking through a pile of bank notes before he gets into a different car—a step up, I notice, from his old broken-down heap—and is driving away.

CHAPTER TWENTY-THREE

*S*am…

"Out!" The command's repeated, this time more urgently. "You don't want me to come in there and get you."

"Don't do anything to get yourself hurt." Drummer's voice comes over clearly, and I jump, hoping the men haven't heard, but of course they can't, as he's speaking directly into my ear.

He's right, it's best if I do what they tell me to do. Now faced with this ugly and scary man, I have no need to fake my confusion or that my body's shaking in fright. Ignoring the offered hand, I jump down onto the sand.

"Strip," the disfigured man tells me. His voice might sound disinterested as though he's done this a hundred times before, but his hungry eyes don't leave me for a second.

"What?" I didn't expect the crude demand. I'm trembling so hard it's difficult to speak.

"Take off your clothes," he instructs more slowly, as though addressing a petulant child.

"Why?" My eyes wide, I look around in horror at the men surrounding him—there are three others with him. None of them look sympathetic; all are just as unpleasant versions of the first, or perhaps that's just how my mind portrays them. All have virtually identical leers on their faces, and four pairs of eyes are focused on me.

"So you can put this on." He throws me a flimsy babydoll nightie which would barely cover my ass, and a top so low it will show a whole lot of breast. "We haven't got all day. Take off your fuckin' clothes now. Or we'll do it for you."

Stripping in front of them is the last thing I want to do, but I don't want their grubby hands on me. "I'll change in the truck," I suggest.

He smirks. "No, you change here."

Yeah, they'd want me to do that, wouldn't they? All part of the humiliation aimed to control me. They want to see my body, but they won't touch. My value is my assumed virginity, Devil assured me of that. Summoning up some backbone, I remember what I've been told. It might be degrading, but it's not going to hurt. Unless I refuse. And that's when their gloves will come off.

But still I try to retain some dignity. "Can you turn around? Please." I add my plea, hating the genuine weakness in my voice.

They laugh, loudly. One slaps another's back. "Fuck, some-one's going to have fun breaking her."

Oh. My. God. Devil promised I'd be rescued, but I hadn't allowed myself to imagine what I could go through first. What had I thought would happen? That a man would turn up, politely ask me to step into a car and make polite conversation on the way? These men trade in flesh, human flesh. If they weren't born that way, they'd have developed a disregard for the people they've stolen and consider them as nothing more than animals. To them, I'm not a woman anymore, I'm a thing, an object, to be defiled and vilified in whatever way they want. Then they'll sell me. They have no better natures I can appeal to; they'll have long lost any semblance of that.

Back in the cocoon of the compound, it had seemed so easy. But now that I'm here, even with the communication device in my ear and the further comfort of the GPS implant, I have to suffer just like any other woman they've taken, even while knowing help isn't far behind.

It's the demand I take off my clothes that undoes me, and I know I've made a mistake. *I can't do this.* The only man who's seen me naked has been Drummer. Without conscious thought, I swing around and start sprinting across the hot sand...

And have the air knocked out of my lungs when Ugly-face throws himself on top of me. I scream as he starts tearing at my clothes.

"Don't fight." Now the voice in my ear is no longer calm, and there's a snarl and a rushed, "Devil, put your foot down..."

The sound goes as if the radio's been switched off. *No, don't leave me alone!*

But I stop fighting, stop resisting, and soon he has me down to my underwear. I hold on to my bra, but he's too strong and gets it off. Then my panties are torn away. I try to cover myself as they all stare at me, one openly jerking himself off in his pants.

"Can we try her out, boss?"

No! I shake my head wildly and try and step back, but rough hands have a hold on me.

"Not this one," the man stripping me snarls. "You can look and feel, but no further than that. She's valuable cargo. Untouched."

"I'd like fuckin' touching 'er."

"You can *touch.*" To my horror he gives his permission. "Just not fuck."

My arms held firmly behind my back, Jerk-off steps forward. His free hand roams my breasts. "Bit on the small side, these. You sure you've got a buyer for her?"

Then he's taking out his dick and pushing it up against my stomach. Closing my eyes, I try to pretend it's Drummer, but it's impossible. There's a rank smell, and he's so much shorter it's impossible to imagine it's my man in front of me. At last, he turns away, and I open my eyes, immediately wishing I hadn't as I watch him tugging at his cock and a stream of cum shoots out over the sand. But he's not finished, he takes some of the drips remaining on his tip and rubs them into my breasts.

"There you go, darlin', now I've marked you, you'll remember me all day. Bet you'd have loved my cock inside you."

Another man lurches up to me, his fists in my hair, holding my head steady as he kisses my mouth. When I refuse to let his tongue probe inside, he bites my lip so hard I gasp, inadvertently opening for him. His tongue tastes foul and his breath smells, while his hands roughly roam over my skin. I sob and gag and want to spit when at last he pulls away.

The last man fondles my breasts and twists my nipples so hard it brings tears to my eyes. He runs his hand down my stomach, and into my folds. "Fuck, she's dry as the fuckin' desert."

Unable to bear the alien touch, my tears are flowing freely now. Being restrained, I can't wipe my nose and snot runs down my face. Freed momentarily I try to escape, but it's only so someone else can take over my imprisonment, allowing Ugly-face to stand in front of me.

"Fuck you're a mess," he tells me. "But don't worry, I like to see a woman cry. Turns me right on, it does." He outlines his hard cock with one hand, then shoves his other between my legs. I rise up on my toes trying to escape him. As the other man holds me tight, he pushes his fingers into me, probing. I grit my teeth and try to send my mind back to better times, but it doesn't work.

Jerk-off laughs. "Don't damage the goods, man."

It makes him draw his fingers away from *there*, but then he's prodding at my backside. I freeze as his finger tries to probe my puckered hole.

He's looking straight in my face. "Wish I could be the one to break you in, sweetheart, but you'll know what it's all about soon enough. And while that fuckin' vibration is doing wonders to my cock, I need to answer this. If you'll excuse me."

I heave a sigh of relief, as with a sarcastic grin he steps away, pulling out his phone. All I can hear are a series of yeses and noes from his end; however hard I strain, nothing of the call itself.

Mouth rapist yells out as he ends the call, "You got the details of the next stage?"

"Yeah, we're heading for the border. Boss man will meet us this side and check the merchandise. Get her loaded up now." He shoves the babydoll nightie at me. I slip it over my head fast, grateful for any covering, however ineffective it is.

At last he steps away, and the men turn to business, pulling me over to a truck and opening the back. The inside is crammed full of women dressed the same way as me. If the state of them is anything to go by, it looks like most of them must have put up a fight. One young girl is holding her hands to a bloody graze on her face; another's nursing a swollen wrist. All are covered in a range of bruises. Only a couple glance up with anything resembling interest as I'm pushed inside, some seem almost catatonic. I can only be grateful my portrayal of a scared virgin was enough to convince them only to put their dirty hands on me. That the men had probably gang-raped the others seems certain.

One man jumps up and cuffs me into the one remaining space. Then, as they slam the door, I hear Ugly-face cry out, "Let's get this show on the road. I'm looking forward to payday!"

"Too fuckin' right," replies Jerk-off. I hear them walk away, and then a rumble as the engine starts.

I sit in stunned silence, my mind trying to come to terms with the crudeness and callousness of my captors while my body tries to balance against the rocking of the truck. I feel sullied and dirty, unable to shake off the feeling of the men's hands as they roamed over me. I don't think any number of showers will ever let me feel clean again. When I agreed to do this, it had all seemed so simple, allow myself to be captured, and then go with the flow. I hadn't expected to be taken by men like them—heartless men who regard women as nothing more than bodies to play with, to torture and hurt. *Why hadn't Devil prepared me?* But if I'd known, I wouldn't, couldn't have played along with his plan. And, according to Devil, they'd have taken me anyway.

"Sam, we heard what happened. Drummer's lost his shit, so I'm taking over communications for now." Devil's voice speaks into my ear. "I won't ask you if you're alright, but could you get some information to me? How many men are with you? I think I heard four. Is that correct?"

Oh, those glorious words go straight into my ear, his matter-of-fact voice reminding me I'm not alone, and that I'm here to do a job; the knowledge grounds me. I glance around, most of the women wear vacant looks, lost in their misery, but the woman opposite is looking at me curiously. I catch her eye while lamenting my previous lack of female interaction hasn't much prepared me for making a friend, especially in the current circumstances. How do you start a conversation with someone who's been molested and hurt?

But she speaks first, "They didn't rape you." Her statement is almost an accusation.

"They touched me," I confirm, giving a little shake of my head. "But they didn't do that. They're saving me," I explain, not having to fake the disgust and fear in my voice.

She's staring at me intently. "You've still got your V-card?" And then, at my nod, she shrugs and continues, "I don't know if that means you're lucky or not."

It depends on who wants to buy me. *But it's not going to get that far.* I hope.

She moves her head around, indicating everyone else. "They sampled the rest of the goods. You got away lightly."

As she draws my attention to the traumatised women sitting around me, I suppose I am the lucky one, but I selfishly I don't feel that way. What they already did was enough. As I shudder, I try to remember why I'm here, and not let my fear conquer me. I need to get answers for Devil and Drum. I decide to test how much she knows. "The men, are there just the four of them?"

"Just?" Her voice rises. "That was fucking enough." A shiver wracks her body and she goes quiet for a moment, before adding, "I haven't seen anyone else, so far."

"Have you any idea where they're taking us?"

She jerks her shoulders again. "I've heard them say Mexico, but from there who knows." Now she looks at me directly. "If you're thinking of trying to escape, you won't have a chance. They're too careful for that."

"Has anyone tried?"

Her head dips in the direction of a woman at the front of the van, whose head lolls forward into her hands, and a moan comes from her bloody mouth. I get the message.

Having drawn my attention to my companions, I examine them more carefully, quickly realising what Devil said had to be true, that these aren't women picked up off the street. Even with their red-rimmed eyes, they're all attractive in one way or another. Some have lithe, slim bodies, some well-endowed, hair which is probably beautiful when properly styled. But fear and terror aren't a good look, so I see no one at their best.

Indicating the clothing, I ask, "Why do they make us wear these?"

"We were kept naked most of the journey. Stopped off last night and told to put these fucking cover-nothings on. Think we're meeting the main man today. He'll want to inspect his merchandise."

The defeated look in her eyes shows she's given up and is accepting her fate. But I can't say anything to give her hope, or even an inkling there might be a chance of rescue. She shakes her head to get the hair out of her eyes and shifts as though trying to find a more comfortable position. But cuffed as we are, that's nearly impossible. My arms are already going numb being tied around my back.

"I'm Sam," I suddenly decide to tell her. Humans have names; herd animals don't.

She gives a half-hearted grin. "Monica. I'd say pleased to

meet you, but…" she ends on another shrug, but she doesn't need to complete her sentence.

The air is tainted with the smell of fear, and when my companion closes her eyes, signalling the conversation's over, the sound of the road beneath us and a muffled sobbing punctuated by groans is all I can hear. Leaning my head back against the side panel, I try to remember that this isn't my destiny, that Drum will be coming for me. But as the miles roll on, my anguish becomes as real as that of the others. What will I have to suffer before rescue arrives? As a tear trickles down my cheek, I fear being free again seems very far away.

I give myself a mental shake. Information, that's what I need to provide. Looking around, I count up our numbers. "Twelve women," I softly murmur as though speaking to myself. "They've kidnapped twelve of us." Then I go silent; there's nothing more I can say without drawing attention to myself.

The journey continues in silence, each of us lost in our own misery. Then we're turning off the freeway, and the truck's bumping over a different surface. Like the rest of the women with my hands cuffed behind me, I sway to one side then the other, yanking on my poor shoulders, unable to balance myself. The others seem to take it in their stride. Presumably, there's been a number of stops on their drive down from the north.

Soon we come to a halt. The doors are opened, and one by one we're unlocked and dragged out, then have our hands fastened behind us again. We're all blinking in the harsh sunlight, and I don't have to act to make my expression match the others' looks of despair.

The threat of guns is unnecessary, handcuffed as we are there's no chance of escape, and, looking around, only desert to run to. Monica told me these men would be quick to punish any sign of disobedience. When we're told to get into a line, that's what we do, obedient as a flock of sheep being nipped at the heels by a dog.

The truck has pulled up next to a couple of cars and standing alongside are two well-dressed strangers deep in discussion. Shuffling, I try to get the short nightdress to cover my ass, but however I try to pull it down, it gives me no semblance of dignity.

I stand much like the others, fidgeting, trying to ignore the leers of the men guarding us. A few minutes pass, then one of the new arrivals starts inspecting the line, beginning from the end furthest from me. Wide-eyed, I see my companions being manhandled. Teeth are inspected, breasts fondled, and hands grab at their asses. Cries and whimpers of objection go unheeded, the man moving on dispassionately, leaving each of the women in fresh tears.

As he gets closer, my legs start shaking so badly I'm worried they won't hold me up. When he finishes his brutal examination of the woman beside me, there's a change. He asks confirmation from Ugly-face, then calls out to the other stranger and points to me. "Hey, Kurt. Here."

A well-dressed man, who apparently answers to Kurt, comes up beside him, and both men give me a visual examination, the look in their eyes making me flinch. "So, Louis, this is the one?" he says.

"Yeah, man. We've kept our hands off as instructed." This from Jerk-off, who sneers and puts his hand on his cock as if he wants a repeat of his earlier masturbation.

"You better have," Louis, who appears to be one of men in charge, replies, his snarling tone suggesting there would have been swift retribution if they hadn't. Suddenly he grabs my breasts, roughly, making me gasp. He raises an eyebrow toward the other man. "Small tits. You sure about this?"

I move to escape his touch, he tightens his fingers around my tender flesh, then takes one hand away and slaps me hard across my face, making me stumble.

"Keep still, bitch."

Kurt looks on dispassionately. "They're on the small side, but I can get them enhanced." He huffs a cruel laugh. "I can have them made to exactly my requirements. The rest of the package is as I expected."

He'd make me get breast implants? Who the hell does he think he is? Then I watch what they are doing—they're talking about money. Confirming a price. What he's going to pay for me. *Oh shit!* This is the buyer. And if my buyer's here, does that mean I'm not going to be travelling on with the other women? How will Drummer find me?

A moment of sheer panic before I remember, *I've got the tracker implanted, and Drummer is listening to everything they're saying.* Drummer will come to save me. This isn't for real.

But they didn't expect me to be separated from the other women. What will Devil do now? This wasn't the plan.

"The rest of them going south?" Kurt, who's apparently paid an extortionate amount for me, seems in no particular hurry to get going.

"Yeah. They're going up for auction." Louis pulls out a packet of cigarettes, taking one out and lighting it. He offers the pack, but Kurt declines. Then he nods at our captors, who seem to know what to do.

"Comfort break, ladies. Go take a fuckin' piss as you won't get another chance." They push and shove the women into a line by the brush, one by one undoing the handcuffs, leaving just one remaining dangling from a wrist. Louis tilts his head toward my buyer, who nods back, and I'm pushed over to join the others. That they've done this before becomes clear when one by one they crouch and, in full view of the men, relieve their bladders, accompanied by lewd comments from the men behind. Any desire I had to pee disappears at the sight, but a kick swipes my legs out from under me.

I want to tell them I'm not a freaking animal but expecting any further protest would be met with more violence, so trying my best to ignore the situation I try to do what they want. Eventually I produce a small trickle. I don't think I've ever felt so humiliated in my life.

A firm grip on my arm pulls me to my feet, and I'm dragged across to one of the cars.

"Well then, she's all yours now." Nodding at Louis, Kurt pushes me forward and a driver steps out of the car. While Louis and Kurt shake hands as if they've done nothing more stimulating than having bought and sold a puppy, the driver opens one of the rear doors and pushes me inside. He wrenches my arm painfully around and cuffs me to the door. With a sinking feeling of dread, I notice the rear windows are blacked out, preventing anyone seeing inside. No one's going to know I'm held prisoner in the car. Swallowing hard, I try to damp down my rising panic. *Drum's heard everything. He knows what's happening. He won't leave me to this fate.*

The driver takes his place up front, and Kurt gets in beside me. Casting a sideways glance, I examine him for the first time. He looks like he's in his fifties, with a paunch protruding from his suit jacket, his smattering of greasy grey hair covers a dome-shaped head. His grey eyes are too close together, his bushy eyebrows meeting in the middle. His nose is bulbous and his mouth thin and cruel. A whiff of body odour assails me, and that combined with the smell of leather makes my stomach churn. It's no wonder this man has to buy a woman. Unless he's got a wonderful personality, which I doubt, on looks alone no one would find him attractive.

His car smacks of wealth, but the soft seats offer no comfort. He thinks I belong to him now. *He's wrong. I belong to Drummer. And he's coming for me.*

"Where are you taking me?" I attempt to get information for Drummer and Devil, but they haven't spoken to me in ages. What if I'm not in range? Now there's no voice in my ear, I'm feeling abandoned and very alone. *But they can still find me. I've got the GPS.*

As the driver switches on the engine, Kurt deigns to look at me. With a leer, he replies to my question, "Oh, you don't need to worry about that. Which city you'll be in won't matter one bit.

You're just going to love your new home." He chuckles, then leaning forward he says something to the driver, who puts his foot on the gas and we're going back down the track, back the way we came.

It's going to be alright. Drummer will know exactly where I am.

But now I've been separated from the other women; they can't track the transport.

To save me, Devil will have to abandon his plan. *Will he want to do that?*

CHAPTER TWENTY-FOUR

*D*rummer…

"Give me the fuckin' mic." Reaching over I try and wrest it from Devil, but only succeed in making him swerve, almost off the road.

"Bloody hell. Give it up, will you? Listen to me."

"That's my fuckin' woman!" The radio's still transmitting, and I can hear everything that's happening to her. The filthy words her captors are spouting. Fuck, they're making her get naked, in front of them. That body, which belongs only to me. That only I have ever seen. How dare they put their filthy hands on her.

"Drum, you'll only make it harder for Sam if she hears you losing your shit. Christ, man, I understand how you're feeling, but *she* doesn't need to know that. What she's going through? That will be hard enough without her hearing the effect it has on you." Devil takes his eyes off the road long enough to glare at me. "If you can't keep it together, then I'm stopping this car and tossing you out on your arse."

I stare at the English bastard who's preventing me from comforting my girl. Slowly I understand he's right, my anger, *my disgust*, would only be piling more shit on top of what Sam's already dealing with. It's bad enough for me to hear it. Fuck knows how she's coping with it actually happening to her. The reality of her situation is so much worse than I had imagined. Surely, there had to be some better way of handling this without subjecting her to such degradation? But without blowing every-thing, and Devil's chance to bring down the whole ring, I can't see how I could stop it now. "Asshole," I throw at him, half under my breath.

When he sees I've calmed down he picks up the mic he'd wrestled from me and speaks to Sam calmly, asking her to give him information. There are four men with them; we already heard that, and they're apparently meeting one of the leaders of the gang today. That's what Devil wants, to catch the men at the top of the food chain and cut off the head of the snake. My leg bounces uncontrollably. All *I* want is Sam safe and back where she belongs, with me. The knowledge of the hell she's going through causes such a churning in my gut. She's *mine*. And those men have their hands on her. Touching her in places only I have known. *No one's going to touch her again.* Ever.

Well, fuck me. The intensity of my feelings toward her gives me pause. The radio's gone silent now; she's given us all the information she can, which leaves me alone with my thoughts as we hurtle down the I-10, keeping a good distance between us and the truck.

Me? Thinking about claiming a woman? That's where my mind is taking me, isn't it? Could I do that? I wipe my hand over my brow.

I'd been given my name when I was still a prospect. Joining the MC twenty years ago, as a wild, untamed youth, it was the trappings of the lifestyle that attracted me. I partook of them all with great enthusiasm. I drank, did drugs—nothing heavy, but illegal just the same. Then there was the pussy. Lots and lots of free pussy. I went through the club whores and hangarounds as though my life depended on it, two, three, or even more fucks a night. If I visited another chapter, I'd go through their sluts too. By the time I'd patched in, I'd picked up my handle and a reputation for banging everything in sight.

Stroking my hand down and over my bearded chin, I admit I haven't changed all that much over the years. My appetite for sex remains insatiable. My disdain for the men who tied themselves to just one woman immeasurable. Why restrict yourself to one pussy when you can have variety each and every night? Big tits, small tits, tall, short, slim, chubby. If they weren't much to look at, I'd fuck them from behind.

I'd never taken time to talk to a woman before; bitches were there to fuck and nothing else. Conversation I'd get with my brothers. But that was before I met Sam. Until I'd met *her* and found we had things in common, things I wanted to talk about, to listen to her views and opinions like discussing her Vincent and the restoration of my vintage bikes. In fact, I suspect just chatting about anything and everything would be a revelation and a joy with her. For once, I want to hear what a woman has to say.

And the sex? Simply mind-blowing, right out of this world. But could I be content with just her decidedly delectable pussy, or would I find myself straying, wanting a change? Sticking to just one woman is an unfamiliar thought to me.

The vision of Viper enters my head. If I tried to commit, would I end up like him? Find myself having the same kind of halfway arrangement that keeps him faithful to his wife while cheating with the whores, even if it is only for blow jobs? His marriage seems to work in that strange way, but somehow, I think Sam would hand me my balls if I suggested a similar compromise.

On the other hand, now that I've sampled her mouth, the thought now of any other woman sucking my cock holds little attraction. There's something more to it with her—not her technique; she still has a lot to learn, but it's that look in her eyes, as though she's giving me part of herself when she sucks me off.

It's not only to give me pleasure and release, but she finds enjoyment for herself too.

She's untutored and naïve, but the things I could teach her...

I'd told her she's mine.

I don't think I lied.

With a slight jump as he interrupts my thoughts, I glance over to seeing Devil tapping the dash and pointing to the GPS. "The truck's pulling off the interstate."

He's got my attention, and I sit straight, craning my neck to see what's he's talking about. "I thought they'd get closer to the border."

"So did I." My companion thinks for a moment. "I don't like this. From the map, it's not a long road and peters out about a mile up. They can't go far in that direction, so must be making a stop and will have to come back this way. Let's pull up and get the boys prepared."

The boys, my brothers, are travelling in a pack a good distance behind us. I've a bad feeling in my gut telling me I'd prefer to plow straight ahead and get Sam back now. But with my president's hat on, I know that Devil's correct. If we don't know what we're heading into, it could all go horribly wrong. And Sam's life, or such as she knows it, is at stake.

Devil slows, then when the bikes catch up, flashes his indicator, and in a pre-arranged signal uses the brakes twice before turning into a rest area and coming to a stop. My brothers pull up behind.

"What's up?" Peg approaches first, along with Wraith. Dart's close behind, taking the opportunity to pull a pack of smokes from his pocket. As Blade nudges him, he rolls his eyes, then offers him one. Soon his pack is being passed around. I wish I could take one; it might help settle my nerves, but I resist and concentrate on the task at hand.

"They've pulled off. Gone down an unmade road."

"Meeting someone?"

"Could be." It seems the most likely reason.

Devil steps forward. "I thought they'd be stopping closer to the border, but this could be the meet. Drum and I will go in slow. Sam's in the back of the truck, and until they stop, we won't know what's happening." He holds his hand to the earpiece he's just inserted, showing he's still listening to what's going on. "They're still on the move."

"So no fuckin' assing about then. Listen up." I get them to shut up, then nod at Devil. It's his show after all. Until I get a whiff that his way's not working, then I'm taking charge, there's no doubt about that.

"We'll follow them. I'll take the SUV as close as I can, but they could hear the bikes so you lot wait here, out of sight. Drummer will keep in touch and tell you what we've decided to do once we know what we're dealing with."

Heart's looking thoughtful. "What if they turn around and come back this way? Could be they just stopped for a drop-off or pickup?"

It's a good point, and thinking fast on my feet I respond, "We'll get Sam to let us know if the truck turns back. We'll be able to hear everything that's going on."

Devil nods at me, I get back in the SUV and we're back on the road again. Once we're moving, we listen intently to the radio transmitting the sounds from inside the truck.

I hate this. Hate feeling so helpless. Hate the fact that my woman is out there without my protection, driving into a hell that any sane person would find hard to imagine. I've seen and done some shit in my time, but abusing women? Raping them? Forcing them into a life of sexual servitude? I can't understand how anyone could get involved in that. Fuck the money. Women aren't objects to be bought and sold. And definitely not my woman.

Before I know it, Devil's pulling over. I get my phone out, ready to summon my brothers as soon as we know what's going down. From the radio we hear voices and shouting, the women are being told to get out of the truck and being helped roughly if

I'm translating the sounds correctly. My gut clenches at an involuntary oomph from Sam.

Devil drives the van behind a clump of brush, then his hand snakes out and fastens around my arm. "We wait."

"No, we fuckin' don't. We move in." I try to wrench myself away, but he fastens his grip.

"Not until we know who's there and what's going down, Drum. We need to get the ringleaders."

He can afford to be calm and wait. It's not his woman who's being hurt. My hands clench as I force myself to hold back and not hit him. Just as I'm about to have another go at him, we again hear speaking and understand why they've stopped.

My knuckles go white as I'm forced to listen to Sam, and the other women, being inspected like cattle. Devil was right, it must be one of the ringleaders who's turned up, and he's making lewd comments on the quality of the goods that's been delivered to him. At first the voices are distant, but as they move closer, I tense myself, realising they're getting to Sam.

"Hey, Kurt. Here."

"So, Louis, this is the one?" It's a different voice now, a cultured accent, American, but I can't quite place a regional accent. I see Devil making notes of the names we've heard.

"Yeah, man. We've kept our hands off as instructed."

"You better have done," the first man snarls out, presumably at his men.

I hear a gasp, explained by the next words.

"Small tits. You sure about this?"

Devil and I exchange looks; the voices are so close he has to be talking about Sam.

Another gasp, and a protest from Sam, followed by a slapping sound that nearly has me shooting from my seat. Christ, it's hard sitting here with no visual, my imagination is conjuring up the very worst that could be going on.

"They're on the small side, but I can get them enhanced. I can have them made to exactly my requirements. The rest of the package is what I expected," the cultured voice says again.

"Fuck!" Devil slams his hand on the steering wheel. Being slightly slower to catch on, he continues, "It's her fucking buyer."

"What does that fuckin' mean?"

"Quiet, Drummer. Listen and we'll find out!"

An amount of money is mentioned, again we glance at each other, not having truly appreciated her worth.

"The rest of them going south?"

"Yeah. Some are going up for auction. Others will go on to their buyers. You can take her from here."

Shit! It sounds like Sam's not going with the rest of the women. Exchanging worried looks with Devil, I start to think fast. It's Sam I'm concerned about. We can approach them now, while they don't expect it. Devil won't get everything he wants, but we can free the rest of the women, and I'll get Sam. Devil will have to live with it, his plan is down the drain now without Sam in the transport—he's fucked. There'll be no way for him to track it.

As I turn to tell him, he waves at me to keep silent. We listen to the instruction for the women to take a piss and then get back on the truck. The men laugh and jeer, obviously enjoying watching their captives empty their bladders.

"Not you." The voice again so close the words are obviously being addressed to Sam. "You're coming with me."

"Where are you taking me?" Brave girl, she's trying to get us the information.

"Wherever I fucking want to, bitch." If I hoped someone with any compassion would be taking her, my hopes would now be dashed. Particularly when I hear Sam's yelp of pain.

I take out my phone. "I'll get the boys down here. We've got to get down there now. Surround them, get the women out now. You'll get one of the ringleaders—"

"Not doing that. The plan is to get them all. Find out where they're holding the auctions, and maybe even round up the buyers. We'll just do this the old-fashioned way without the GPS. Follow the transport."

I throw him a look of utter disbelief. "Someone's fuckin' taking Sam to God knows where, and you want to go after the fuckin' slavers? That's not what I fuckin' signed up for."

But Devil's not listening to me. "Tell your boys to stay out of sight," he instructs quickly. "They're on the move."

Thinking fast, I do what he says. We've obviously missed our chance to take them here. Once we're all together we can stage an ambush. Whatever Devil says, I am not going to let Sam be separated from me. So, I get the boys ready to move as Devil manoeuvres the car around, and we're speeding back up the track. But Devil doesn't come to a stop, he joins the freeway, heading in the direction that we've just come from. For a fleeting moment I believe he's changed his mind and he's going to be following Sam. I tell the boys to get their engines started. Then Devil stamps down on the gas, makes a U-turn, and starts heading slowly back in the other direction, watching out for the truck that will soon be exiting the turnoff.

"What the fuck you doing?" I yell at him.

"Continuing our mission. We've just got to follow the transport."

"But Sam—"

"Sam's one woman, Drummer. If we lose this chance to put a stop to everything now, how many others will be taken to be abused? And we know where Sam is; she's got the GPS implant. We can retrieve her later."

Retrieve her later? He makes her sound like a dog that's been dropped off at the pound. How much later? What will she suffer in the meantime? "I don't give a fuck about the other women! You promised no harm would come to Sam!" Not even needing to even think about it, I take my gun from its holster and point it at him. "Turn this car around now, or I'll shoot you, Devil."

Devil laughs. He fucking laughs. "You didn't check your weapon when the ATF handed it back, did you?"

Suspicious, I do so now. Stupid fucking schoolboy error. There are no bullets in it. I check my pockets for my spare ammunition. It's all gone. Being in such a rush to get moving, I'd forgotten the basics. Without wasting time, cursing, I call for my brothers. Devil can't go any faster, or he'll be within sight of the truck. Soon the bikes come alongside. I open the window of the van and wave at the bikes following; they pull over. Using my phone, I give them one further instruction. Devil tries to stop me, but he can't drive and fight me at the same time.

"When I give the signal, shoot the tyres out on this SUV." Devil knocks the phone from my hand, but it's too late, his action confirming that unlike mine, my brothers' guns weren't tampered with.

"Fuck, Drummer. You can't do that. Stop this mission, and I'll have the FBI pick you up for real. And this time they will search your compound. Thoroughly."

Right now, I don't give a shit, knowing I'll happily go to prison for life if it means Sam will be safe.

CHAPTER TWENTY-FIVE

*S*am...

There's no voice in my ear. No one comfortingly telling me they're on their way to save me. *Something's gone wrong.*

Devil wanted the ringleaders. He's followed the transport instead. Shit! Am I already out of range? What if the tracker's not working? As I glance at the man called Kurt sitting beside me, the man who thinks he now owns me, tears start trickling down my cheeks as I start to wonder whether being this man's plaything for real will indeed be my fate.

What if I never see the president of the Satan's Devils again? Or my father, who I only recently found? I've not even had a chance to learn much about him. Why hadn't I gotten to know him when I'd had the opportunity? Or spoken more with the other men that I've come to respect? And their women too? Me and my bike, my skills as a mechanic, I'd thought my life was stretching out in front of me with no sign of an end. But now, my hopes, dreams, and expectations might all have been taken from me, and I'm staring a totally different sort of life in the face. I'm pinning my rescue on one man. Am I wrong to think I mean so much to him? Has he abandoned me to complete Devil's mission?

As my fears grow, I'm unable to stifle the genuine sobs that start coming from my mouth. It's too much. Why did I ever agree to this? Drummer was right, I should have stayed under their protection. I'm frightened and scared.

The car drives on. Now we're off the side road and out onto the highway, heading back the way we'd come. As we pass other vehicles I lean forward, trying to wave my free hand to get their attention, but I can't make myself seen. We race past, a car with a woman held captive inside and no one notices. My captor, however, doesn't miss what I'm doing—he pulls back my hand with a sharp tug and chuckles. Loudly. He continues to hold onto me with a sweaty palm. His fingers move against mine in a mocking caress. "No one can see in. No one's coming to save you. Just accept it, girl, stop fighting it. I own you now. You're mine."

It's a wretched twist that Drummer had said the same words to me. Wrenching my hand out of his grasp, I spit out at him, "I belong to no one. You can't own another human being."

His beady eyes crease and his lips turn up into a parody of a smile, which sends shivers down my spine. He reaches out and touches my cheek, then his fingers close on my skin, pinching it painfully. "Oh yes, my dear, I think you're going to find that I can." I try to pull away, but he waits a moment before releasing me. Just his touch has me cringing, and I'm unable to prevent a shudder. It simply elicits another laugh.

"Oh, I'm going to enjoy training you to respond to me," his voice rasps. "And, just for the record, my dear, your tears and pain make me hard." To punctuate his words, he places my hand over his groin, making me feel him behind his tailored suit.

Bile rises into my throat.

Then he grabs my hair, pulling me done roughly, so my face is in his crotch. As he does so, he accidentally bares my neck.

"What the fuck is this?" His fingers quickly find the small raised lump and probe it, none too gently.

"It's an insect bite." I offer up Devil's explanation, but a rough tug on my hair and having my face slammed back down shuts me up.

He traces it. "You been tagged?"

"No, what?" I try to act surprised. "I got bitten."

"Best we don't take any risks."

"Should we stop and try to cut it out?" The driver sounds concerned, but not about me.

"Need to check what it is first. Poke around too deep with a knife, and I might hit a nerve, it's at the top of her neck." Kurt sounds doubtful, and I hope he won't want his property damaged.

No, don't do that. I don't want to be paralysed.

"Bradley, you got a jammer?"

The driver, *Bradley*, helpfully reaches over and opens the glove compartment, extracts something and waves it at his employer. Without saying anything, he plugs it into the cigarette socket.

"Thank you, Bradley." Kurt stares at me. "I'll get a doctor to see you as soon as I can. If it's a tracker, he'll remove it. But for now, the jammer will do its job." He tightens his hand painfully in my hair, pulling some strands out by the roots. "And if turns out you've been tagged, you'll have some questions to answer, girl."

As I suppress a tell-tale shiver, Bradley announces, "Dust storm ahead, sir."

The driver's words turn my thoughts to the weather and distract Kurt too. He releases my head and I remove my face from his groin. Sitting up, looking ahead through the wind-shield, I see it's true, the precursor to an Arizona summer monsoon. I might not have been in the state long, but long enough to know the ferocity of the sudden storms. *Is it possible we'll be forced to stop? Could I have a chance of escape?* Tugging unobtrusively, I try to loosen the handcuff, but it's futile, there's no way I'll be able to jump out of the car, even if it comes to a halt. Unless I can knock Kurt out, steal the handcuff key and overpower the driver. While I might be desperate enough to give it a try, there's not much chance of success.

Don't fight them, Devil had told me, *or you'll get hurt.* But what sway do his instructions hold if he's forsaken me? Left me to my fate? Is getting hurt while trying to escape worth the risk?

"Sir?" Once again the driver speaks, getting Kurt's attention. "There's a group of bikers coming up fast behind us."

"Shit!" Kurt pulls himself up to look out of the rear window. "Step on it, Bradley, I don't know who the fuck they are, but I don't like it. Lose them." Following his instruction, the engine roars as the car picks up speed.

I turn too, they're only just in sight but drawing closer. A wave of elation rushes through me. I'm going to be saved. The bikers will be armed. They can surround the car and stop it. I knew they wouldn't let me down. My heart starts beating faster at the thought I could soon be free, when the car shoots forward again. Looking around the driver's seat, I see the needle on the speedometer already touching the 100-mph mark and still climbing.

Then the rain starts. Soon it's as if we're driving into a solid wall of water. Bradley slows his speed, the car fishtailing across the highway, but he regains control fast. Now I can't even see the bikes through the rain lashing down. Knowing four wheels are better than two in this downpour, my brief expectation that rescue might be at hand starts to fade.

"Flood coming up."

"Go through it," Kurt replies tersely.

With a quick nod, the car lurches forward. Suddenly we're driving through the torrent, crossing the road, with water cascading over the roof. Bradley fights the wheel as the tyres lose traction. *Oh God, please let us crash or break down…* But the water's not quite deep enough to stop us, and with Bradley's expert handling, we're across and out the other side.

I stare out the back window, but the bikes are no longer in sight. Even if they've got the radio with them, I must be more than half a mile away now, and there's no way they can hear me, and the GPS signal is being blocked.

Drummer had tried to save me and failed, through no fault of his own. Despite my plea, God's not on my side, and even the weather is against me. I really am on my own.

"Bikes haven't been able to cross." Bradley checks the rearview mirror and starts laughing. Kurt joins in. Their triumphant jeering doing nothing to help the churning in my stomach. Unless I can do something to get out of this myself, or a miracle happens, Drummer won't be able to locate me. I pray the torrential rain will hold us up and force us to stop, allowing the bikes to catch up again, but Kurt must have the devil on his side, as well as a good driver, as we proceed at a steady pace heading north. I'm noting the directions, but what good will it do me? Even if I could offer my location, I'm too far away for anyone to pick it up.

Kurt's arm comes around my shoulders, pulling me toward him. "Can't wait to start having some fun with you." As he murmurs the words into my ear, his hand slips south, under the barely-there dress that I'm wearing. He toys with my nipple. My body betrays me as it peaks under his touch, an automatic reaction, but one he appreciates. "You're so responsive," he continues, before pinching it hard, making me yelp. "Oh, yes, pretty baby, I'm surely going to enjoy possessing you, knowing I'll be your first, that my cock will be the first, and *last* to be inside you."

He grabs my hand, putting it on his crotch again, moving it up and down as if proud of his size, showing me just how much he's looking forward to defiling me. I try to pull away; his fingers tighten sharply round my wrist, nails digging in hard enough to draw blood. Seeing the damage, he lifts up my arm, sucking the red drops into his mouth, his tongue sweeping out to lick his lips in appreciation. "Is this what your virgin blood is going to be like when I take you? Hmm, I can't fucking wait, my dear."

But I'm no longer a virgin. What's he going to do when he finds that out? A whimper escapes my lips.

"Not much of a conversationalist, are you, darling? Not that I mind. No, I've got other uses for that mouth."

Just the thought makes me gag. "What are you going to do with me?" I ask, not actually wanting to know, but I'd rather keep him talking and his mind off anything else.

He laughs, it's an evil sound. "Anything I fucking want. And you're going to take anything I want to give. Your life from here on in is to serve me. Any way I want to be served. In fact," he pulls away and turns my head toward him, running his fingers over my lips, "I'm tempted to start right now with that pretty mouth."

No, don't! Inside I'm screaming.

"What do you think, Bradley? Shall I try her out?"

I can see the driver in the rearview mirror, and the sneer on his face does nothing to reassure me. To try to distract him from whatever he's got in mind, I quickly ask another question. "Why me? Why did you pick me?" If my voice sounds slightly hysterical, there's nothing I can do about it.

Again, his clammy fingers reach out and touch my face. Turning me toward him, he gazes at me, soaking in my features before he deigns to speak. "Because you're quite beautiful, pet. Just my type. Exactly as Jackson knew you would be when he first laid eyes on you. When he found out you were a virgin... Well, that was just the icing on the fucking cake."

"How the hell did he learn that?"

"Your colleagues were quite forthcoming. Jackson acted as though he was interested in asking you out, of course, and they laughed and told him he wouldn't have a chance. That it was unlikely any man would ever get close to you, as you didn't seem to know what your pussy was made for. But don't worry, I'm going to enjoy teaching you all about that. And I at least, will delight in your lessons."

While not doubting the mechanics I worked with would have put it in quite such crude terms, I have to agree, I'd had a reputation for not being interested in the opposite sex. Before Drum, I hadn't thought anything could be better than bringing an old engine to life.

"I'm twenty-six, a mechanic. I don't wear nice clothes or makeup. I don't understand how I can be your type." I've no real hope I can dissuade him, but I have to try.

He gives a hearty laugh. "Don't worry about nice clothes, darling, or clothes at all. You won't need them. And your tears will be makeup enough for me." He gives me a considered look. "And your age? Well, I expect you to be made of stronger stuff than my younger pets. You'll be more fun and last longer."

I latch onto something he's said. "You have other women?"

Another guffaw. "No, I much prefer just the one at a time. I'm monogamous you see. Aren't you lucky?"

I go cold and get chills. Reading between the lines, it's not hard to guess what happened to his previous women, and I very much doubt they are enjoying any kind of retirement package.

"Step on it, Bradley. I'm getting impatient to be home."

As the car picks up speed, I continue to hope the rain will slow us down, being in no hurry at all to reach my destination. But it's easing off now, little more than a drizzle, and when the sun comes back out, it does nothing to brighten my mood. They could be taking me anywhere. Looking at the clock on the dash, and doing a quick calculation in my head, I'm conscious that six hours have already gone by, leaving only twenty-four more of battery life of my earpiece. Much good that piece of spyware is going to do me. Drummer will need to be within half-a-mile range to get back in contact, and there's a slim chance of him locating me within the next day. *Slim?* There's no freaking possibility at all.

The only plus point is that Kurt seems content to wait and doesn't make good on his threats to force me to give him head in the car. Instead, he satisfies himself with cruelly fondling my breasts and tweaking my nipples, causing such pain until I protest and wriggle, trying to get away. Then he grips me harder with one hand, and his other wanders lower and starts to explore my panty-less nether regions. Divorcing myself from his molestation of my body, I blink back tears and look out the window, watching the road signs go past.

We're heading toward Phoenix, but just on the outskirts of the city turn off the freeway, and soon we're heading into a sparsely populated area with huge houses in large grounds set back from the road. *I want this journey to end so he removes his filthy hands from me. I never want to arrive so he can carry out his threats.*

Conflicting thoughts are still going through my mind as Bradley pulls the car up in front of a set of sturdy security gates and waits for them to slide open before driving inside. There's a guard waiting by a control panel and another I can see patrolling the grounds. *This just keeps getting better.* Taking in as much as I can, I note all the obstacles to any escape.

The car continues up a short driveway and stops in front of the main entry door to a huge freaking mansion. Before getting out, Bradley reaches again to the glove compartment and extracts something. He unplugs the jammer from the 12volt socket, and quickly plugs it into what I now recognise is a portable battery unit and hands the whole package to Kurt. Great. I'd had the slim hope the GPS signal would be able to be picked up once we'd left the car, but my captors seem to have thought of everything.

If I'm going to get out of this, it's down to me. I can no longer bank on help from anyone else.

CHAPTER TWENTY-SIX

*D*rummer...

At the threat of disabling the SUV, Devil pulls immediately onto the hard shoulder. We've come back just about level with the turnoff again, and as a late model Jaguar pulls out, I realise Sam must be inside. Devil might have confiscated the mic, but I've heard everything that bastard said to her, and know how fucking scared she must be. Remembering the half-mile range of her earpiece, I know we've got to stay close if we've any chance of continuing to hear what's going on and being able to reassure her.

Having told Wraith to hold off firing, for now, I turn to the man beside me. For a second time in one day, I'm in a situation that reduces me to begging. "Devil, please!" I turn in my seat, frantically trying to keep my eyes on the car as it disappears into the distance.

Suddenly Devil thumps the steering wheel and makes a decision. "Get out, Drummer. I'll go on alone. You go after your woman. You won't be able to speak to her. The radio equipment's a fixture, and if you're not quick, you'll lose her. But I'll keep tracking her on the GPS. If she gets out of sight, give me a call."

I can't open the door fast enough. But even though rescuing Sam is foremost in my mind, it's not that I don't give a fuck about the other women. I do. "Devil, I'll take some of the boys with me, the rest can go with you."

His face brightens as he throws me a quick nod. "Cheers, mate. Appreciate that." I get out of the car, running over to the waiting bikers. "Wraith, Blade, Viper, Beef, Bullet, and Mouse. You're with me. Peg, take the rest and follow Devil. We're splitting up." I point to the car disappearing in the distance. "Sam's in the Jag. Devil's going on with the tracking equipment. We won't be able to talk to her but—"

"Fuck it!" Viper's face has gone white. "That's my daughter. What the fuck have you done? She'll be lost, a-fuckin-lone, if you can't talk to her. Get Devil to give us the radio. What if we lose her?" He gets off his bike and comes toward me. "I knew this was a bad fuckin' idea!"

"Viper! Pipe the fuck down and get back on your ride. We can't take the equipment, it's built into the SUV. Dart, lend me your bike? Go with Devil?" Dart wastes no time dismounting his Harley, and I'm astride it as soon as he's running off and taking my place in the passenger seat next to Devil. Tyres spin, gravel flies, and the SUV disappears in a cloud of dust. The brothers not coming with me right behind it.

"Right, Brothers, we're doing this fast and quick. We surround the Jag—Wraith, you're with me up front, Bullet and Blade to the sides, Viper, you, Beef, and Mouse stay behind. We'll block him in and force him to stop." Then I remember. "Wraith, chuck me some extra ammo, will you?" He does so; I load my gun.

Viper's still glaring at me, but he's back on his bike at least. I start my engine, then throw my arm forward.

It's been barely a minute since I jumped out of the van, but that means the Jag has now got a good start and is way ahead. With no time to lose, I twist my throttle, kick up through the gears, getting up speed on the main highway. Soon the car's in sight. Just a little more throttle and we start drawing closer. I'm in charge, in control, and I have a plan. Soon Sam will be riding bitch behind me, and I'll be taking her home. And the man who tried to take her from me? Well, he'll be dead.

I'm close enough to see the model now. Fuck, he's got a 3 litre V6 engine under his hood, and right now he's increasing the power. The distance opens between us again. But we've got modified Harleys and know how to ride them. I allow myself a small smile knowing we've got this in the bag, until I see the dust storm approaching.

Shit. Everything's against us, even the weather. The monsoon will most likely force us to stop. But all's not lost, the car won't be able to go through the washouts either. With my left hand I try to adjust my bandana, having dust flying at your face at one hundred miles an hour is not my idea of fun. Lightning flashes above, a crack of thunder so loud I can hear it over the sound of the road rushing beneath me. Now comes the rain, forcing me to slow, knowing it would be suicidal to continue at this speed.

But the car's slowing too, and I'm still keeping him in sight. I see a shower of water cascading over the car as he goes through one of the floods. Christ, the driver must have a death wish. I see the back swing out, but he gets it under control, and he's through and safely out the other side. The torrents of water build up so fast, and in the few seconds it takes me to get there, it's now deep and all over the road. Breaking gently at what now looks like a raging river, I come to a halt, my brothers pulling up alongside me. The Jag is already disappearing into the distance.

"Fuck!" Wraith comes up alongside. He's said it all in one word.

A pain so sharp it takes me by surprise slams through my chest. Sam's gone. He's got her. Our plan should have, *would have* worked if it hadn't been for the summer storm.

Now I have a physical ache in my jaw; Viper's fucking hit me.

"You bastard!" he shouts. "You fuckin' let her get into this." Covering his face with his hands he rakes his fingers down his cheeks. "I might never see her a-fuckin'-gain, and that's on you, Drummer."

"Calm the fuck down, Viper. She's got the GPS. I'll call Devil and he can track where they're heading to." Rubbing my bruised chin, I glare at him. We haven't lost her, just simply no longer have eyes on her. Forcing my rage back down, I take out my phone and place the call. "Devil, we lost her. Got caught in a flood. The car crossed over, but we had to stop."

"That's fucking bad news, Drummer." There's a brief pause before he continues, "They must suspect she's wearing a tracker and have a jammer in the car. I'm sorry, Drummer, but the tracker isn't giving me anything. Without it working, I have no bloody idea where they're taking her."

I feel the blood drain from my face. She's gone. Unable to accept it, I raise my head, ignoring the droplets of water falling, stinging my skin like pellets of ice. Opening my mouth, I roar in frustration.

"What the fuck, Prez?" Viper grabs my cut and screams at me.

Lowering my head, I rub away tears disguised as drops of rain, bringing myself under control and forcing my emotion away. "They've jammed the GPS signal." My eyes meet his. For a second, I think he's going to kill me, but instead, he falls to his knees, his head in his hands. He's wailing.

The others group around me, but there's nothing to be said. Nothing to do. We've lost her.

"I got the license plate," Mouse says, noting something on his phone. "Need to get back to the clubhouse so I can trace it."

At least that's something positive, and if anyone can find her using technology, it will be our computer guy. I'm not going to give up. *I will never give up.* Rubbing my jaw, still stinging from Viper's blow, I speak the words to reassure her father while feeling utter dread settle in my heart, recognising all I'm giving him could be false platitudes. "We'll find her, Viper. We'll fuckin' find her." We have to. The alternative is just too horrific to think of.

The storm has caused the temperature to drop nearly forty degrees. Dressed for the heat of the day, we're wet and cold. But in the middle of nowhere, there's nothing to do but wait it out. While it's not going to do much good, I reach into the pannier and get out Dart's waterproof poncho that I'd expected to find there, my t-shirt and cut are already drenched and heavy, but we won't be moving for a while. Around me, my brothers are doing the same, while up above us the heavens provide a spectacular show of the fireworks of the gods. Then we've nothing to do but twiddle our thumbs, impatiently waiting for the deluge to cease, and the floods to dissipate.

Wraith points to the water roaring across the road in front of us. "Want to backtrack and see if there's a way around it?"

I consider his suggestion but quickly reject it. Most of the routes we could use would be blocked to some extent, and riding in this weather is just too fucking dangerous. As much as it pains me, I shake my head. "We'll wait it out."

"Sam's gone, Drum. What are you going to do about that?"

Whatever I fucking can! Viper, back on his feet and lurching forward, looks like he's coming for me again, pinpointing me as the target for his frustration and fear. But he's already got one good lick in, and whatever the situation, I'm his fucking president, and he's not going to get another chance. "Be fuckin' careful what you do next, Viper," I growl, my teeth showing. It's enough to remind him just who I am, but the look of desolation on his face, probably mirroring the one on mine, undoes me.

The rain continues to pour down; half an hour passes. The feeling of hopelessness makes time tick by slowly. A car passes us, ignoring the 'do not cross the road when flooded' signs, and, we watch on, finding a moment of light relief as predictably it gets caught in the current and ends up with a thud against a telephone pole. The driver gets out, loses his footing, and is almost washed away by the power of the water. Arizona doesn't have a stupid driver's law for nothing. While our mood isn't conducive to outright laughing at his plight, Wraith manages a half grin, and Dollar raises his eyebrows in amusement. We don't go to help. He got into it; he can get himself out.

The rain begins to ease. Once it stops completely, the flood waters soon start to ebb. Waiting for it to fall to a passable level is exasperating, and I'm bouncing with impatience to get moving again. We pack away our soaking ponchos, our wet leather cuts quickly starting to steam in the renewed heat of the sun. Then, as soon as the torrent has sufficiently eased, we get back on our bikes, carefully cross the part of the road that's still submerged and, at last, are on our way.

We alternate exceeding the speed limit when we can and needing to pick our way through other diminishing washouts, and it seems an awfully long ride to the compound. When we arrive, Joker's there to open the gates, his mouth falling open in amazement as we tear through, spitting up gravel as we speed up to the clubhouse, backing our bikes into a straight line. Mouse is gone before I need to tell him.

The women are waiting inside. Knowing none of us are in the mood for their services, I tell the sweet butts to get lost. Although their faces show a mixture of relief and incredulity, I offer them no explanation. The old ladies get afforded deeper respect.

Sophie runs up and jumps at her man, her hands clinging to his cut. "Wraith, what's happened? Why, how are you back? I thought you'd be in prison?" I watch her fingers tighten on his leather. She had no reason to think she'd see her man for a very long time unless he was across a table dressed in orange. Wraith's arms go around her, holding her tight, causing a sudden rush of jealousy. Wishing I had my woman here to hold, impatient to initiate any action to find her again, I suppress my immediate impulse simply to tell them to hurry it up, allowing them their special moment.

Sophie's brief moment of pleasure fades as she pulls away from her man, telling us, "Sam's missing. She's been abducted! And Roadrunner's been shot! We didn't know what to do!" Her eyes are reddened, showing she's been crying.

Wraith encircles her in his arms again, resting his chin on her head. To incredulous stares, and with my unspoken thanks that he's stepped in and is doing what I should have done, he explains to her, and everyone else left behind about the fake ATF raid, and how we were supposed to have been following Sam.

"We fuckin' lost 'er." Trust Viper to blurt it out.

Sandy's hand goes to her mouth to cover a gasp. "No!" she cries out in protest. "Viper, no." Then she's in his arms, giving him comfort.

"Where's Heart? And the others? Why haven't they come back too? Where are they?" Crystal walks over to me, a desperate urgency in her eyes. "Are they in prison? Why weren't they released?"

I rest my hand on her arm. "They're fine." Or rather I hope that they are. With disbelief, I realise I haven't given a thought to the rest of my brothers, so caught up in my concern about Sam. "They're on club business." She's been an old lady for a long time; she'll understand, even though she won't like it. Squeezing my fingers, I put a brief pressure on her arm while wondering what I sent my men into. Should I have left more with Devil? Or should I have brought everyone back with me, now that it's no longer our fight? Fuck. Have I made all the wrong decisions today? I turn away from Crystal. The rush to find Sam has me twisted in knots. It's the first time I've ever let a bitch steer me by the dick. I don't know what I'm doing anymore. I'm acting as her concerned lover, not as a president of an outlaw MC.

I've got to start thinking of the club and those who depend on me. "What's the news on Roadrunner?"

Joker's still staring at me as though I'm an apparition.

"Well, man?"

With a shake, he comes back to himself. "Doc's with him. Bullet was a through and through, but he lost a lot of blood."

"He going to be okay?"

"Yeah, Doc thinks he'll pull through." Well, at least that's something off my mind.

"Anyone want a cuppa?" The dulcet tones and very English offer come from Sophie. But I need something a damn sight stronger. Going to the bar, I nab myself a beer and take off for Mouse's office. Inside, the half-Navajo nerd is tapping away on his laptop, ash from his joint overflowing onto his desk.

"Got anything?" I approach and put my hands flat on the desk, looming over him.

"Yeah, of sorts. The Jag belongs to a Kurt Regus. A businessman based out of Phoenix."

Rolling my head back on my shoulders I let out a sigh of relief, that's the right man. We'd heard the other man call him Kurt. It seems this is going to be easier than I feared. "We got an address?"

Mouse partially closes the lid of his laptop, his dark eyes staring up at me. From the worried expression on his face, what he's going to tell me isn't going to be fucking good news.

"Spit it out, Brother." I lean back, realising my posture must be threatening.

"Fucker's got a shell company. Owns a shitload of businesses and residences. Nothing registered under his name. Of the residences, there're a couple in Phoenix, one up in Flagstaff, two more in California, and one in Vegas."

I smooth my hand over my hair. "Never was going to be that simple, was it?" I swallow down the whisper of hope I'd fleetingly felt. "Anything stand out?" Those places are scattered all over, and we need to head for the right one. I can get Red to check out the Vegas one, and, depending on location maybe Snake can check in California. Otherwise, he'll have Sam in his hands for far too long. Long enough to… No, I can't think about that.

"He'd want to take her somewhere isolated." Mouse lets me in on his thoughts.

"And somewhere where he has access to her," I add. "Is he married?"

"Nah, divorced. Separated from his wife a couple of years ago. No kids."

"So he could take her to his home." But where would that be? I start to pace, both hands now tunnelling through my hair as I think. "He got any criminal record?"

"Nothing that's stuck. There have been a couple of investigations into him for fraud, but they were dropped before they got to court."

"Money?"

"He's loaded."

"Okay." I draw out the word as the little I've been told sinks in. "Make a list of the residential properties his company owns, see if you can find out who lives there. If we can't narrow it down, we'll have to pay them all a visit." But that could take some time, even with the other chapters helping.

Mouse is tapping his fingers on the desk. "What about the ex? Could she have any useful information?"

I pause my steps and retrace them to stand in front of him. "Depends on whether she knows his appetites. Could have been a reason for the divorce, I suppose. He paying her?"

Now he's got his hands over the keys again. How Mouse does it, I'll never know, but he seems able to get all information for the club that we ask for. After a second, he turns the screen around to face me. I whistle through my teeth. As an alimony settlement, she must have hit the damn jackpot.

Meeting my eyes, Mouse nods. "Doubtful she'd want to risk losing out on that. And a dead man can't pay her fuckin' bills."

Mouse knows me too well. Regus isn't going to prison for

holding a woman captive. I've got my eye on a nice cosy hole in the ground especially for him.

A knock on the door, and when it opens, Wraith steps in, jerking his chin toward me. "Viper's going fuckin' crazy out here. Smashing stuff. Stopped him from coming in here, but man, he's taking it bad. Sandy's crying as he booted her away saying she didn't understand shit. You got anything to tell him?"

I give a slow nod. "We know who, just not where yet. Mouse, see what you can dig up in the next half hour then we're in church, okay?" I wait for him to signal his agreement, and then turn around to my VP. I'm worried as fuck about Sam myself, but now I've got to act like the prez and calm down my brother. "I'll come see to Viper."

Wraith hadn't been kidding about Viper. Bottles have been smashed and glass litters the floor; chairs and tables are over-turned. Sandy's in tears and the girls sit huddled into a group trying to comfort her, their posture shielding her from the fury of her man.

"You don't understand shit!" Viper's screaming at her. "Don't pretend you know how I'm fuckin' feeling."

Wincing on Sandy's behalf, I'm aware how much Viper will regret his outburst once he calms down. He loves his wife in his way. For fuck's sake, I nearly lost Sam before I got to know her because he didn't want Sandy to be upset. And now he's fucking destroying her with his words.

"For fuck's sake man, calm down." I put myself between him and the women. "Shut the fuck up and listen to yourself. It's not down to Sandy she's gone."

Viper's eyes burn into mine. "No, that's on you! You fuckin' set her up." As I stare him down, some of his rage starts to fade. "What's happening to her, Prez? What the fuck is that bastard doing to her?"

I've got no answer for that, I just have the same dreaded feeling in the pit of my stomach as I expect he has. Seeing him start to calm, watching the tears silently rolling down his cheeks,

I take his arm and lead him to the bar. Marsh is there before us, beers already opened. Jerking my chin in thanks, I take one and swig it down. Wiping my beard, I turn to Sam's father. "Viper, Mouse is getting some info. We'll have church in a few and decide on a plan. We'll get her back. We have to." The sight of his wet eyes is making mine water too.

Fuck, Sam. Where are you, and what is that motherfucker doing to you?

CHAPTER TWENTY-SEVEN

*S*am…

The size of this place astounds me, but I should have expected it from the amount he'd paid when he bought me. Kurt certainly isn't hard up. But I doubt any life of luxury is in my future. My thought immediately confirmed, when I'm uncuffed from the car and pulled roughly out. I struggle and to try to break free, intuitively knowing once he gets me inside, I'll be lost. But Kurt laughs and gestures to one of the guards waiting just inside the doorway. He comes out, his face impassive, and throws me unceremoniously over his shoulder and, ignoring my kicking and shouting, carries me into the building.

He doesn't need to ask instruction as to where to take me, heading straight for a door which reveals stairs leading down into a basement. Kurt follows behind and switches on the lights, bare-naked bulbs in the ceiling illuminating the room while he waves to the guard to put me down. He does so but keeps tight hold of me. I'm allowed a moment to stare at my surroundings.

"Welcome to your new home. I trust you'll be very comfortable here." His smirk reveals the falsity of his salutation, along with his gesture that draws my attention to items of equipment which look like they wouldn't be out of place in a medieval torture chamber. There are things resembling sawhorses, and a large frame shaped in an X, a St. Andrew's Cross I think it's called. Hanging on the rough stone walls are all manner of whips and other implements. With wide-open eyes, I gaze around. I struggle, but the guard holds me firm.

The furnishings, my situation, the thought that this man is going to keep me here and do unspeakable things to me causes my stomach to churn. An unstoppable stream of vomit comes out of my mouth, causing the guard to swear. Kurt comes over quickly, avoiding the pool at my feet and slaps my face hard, growling with disgust, but his eyes seem to crease in amusement as if my reaction wasn't unexpected.

"Chain her up."

Again, compliant and almost bored with his duty, the guard drags my body across to one wall, my futile struggles making no impact on his muscular frame. He pushes me down until I'm sprawled on the floor, then fastens a shackle around one of my hands and locks it tight.

Kurt dismisses the guard with an instruction to clean the vomit up, then walks across to me, picking up a knife from a table as he approaches. He cuts through the flimsy garment I'm wearing and takes a step back to admire the view. I try to cover my nakedness with my free arm, but that only makes him rasp out, "Take your hand away. Let me see what I own."

As I refuse to obey, he threatens, "I'll shackle your other hand too."

Not wanting to lose the little freedom that I have, I reluctantly do what he's asked. His eyes burn into me, making me feel dirty from his manic stare. Then with a little nod, he explains, "I'm afraid I'm going to have to leave you waiting in anticipation for a while. I've got a doctor to call, of course, and there's work I have to attend to. You can stay here and dream about all the fun we're going to have when I come back." He cups himself, rubbing his cock through the material of his pants. "I want to take my time with you, without distractions. Oh, I nearly forgot. Silly me." He places the battery pack with the jammer just out of my reach, but close enough to be effective. It's glowing green light, showing it's fully charged, seems to mock me.

"Right, my pet. I won't be long, I promise you that. I won't keep you waiting long for some fun."

I can wait forever; I want to tell him. I watch him walk up the stone stairs and disappear through the door, hoping whatever he has to do will take a very long time. In fact, I'll be quite happy if he never comes back.

As the door closes behind him, immediately I start tugging on the shackle, but it won't budge, as it's bolted firmly to the wall. I want to scream in frustration, but am scared any sound might bring him, or one of the guards back. So instead, I cry, curling myself up into a ball. Scared, terrified, and dreading what will happen when he returns.

I've never thought of myself as a weak person, but this is too much for anyone to bear. Tears running down my face, I twist and turn, trying to get comfortable on the hard stone ground. The actions cause a tug on the shackle again. Some part of my brain is still working. *The shackle's got a mechanical lock.* With my free hand, I examine it. I don't have a key, but... Wiping my face with the back of my hand, I force myself to concentrate on something other than giving up or giving in. That isn't me. I look around for something, anything. It's useless. To open the lock, I either need a key or something to manipulate it with, and there's nothing within reach that will help.

But the thought that I could perhaps free myself if I could get hold of a tool, gives me something to focus on. Judging from the devices hanging on the walls, he thinks he's going to break me. But I've a new desperation to fight.

Time passes, the green light glows steadily, the hope it might fail before the promised doctor arrives fading by the minute. Then the moment I've been dreading arrives when the door opens again, and Kurt descends the stairs. He's changed out of his suit and is now wearing a loose pair of sweats and a t-shirt. His clothing might look casual; his expression is not. There's a look of glee on his face that's almost rabid.

I've never been a helpless female; I work in a man's world. While there are hoists to help with the heaviest lifting, my arms are muscular, and my upper body strength is strong. I'm not going to make this easy for him. As he stalks toward me, my posture stiffens. My hand is cuffed about a foot off the floor, so I haven't got very much to work with, but my legs are free.

Now I want him to come closer. In my head, I'm encouraging him on. What I'm about to do will most certainly enrage him, but if I do it right, I might render him incapable...

Swallowing rapidly, forcing myself to wait until he's near enough, the look of fear on my face no pretence. I shuffle back slightly, looking like I'm retreating while using the wall at my back to brace against. And now it's time; I shoot out my leg, the heel of my foot connecting hard with his crotch.

He lets out a satisfying scream of pain, so shrill it could have come from a woman. Which, presumably, is what his guards think, as none of his men come to investigate as he falls onto the floor, curling around himself and hugging his knees to his stomach. The pain takes away both his breath and his ability to speak for a moment.

But my reprieve doesn't last long. After a couple of minutes, he starts to straighten, his eyes blazing in my direction. When his breath stops coming in pants, he raises his head. "You fucking cunt! You're going to pay for that!"

As he gets to his feet, he staggers. Still in agony, he bends with his hands on his knees. He looks around the room, his eyes fix on something. A twisted grin comes to his face as he limps awkwardly to the wall covered in the implements of his preferred form of torture. He considers for a moment and then takes down a long whip. As he turns back to me, I see his eyes are watering and creased with pain and sweat is pouring down his face. I hurt him good.

Now he's going to retaliate. But if he's angry because of the hurt I've caused him, it's nothing to the fury I feel knowing he believes there's nothing wrong in keeping a woman for his personal satisfaction. As he swings the whip, possibly not with the same intensity as he would if he wasn't injured, I let it fall across my breasts, forcing myself to ignore the burning smart of agony, and snake out my hand, grabbing hold of the tail and jerking hard before he can pull it back.

His eyes widen as I take him by surprise—he obviously hadn't expected a mere woman to fight back. This time I'm in charge and I've got the weapon. I slash the whip down on the floor with a loud crack, feeling a sense of satisfaction as he takes a step back. I flick it again, using all of my strength. The sound of the whiplash echoes like a pistol shot.

Stepping back out of reach, his face grows red, and his hands bunch into fists. "Put that down. You're just making it harder for yourself."

Doubting that very much, I shake my head. He was going to whip me, and there's no way of knowing how far he'd go before he stopped. I watch as indecision crosses his face, and wonder what will be his next play? He could call down his men; it might take a while for them to overpower me, but eventually they will. But will he want to lose face? I'm banking that he's a coward and wouldn't want his employees to know that a woman has gotten the better of him.

That he's still hurting is plain to see. Rape, at least by him, has to be off the cards, at least for the moment.

Finally, he breaks the stalemate and speaks, "So that's the way you want to play it, is it? I'll enjoy breaking you. Let's see how feisty you are without water or food." He pauses, his hands start to relax, and I let out the breath I've been holding. "This can only go one way, girl. There's no rescue coming; no one knows where you are. I *will* break you. And I'll enjoy doing it. Now I'm going to enjoy inflicting a lot of pain while I do so. I'll leave you to think on that for a while. But believe this, you're going to pay for what you've done today."

Turning, he makes his way up the stairs, and after he slams the door shut, I hear a key turning in a lock.

I roll my head back on my shoulders trying to rid myself of the stiffness in my neck and allow myself to enjoy a moment of relief. But not for too long. I might have won this battle, but the war is far from over. A shiver runs through me when I consider his promise of painful retribution, and I won't stand any chance cuffed to this wall. Once again, my eyes flick left and right, searching for something that could help. I see it. When Kurt had bent over, a pen must have fallen out of his pocket. Now if I can just get that over to me.

Flicking the whip, it takes a few tries, but at last the pen is within my grasp. It's a fancy one, but I don't care what its value is as I take it apart. The nib might be too thick, but at least I can try. Twisting my body around, I rise up on my knees and attack the shackle, my hands slippery with blood that's flowing from my breasts, opened by the sting of the whip. Using the remainder of the flimsy dress I'd been wearing, I dry them as best I can and carry on. Wiggling the end of the pen this way and that, finally I unlock the mechanism, and it falls open. *I'm free.*

Wasting no time, I take the battery pack and unplug the jammer from it then place it at the furthest end of the room. Hoping the walls aren't thick enough to block the signal, I rub the back of my neck, trusting someone will still be watching for the tracker to flare into life again. *What if they've given up?*

No. I can't think like that. Drummer, Viper… They'll be coming for me the instant they know where I am. In the meantime, I can't rely on others to rescue me. I start to explore my prison, hoping there might be something I can find to help me escape, or, at the very least, something I can use to defend myself during round two.

CHAPTER TWENTY-EIGHT

*D*rummer...

"I say we get brothers out to all his properties." Viper's dabbing at his eyes, which are already red and raw. From time to time he's swiping away a tear which escapes and runs down his cheek. Seeing the difficulty he's having sitting still in his seat, I empathise, as I'm having the same problem, finding it almost impossible to just sit here chucking ideas around and not leaping into action. But for now, doing nothing is better than wasting time heading out without the information telling us where we should be going.

"We can't do that," I start, with every intention of explaining we could end up going to the wrong locations, but Sam's father is not in the mood to listen.

"Why the fuck not?" His frantic gaze goes around the table, drawing my attention again to the fact that over half the seats are empty.

"Shut the fuck up and listen, Viper. We're too thin on the ground. It would take us ages to get around all the shit he owns, and you can bet you're fuckin' life he's gonna have them well guarded. A man like that would."

Joker's nodding. "Agree with you, Prez. We gotta do this smart."

Viper gets to his feet. "Mouse, give me that list you got, and I'll fuckin' go myself. I'm not going to sit here on my ass knowing Sam's probably being raped and hurt."

Wincing inwardly, wishing he hadn't put it quite so bluntly, I know I've got to get some sense into him. He'll end up getting himself killed if he carries out his suggestion. "Mouse is gonna give you fuck all, Viper. Now sit back down and shut the fuck up. You're the one wasting time."

Viper's eyes burn into me, but he kicks out his chair and takes his place again. I wait for just a second longer to make sure he's going to stay put, then jerk my chin toward Mouse. "What you got for us?"

Mouse looks at his laptop screen. "He's got a few warehouses, he could have taken her there. But I'd put my money on him keeping her close. Why buy a slave and not have her on tap? I've done more digging and this," he turns his screen so I can view it too, "is his main residence."

"Let's get going then."

"Viper!" This time it's Blade who's spinning his knife and stops it as it points toward Sam's father. The enforcer's sharp tone and action have the desired effect. Viper huffs but stays in his chair.

"What's the security like?"

I nod at Wraith, appreciating the question, then turn to Mouse as he answers, "Top of the line. There's a security guard on the gate. High perimeter fencing, which must be alarmed."

"Any way of knowing exactly how many employees he's got?"

"Nah, Prez. Whatever goes on in that house, he keeps private. There's no off-site storage of the security footage, but I have managed to get hold of this." He pulls up a photo of the house and shows it to me. It's better than nothing, but still not a lot. It's a large two-storey building.

I lean back in my chair, propping my foot up on the heavy wooden table, looking around the room. With the men I brought back with me, together with Joker and Lady, that makes nine of us in all. Marsh, being a prospect isn't around the table, but I'll need to leave him here at the compound. We've no idea how many we'll be going up against. Fuck, why did I let my brothers go off with Devil when I want them here to help me save Sam? Everything about this situation is fucked up. Christ.

I'm not comfortable with putting all our eggs in one fucking basket. If Mouse is correct, then maybe we can rescue her. If he's wrong, we might lose her again.

As I've needed to keep in touch with Devil, I've left my phone turned on. When it rings, and I see it's him, I lose no time answering it. "Speak to me."

"What?"

"Fuck. Where? On Sonara, you say?" I flick my eyes toward Mouse; he's looking excited and nodding furiously.

"Yeah, that's one of his properties. His main residence, we've already earmarked it."

"I'll let you know. Take care, man."

All eyes are on me when I end the call. I stand. "She's fuckin' there. Her GPS has just kicked back into action. We're going. Now." Viper's already on his feet and opening the door. "Viper, Brother, wait a fuckin' minute." When he pauses, I address everyone. "We've got to take care. We approach quiet, you hear me? Check out what we're dealing with before barging in. Won't do Sam any good if we fuckin' end up dead. Viper, you feeling me here?"

Viper turns, hope shining from his face. He gives me a considered look, then a sharp nod. "I got you, Prez."

"Okay, let's get fuckin' rolling then."

We don't waste a minute as we head for the bikes and start our engines, peeling away from the clubhouse and out of the gates heading for the outskirts of Phoenix. It's our one piece of luck Sam wasn't taken further away. *Two hours, darlin'. Just hang on for two more hours.*

Another fast ride, throttles turned all the way, we race up the interstate, with myself in the lead, Wraith and Blade behind me, Viper and Beef behind them, followed by Joker and Lady. With Mouse and Blade bringing up the rear in the crash truck. I might not have all my brothers with me, but apart from the new guys who are still an unknown, I have nothing but confidence in the ones who are. My only concern is that Viper might go off half-cocked, but I'll be watching him closely and pulling the plug immediately if it looks like he's going to go off on his own fucking plan.

We head toward a suburb south of the city, and after we turn off the freeway, it's clear we're riding into the area where the rich motherfuckers live. As desert gives way to a more populated area, the houses are large, built back from the road and secluded behind impenetrable-looking fences. If these are an example of Kurt's residence, I'm going to have to start drumming up some ideas how to get us inside.

Checking off the numbers as we pass, I spy a utility yard, a paved pull-off area with boxes probably full of electronics and circuitry of some sort—not that I give a fuck at that moment, but it's a useful place to stop. I wave at my brothers then give the signal to cut the engines. Coasting up to it we park our bikes as best as possible out of sight. This seems to be the closest we can get if we don't want to be heard. For the rest of the way, we'll be on foot. As soon as we stop, Mouse has gotten out his laptop and is tethering it to his phone. I motion to take off our cuts, and we put them in the crash truck while the computer guy does his job.

"Yes!" As he fist pumps the air, I raise my eyebrow. He's grinning. "I can hack into their security from here. Cameras are going to stop recording... now."

That's great news. Now we can be sure they won't see us going in. "Wraith, you take Bullet and Beef and keep an eye on what's going on out front. And stay out of fuckin' sight. I'll take the back, the rest of you, with me." Meaning I can keep Viper close by.

As quietly as burly bikers can, we move stealthily forward; this isn't our first rodeo. Lady and Joker fit in as though they've always been with us. I position my team where I want them.

"You've got a guard heading in your direction," Wraith speaks into my ear. I motion to the others to stay down and watch as he comes into sight. It's clear he's being slack and not expecting trouble—he's texting someone on his phone, only making a show of doing his rounds.

"What you got there, VP?"

"One guard on the gate looking fuckin' bored."

"Can you take him?"

"Oh yeah." My lips curl as I hear the confidence in my VP's tone.

"When the guard coming our way is out of sight, we'll cut the fencing and get through. I've seen no movement inside. You?"

"Nothing."

Blade's got the wire cutters and doesn't need any instruction; he starts doing his shit directly when the guard turns the corner. Silently we all slip through, keeping low and taking advantage of the ornamental shrubs conveniently placed to give us some cover. Soon we've made it, unchallenged, to the back of the house. This is too fucking easy.

"We're in," I tell Wraith. Joker's carefully peering into the windows, moving from one to the next. The shake of his head tells me there's no one to be seen. Motherfucker must put one hell of a lot of faith in his security system and guards.

"Your guard is coming back. Southside." I wave Blade and Mouse forward to the corner of the building. They take out the guard with a quick blow to the head and have him bound, gagged, and hidden in less than a minute. Fuck yeah, my boys are good.

"Taken care of. I'll come to the front." Leaving the others

behind, I make my way carefully along the side of the house, but again, no alarm is raised. I get to the corner and raise my weapon.

I can see Wraith step into sight, flanked by Bullet and Beef, guns ready in their hands. Through my earpiece, I hear what he's saying. "Drop your weapon and open the gate. That's it, take it out carefully."

I can see the moment when indecision strikes, the guard wondering if he has a chance. But Wraith stops that dead. "Take a look behind you if you're thinking of being a fuckin' hero."

He glances around, sees me to his rear. Whatever he's paid is not to be enough for him to take a bullet for his boss. He presses a remote, and the gates start to open.

"Blade, entry in five."

As Bullet deals with the guard in the same efficient way as his brothers had done the one out the back, Wraith and Beef run toward me. We crash through the front door at the same time as I hear glass breaking out back. A man stands frozen to the spot, startled by our unexpected entrance. As his mouth drops open, his hand goes to his belt.

"Stop right there," I tell him. But he doesn't, stupidly continuing the movement toward his gun. I fire once, a muffled pop courtesy of my silencer, and the guard drops to the ground, a neat hole in his forehead.

"Nice, Prez." I acknowledge Viper's compliment with just a small nod.

"Viper, you, Joker, and I, we'll take upstairs. VP, you, Bullet and Lady see what you can find down here. Blade, Beef and Mouse, check garages and outbuildings."

We split into the three groups. Walking quietly is damn near impossible wearing motorcycle boots, but we manage it. The blatant wealth of the house's owner is apparent everywhere—this Kurt fucker is clearly rich as all get-out and isn't ashamed to flaunt it. I'd bet good money all the vases and such are genuine antiques. But we're not here to steal, we're here for a rescue. A rescue that's looking more unlikely by the minute. Each bedroom and bathroom we find is empty. Oh, the house is lived in, alright, it's just there doesn't appear to be anyone at home. And no sign of Sam or of any woman's occupancy.

Exchanging frustrated looks, we head back down and find Wraith, shaking his head. "There's a cook in the kitchen, and, according to her, no one, except the guards, are around."

"No sign of Sam?"

"None. Upstairs?"

"Nothing." Have we come to the wrong fucking place after all?

I place a phone call. "Devil, she's not here. Have you got a new location for her?"

Going cold, I listen to him tell me her GPS signal still shows she's here. But she's not. A chill runs through me. Could they have cut the tracker out? Shit! It could be hidden anywhere in the house. To lead us into a trap? Unlikely, we wouldn't have taken the guards out so easily if it was.

I'm not yet satisfied we're in the wrong place. But where could she be? "Where's this cook? She alive?"

Wraith nods, and points in the direction of the kitchen.

"I'll go question her; you go make the guards talk. We need to know where she fuckin' is."

"I'll do it; I'll make them fuckin' tell us." Viper's face is twitching, his skin glowing red, his eyes moving back and forth in panic. "We've gotta find her, Prez."

He needs something to do. Feeling pity for the guards, I send him out with Blade. Wraith follows me to the kitchen. The cook is trussed up, her eyes open, her throat working as she swallows hard. I rip off her gag. "Where's the girl?"

Her brow creases. "What? Whaaaat girl?"

Her reaction looks genuine. "Your employer, Kurt Regus. He brought a girl here earlier."

She shakes her head. "I haven' seen no girl. But I've been in the kitchen most of the day. I was just clearing up after dinner. I don't get to see nothing." Glancing around I see what she's just taken out of the dishwasher, a lonely plate sits on the side.

"You live in?"

She shakes her head. She's trembling, her body jerking in little movements showing her fear. "Kurt usually keep a woman here?"

Another shake of her head. Fuck, is this a dead end? It's starting to seem more likely that somehow he's removed her tracker and taken her elsewhere.

I know from experience when someone's telling the truth, and this woman is so scared a puddle of urine has appeared on the floor. Accepting she's told us everything she knows, I slam my fist against one of the cabinets, leaving a large hole in the expensive wood. "Fuck it!"

Returning to the entrance hall, I find Viper's returned, his hands, bloodied. He's shaking his head. "We're in the wrong fuckin' place, Prez. The guard's say she's not in the house. He's telling the truth, I'm sure on that. What the fuck do we do now?"

Rolling back my head, I let out a sigh. All eyes are on me, waiting for me to tell them what to do next. Viper's shaking in his desire to get searching again. And me? Well, fuck, all I can think of is Sam and all manner of hell she could be suffering. As I try to work through our limited options, my eyes look around the hall and focus on a curtain hanging on a rail under the stairs. It strikes me as an odd place for a curtain.

"You look behind that?"

"What?" Wraith looks round, his eyes creasing before flicking to mine. With a few long strides, he's moving over to it, pulling the curtain aside and revealing a door.

"Shit!" I'm beside him in seconds. We've been asking the wrong fucking questions. She's not in the *house*. She's in the fucking basement! She has to be. The door is locked. I don't waste time hunting for a key. "Stand back!" Speaking, while simultaneously pointing my gun, I shoot out the lock. The door swings open

—it's a heavy motherfucker with soundproofing on the other side. Suddenly there's a shrill scream, a man's voice cursing, and then a cry of pain. It's Sam. We've found her. And she's being hurt.

Holding myself back with great difficulty, cautiously I start to make my way down. Viper almost pushes me off balance in his hurry.

"Careful, man," I admonish him in a growl, the fucker takes no heed.

Pushing me hard against the wall and out of his way, he's descending in front of me. Throwing caution to the wind, I'm right behind him, barrelling into him as he comes to a sudden halt at the bottom. There, in front of us, is the man who I assume is Kurt, and he's crouching behind Sam who's shackled to the ground, one arm around her throat, and another holding a gun to her head.

"Not one step further, or I shoot her."

Sam's naked, her eyes wide with panic.

"Don't worry, babe. We fuckin' got you now." I force my voice to sound calm and reassuring.

"I don't think you fucking understand. I'm holding all the cards here. She's dead if you take one step further."

I've been in situations like this before. "Shoot her, and you're not going to see daylight again. Let her go, and I'll guarantee you're walking out of here alive." And that's the truth. It was part of the deal I'd made with Devil. Deliver him alive and able to answer questions. Nothing to say he needed all his limbs in working order.

Taking a step into the basement, I give my brothers room to stand beside me. Each of us with a weapon in hand. While giving the rich prick time to realise this is one situation where he's not going to wriggle his way out of, my eyes alight on Sam again, seeing the bruising on her head, and the open, bleeding cut across her breast, and another down the side of one arm. My whole body tenses with rage while I try to read her expression.

Have we gotten here too late? Has he done *that* to her, too? A growl comes to my throat, I swallow it down.

I don't ask if she's alright, I can see she's not. My arms itch to hold her, but when I take another step, he presses the barrel to her head, and his fingers twitch on the trigger. If I'm not careful, he'll shoot her by accident.

"I can pay you." His voice has gone up an octave. "Just leave me with the girl. She's special to me, so name your price."

"Why is this girl so special to you?" It's Blade who asks, while I think she's fucking essential to me. Just seeing her, hurt, afraid, but keeping her cool, staying strong and not moving, she's fucking amazing in my eyes. My enforcer is just trying to keep him talking. Like me, he'll have seen Kurt's finger on the trigger is none too steady.

"Just look at her." Now his voice sounds creepy. "She's so beautiful. Just waiting to be corrupted."

Oh yeah, she'll be corrupted all right, just not by him.

I stare at Sam, willing her to believe there's no sum large enough to tempt me to leave her with him, even if I thought Viper would let me get away with it. She blinks her eyes, and I'm sure it's a sign she understands. My words say something different. "How much you talking?" I use his distraction, and his momentary hope to inch closer. I feel Blade moving a little way off to my right.

Kurt's eyes flare with interest. "A million? Two?" I suppose it's pocket change to a billionaire.

My VP knows what I'm doing. "Prez, we could do a lot with that kind of money. It's a good fuckin' deal for the club."

The gun lowers an inch. But I need it away from her.

"Two and a half," I barter.

The taut lines on Kurt's forehead begin to smooth out, and a slight smile comes to his face as he begins to think that he's won. Not surprising. In his world, you can buy anything. The gun moves away, and as soon as it's no longer pointed straight at Sam's head, in a blur, I see a knife fly across the room, embedding itself in Kurt's right hand. I leap forward, taking charge of his weapon and pistol-whip him across the face. And that's just for starters; he's had his hands on my woman.

Sam gasps and falls forward. Dropping to my knees, my arms are there to catch her. Her fingers grasp at my arms, pulling me to her as if she's never going to let me go. I hold her, kissing her hair, *never*, I vow silently, *I'm never letting you go again.*

And then Viper's here too, crouched on the floor trying to take her from me, ending up with his arms awkwardly around us both. He's crying openly, his tears setting off hers. My own eyes are wet.

"Found a key, Prez." Bullet's pulled the prone body away and searched his pockets. The key fits the shackle, and she's free.

Now I'm standing up, cradling her like a baby.

"Prez." Lady's taken off his t-shirt and is handing it to me. I gesture, not wanting to put her down. Viper takes it and puts it over her head, then we both manoeuvre her arms into it. A little awkward, but it does the job. While I carry her upstairs and out of the house, I leave my brothers to bring up the trash.

Blade's run ahead, and the crash truck draws up in front of the house. Kurt, tied and gagged, is thrown in the back, and I go to put Sam gently in the passenger seat, but she shakes her head violently.

"Don't leave me," she cries, her eyes pleading.

Making the decision quickly, I tell Blade to bring back my bike. I have no desire to take my hands off her, not for a moment.

"I'll drive." In the same frame of mind, Viper tosses the keys to his bike to Mouse.

CHAPTER TWENTY-NINE

*S*am…

I'm safe. Just thinking those wonderful words helps to slow the frantic beating of my heart. *Drummer came for me.*

I hold Drummer so tightly, unable to release him but he doesn't seem to care, sitting beside me in the truck with his precious leather cut on the seat next to him. I can't stop shivering, violent tremors wracking my body, knowing my rescue had only just been in time. He'd come only minutes before I would have been raped.

Left in the basement, with no watch or phone to advise me, I had no way of measuring how long Kurt had left me alone, but it had been probably no more than a couple of hours. When he'd returned, though he'd evidently recovered enough to torment me, his posture was stiff, as though still in some pain. But my self-congratulatory feelings didn't last long. Initially it had been a standoff. I was free now, no longer chained to the wall, and I threatened him with the long whip. But he'd come prepared; he'd brought a gun.

I knew my brief freedom was lost when he threatened to put a bullet in my leg, saying it didn't matter to him if I was unable to walk. The cold, unfeeling set of his eyes told me he'd have no problem following through with his threat.

With the weapon targeting me, I'd reluctantly put down the whip, and allowed myself to be shackled once again to the wall. Then he'd snatched up the whip and used it again, punishing me for my rebellion. Once, twice, I'd put my free arm around my torso to protect me, ending up with slashes from my wrist to my shoulder. A sharp, searing pain opening up my skin. Then he'd come closer, taking my hair, pulling my head back and pressing his mouth to mine. With a sharp pinch to my nipple, I'd gasped and opened my mouth. He'd thrust his tongue inside. I tried to bite him and got a hard slap around my face as a reward.

It made him laugh, his face twisted and cruel. "Damn girl, you taste good. But we'll use a dental gag when I want my cock in there. Can't risk your teeth on my cock." *What's he talking about?* But while I might not know exactly what he was suggesting, he hadn't needed to draw me a picture.

Then it was time for payback, for me kicking out at him. His fisted hands flew at me, starting on my breasts. He'd pinned my free arm to the wall so I couldn't escape, then kneaded and twisted, pinching and hurting. Then he pushed his fingers up inside me. Probing, pushing up rudely into my dry channel, mimicking what he'd have been doing if I hadn't damaged him. Oh, God, did he hurt me. When I tried to press my legs together, he'd done worse, kicking apart my legs and sending his boot-clad foot hard into my most tender parts. Then it was a fist to my stomach, stealing my breath and sending bile rising into my mouth. At that point he let me go, a quivering mess on the floor. A kick to my ribs and I screamed.

His hand went to his belt, and as I widened my eyes, he'd sneered at me coldly. "I'm waiting no longer. You thought you incapacitated me, but you're a stupid fucking bitch. I'm hard for you, girl. Been hard since I first saw your picture. My balls might be throbbing, but they'll be better for some release. Now I'm going to have that virgin pussy, and I'm going to enjoy making you bleed."

I screamed, not thinking anyone would hear me, knowing there was nothing I could do to prevent being raped.

It was then, when I'd given up all hope, I heard a shot. I let out another loud scream as Kurt's eyes flew to the stairway. In a split second, his posture changed from aggressor to one defeated as the mass of men poured down the stairs, Viper, and thank God, Drummer, in the lead. He pulled me against him and put his gun to my head, pressing so hard into my temple he bruised my skin.

In the next few minutes, so many emotions whirled through my mind that I ended up dizzy. Elation that Drummer was there, horror that Kurt was going to kill me. Disgust when I thought for a split second the bikers were going to accept his extravagant offer, fear that they would, hope, at the expression in Drummer's eyes—or was it just wishful thinking he was trying to persuade me that was the last thing on his mind—that he wouldn't consider it for a moment. Then I watched as Blade threw that knife, showing his skill with the weapon that carries his name, Kurt dropping the gun... And, at last, Drummer taking me in his arms. I knew I never wanted him to let me go again.

Now safe in the van, as my torture replays in my mind, shudders shake my body. I'm crying and sobbing, my fingers twisting in Drummer's shirt. He's speaking to me so softly, murmuring quietly, over and over, "Hush, you're safe now. I've got you, I've got you."

The van's moving fast. Glancing up through my tears, I see we're back on the interstate. Suddenly there's a thump from the back, and I jump and cry out, remembering they've brought Kurt along for the ride. Why, I'm not sure. I'd been certain Drummer would kill him.

"It's alright, he can't hurt you, babe." Drummer's strong arms wrap around me, I stifle a groan as he squeezes my sore ribs. "I promise you, he won't hurt you ever again." He turns my head so I face him, his eyes examining me. "Forget him." His eyes look over me, his gaze tormented. "Sam, he'll pay for what he's done to you." He stares into my eyes, trying to read the answer there as he asks, "I need to know, did he...?"

He can't say the words, and as another violent shudder goes through me as I remember just how close it had been, I can't bring myself to speak.

Drum's face grows black, his mouth tightens, and it's now he asks, elucidating every syllable so there can be no misunderstanding, "Did he rape you?"

I shake my head in denial. "No, not with, but..."

"He touched you," he growls.

I give a faint nod.

"He hurt you."

At my second nod, he gets out his phone and wastes no time when it's answered. "Doc, you still at the club? Stay there. I need you."

"No, Drum," I don't want anyone touching me.

Drummer ends the call, ignoring my protest. His steely eyes gaze into mine. "I need to know exactly what the motherfucker did to you, so I can make him pay."

At that moment, there's a muffled groaning from behind me. I don't want to relive either the things he'd done or the fear and disgust I'd felt. Not when my tormentor is lying behind me savouring my suffering and pain. I don't want to give him the satisfaction of knowing just how much he hurt me, or that he's left mental scars along with the physical. He'd wanted to hurt me. I don't want to leave him the gratification that he had.

Drummer's phone rings, he answers, "Speak to me."

"Uh huh."

"Right."

"Who?"

"Fuck."

"Yeah, we got him."

There's a pause while he considers his answer, then, "Yeah, alright. You're making us get a bit too friendly with them. Not sure as to how much I like that."

Then a chuckle. "Yeah, it will damage our fuckin' rep."

He ends the call without a goodbye. Sniffing, I wipe my eyes and raise them to his in silent question.

His eyes soften as he returns my gaze. "That was Devil. The truck got to the meet point, and the boys surrounded them. There was a gunfight, but they weren't prepared. The brothers captured most of the ringleaders and freed the women."

"Oh, thank goodness for that!" I'm embarrassed. Overwhelmed by my predicament, I hadn't given a thought to the rest of the women. Then I go back to what he said. "Most?"

"Yeah, it's good news, babe. One got away, but they rounded up the others."

"Anyone hurt?" Viper calls over his shoulder.

"Slick took a bullet to his arm. Only a graze."

Oh, God, I'd forgotten. "What happened to Roadrunner?" As I remember him lying on the ground and how I left him bleeding out, I freeze. "Is he… is he dead?"

Drum shakes his head. "He got hit pretty bad, darlin', but the bullet went straight through. Doc's looking after him at the club. He's a strong son of a bitch, he'll recover. And that's down to you, darlin'. We got Doc on his way as soon as we heard. You did good letting us know." Drummer strokes my hand. Now he raises his voice so Viper can hear. "Devil's bringing everyone back to the compound. The men they've taken captive and the women they've freed. Reckon Sandy and the ol' ladies will help looking after tbe bitches we're bringing back?"

Viper flicks his eyes in the rearview mirror. "You know our women, Drum, they'll be falling over themselves to do what they can. What's that all about, though, Prez?"

Drummer scoffs. "Seems the FBI wants us to do it a favour, as they're doing this on the lowdown. They need somewhere to keep the fuckers out of sight and secure, and somewhere the women could be safe while they round up the one that got away."

"But, Drum?" I start, my brow creasing. "I thought the feds were set up to deal with situations like this. Don't they arrange counselling and support for people who've been trafficked?"

He squeezes me gently. "Right now, I don't give a fuck what favours they're asking or why. Getting you back to the compound is the most important thing. Perhaps the feds need to get their ducks in a row before taking the women and captives away. Fuck, Sam..." He breaks off, and I swear his eyes are watering, and he's thinking about what could have happened to me.

At last I make my fingers unfold, releasing my grip on his shirt. Reaching up, I touch my hand to his face, a tactile reassurance I'm here and alive.

"Something about that I don't like, Prez. Us doing favours for the feds."

"Me neither, Viper. But we'll do what we can. It's looking after the women I'm more worried about. Joker and Lady can show if they're willing to get their hands dirty and throw in with the old ladies and Marsh getting things ready."

"There's the block at the top, Prez, the one we use for visiting clubs. Reckon we could get half the women in there if we put some more cots in there, and perhaps the one next to it?"

"As long as the sweet butts don't go on a recruitment drive." Drum tries to lighten the mood.

"Wouldn't hurt getting some new pussy."

I can't help it; I flinch as I hear them so casually refer to girls providing them with sexual favours, and especially hearing my dad talking so casually about it. Drummer senses me tensing up. "It's alright, babe. Remember, the sweet butts are here by choice; it's not the same as you or the other women captured by force.

They can walk away at any time. They're well recompensed for providing their services—we take care of them, feed them, house and protect them."

I can't understand how women can do that, not voluntarily, then I remember the things they had said to me. "They don't like me, Drum." I hate that I sound like a whiney little girl.

"Only because they don't yet know your place, sweetheart."

I'm hurting and sore. I want this drive to be over. I want to heal. But then? I've no idea what the future is for me. I mumble, "I don't know what my place is either."

Now it's Drum's turn to tense. After a slight hesitation, he pulls me to him and nuzzles my hair, tracing his lips down my cheek until they meet mine. I open for him, and he sweeps his tongue inside, immediately erasing all memories of Kurt's assault on my mouth. But all too soon he pulls away and tucks me under his arm again, and I feel his beard grazing the top of my head. "Your place, if you want it, is with me." His voice is soft, low, but full of conviction.

I don't know how to answer him. "Drum, I—"

"Shush, don't say anything now. But know that's what I want, darlin'."

Their prisoner is fully awake now, stirring and kicking at the sides of the van. While Drummer assures me Kurt can't get free, the sounds coming from the man who hurt me stops me from analysing anything else that's been said, the wounds on my body and in my mind still too raw. The muffled shouts through the gag start me shaking all over again, and I remain on edge until finally we enter the compound.

When the van comes to a halt, I don't need to move as Drummer lifts me out and carries me over the hot ground. The sun is setting in the sky, glorious orange streaks reflecting into the storm clouds above. But what would be a wonderful sight is ruined by seeing Kurt dragged out of the van and being dumped unceremoniously on the ground, before being picked up by

Wraith and Blade and carried away. I catch his eye before he's taken out of view and can feel the force of his hatred directed toward me. And strangely too, something which suggests unfulfilled desire. It chills me.

"Where are you taking him?" I ask nervously. Scared he might be able to escape.

"They're taking him to the storage room. Don't worry, he won't be getting out."

"What are you going to do to him?"

Drummer shakes his head. "Club business, darlin'. But you won't ever be seeing him again. I promise you that."

I frown. I would have thought in this instance at least, I deserve to be told, but as he carries me into the clubhouse, he's clearly not going to say any more. As we enter the main room, there's a man who've I've not seen before, standing, waiting. He's dressed as a biker but isn't wearing a cut.

"Your patient, Doc," Drum calls out as he marches with me still in his arms. "I'll take her out back to my room."

I hear a gasp and a woman's voice calling out, "Sam! You've got her! What's the matter with her? Is she alright?" I recognise Sandy's voice, but it sounds different, bursting with emotion.

Drum doesn't stop to answer, just carries me through and places me on a soft bed. The mattress sinks as I land on it, and even in the state I'm in, I question if it's the bed Drummer uses, and just how much action it must have seen. Automatically I pull the t-shirt down to make myself decent, grateful Lady's a big man and it's long enough to cover my thighs. Drum sits on the bed beside me and takes my hand as though he's as reluctant as I am to lose contact, for however short a time.

"Do you want to give us some privacy, Prez?" Doc enters the room, his voice is deep, a little scratchy, but for all that, calm and comforting.

As I grab Drummer's hand harder, he squeezes back. "Not unless Sam wants me to."

"Stay, please." My voice comes out hoarse. I look up to the man staring down at me. "Are you a real doctor?"

His stern features rearrange themselves into a grin. "Ex-Army medic," he explains. "I'm qualified for the basics, but if you need more extensive treatment, you'll have to go to a hospital."

Shaking my head, I dismiss that option immediately. "I don't want to go anywhere." I take a tight hold of Drum's hand.

Doc steps next to the bed, his eyes appraising the external damage he can see. "I'll make a deal with you. You let me take a look at you, and we take it from there?"

My frightened eyes flit to Drummer. He raises my hand to his lips and kisses it. "Let Doc examine you, darlin'."

I shake my head. Drummer's the only man whose hands I want on me.

"Talk me through it then, tell me what he did to you." Doc's voice is matter-of-fact, particularly when he adds as though it's as insignificant as an enquiry about the weather, "Did he rape you?"

"No, he couldn't." But he was going to try.

Drum snorts. "He couldn't get it up?"

"Not after I kicked him, no."

"Good girl." Drummer breathes a sigh of satisfaction as Doc laughs loudly.

After swallowing a couple of times, I continue, "He kicked me, hard. There." I don't need to explain exactly where there is. "And he put his fingers…" They fill in the gaps for themselves. Drummer snarls and Doc throws him a warning look. "He kicked me in the ribs and whipped me."

"Prez, pull the sheet up to her waist, will you? And then lift up the shirt. I need to take a look, sweetheart."

As he's doing all he can to preserve my modesty, I let him. Gentle fingers, at odds with the size of the man, run over the bruising that's already starting to purple. He's so matter-of-fact that strangely I feel no embarrassment exposing my breasts. A sharp indrawn breath from Drummer, and a tightening of Doc's features before he opens his bag to get out some antiseptic wipes and cleans away the blood from the lashes of the whip. I hiss in air through my teeth; he pauses for a moment, and at my nod carries on.

He continues cataloguing my injuries, studying me carefully, feeling down my arms, pausing at the red ring left by the shackle. After a few moments he straightens.

"I don't think anything is broken, and the cuts don't need stitches. You'll be sore for a while. Any bleeding down below?"

"I don't think so."

"Hmm, again, you'll feel bruised and sore for a while, but if there's no blood, I doubt any serious damage has been done. I won't ask to examine you, sweetheart. I think you've been through too much for that."

I attempt a small smile to thank him.

"I'll leave you some painkillers. Your probably dehydrated, so drink lots of water. And if you can manage it, have something to eat. Then sleep and rest. Prez, I can leave that to you?"

"Yeah," Drum confirms, his voice catching. "I'll make fuckin' sure she's well looked after." As Doc packs up his bag, he adds, "Any more news about the prospect?"

"I'm just gonna check on him now."

Drum nods. "I'll come out with you and check." His hand touches my chin. "Sam, I don't wanna leave you, but there're things I need to be doing. I'll send someone in to sit with you, okay? Viper will want to see you if you're up for that?"

It's understandable he can't stay glued to my side, he's the president after all. Much as I want him to stay close, I know I need to be strong and let him go. Drummer bends over and places a kiss on my forehead, then gets up from the bed, and after a sorrowful look which screams his reluctance to go, he starts to follow Doc out as he opens the door.

As soon as it's cracked Viper tries to push his way in.

"I want to see my daughter," he demands. His face is set.

Drum looks over to me, raising his eyebrow. When I nod, he stands aside and lets my father come in.

"We'll need you at the storage unit," his prez tells him firmly. Whatever's going on, it seems Viper needs to be part of it.

Viper gives a sharp nod. "Don't fuckin' start until I get there, Prez. I want to make sure that motherfucking bastard can't ever hurt a woman again."

Drum slaps him on the back and then leaves us alone. Viper stands by the door, his back leaning against it, staring at me as if trying to convince himself I'm here in the flesh. His eyes open wide as, for the first time, he can properly see the bruising discolouring my face and the marks from the whip on my arms. As though a switch is thrown, he moves quickly, crossing over to the bed. When he comes closer, I see his eyes are bloodshot and rimmed with red, and that they're beginning to water. It's then I understand he's not only here to give comfort to me. Reaching out my hand, he looks at it, takes it, and clasps it in his, squeezing it so tightly it's borderline painful.

"I'm alright, Viper," I try to reassure him, knowing if he breaks down it will start me off again too.

"I thought I'd lost you," he stammers, his voice breaking. "Sam, when the fuckin' signal was jammed, I thought I'd never find you again."

"I'm here, Viper. I'm sore but safe. You and Drummer saved me."

His eyes narrow. "That fucker, he'll get what's coming to him for what he did to you. I promise you that."

I turn my head away, not wanting to know about their retribution. All I need to know is that Kurt will never be able to hurt me again. I wish I could wipe everything that had happened from my brain, wondering if I'll ever be the same person again.

We sit, holding hands, neither quite sure what to say. Viper doesn't ask me to relive my ordeal, and I'm grateful for that. I don't know him well enough to make small talk, well, thinking about it, all I know about him is his preference for blow jobs and I'm certainly not going to get into a conversation on that subject. But it's comforting having him close. I'd rather not be left alone with my thoughts right now.

We're not given long before there's a knock at the door, and a cautious head peers around. "Can we come in? I've got food."

"Sophie! Yes, come in." I sit up, pulling the sheet up over me, wincing as I do so. She's carrying a tray, and Sandy and Carmen are following her, the former carrying a bottle of water in one hand and a cup of something in the other. A welcome waft of coffee comes over to me.

Another squeeze of my hand. "I think, sweetheart, that's my cue to go." Viper stands, appearing more pulled together than he had when he came in. I nod to show he's leaving me in safe hands. "I'll see you later, darlin'."

Sophie stands aside to give Viper room to get out, then she smiles at me. "I was going to make you a cup of char, but Sandy said you'd prefer coffee."

I cock my head to one side.

"Tea. *Hot* tea," Sandy interprets and clarifies with a shudder.

"What?" Sophie questions her. "It's a great cure-all. Just because you heathens like it iced."

"Soph, it's over a hundred degrees out there!" As Sandy passes me the steaming cup of coffee they laugh, and even my face twitches with the beginnings of a smile.

I pull myself up in the bed and wince again as my sore body rebels. None of the women miss it. Sandy's eyes narrow. "What did he do to you, hon?" She points at the blood drying on the t-shirt I'm wearing. For some reason, it's easier to tell them than it was cataloguing my injuries to Doc and Drum. When I finish, they all look at me with similar expressions of sympathy, and it's Sophie who rests her hand on my arm.

"He actually kicked you in the fanny?"

I shake my head to correct her. "No, not my ass. My... you know..."

Sandy barks a laugh. "She means your pussy, Sam. She speaks a different language. But don't worry, I'll interpret for you."

This time a giggle escapes me. And just like that, I know I'm on my way back.

CHAPTER THIRTY

*D*rummer…

If it wasn't for two things, my duty to my club and the desire to seek revenge on her behalf, nothing could have dragged me away from Sam. I'd wanted to stay there with my arms around her as if only by physically touching her, I could reassure myself she was really here. *She's going to be fine*, I tell myself. Sam hadn't been destroyed. She's been knocked down. Hard. But now she's picking herself up. Fuck, she's one courageous woman.

My mind a little more at ease, I continue on my way, ready to deal not only with the fucker who thought he was man enough to own her, but also with the shit Devil's bringing my way. Walking into the clubroom I'm only just in time, as a rumble of bikes arriving warns me all hell's going to break loose in just a few minutes.

Seeing Crystal and Marsh behind the bar, I quickly summon them over, turning first to Heart's old lady. "Need you to get the lazy sweet butts out of their beds and do me a favour." I jerk my head toward the front of the clubhouse. "Pretty soon we're gonna have a dozen women who need clothing and shit, and somewhere to hole up for a while." As her eyes crease, I see her brain kicking into gear.

Joker and Lady were sitting at one of the tables, and as they hear my words they come over.

"What do you need us to do, Prez?" Now that's what I like. The boys from Vegas are steadily going up in my estimation. I jerk my chin toward the prospect. "Marsh will show you where we keep the spare cots. Can you take them up to the guest accommodations? Crystal will show you where I mean." As the rooms we keep spare for visiting club officers are located near the sweet butts' residence, she can kill two birds with one stone while she's there. "Crys, can you get the girls ready to settle the women in, pull together some decent shit they can use? I'll get Doc to come up when they're ready. Some of them may have need of his services."

"On it, Prez." Joker nods to Lady and Crystal, who dip their heads in agreement. Marsh is already by the door waiting to get started.

Having this old vacation resort as our compound pays dividends, as we've got room to spare. The work we've done recently to fix up more of the burned-out units means we're able to house what we've got coming in. It won't be luxurious, but far better than what the women had been expecting, and a welcome reprieve from the life of servitude they'd been headed toward.

That arranged, I go out front where my brothers are parking up, backing up neatly in line in front of the clubhouse. While his arm's covered in blood, Slick is at least dismounting his own ride. Peg is first off his bike. I wait for him to come to me, noticing he looks tired and drawn.

"Roadrunner?" It's just like him that his first thought is to enquire about our fallen brother.

I wave my hand in a so-so movement. "Lost a lot of blood. Doc's got him hooked up to an IV. He should be okay."

Devil parks up the truck and opens the back doors. There are three men inside, injured and groaning. I shout for Blade, Dollar, and Beef to take them to join Kurt. Now the transport carrying the women pulls up alongside, Dart driving.

"You got a doctor here?" Devil asks, his eyes flitting around.

I point to the vehicle he's just stepped out of. "Not for them, I suppose?"

"No, fuck it, leave them to suffer. They're not going to croak on us." He gives an evil grin as he adds, "Yet."

"I've arranged for him to look at the women once the girls have got them settled." I narrow my eyes. "What's all this about, Devil? We're not set up for this. Sure, we can give them shelter, but they need the services the feds' Human Trafficking Task Force can provide."

"I know, Drummer, I know." Devil's shaking his head. "Seems it's taking them time getting a team together. Hopefully they'll get their act together quickly and the women won't need to partake of your hospitality for too long."

My eyes are now slits. "I shouldn't be having to fuckin' house them at all. They've been through some shit, man. They need proper care. Haven't we done enough of the feds' dirty work for them?"

He shrugs. "I know nothing more than what I've told you."

"And them?" I point to the struggling men being led away up to the storage unit. "Surely, they should be in custody?"

Another shrug. "Drum, look at it this way. Surely, earning points from the feds must help your crew?"

He may have a point there. Seeing activity all around, men being taken one way, women another, brings me to focus on what needs to be done and put the whys of it to the back of my mind. For now.

Jill, one of the club whores, comes running through the door. "Hey, what the fuck you doing here? Thought I told Crystal to tell you you're helping her?"

She skids to a halt in front of me, a sullen look on her face. "I've been helping Doc with Road."

Strange. "And? How is he?"

Her face becomes more animated. "He's doing fine. Doc's just set up a new IV." I don't understand why she's acting so concerned. Hmm, there couldn't be anything between them, could there? It wouldn't be the first time a prospect's been grabbed by his cock. *Interesting.*

"Doc thinks he's gonna make a full recovery," she beams.

"Well thank fuck for that!" I'm genuinely pleased. My irritation with her slips away. "Look, we've got twelve traumatised women." I break off to point to where they're standing. "Help Crystal get them settled, will you? Then you can help Doc up there. And Jill, remember, these women have been through things you couldn't even dream of. I'm relying on you and the others to help them."

She pouts. "I'd prefer to stay and help with Road…"

I don't have to do anything more than glare at her.

She gives an exaggerated sigh. "Oh, okay, Drum. If that's where you want me." She walks off in a huff. Road and a sweet butt? Well fuck me, I'll have to warn him about that.

Having done everything I can to ensure the women are taken care off, it's time to get to business. "Church, now!" I shout at the top of my voice, then more quietly to the man at my side, "Devil, I want you there too."

He gives me that grin, the one his scar makes appear like a sneer and which does nothing to make him look friendlier.

"I'd like to come in, too." My attention snaps to a stranger standing by the door; I hadn't noticed him before. When the fuck did he arrive? I must be losing my game not to have noticed. He had to have snuck in during all the commotion.

I jerk my chin and raise my eyebrows, and get a bad fucking feeling even before he opens his mouth, my concern consolidated when he introduces himself. "Agent Haughton. FBI. Human Trafficking Task Force"

Now that gives me fucking pause. Invite a fed into our church? Well, at least he's playing for the team we need on board. Hopefully he's here to arrange to take the women. But a fed listening to the brothers? Having any outsider there is bad enough, but the fucking enemy? Pinching the bridge of my nose, I realise I don't have much option, and best not to antagonise him. As Devil had said, we're doing a favour for them which could prove advantageous to have in the bank. Giving a slow nod of my head, I cross over to greet him. When the FBI agent reaches out his hand, I act gentlemanly and shake it, then lead him into the room where we meet.

The brothers walk in. My VP to my left, my sergeant-at-arms to my right. Next to Wraith sits Dollar, our treasurer, Blade, our enforcer sits next to Peg. The rest of the brothers take their normal places. Our secretary, Heart, pulls some paper toward him and takes out a pen. Mouse, the last to arrive, plants his laptop on the table. They're all talking loudly, the group who'd rescued Sam catching up with the rest who'd been with Devil. With a dozen different conversations going on, fuck knows what they might let slip, so I put a stop to that shit.

"Shut the fuck up!" I rap on the table with the gavel. "We all want a fuckin' update. Marsh?" I call to our prospect who's hovering by the door, not sure if I need him or not. "Grab a couple of extra chairs, will you? And then fuckin' make yourself scarce."

"Could do with a beer, Prez."

"Good call, VP. And Marsh, see to that as well." I suspect we're all feeling dry.

"Perhaps I can start?" Devil cuts in, his cultured English accent sounding alien in the room.

I wait until the newcomers have seats, and then hold up my hand. "In a minute, Devil, but first, brothers, I'd like you to meet Agent Haughton, FBI. He's from the Human Trafficking Task-force." If I've placed emphasis on the word FBI, it's entirely intentional. Hard looks are thrown at him, and quizzical ones toward me. But I'm satisfied they've got the message—to zip up their mouths or be fucking careful what they say.

"Right, Devil, the table's yours."

Devil glances around. "Okay, this might be going over some things you are already aware of, but as you, Drum, were on another mission, let's get everyone up to speed." He pauses and waits for nods of acquiescence from around the room. "Right, as you know, we expected the transport to stop this side of the border so the merchandise could be inspected, and that's exactly what happened. The man, Louis, Louis Cardell as we've since found out, met up with the truck, and four others joined him. A Vincent Carter, a John Bowell, a Mitch Maclaine, and one other. The plan had been to split up the women and take them in small groups.

"Your men didn't wear cuts." He nods toward Peg, and I offer a chin jerk to the sergeant-at-arms to thank him for remembering to get the brothers to remove them. "There shouldn't be anything to link the raid back to you. With the help of your men, just as we planned, we were able to surround the leaders of the ring who, as we expected, turned up to inspect their merchandise. John Boswell was killed, as were the four men who'd been with the transport, and there was one casualty on your side, as you know." His face falls as he sends a look of apology toward Slick, who's sporting a bandage on his arm.

"It's nothing," Slick assures him.

"One got away." I'd analysed what he'd been saying and hitched onto the man with no name.

"Yes."

"But we've taken three of them out of action."

The agent jerks his head. "They're enjoying your hospitality at the moment, and we're grateful to you for that. We wanted somewhere out of the way where we could talk to them."

He might be showing his appreciation, but I've still got a bad fuckin' feeling about this. I glare at him. "Because you've got a leak in your own pond."

"Look, Drummer, as far as the gang knows, it was an MC who wanted to cash in on their stock. By using your men, they don't know the feds are on to them. That means we can watch and wait, keep an eye on who's getting twitchy on our end." He starts mumbling something else, but I stop listening.

The words he's just spoken rearrange themselves in my head and I come up with a whole different meaning. *It was an MC.* But not just any MC. It was us. And what's the betting they've set us up, so we get the blame? And any blowback. My men might not have identified themselves, but that won't make a difference. I start to suspect we've been dropped in it, and now war is approaching our door. Wraith's cottoned on, Peg too. Mouse is busy looking up the names we've been given.

"We weren't wearing cuts," Peg speaks softly.

Rage rises inside me. "Won't make no fuckin' difference. They'll know, won't they Agent Haughton?" To his credit, the agent returns my steely stare, it matches the one I use that normally no one stands up to.

After a second, he gives the rest of it up. "It's been reported in our organisation."

"And your mole will take it straight to the slavery ring."

He shrugs. "We're setting a trap."

"They'll be coming for us." Beef thumps his meaty hand on the table.

"And we'll be ready," Devil says firmly.

"Fuckin' Christ, I thought we were done with this." Viper's been through too much already. His hand, none too steady, reaches for his beer.

Dart lights a smoke, and without having to be asked, he slides the pack across to Blade. As twin plumes rise, I push down the urge to reach out and take one too. Heart's looking crushed; he's got his young daughter as well as his woman to think about. Rock's spinning his gun. Young Shooter's gone white, obviously remembering all too well the last time trouble came so close.

"How many, and who are we dealing with?" Joker takes the words out of my mouth.

But first I want to know something else. "Any cartel involvement?" That would be bad.

"No, the cartel gets involved when the goods are south of the border. They'll be pissed at the gang but shouldn't come after you."

I raise my eyebrow at the agent. "But you can't be certain of that."

He shakes his head. At least that's an honest answer. Perhaps the first he's given.

"Thing is, Drummer, we need to get info out of the ringleaders we brought back."

Suddenly my hand thumps down on the table. "Why the fuck did you let one escape?"

Peg growls beside me. "I had a bead on him, too. Devil knocked my aim off."

I stand, my chair crashing to the ground behind me. Leaning with my hands on the table I spit out, "How dare you paint a fuckin' target on this club!"

"Bait," Agent Haughton admits. "We want to catch our mole."

Bait! Fucking brilliant!

In a tone that suggests he's used to getting his way, Devil speaks up. "We've got four men to interrogate." I notice he adds no explanation for his part in letting one escape.

"Be my fuckin' guest." My eyes flick toward the FBI agent; with him around we're not getting involved.

Agent Haughton shrugs. "I don't care how you do it, Drummer. But it's on you to make those men talk. It's your club at risk if you don't get the intel."

"You bastard!"

I'm not the only one on my feet. But the FBI agent must have nerves of steel; he stays put, just raises his eyebrow in question.

I can see he hasn't left us with any choice. The information will be leaked, and the trafficking ring will know the Satan's Devils took their precious cargo despite the precautions Peg took. They'll be coming for us, to get them back. Haughton's right, *we* need to learn as much as we fucking can. I point my finger at Mouse. "Anything?"

"I'm digging deep. Might take me a while."

Tunnelling my fingers through my hair, I swear under my breath. We've got women and a child here, and now it's up to me to keep them as well as my brothers safe.

I let my breath out with a sigh. "Blade, Peg. Go see what you can get out of the fuckers. Tongue, Viper, you go with them." Noticing Shooter's put up his hand, I give him a nod. "Yeah, you too, Shooter." Our newest and youngest member; I'm warmed he wants to be involved, before we patched him in I had my doubts he'd make the grade. Dart puts his hand up too, quickly followed by Rock. I jerk my chin at them all. Glad to see they're wasting no time getting to their feet.

"Ok, Joker and Beef, go see how Crystal's doing with the women. Oh, and one last thing. I never fuckin' want to hear them referred to as merchandise or stock. Ever a-fuckin'-gain." I glare pointedly at the FBI agent.

Dollar and Bullet follow the others out, which leaves me alone with Devil and Haughton. "You gonna be in on this?" After, as expected, they confirm they are I rub my temples with the heels of my hand, wondering what blowback we can expect from the feds. We're letting them see our interrogation methods, which sure wouldn't get approval under the Geneva Convention.

But what else can I do? "I'll take you up in a couple of minutes." I want to check in on Sam first. "Wait for me at the bar." I walk out of the room, wondering how this fuckup of a day can get much worse. Immediately it is obvious it can. As soon as I get outside, even though it's dark now, in the light from the clubhouse I see Sam, Sandy's arm around her, walking out.

"Hey! What the fuck you doing?"

Sam's eyes stare into mine, her features fixed. She's now wearing a clean t-shirt and a pair of shorts, purple-black bruises adorning her legs. "I'm going to see the women that were brought in. Crystal needs some help, and I know some of what's happened to them. They won't trust the men, or not without reassurance."

"You should be resting up."

She sighs, comes over, and puts her hands on my cut. "Drum, I'm sore, but that's all. And I won't be able to rest if I don't do all I can for them. Jeez, Drum. What they've been through?" She shakes her head.

Rolling back my head, I close my eyes and take a deep breath. A president's woman has got to have strength, and Sam's showing she's about as strong as any woman I've ever known. It's what I'd do if I was in her place. Looking back down at her, I softly caress her hair, grateful when she leans into my touch. "Just don't overdo it, okay? I'll be there as soon as I can."

She smiles. "You go and do your prez things, and I'll see you later."

I stay where I am, watching her limp stiffly away. Fuck, she's going to be the death of me. Then, seeing Devil and Haughton waiting, I go out back where I find Doc finishing up with his rather impatient patient.

"I'd rather he go to a hospital."

Roadrunner's face twists with pain but is set in a glare. "I don't need to go. You said nothing vital was hit."

"I said I didn't think the bullet went near anything vital," Doc corrects him.

"I trust you, Doc."

Doc's face doesn't seem to reciprocate the faith the young prospect has in him. "I don't want you to move. You stay put until that IV runs out. If you don't, I'll have an ambulance here faster than you can fuckin' blink."

I add my bit, "And if you want to patch in, Road, you do exactly what Doc's telling you to do. Understood?"

As Doc and I both direct our best glowers toward the prone

man, he seems to shrink back on the bed. After a moment he gives a slight nod. "I hear you, Prez."

With a shake of his head, Doc turns to me. "I'll go see to the women, then come back and check on this one."

Returning to the clubroom, I signal to Devil and Haughton, then lead them out back to the innocently named storage area. A place we don't often use for anything but keeping random stuff, and a location which comes into its own when needed, sufficiently out of the way so we don't need to be quiet.

Kurt's already strung up, stripped naked. His cock he was hoping to use to deflower an unwilling virgin, swinging limp and flaccid. His eyes are wildly flicking left and right. So far, apart for the rough treatment dragging him in, no one's laid a hand on him. They'd been waiting for me. Throwing him a look of disdain and having to keep my hands curled by my thighs, I take Devil and Haughton off to one side and then lean back against a workbench, leaving them to make themselves comfortable as they see fit. I incline my head toward Blade.

Kurt starts spluttering before the enforcer's taken his first step toward him. "I have money!"

Yeah, tell us something we don't know. We know what he paid for Sam, and we've seen his house.

"You can have the woman."

We've already got her.

"Look, you're making a mistake. I'm a businessman. I'm well respected. The police will come looking for me. You don't want any trouble. Let me go and I'll keep quiet."

He wanted to hurt Sam, to break her, but is shit-scared of pain for himself. Blade looks toward me; I give the nod, working to quell the rage burning inside me. He picks up a baseball bat we leave here and smashes it against one of Kurt's legs. There's an animalistic scream that seems to hang in the air. Stoically hiding my wince, I force myself to look steadily on, as it's clear with the one strike Blade's broken a bone. Now there's pressure on Kurt's shoulders as he tries to balance on just the one leg. After his initial bellow of agony, he's whimpering like a baby.

Now that Blade's softened him up, I push off my perch. "How did you hear about Sam? Tell us everything about the gang you were dealing with. Who were your fuckin' contacts? You tell it all and we let you live. Blade, here, will be giving you some encouragement if you stop fuckin' talking unless it's to take a breath."

The pain's already making him shake, but the tone of my voice makes it worse. He knows I'm fucking serious.

Blade's taken out his knife, lovingly sliding his fingers over it. It's his weapon of choice.

"They'll kill me," Kurt rasps.

Another nod toward Blade, a slash across his stomach. Not too deep, but enough to sting. Seeing his own blood dripping down his legs is all it takes.

When at last Kurt stops spewing every detail he knows, I glance across to Haughton, who gives me a nod. We've learned a lot about how the buyers are fixed up with their women, and the one name that he knows of the person who was the scout for Sam. He doesn't know much, has only dealt with Louis, but some of the background should help.

"May I?" The agent steps forward, I grant my permission with a nod. "Who got you into this?"

As he speaks in a calm voice, it's clear Kurt hadn't noticed the agent, wearing his jacket identifying who he is, was present. A whole new level of fear comes into his eyes. Once again, I lean back against the workbench. *This will be interesting.*

Haughton continues, "How did you learn about the ring?"

Kurt's in pain already, but now a stream of urine runs down his legs. Catching Devil's eye, I slowly dip my head. Kurt knows something.

The agent indicates Blade. "Shall I let him loose on you again? Pull out your teeth?" He sneers. "After what you tried to do to their president's woman, I reckon you might be saying goodbye to your cock."

I raise my eyebrows. It seems the agent is relishing being able to call on our interrogation methods that wouldn't be allowed in his organisation. *He's enjoying this.*

Kurt starts to cry. "You can't let them do that. You're a fed."

A disinterested shrug. "I'll just turn my back."

There's a moment of silence, then Kurt speaks again, he sounds defeated. "If I tell you... I'm dead."

Another shrug. "And if you don't, you're not very far away from that. Doubt it will take long to bleed out once they cut off your dick."

Tears streaming down his face, mingling with the blood and urine on the floor, Kurt's chin drops to his chest. Haughton nods at Blade, who once again removes his knife from his sheath and steps forward, his hand aiming toward the flaccid cock that seems to have shrivelled up even further.

Kurt's eyes follow the blade until it's almost made contact, and at the last minute gives it up as he rasps out the name of a prominent senator.

The agent's eyes open wide as he queries he's heard correctly.

"Yes," Kurt agrees, his mouth twisted in pain.

Haughton's beaming as he slaps me on the back. He looks like he's won the fucking lottery.

"Got what you wanted?"

When he clarifies that indeed he has, and it's over to me again now, I jerk my chin at my men. "Gag him," I instruct.

As Blade and Wraith move forward, Kurt realises his suffering isn't going to come to an end, and he screeches out. "Get me down, you can't leave me up here!" Then his begging stops. He can't say anything at all with a rag stuffed in his mouth. We've three more to interrogate, and the sight of him strung up, his stomach bleeding, his left leg useless, will help loosen them up.

My first officer position in the club was as enforcer, so I know exactly how Blade is feeling, though his face will give nothing away. He's treating the men he's questioning as though they're nothing more than a side of meat he has to cut up. His knowledge of anatomy means he can make it hurt, but not do enough damage to kill—unless I give the signal of course. Afterwards, he'll get drunk and fuck whores, berating the loss of one more piece of his soul. But the job needs to be done. And we've just proved our methods of questioning are a lot more successful than those of the feds.

One by one we grill them. Haughton's making notes in a book, Devil's jotting them on his phone. Names, locations, pickup and drop-off points, and their contacts in the cartel. Now we have some idea of the size of the organisation we're facing and where the rot stems from.

When we come to the end, I raise an eyebrow toward the agent. If I had my way, I'd end this now, finally and for good. Leaving these men breathing, wasting money on a trial when they're , guilty as hell of ruining the lives of hundreds of women seems a waste of time, space, and air to me.

Haughton's conscience may have allowed us to interrogate them, but he baulks at my final solution. At last, he calls for some transportation to take them away, and asks for a doctor to be ready as they'd apparently been in a fight. Yeah, with the losing end of Blade's knife and baseball bat.

CHAPTER THIRTY-ONE

*S*am...

The compound rests in the foothills of the Coronado Forest and rises toward the back where the women have been housed. Seeing me struggling, Sandy puts her arm around me to help me up the slight incline. As we approach the houses, the sound of weeping reaches me.

Pushing in through the door, I find, at least for now, all the women have decided to stick together in one of the buildings instead of spreading out to the second available unit next door. Their time together causing a bond to form between them. I can relate to that, as my eyes meet those of the one woman who'd not been too broken to speak to me in the transport. I'm not surprised to see it's her, Monica, who's comforting the rest.

Crystal had called on the other old ladies to help. Carmen and Sophie are already here. Sandy, having stayed to help me dress and then lend me her arm on the way up, is meeting the abused women for the first time, and I see by the worried glance she throws toward me that it's only now she's realising just what they, and I, have been through. Some are sobbing, possibly with relief that they're free, some are simply staring into space. There's a low murmur of conversation, and in snatches I catch mostly disbelief in their rescue, tinged with concern and suspicion about the bikers who saved them.

The old ladies have been busy. Already they've got coffee brewing, the welcome scent pervading the air, and food on the go. Doc's beaten me here too, but like Joker and Beef, the three men stand in a corner, the women shying away from them, their ordeal making them fearful of anyone of the opposite sex.

Some of the women had been with their captors for weeks. I, only a few hours, but that was enough for me to have some insight into how they're feeling. I give Doc a nod, then pick on the person I think might be the bravest. Going over to Monica, I touch her arm. "Doc, the man without a cut over there, he wants to examine all of you. See if you need treatment. If you go with him, the others might follow."

She grabs my hand, with her other she touches the bruises on my face as if confirming I was indeed one of them too. "Do you trust him?" Her voice is tentative; she too is wary of any male.

"I do," I say, confidently, with no doubt in my voice, able to vouch for him due to the sympathetic way he'd treated me. "He's a good man. He knows what he's doing. He's not like the men who stole you." That I show no misgivings about the medic's skills and can confirm he's got no ulterior motive seems to calm her.

Her eyes search my face. "Will you come with me?"

"Of course, I will." I squeeze her fingers in mine and lead her across to where Doc's waiting by an open bedroom door. Joker and Beef step back, giving her a wide berth. Nodding to them, I give an inward smile. They're doing everything they can to appear non-threatening, but it's an uphill struggle. Tall, muscular, rugged-looking bikers wearing cuts have their work cut out to appear non-threatening.

Doc's examination is quick and non-invasive, instead asking her about any concerns. Like me, she's got bruises and scrapes and admits to being raped. It's then he leaves us for a moment and goes outside to make a call.

When he returns, it's to tell us, "I've spoken to a friend of mine, she works at a women's clinic. She's gonna come up with some rape kits and tests for STDs. If we do this the right way, we can get evidence to put the bastards who did this to you away." His kind eyes find Monica's.

Monica glances at me, and then back to Doc, a tentative nod is her only reply.

I stay while Doc examines the others, the awfulness of their ordeal lessening mine. At least I wasn't raped by multiple men, used and abused. In Doc's view, no one needs to go to hospital, though he confides they'll all need therapy to fully recover, if indeed they ever do. When the nurse arrives, she brings a female colleague to help. All the women want me there to support them, and again, I'm happy to help.

By the time Drum, Devil, and another man appear, we're well into the early hours of the morning and I'm overcome with tiredness. Doc fills them in; the stranger seems pleased with the steps that have been taken.

He then steps forward, introducing himself as Agent Haughton. He addresses the women, letting them know the services that the Human Trafficking Task Force will be able to offer. I'm interested in learning this includes providing them with shelter, food, and clothing if they require it, and the counselling which they most definitely need. But the best bit of news that helped cheer us all up is that the four men who'd been with the transport had all been killed, along with one of the leaders of the trafficking ring, and that they'd captured three of the others. Knowing the men who'd molested them can't ever hurt anyone else was the best news they could have heard.

"Should have cut off their fucking dicks," Monica grumbles, and her comment even brings forth a weak laugh from a couple of the other women.

When Haughton concludes his speech, Drum puts his arms around me, and I lean into his touch, barely able to support myself anymore. Pulling back slightly he examines my face. "Come, you're worn out. You've done enough, Sam."

I have to agree. We're already at the top of the compound so his house is quite close, just a little way away, secluded from the other buildings. Keeping one arm around me, he leads me over the sandy ground. Above us, the moon hangs in a star-laden sky, but I'm too tired to appreciate the sight. Reaching his front door, he opens it and leads me through the lounge area and straight into to the bedroom. He prods me over to the bed, where a gentle pressure on my shoulders has me sitting down.

Taking his hands away slowly, as though reluctant to break the contact between us, he maintains our connection with his eyes. "You hungry? Want anything to drink?"

The stress of the long day before and the tension of supporting the abducted women catches up with me now that the weight's off my feet, and there's a soft mattress underneath me. "No, I just need to sleep, Drum."

Slowly, non-threateningly, he folds to his knees, and his hands go to the button of my shorts. "Let's get you undressed then."

I welcome his assistance, suddenly overcome with weakness. As though I were a child, he undoes the zip and encourages me to lift my hips so he can remove them completely. He leaves my underwear on.

"Do you want to sleep in your shirt?"

For some reason I do. It's not that I believe he'll take advantage of me, but having been naked in front of Kurt, I need the illusion of protective armour now. But my bra will be uncomfortable, so I slide the straps down my arms and reach around to undo the clasp and pull it away without removing the t-shirt. Drum doesn't miss that I'm avoiding his more intimate touch. His eyes narrow, and his mouth thins, but I know the anger he's trying to rein in isn't directed at me.

He pulls back the sheet and I slip underneath. Then, after adjusting the air conditioning, he strips down to his boxers. As he slides in behind me, there's a moment of hesitation, and then he pulls me into his arms, spooning me. The warmth of his body behind me makes me feel safe, and I close my eyes.

The combined effect of the trauma of the day and the painkillers I've taken, mean sleep comes fast.

I'm back in that basement, tied to the wall. Kurt is standing over me whip in hand, telling me that he owns me. I scream to escape.

"Hush, you're here. With me. You're safe." A hand smooths my back, a gentle caress.

Without gaining full consciousness, the nightmare vanquished, I drift back to sleep.

The next time I awake, I'm alone. I stretch, wincing at the bruises and my sore muscles. Bright light streaming in through the gap in the curtains suggests I've slept well into the day, but it's done me good, and I'm feeling better, mentally and physically stronger. Just as I'm wondering where Drummer has gone, the door to the bedroom opens and he walks in with a tray laden with coffee and a delicious smelling breakfast that immediately makes my mouth water.

Gazing at the tray he's placed on my lap, I look up with a bemused grin. "You cook?"

He huffs and looks sheepish. "Can't take credit. Soph brought it up." He takes one of the overloaded plates for himself and leaves the other for me. Soon I'm tucking into the most scrumptious bacon and eggs I've ever tasted.

He looks on, his steel-grey eyes examining me. "How you feeling today?"

I try an experimental wriggle. "A lot better."

"Want more painkillers?"

No, I don't want more tablets, but… "I want you."

He runs his hands through his hair, then bringing them down, removes the tray and puts the empty plates and cups on the floor. "Sam, I don't want to hurt you."

"Drummer, you won't." My mouth forms a frown. "I need

you. I need this. I need to know I'm here with you, and that I'm safe. That I'm *alive*."

He inches closer, his weight making the mattress dip. Reaching out his hand, he smooths it down my cheek and I lean into his touch. Snaking out my tongue, I lick his palm, his taste a mingling of saltiness and soap. Risking a glance up to his face, I see his eyes darken. His free hand comes around, and his fingers tangle in my hair, then tighten as he pulls me toward him, his possessive action triggering a throbbing in my loins.

His mouth hovering above me, he waits for a second, analysing my reactions. Then he lowers his lips, a gentle brush across mine, completely at odds with the firmness of his hold on my head, a dominant action despite the tenderness of his touch.

Gradually he increases the pressure, his tongue seeking entry, and I let him inside. He starts making love to my mouth; there's no other word for it. So tenderly, his actions so tempered, I get lost in the feel, the taste of him sends tingles down my spine. It's a kiss from a lover.

Impatient for more, I reach up my hand, trying to increase the pressure. But he ceases all movement, lifting his head away enough to get out the words, "This is my show, Sam." His fingers caress my face, tracing the bruising.

"You won't hurt me."

"I could. You're injured, darlin'."

I need him so much, need him inside me, need him to erase the memories of the other men's hands. "I don't care."

"But I fuckin' do." His mouth works as if he wants to say something else, and then a little shake shows he's dismissed those exact words. "Sam, it killed me when you went missing." The twisting of his face shows just how much it must have pained him. A man who likes control over everything—his club, his men. His woman. *Is that what I am?*

Is his reluctance due to something else? That another man's touched me? I shiver for a different reason.

He doesn't miss it, loosening his hold on my hair. "What's

up, Sam?" His mouth turns down. "I knew this was too soon." I feel my eyes growing wet, a tear escapes, and he wipes it away. "Oh Sam, it's over now. I've got you. I've fuckin' got you."

But worrying his hesitancy might have a different cause, I have to ask, have to know. "Does it bother you, Drum? What you heard those men do. What Kurt did…"

He rears back, the cold steel of his eyes suddenly blazing with fire. "What the fuck you asking?"

I swallow. "You might not want me…"

"Because another man's had his fuckin' hands on you?" His fingers rake through his hair, brushing it away from his face, the action revealing the slight greying at his temples. "Christ, Sam. I want to touch you all over, kiss you everywhere. I want to take every fuckin' memory of those motherfuckers' hands on you away. They touched what was *mine*. Oh fuck, babe, is that what you really think? That I wouldn't want you now? You couldn't be more fuckin' wrong."

"But you were kissing me as if you didn't mean it. Like you didn't want to."

"Sam, Sam, Sam," he says, as he takes my hand and places a light kiss to each of the fingertips and then to my palm. "I fuck women, Christ, you know that. That first time with you…"

I shake my head. "Drum, you didn't know."

"Hush, let me finish, will you?" His fingers now cover my mouth. "I fuck. But for the first time in my life, I want to make love. And fuck me, I must be doing it all wrong if you think I don't want you. You're going to have to help me out here; I don't know what to do." His face twists in a self-deprecating grin. It makes him look boyish and younger.

Then his words filter into my brain. *He wants to make love to me?* I give a short laugh. "I don't have any experience in that area, either. It's only been you, Drum."

He chuckles. "Then let's play this by ear. We'll find our own way to do it, no need to try to copy someone else. You up for that?"

I nod, knowing I'm giving him back the control he desires, and settle back to enjoy the ride.

Again his mouth meets mine, and immediately I open my lips. Now understanding, I let our tongues slide together, mating gently, enjoying the unhurried pace which works to ramp up my desire. I writhe under him as my arousal grows, feeling his hard length pushing against my side. He kisses me until my senses are full of nothing but the scent of his soap tinged with leather and the touch of his mouth on mine. My eyes close as he takes me to new heights.

Gradually he pulls away, his lips slowly leaving mine, and I watch him as he takes the bottom of my t-shirt and begins to draw it up. I lift my body so he can remove it completely. As his eyes land on the scars already forming on the whip marks over my breasts, his face tightens, and gently, oh so gently, he traces each one with his fingers. When his eyes flit to mine, I give a dismissive shake. I don't want to discuss them. Not now. It's enough that while they upset him, he can ignore them.

He moves his mouth over my breasts. First one, then the other, teasing the already hard peaks of my nipples until they stand even more erect. His tongue circles each aureole until I'm bowing my back, silently asking for more pressure as shooting sparks fly down to my clit. I feel him smile against my skin, and then he's trailing kisses down, over my stomach, pausing to lick at my belly button, causing me to giggle and squirm.

"Mmm, ticklish, eh?"

There's no need to answer, as slowly, oh so slowly and teasingly, his mouth moves south. Now he's shuffling down the bed, rising to his knees, the loss of his body heat and the air conditioning causing goosebumps to rise on my skin. Gently his hands grasp the sides of my panties, and, with a wicked grin, he tests the material, then pulls hard, and I'm naked. I grin, knowing my man is still in there, despite the atypical gentleness he's showing.

He breathes on my clit, the warm huff such a sharp contrast

from the cool air that I rise off the bed. His hand pushes me back down.

"Tell me the truth, Sam. Are you sore? Bruised? I don't want to hurt you."

"A bit tender, but I'll be fine."

"I don't want you, fine, darlin', I want you writhing with pleasure."

Oh God, I want that too.

"Tell me if anything I do causes you pain."

As I nod my agreement, he, at last, puts his mouth there. Where I want it. Sucking my clit gently into his mouth, then moving his tongue down I feel him start lapping at my wetness, at my cream. He groans. "Fuck, you taste so fuckin' good, darlin'." The vibration of his voice makes my muscles tighten.

The sensations are driving me insane. I push up toward him, wanting more contact. Any residual pain completely obscured by the other wonders he's doing to my body. Writhing again, I moan gently. Taking pity on me, he pushes an experimental finger inside, watching me carefully for any sign of discomfort or unease. But I've missed him so much, wanted this, needed this, my cries of satisfaction spur him on. He adds another finger, curling around. When he feels my body tighten, he leans over again, taking my clit between his teeth and circling his tongue around.

It's been such a gentle journey, but now I've reached the end and am soaring over the top. My head thrown back, I suck in a deep breath then stop breathing, my muscles pulsating and contracting. The orgasm seems to go on forever. Perhaps not the strongest he's given me, but one still powerful enough to bring tears to my eyes. With a gasp, my lungs start heaving again.

Opening my eyes, I see him dispensing quickly with his boxers. Now he's pushing inside me, slowly, taking his time as he pushes through tissue swollen by my climax. He gains some ground and slides out again, my moisture slickening his way. He pushes back in, then out again gently, going slow, being so careful not to hurt me, his muscles strain with effort, the V-twin engine of his tattoo vibrating with each movement.

Briefly, I drink my fill of the offering in front of me, and then when my eyes have seen enough, I reach for him, pulling him down to me, and raising my legs, dig my heels in either side of his spine. Then he's as deep as he can go inside me, up against my cervix, a slight pressure that's more pleasure than pain.

Still keeping himself under tight control, he starts to thrust languidly, a long pull out, a deep push in. Over and over and over. Each time hitting that spot inside me, forcing cries of incomprehensible encouragement to fall from my lips. His measured onslaught and unhurried strokes allow me to feel everything, and when his cock swells, it hurtles me again to the edge. With a loud scream, I go over, and he increases his momentum. A few short pumps and he's coming inside me.

His roar of triumph announcing his completion, he collapses on top of me, then moves to his side. "Fuck, woman. Sam, fuck." He pulls me in close, holding me tight to him. "Christ that was so fuckin' good." Then he chuckles. "Was that making love, d'you reckon?"

I smile against his skin. "Whatever it was, it was fucking good."

"Yeah," he laughs. "I know how to give my woman a good fuckin'."

When our breathing returns to normal he pulls himself up on one elbow and looks down at my crotch, his hand gently smoothing across my mound. "Did I hurt you?"

Shaking my head, I touch my hand to his face. "No, Drum. You didn't."

"Hmm." For some reason his smile disappears, and his lips purse.

Have I done something wrong? "Drum?" I venture tentatively.

"Didn't use a fuckin' condom babe. Fuck, I lose my mind around you."

Tensing, I'm more worried about his reaction than mine.

Kids? A baby? Do I want that now? He's called me his woman, but that's just for now, isn't it? I can't fool myself, he's not a man who'd want someone permanent.

His hand now smoothing my brow, his expression one of concern. "I'm sorry, babe. This making love thing got me carried away. But we'll deal, okay?"

Deal. Yes. But that doesn't mean he wants me. "We don't need to deal, Drum. I can—"

"Babe, whatever you're thinking, just stop right now. You're my woman, right? My fuckin' ol' lady. You're *mine*." His intense eyes stare into my wide-open ones.

"Your... your ol' lady?"

"Guess I should have asked you first before branding you with my cum. But yeah, that's what I want, darlin'. Never gonna want another bitch again after you."

The words come easily. "I don't want another man."

He rolls me into him, kissing me gently before saying, "Guess that settles that, then."

CHAPTER THIRTY-TWO

*D*rummer...

Sam falls back into another exhausted sleep. The worry, stress, and fear of the last few days have taken their toll. And it's my job to heal her.

Rising, I leave the bed and just stand for a while, watching as her chest gently rises and falls, relishing the reality that she's here. Everything I said to her was true, even if I could never have predicted I'd be saying such things. Fuck, I hardly recognise the man I become when I'm with her. Maybe it would have taken longer if her abduction hadn't forced me to come to terms with my feelings, but even if she hadn't been taken away, compelling me to envisage a life without her in it, I would have come to this place eventually. She's mine. I don't want or need anyone else.

I haven't told her the words, but I love this woman.

And forgetting a condom? I've never done that before in my life, reaching for the protective latex an automatic action. But shit, it had felt so good to be skin to skin inside her. Although I hadn't realised what was making it so spectacular at the time, I'd only known the experience was unsurpassed. *We'd made love.* For the first time in my life, I knew I couldn't apply the term fucking to describe what had transpired between us.

Had I known on some unconscious level? Had I wanted to mark her and truly make her mine? *If I'd realised I'd gone without protection, would—could—I have stopped?*

I've got no answer for that. Shaking my head, it dawns on me that the possible implications hold no concern for me. If I'd forgotten with anyone else, I'd have been tearing my hair out with worry. I want Sam in my life. All of her. I want everything that has to offer.

I shower and dress, then, donning my cut, make my way to the clubhouse. My brothers had me covered in my absence, allowing me the one uninterrupted night with Sam that I needed before entering the fray again. But in order to keep *my woman* safe it's time to immerse myself in my role of president and take part in a council of war.

As I enter the clubroom, young Amy comes barrelling over, crashing into my legs, Crystal hot on her heels. She'd been aiming for Heart and I'd inadvertently gotten in the way. As her father steps forward, swinging her up in his arms, I get a tight feeling in my chest. Seeing the look of tenderness on my brother's face as he tickles his daughter, her response a peal of giggles, I recognise my unfamiliar reaction as envy. Never having given much, if any, thought to having a child before, the emotion slams into me, taking me by surprise. *Could I have put a baby in Sam's belly already?*

When I notice my contemplation has brought me to a halt, I make my feet move toward our meeting room where my brothers are ready and waiting for church. As last time, we have two extra seats filled by Devil and his cohort, Agent Haughton.

I toss them a glare and curse under my breath as I take my seat, annoyed at not having been asked to issue an invitation. Once again, we'll need to keep tight-lipped about normal club business. Banging the gavel loudly, I call everyone to order.

Once quiet has settled, I get the meeting started by asking for an update. "How are the women, Joker?"

He sighs. "About as well as can be, Prez. A couple want to go straight home. I spoke to the agent there," he breaks off to point his pen at Haughton, "and he said to persuade them to stay with the others until he can arrange transportation to take them. The task force can give them any assistance that they need."

I nod. "Yeah, they're better off together for now." My brow furrows, and I look Haughton's way. "But how long you talking about? You already called in your folks to collect the women? They're going to need specialist help."

"They should be out of your hair later this morning."

He's given me no reason to trust him, and his blank face suggests there's something I'm not cottoning onto here. On the face of it, it sounds reasonable, but while he's trying hard to temper his expression, the agent has got a shifty look in his eyes. He keeps looking away as if unable to meet mine.

Raising my brow, I turn toward Devil. The distortion of his scar makes him impossible to read. But from the intense stare he's giving me I become certain he knows something, or at the least, is putting two and two together. And that something is what I'll need to find out. I make a mental note to get him on his own after the meeting if whatever it is doesn't come out here first.

"Prez?" Beef draws my attention with his hand, and I nod for him to spit out whatever's on his mind. "Jill, Allie, and Pussy have been helping out with the women." I know that. I was the one who directed the sweet butts to assist while hoping they'd stay in the background as their chosen way of life might have bad connotations for the kidnapped women.

"And?" I snarl, fearing I'm going to be told they've upset them.

"Turns out a couple of the women are quite interested in staying with us. As sweet butts," he clarifies, in case I don't understand.

My eyebrows rise, I didn't see that coming.

"Fuck, yeah." Tongue bangs the table.

"Shut it, Tongue. Beef, what's that all a-fuckin'-bout?"

"I've had a chat with them. The girls in question worked a strip club before, one which allowed up-close-and-personal with the clients. They weren't as badly hurt as some of the others as they didn't fight back when those motherfuckers had their way with them. They've been talking to Allie, understand that we provide for them here, and from what they've seen of us, have an appetite for biker cock."

Rock leans back and makes a show of thrusting his hips. "Happy to show them mine."

"Rock!" I growl. He sits forward again.

Hmm, well, with getting extra members in and losing the sweet butt Chrissy, I'd be lying if I said we couldn't do with some extra whores.

"The ol' ladies would be outnumbered." Heart's frowning. "It's a good balance at the moment. After the trouble we had with Chrissy…" At my glare he stops talking. Agent Haughton doesn't need to know about any of that.

I know something he doesn't. An unusual smile spreads over my face. "That can be evened up. Sam's gonna be my ol' lady."

"Fuck me!" Wraith stares at me.

"I'd rather not," I reply in all seriousness.

"Huh! Not that I didn't see it coming, but I thought it would take you longer to put your patch on her!" A smile spreads over my VP's face.

Dart reaches for his smokes. "Congratulations, Prez." His words are echoed around the table. One bit of much-needed good news for once. "This calls for a fuckin' party!"

Yeah, like we don't have enough parties around here, but there's not going to be any partying until we've got out from underneath the slave traffickers' threat.

I'm staring at the one brother who's said nothing as yet, and my leg bounces under the table. While I want to know what he thinks, nothing he can say will alter my mind. I just need to be forewarned if I'm likely to get his fist coming my way again.

Viper's staring at me, his face blank and unreadable, then it splits into a wide grin as he slaps his hand onto the table. "Fuck, yeah. Good on you, Prez. That's mean's she's sticking around! Fuck yeah. Fuckin' ace." Well, it seems I've got his parental approval.

"Wench staying on as a mechanic? She's a fuckin' good one."

"Doubt if I'd be able to stop her, Blade." I bark a laugh at the thought. "And her name's Sam. Wrench if you must."

"Fuck, Prez, she's got you wrapped around her little finger already."

I glare at Slick until he can no longer meet my gaze. He's probably right, but I'm not letting him get away with that.

I get back to the original proposal. "Beef, tell the girls if they want to swell the ranks of our sweet butts we'll consider it. If they've got nowhere else to go and want to hang around for a bit, then we'll give them a try. You know what you gotta do, Mouse?"

Mouse's eyes flick toward the fed, and then he jerks his chin toward me. He knows I'm asking him to do a full and illegal investigation into their backgrounds. Whores get to know too many of our secrets, and we need to be able to trust them. If they betray us, the result isn't pretty. The body of Chrissy, rotting up in the woods, can testify to that.

"Right." My gaze settles on the agent. "Now, down to business. What are we up against?"

There's a slight look of disappointment on his face, as though he was hoping we'd let slip any tasty morsels. He clears his throat and looks down at his phone. "Your boys got us some good info from their work on the prisoners, Drummer, and I've had our team look into what they gave us. This was an organised ring, we got three of the five men at the top, one escaped, as you know, and one was killed when you took out the transport.

There are normally five teams. Each goes out with four men. We got this lot in custody. We can assume that leaves another sixteen bodies they can call on."

That's not bad odds; we'd be about matched in numbers.

"What about the senator?"

He stares at me steadily. "Not your business, Drummer. You can leave that with us."

I thought that would be the case, but I'll be interested in watching how that plays out. Fucking politicians can get away with anything, and I wouldn't be surprised to learn, sometime in the future, that he'd retired due to ill-health. But how it's resolved is fed business and won't affect the club. That's what's important.

I frown. "You've dropped us in it, Haughton. I know you want to use us round up the rest of the ring. Is there anything else we should consider?" I'm still convinced he's playing his cards close to his chest.

Once more he looks away as I catch his eye. "Of course, there are some rich pricks who they buy for. It's possible they'll be able to call on more support. And again, there's the cartel."

"They wouldn't come north of the border, would they?" Peg's tapping his fingers against his mouth. "Would it be worth it?"

"Got some nice stock, er, sorry, Drummer, women that they've lost. A lot of money's been spent getting them this far, and the cartel's left with having arranged an auction that's now without any goods, er, women."

Okay, so now that we know what we're talking about, we have to prepare for an army. "Agent Haughton? You're arranging the FBI support?"

He shifts uncomfortably. "I'm returning to the office after this meeting. We'll see what we can do." His vague non-commitment can be easily translated. He's got most of the ringleaders and the name of the man at the top. It's not his concern if the foot soldiers come to pick us off. When he stares straight at me for his next statement, I know that's the truth. "I'll check if the transportation is on its way for the women."

My suspicions are fast coming home to roost, and just like that, it all falls into place. Suddenly my desire to get the women off the compound does an abrupt one hundred and eighty degree turn. I need as many bargaining chips as I can get. "Been reconsidering that, Agent. If what's left of the slavery ring, and possibly even the cartel, are determined to take them back, it's safest not to move the women. We can best protect them here." I lean back in my chair, balancing on two legs for a moment. "Take them off site, and you could be followed. We can lock the compound up tighter than a gnat's ass."

"I've arranged—"

Now I sit forward, my chair slamming back down to the ground. Pointing my finger toward him, I snarl, "I don't give a fuck what you've arranged. If you're not staying to help, you can unarrange it. The women stay here. Under our protection. Until this is ended. You leave? You go alone."

The agent's eyes flit toward Devil. "That wasn't what we agreed."

Devil shrugs. "Drummer's got a point. Take them out, and you could be ambushed. Best way is to provide support to the Satan's Devils and help them beat whatever's coming their way."

Haughton sneers, and his hand pounds down on the table. "You're suggesting the FBI provide men to defend a motorcycle compound?" At last, some honesty from the agent. They're not going to help us at all.

Another dismissive gesture from the scarred man. "Why the fuck not?"

As Haughton stares back at him and doesn't say another word it all falls into place.

"I think your time with us is over, Agent Haughton. If we're on our own, we'll make our own plans." Jerking my chin toward the door, I emphasise my desire for him to leave.

Peg gets to his feet, his huge frame intimidating. "I'll show you the way out." It's not an offer.

The agent turns to Devil, who looks at me instead. "You stay," I instruct. I want to know exactly what he's been hiding.

As Peg escorts Agent Haughton from church, I look around the table. "Anyone got any objections to Devil being in on our planning?" We might not know the man, but we got to know his colleagues from Grade A at that bizarre wedding we'd attended.

"Grade A's fine in my book." My VP gives his opinion, nodding at the Englishman.

Devil's been listening intently. One side of his mouth turns down; it now matches the other, and he holds up his hands in supplication. "Drummer, you have my apology. I might have had some inkling as things didn't add up, but I didn't know this is what he intended."

"Can't trust the fuckin' feds." I should have known that from the start. I shake my head, furious at my stupidity.

Seeing my anger, Shooter's looking puzzled, his expression mirrored by Lady. I jerk my chin as permission Shooter can speak. "Prez, what's going on?"

But it's Devil who answers, "Feds want to get the women out of here, and then let the slave traders take out the club. I expect they want you to kill each other. Get rid of two birds with one stone—a human trafficking ring and an outlaw MC. Shit, I didn't see this coming, I'm sorry, Drum."

Wraith's fingers are drumming on the table. "We've got this." His eyes take in his brothers sitting around the table, and nods at me. "We don't need the fuckin' feds. I'll call Red. He'll send us some help."

"And I'll speak to Snake; he owes us a favour." Getting members from the Las Vegas and San Diego chapters would help. "Anything Grade A can offer?" I incline my head toward Devil.

"Sorry, Drum, I, er, I'm working on my own at the moment, as an independent contractor to the feds. Well," his mouth twists again, and I interpret it as a grin, "until I resigned about, oh, two minutes ago. Bloody bunch of pansies." He grows serious again. "I'll be putting a team together soon that I'll be able to call on, but for now I'm on my own. But I'm here to help you." He nods sharply to confirm he's on board.

"Thanks, Devil."

"Right. Ah, Peg. You've seen our guest safely off the premises?"

As Peg retakes his seat, he nods in my direction. "Indeed I have. Checked who was out there too. Marsh is at the gate. In light of what's gonna go down, I want one of the fully patched members there at all times." He's right to get straight on to that. If trouble's coming our way, we'll need early warning. And a first line of defence.

"I'll take first watch."

"Your arm good enough, Slick?"

"Yeah, Doc patched me up. I'm good."

"Okay, we'll work up a rotation." I tap my fingers as I mentally go through what we need to do. "Guns. Get them back out of stock."

Rock puts up his hand and nudges Beef. "We'll get on that." The allusion to our armoury causes a round of laughter. It's a source of amusement that although the ATF agents might have said they weren't searching, we'd hidden what we didn't want them to stumble across. Extremely well. When the compound was a resort, it had three swimming pools, one of which has been filled in. The other just looks like it has. Underneath is our bunker, useful for all manner of things.

"What armament have you got?"

If he's going to be fighting beside us, I've no problem with filling Devil in. We spend the next few minutes going over our weapon and ammunition status. We're in a healthy position.

"Drum, I don't want to be telling you your job, but are you considering an offensive as well as your defence?"

"What you suggesting, Devil?"

He puts his ideas forward, and I like them a lot. I like them so much, I actually smile.

"Right, fuckers! You all know what to do. Church fuckin' over!"

Following my brothers out, I detour to the back room where Roadrunner's staying, finding Jill must have snuck back down to be with him. He's sitting up drinking some kind of soup. From the expression on his face the sweet butt has probably made it herself, and exemplifies they're not employed for their culinary skills. But he's manfully spooning it down, a grimace for me, and a smile and a *thank you* for her. I wonder whether we'll have another vacancy in the sweet butt rank soon, though it is unusual for one to become an old lady. But Road's a new prospect; I'll have Wraith take him aside. Perhaps give him shit for monopolising one of the whores. The thought amuses me, but I'll be kind. I'll wait until he's healed.

"How you doing today, Road?"

"I've had worse coming off my bike." Recalling he rides in trials on a pocket rocket, I reckon he's used to some spills. "Fed up with lying here. But she won't let me get up."

"Just following Doc's orders," Jill rebukes him sternly.

"As long as he's not slacking off."

Road makes to get out of bed; I hold out my hand. "Nah, man, I'm messing with you. You take the time to heal. You're no use if you pass out from loss of blood. When's Doc coming back to check you?"

"Later today," Jill answers for him.

I consider her carefully. "The boys will be wondering where you are." I test out the waters.

When her face drops, I have my answer. Confirmed when Road says, "I'll be fine, Jill, if you've got things to do."

Or in other words, bikers to do. My lips curl at my inward joke.

That's interesting, seems like it might be a bit one-sided. Just another sweet butt trying to snag a brother. Not that he's patched in, yet, of course. But maybe that's why she's latched onto him. Get him hooked before he's aware of our ways. I wouldn't be at all surprised.

CHAPTER THIRTY-THREE

*S*am...

As I stretch, I groan. My ribs hurt and all my other muscles seem to be making themselves known and protesting in one way or another. Despite how gentle Drummer had been with me, he's still left his mark on me. And perhaps more than one. As I move my legs, I can feel a stickiness between them, and our omission comes back to me.

We didn't use a condom. Oh my, what if I'm pregnant? Could I be? Doing a quick calculation in my head, I couldn't say one way or the other. But Drummer didn't seem worried, and I am, apparently, officially his old lady. *Wow.*

Am I okay with committing to him? Staying here for the rest of my life? Working on bikes, living with bikers? Being able to get to know my father? Belonging? Hell yeah, I am. A grin spreads over my face. I'd lost the only parent I'd ever known but have found another. And while some of his ways seem strange, or scratch that, downright disgusting to me, there's no doubt that having accepted I'm his daughter, he seems to care. I've found a family, something I didn't think I'd ever have again, and Viper had found he's sired a child when he didn't think it was possible.

Sitting up, I see my pack lying in the corner of the room and going to it, pull out some fresh clothes, noticing I'm down to my last. I'll have to buy some more soon, or at least do some washing. I hadn't been able to bring much with me in my saddlebags, but if I'm settling down, I can treat myself to a new wardrobe and garments more appropriate for the Arizona climate. After a quick shower, which helps to loosen me up, I explore Drum's house, finding a small laundry room behind the kitchen. I'm just filling the washing machine when I hear a voice calling.

"Hey, Sam, you here?"

"Yeah, out back," I yell.

It's Sandy. She comes in, stands and watches me, and must see how stiff I am as I move. "Shouldn't you be resting?"

"Nah, moving around is helping to loosen me up."

"You scared the shit out of Viper, disappearing like that." She moves closer, her hand touches my arm. "And me."

She's nothing like my mother, not even close, apart from similar coloured eyes, no looks or mannerisms in common. And that perhaps helps. Officially, she's my stepmother and could become another important person in my life. Now I have the chance to get to know her, too. I huff a laugh as I answer her, "I didn't do it on purpose, Sandy."

"You must have been so scared. You're one brave woman, Sam." She looks down at her hand, still touching my arm, and puts a little more pressure into her touch. "You're good for Drum. He needs a woman with backbone beside him."

I cock an eyebrow in question, to be greeted by a grin. "I've seen the way he looks at you, he's besotted by you." Then her face falls. "Though I have to warn you, he may not stick around for long. He's not the type. You try and hang onto him, you hear me?"

I feel a moment of uncertainty. Until Drummer's told Viper, I don't think I ought to tell her exactly how far our relationship has progressed. "I hear you, Sandy. And I intend to do just that."

"Oh, love." Suddenly she's pulling me into her arms. "Viper

loves you, and you're a part of him, so I love you too." She breaks off, sounding a little uncertain. "I can't take the place of your mom, but I hope, while you're here, we'll become good friends."

Hugging her back, fighting to keep the tears from my eyes, I tell her, "We already are. Hey, I'm done here. Would you like a coffee?" As she nods, we go to the kitchen, and I start opening cupboards to find where everything's kept. Soon we have steaming cups in our hands. She asks me about life with my mom, I ask her about life on the compound, the conversation flowing easily between us.

We've just finished our drinks and I'm rinsing out the cups when the front door bangs loudly and a male voice shouts out, "Hey, honey, I'm home... oh shit." Drummer's face falls when he comes into the kitchen and finds I'm not alone. There's a red tinge under his tan.

Sandy doubles up laughing, and soon I join in.

We both get the death stare, and then he chuckles too. "Always wanted to try out that line," he smirks. "Just didn't expect it to be in front of fuckin' company."

"Oh, Prez. Your rep's sure gone downhill now." Sandy giggles at his forlorn expression. "Well, I think that's my cue to go." Coming over, she plants a kiss on my cheek and whispers into my ear, "Told you you'd be good for him."

"Come here, woman." Drum beckons me to him as the door closes behind Sandy. He enfolds me in his strong arms, making me feel protected and safe. With a finger under my chin, he raises my face, appraising me, and apparently satisfied with what he sees, lowers his mouth to mine. His hands run up and down my back, immediately his touch starts sending sparks shooting through me and he tightens his hold.

"Ouch."

"Oh, fuck, Sam. I'm sorry."

"Drum, don't worry. It's just my ribs. I'm still a bit sore."

"Fuck, I should've remembered." He lets me go and takes a

step back. Brushing his hands down his face, he gives a shake of his head. "Wouldn't take much for me to strip you and take you back to fuckin' bed, but I came up to get you. I need you down at the clubhouse, now."

I wish there was time for another round, especially when I see him ruefully adjusting his cock in his jeans, but I know the club comes first. I tilt my head on one side. "Problems?"

He sighs. "Yeah, problems." Taking my hand, he places a kiss on my palm. "Things are gonna get rough, darlin', you need to know that."

And here I was, thinking I'd found my happy place. I stand a bit straighter. "What do you need me to do, Drum?"

He moves so fast, his hands now in my hair, his fingers tightening almost to the point of being painful as he forces me to look up at him. "Fuck, Sam, what did I do to deserve you?" His eyes blaze into mine. "Here you are, hurt and injured, recovering from the most traumatic thing that can happen to a fuckin' woman, and you want to know what I need you to do? Sam, I should fall to my fuckin' knees and worship you."

I can't move or speak, the intensity of his words taking me by surprise, stealing the air from my lungs, as he continues, "I never believed I'd take an ol' lady. Never thought that fuckin' day would ever come. But that was before I met you. You're so damn fuckin' strong. You're so fuckin' perfect, everything I could ever wish for. You slay me, woman."

Again, his mouth crashes down onto mine, the feeling of being controlled by his grasp of my head sends another rush of arousal through me. Then he lets go of my hair, his hand cupping my scalp lightly. He's had a beer, the flavour mingling with the leftover taste of my coffee. I'm breathing in the scent of stale cigarette smoke and the perfume that's all his, and as our tongues slide together, my legs feel weak as if I'm getting drunk on this man.

People waiting on us or not, soon we're going to be stripping off each other's clothes. But then his phone rings.

A last gentle touch, then he's moving away. Pulling out his phone and snapping into it, a scowl darkens his face.

"Yes, VP. We're on our fuckin' way."

I laugh at this expression; I can't help it. He's aroused and frustrated. Putting his phone away, he spins around to face me.

"You think this…" he growls as he exaggerates trying to get himself comfortable in his jeans, "… is funny?"

I only laugh harder. He stalks toward me once more, a dark threatening scowl on his face which he makes sure I'm noticing. "Woman, I'll have you know, grown men tremble when they see me like this."

Now I raise my eyebrows, and then wave down toward his cock straining at the zip of his jeans. "Really? Grown men? Tremble at… that?"

"Oh, for fuck's sake." Barking another laugh, his hands rest on my shoulders and he turns me around. "Clubhouse, now." He slaps my ass lightly, then adds, "And let's hope I get myself under control or you might just see them quivering at the sight of my tremendous weapon."

I'm still giggling as he pushes me out of the house and down the track toward the clubhouse. Glancing at the man walking by my side, I'm full of wonder of how fast everything's happened, my abduction seeming to be the catalyst that caused us both to validate our feelings for each other.

As we come to the clubhouse, I put my hand on his arm, stopping him for a moment, looking down pointedly. "Just want to check you're decent."

"Fuck, woman, keep staring at my cock like that and I won't be." Taking my hand, he pulls me into the clubhouse. "Now get inside."

As we walk through the door, two things hit me at once. First the noise, hollers, and shouts of congratulations and 'welcome to the family' that I'm greeted with.

Viper's grinning like a loon as he approaches. "Give your old man a hug?"

I take it Drum's told them all, and that Viper welcomes the news. I let him put his arms around me and squeeze me against him. As I struggle for breath, suppressing a wince at the pressure on my tender ribs, I notice the second thing, that I'm the only woman present. Out of the corner of my eye, I see Wraith approaching his prez.

Drum leans over and says quietly, "Sophie okay with all this?"

"Yeah, I think she was relieved."

What's that all about? But I'm not in the dark for long.

Pulling me across to a table, Drum sits me down, and waggling his fingers asks Marsh for a couple of beers. They appear within seconds. We're joined by the VP, the sergeant-at-arms, Bullet, Heart, and Blade. As they look at me in expectation, I shrug and turn to my man.

"Sam, I've claimed you as my ol' lady."

I nod, still not understanding.

"That gives you a certain status in the club, and that's why you're here." Drum swigs his beer as though taking a moment to gather his thoughts. "You need to know some shit. The feds have dropped us in it."

Processing what that might mean, I keep quiet, certain there's more to come.

"The slavery ring. We broke part of it, but not all. We're expecting trouble; they're coming to get the women." At my gasp, Drum covers my hand with his. "We're gonna keep you safe, Sam, no one's gonna get their hands on you again."

This isn't a time for me to get hysterical, I don't like hearing what he's explaining, but if it's something I've got to face up to, I'm glad he's sharing it with me and not keeping me in the dark.

"What do you need me to do?" I repeat the question I asked him earlier, realising if he's sharing club business, there's a good reason for that.

"Fuck, she's a good one, Prez."

I smile at the unexpected praise from Peg.

"We need you to keep the women occupied and calm. Our plan is to keep them up at the guest guesthouse, out of the way. We'll leave a few men with you, but if, when, the shooting starts, you're to keep them together. I can't have a dozen women running around screaming and getting in our way."

That's not going to be an easy task. The traumatised women are probably going to go apeshit if they think there's a risk they'll be captured again. Quickly I start running through the best way of handling them, putting my personal fears to one side.

"Do we know when the attack's coming?"

"Soon. Today, we think." Drum nods his head toward the offices out back. "Mouse and Devil are listening to whatever they can pick up."

"Sam, we've got a handle on this, but it could get bloody." The VP's staring at me, trying to read the thoughts behind the expression on my face.

"I'll need to get my gun, Drum. I want to be ready, just in case."

"You know how to use one, darlin'?" This from Peg.

Thinking I'd already demonstrated that the morning Drum and I were chased, the look of such disdain I throw him causes Blade to laugh. "Looks like she can manage one just fine to me."

"Okay." Drum puts a finger and thumb to the bridge of his nose and pinches it. "I'll send Marsh up with you—"

"Sorry, Drum, but can I have Joker and Beef as well? I noticed yesterday, they seemed to be the least threatening."

"Beef?" Bullet scoffs a laugh. "He never stops talking about pussy!"

A grin spreads across my face. "He's upfront about what he wants but knows 'no' means 'no'. They don't mind his flirting as he doesn't come over as threatening. Joker's the same, he makes them laugh. The women have gotten used to them and will be more relaxed with those two around."

"Good call, I'll do that." Drum punctuates his sentence by giving me a kiss, making the others chuckle.

"Pussy whipped already, Prez?" Drum flicks his middle finger toward them, but there's a twinkling in his eyes despite the seriousness of what they are planning.

Slick comes across. "All set up, Prez."

Looking at my man, I see his face tighten, all levity fading away. He looks at me for one long moment, drinking in my features as though he might never see me again. The thought that he and the others will be putting themselves in danger scares me. I take a deep breath, knowing better than to let any of my own fear show. Drum needs to know he can rely on me to do the task he's assigned me, and not to see the panic I'm keeping hidden inside.

No lingering goodbyes, I just touch my hand to his cheek, trying to stop its shaking. "Go do your thing, Drummer."

His fingers cover mine, then moving it down, places a kiss to my palm. The flare in his eyes shows he knows exactly what I'm doing. Then with a nod, he turns away. "Beef, go get Sam's gun from her bike with her. Then you, Joker, and Marsh get up the top of the compound.

"Be safe, Sam." His voice breaks as he whispers into my ear.

It's hard to keep the hitch out of mine as I reply, "You too."

CHAPTER THIRTY-FOUR

*D*rummer...

Slick's announcement tells me I need to take charge, but I linger a little longer watching Sam leave. Our plan should keep all the females safe—sweet butts, old ladies, and the women we rescued—only putting them at risk if our defence fails. Like my brothers, I'm ready to put my life on the line to protect them, and to save my club. But the best of plans can go wrong. What if I never see her again?

When she disappears out of view, I put an end to my introspection. No space for misgivings now.

Mouse emerges from his hole. "Prez? Just heard chatter. They're on their way."

"Any indication of numbers? Or anything else to let us know what we might be facing?"

"That's a no. Sorry."

That would be too much to hope for. It's time to get this job done. I get to my feet, circling my hand in the air to indicate my brothers should gather around me.

Devil approaches, giving me a nod. "You ready to get moving?"

"Yeah. You got the boys briefed?" At his confirmatory dip of his head showing the Englishman had been getting shit organised while I'd been talking to Sam, I jerk my chin in appreciation, then continue, "Right, let's fuckin' get to it then."

Devil slaps Slick on the back and they move off, followed by Lady and Shooter. Dart's close behind, and like Slick has a heavy canvas bag slung over his shoulder. Moments later we hear the sound of bikes starting, then roaring off.

Before I can leave the clubhouse my phone rings. "Speak to me."

"Great!"

As soon as I end the call, it rings again. "Yeah?"

"Got you."

My VP is looking at me expectantly; I don't keep him waiting long. "Red and Snake are in position."

"Fuckin' ace." I have to agree. It means we've got the backup we need.

I glance around the remaining men. "Let's get this party started!"

"What you fuckers waiting for?" Peg's snarl encouraging them, I lead the men outside.

We each know what to do. We'd discussed the tactics in church, acting on Devil's suggestions. A very useful man to have around I'd learned—he used to be a member of the elite British Forces, an SAS officer, and we'd done well to listen to what he had to say. While the ultimate aim is to defend the compound and clubhouse, we made the decision not to be sitting ducks letting fuck knows how many get close enough to pick us off. No, we're going to be the ones directing this show. We're taking this fight to the front line.

Exiting the door, I hug Peg to me, slapping his back. "Good luck, man. Take care."

Then I do the same to the VP. All around me, men are hugging and wishing each other luck and to stay safe, then the salutations over, I go to my bike along with Blade, Tongue, Bullet, Rock, and Heart. The second wave, led by Wraith, follows us down to the compound gates. The gates slowly slide open and I lead my group through, casting an eye behind me to take one last look at the place I've called home for so many years. Its protection always top of my agenda, but now even more important as it houses my old lady. My vow, as I leave the club behind, is to do everything I can to keep her safe and out of harm's way.

The small group I'm leading head for the ramshackle buildings just below the compound. The original vacation resort had offered hiking in the foothills for the guests' enjoyment, and these falling-down sheds had once served as stabling for horses. Being outside our boundary, we haven't bothered to restore them, but today they'll do as a place to keep our heavy metal rides out of sight.

As the other group, led by Devil on a borrowed bike, thunder past, I watch them go. My eyes, drawn to the desert, take in the saguaro surrounding us. It's hard not to imagine we're taking part in a western, playing the role of cowboys defending our homestead—the only differences being we're on steel horses today and not acting a part.

Once we're parked up and bikes hidden, I wave for my group to gather round me, nodding at Blade.

"Prez?"

"Rock, take Tongue and Bullet and wait on the other side of the track. You got your phone switched on?"

"Yeah."

"Blade, Heart, you're with me. As soon as we know they're coming, Heart and Tongue, you do your shit, okay?"

"Got it Prez." Already both men are assembling their M40A3 sniper rifles. They both served as Marines and I'll just be leaving them to get on with what they know best. The way I've placed them is one pair on either side of the track. Bullet and Rock will serve as spotters, and I'll be keeping an overall eye on things.

"Our job is to stop any that get this far from reaching the compound, okay? Tongue and Heart will start taking them out, the rest of us step in when they get closer." And if they get past us, Wraith will lead the last stand.

"You want us to go further down?"

We hadn't discussed this. "Leaves you exposed."

The two snipers look at each other and shrug. "I'll take that risk," Tongue offers, and Heart nods in agreement. Christ, Crystal would have my balls if anything happened to her man.

We sort out our other weaponry, each taking one of the semi-automatic M-10s Wraith had picked up from over the border not so long ago, and of course, making sure our Glocks are fully loaded and we've got enough spare ammunition.

Once we're suitably armed, I point down the track. "Go choose your positions. And for fuck's sake, don't shoot each other!"

Nervous laughter accompanies my statement, a few more man hugs and the snipers and spotters start walking down the road spotting a location to set up. There's no rush as yet, we'll get an early warning from the others closer down toward the highway if anyone's about to approach us.

Tongue goes with Rock; Blade stays by my side. We find cover behind some low-growing shrubs. The enforcer pulls out a crumpled pack of smokes which appear to have been in his pocket a long time. When he sees me watching him, he gives a rueful shrug. *Sneaky bastard, he must have had them all along.*

My phone vibrates in my pocket. I don't delay answering when I see that it's Red.

"Got some suspicious looking fuckers coming down from Phoenix way. Reckon they're what you're waiting for."

"How many, Red?"

"Three trucks. Hard to say how many's inside."

"Okay, just follow behind when they get ahead of you and keep out of sight."

"Will do, Drum."

Quickly, I update Devil. "All set on your end?" Devil and his team are a quarter of a mile down.

"Yeah, we've got the stingers in place."

"Everyone know what to do?"

Devil's laugh comes down the line. "Your men can't bloody wait to start playing with their new toys. Slick and Lady will get busy. Me, Dart, and Shooter will give them backup." I grin, knowing they've got grenades and a launcher, they should be all set.

As soon as I end the call, my phone vibrates again, this time it's Snake. "Got a couple of trucks slowing down like they're looking for the entrance."

Shit! That's more than I expected, and they're coming from two different directions. Quickly, I update the Englishman again, then thank fuck there's only one vehicular entrance to the compound.

Devil's been thinking fast. "Assuming they stay as they are and don't group together, we'll let the first trucks go past us. I'll stay here with Lady and Shooter and send Slick and Dart further up and lay the second stinger across there. We won't have a chance to stop them all otherwise. This way we can hit them in two waves."

"You need more men with you?"

"Hopefully not, the grenades should do the trick."

Quickly I contact Red and tell him to hang back and wait for Snake, not wanting him to get caught between the two parties.

Yeah, that was the plan, to disable the trucks and before the occupants can react, chuck grenades inside. We're not wanting to take anyone alive today. Fuck the feds if they're expecting anyone left to question. And any the grenades don't take out, we'll finish off with the guns.

It's Devil again. "First two trucks have gone through. We're setting up the other stinger now for the next three."

"Great."

In the unlikely event a truck will not be incapacitated by the sharp metal prongs, my team will take them out, and if they get past my boys, then it's up to Wraith to protect the compound.

Coming up behind to form a pincer movement will be the men Snake and Red have brought with them.

I know the first stage has worked as I hear the sound of the grenades exploding, followed by shots firing into the air. A second wave of explosions sounds from further down the track where Devil must have stopped the last trucks.

"First truck hit the stinger, the one behind couldn't get past," Slick tells me quickly. "Grenades did their job. We followed them up with the M-10s. No survivors."

"Third truck's been stopped. All dead," Devil confirms.

Well fuck me if this plan's not going smoothly. I wipe sweat off my brow that's not just caused by the heat of the day.

Snake calls in, Red's on the same line. "They've learned fast. Two trucks have gone off road. Drum, they're headed your way."

Red butts in, "Drum, I'll team up with Snake and we'll come up quiet from behind. Don't worry, man, we'll have your six."

"Got it, Red. Keep me updated. And take fuckin' care." I want no Satan's Devils dead today, from whatever chapter.

There's rapid gunfire in the distance, and now it's Devil on the line. "They're coming up past us. We're under attack but holding our own. Watch yourselves, some have exited the trucks and managed to go wide on foot. We've got the others pinned down. Keep eyes on your flanks, Drum."

The sound of gunshots ringing out makes my trigger finger itch. I want in on this fight. Moving under the protection of my cover, my eyes flick around, watching for anything out of place.

I see men circling around, more organised than I'd given them credit for. I count ten in all, and then two fall, taken out by my snipers. Another couple drop before the others respond and start firing back.

Taking advantage of the brush to hide them, they're giving each other cover, making it hard for Slick and Tongue to take aim. But I haven't revealed my position yet, and now I've got two in my sights. I set the M-10 to single-fire, get off a shot and one man drops like a stone, the other ducks down.

For a moment, it's a standoff, then I see something move, ease sideways and shoot, then move to the next piece of brush hoping to take someone unawares. But I've exposed myself. A sudden intense burn hits my right arm, making my semi-automatic drop from my hand. Undaunted, I take out my Glock with my left. I might not be ambidextrous, but I can shoot well enough with my handgun to lay down covering fire.

Shots cease momentarily while each side waits for the other to make a mistake.

Then new guns enter the battle. Red and Snake have appeared and start taking the attackers out from behind. There're screams and men falling, dead bodies hitting the ground. I risk standing and running, firing as I go. We've got our enemy surrounded, there's no escape.

Realising their precarious position, they become reckless and attempt a retreat. The sniper rifles keep firing, and more bodies drop.

Then, all goes silent. It takes me a moment to realise there's no one shooting back.

Down the track a plume of thick black smoke billows high into the air, one of the trucks must have caught on fire. That's just what we didn't need. Although we're a long way from Tucson, a reason the original fire at the complex took such a strong hold, that won't stop people we don't need interfering coming to investigate. I start turning my mind to the cleanup.

"All clear!" Blade shouts.

Cautiously, I wave Dollar out from his hiding place and stand up. Blade comes over, grimacing as he sees the blood streaming down my arm. "Prez?"

"I'm okay, where's Tongue?"

"Here, Prez." He's limping, it looks like he's taken a bullet to his leg.

"Tongue, get yourself up to the compound and see Doc.

Blade, Dollar, you're with me. Let's get the bikes and see what the fuck is going on." I pause as I see two men approaching. "Hey, Red, Snake! Thanks for your help." Red reaches my side; I clasp his hand and hug him to me. "Your men okay?"

Red nods. "One took a bullet, but he'll live."

"I owe you one, man." I nod toward Snake, who waves away my heartfelt words of gratitude.

"Least I could do, Drum, after that fuckin' fiasco with Buster. Man, I'm sorry about that." He clasps my hand, then notices the blood. "You okay, Drum?"

"Just winged me. Red, Snake… We couldn't have done this without your help."

"Satan's Devils stick together, Drum," Red says, slapping my back. He eyes the black smoke rising into the air and puts it together with the faint sound of sirens that can be heard in the distance. "That gonna cause a problem?"

Yeah, it fucking could. "Best get down there and do what we gotta do. Blade, Heart, all you fuckers. Come on!" I wave my men to me. Wasting no time, we extract our bikes from the tumbled-down stables, and with our Vegas and California brothers riding bitch behind us so we can take them back to their rides, we proceed carefully down the road, keeping our eyes out for any attackers we might have missed. The smarting in my arm means I can only just hold the throttle with my right hand just enough to twist it, but for now the adrenaline's deadening the pain.

The sound of engines reaches us as Devil and the others appear. Quickly counting up, I see we've lost no one. We've successfully stopped them getting to the compound, and for the first time, I feel the relief flood over me, together with a sudden wave of weakness that we've kept Sam safe. I shake off the light-headedness, knowing my work is far from done.

Devil jerks his head indicating the direction behind him. "We've got a couple alive if you want them?"

Lifting my chin toward him in thanks, I agree we'll take the prisoners. And this time, whatever information we extract, we'll keep to ourselves.

Peg walks up, cocking his head in the direction of the faint siren noises that can be heard in the distance. "We need to get these fuckin' bodies out of sight and fast."

Using my left hand, I hunt out my phone. "Wraith, it's done."

I wait for him to have his own moment of reprise. It means his old lady's safe too. Then I interrupt his questions. "Got the law coming. Send the tow truck. We've got trucks and bodies to move. I need everyone down here. Now."

Red's nodding. "We'll help." Without further delay, he turns to his men, giving them quick and precise instructions as I look around wondering how the fuck we're going to hide the signs of our fight. The first truck has blown out tyres, the second and third smoking heaps, the last two are at least driveable.

But Satan's Devils know how to work together, all being brothers no matter what chapter we're from. We've got body bags filled, moveable trucks driven to the compound, and one of the burned-out heaps towed as well as prisoners escorted to the storage room in very short time. And without a moment to waste as the wail of sirens are getting louder, growing close fast.

Wraith tears off his t-shirt, binding my arm and shoving a fleece at me. Despite the temperature being in the hundreds, I put it on, hiding my wound, hoping the blood won't seep through. A welcome crack of thunder echoes from above, rain starting as heavy spots, quickly increasing to coming down in sheets.

The final burned-out truck is being hitched onto the tow truck as the first police car comes up and slows when he sees me waving him down. Wraith comes and stands beside me, Slick continues the business of fixing the tow to the truck.

"Officer, can I help you?" I speak loudly to make myself heard over the rain.

Getting out of their cars, having put on wet-weather gear, the police officers surround us. Most of mine, and Red and Snake's men, have gone ahead to the compound to get dry and so our large numbers don't make us look suspect.

One of the officers indicates the truck and says in a voice laced with distrust, "We saw the smoke from Tucson. What's been going on here?" His eyes are narrowed, and he waves a couple of his men to start poking around. There's not much to find; this truck's the most badly burned out, and all the bodies have been removed.

It's my job to allay his suspicions. Still mounted on my bike, I lean forward casting my eyes upwards for a second, waiting for the loud rumble of thunder to fade. "Fuck that was some show wasn't it? Poor fella." I stop to indicate one of Snake's men who's stayed behind, now minus his cut, and looking like any other concerned delivery driver. "He was driving in to make a drop, and the darn truck got hit by lightning." God must be on my side, as another brilliant flash streaks across the sky, with almost simultaneous thunder following, showing the storm is right overhead.

The officer's eyes widen, and he tut-tuts before he speaks. "Storm's only just started."

I huff a laugh and give a shake of my head. "Not here, Officer, been going on for a while. Reckon it's heading Tucson's way now." A story that would be hard for him to discount.

Snake's man comes over, he's wringing his hands. "I was lucky to get out, sir. All of a sudden, poof. Whole damn truck went up."

The officer clearly doesn't believe us and walks around the truck. "What were you carrying?" he asks, the question sounds casual, the tone he asks it in is not.

"Gas. For the shop up at the compound."

Devil comes up to join us, swinging his arm over the San Diego man's shoulders. "Poor bugger," he starts to explain. "Soft top on the truck, lightning must have shorted the electrical systems." He points to a hole in the asphalt. "Went around the car and into the ground. Rear wheels hit the hole, must have caused a jolt and the gas cans fell over. Then, boom." He throws up his hands. "Big shock to us all, as to you, I expect." Well, the pothole was caused by a grenade, but Devil's explanation should hold up.

Again, the officer's eyes narrow, and he seems taken aback at Devil's English accent. "And you are?"

Devil passes him a business card. "Jason Deville," he identifies himself. "A security consultant. I've investigated fires before, helps with prevention. I'm assisting Mr Drummer here with security for his club's businesses."

The officer turns as the fire chief comes up alongside and asks his opinion. "What do you think?"

Looking at me, a challenging look in his eyes, the fire chief shakes his head. He sounds sceptical, but admits as he replies, "I've seen stranger things. Unlikely, but possible."

Now the officer calls the men who'd accompanied him, and who'd been poking around. "Find anything?" he asks them.

One shrugs. "Story seems as though it could fit."

Another adds, "Can't do much unless we take the truck in. It's riddled with bullet holes."

The officer in charge spins around back to me. "How do you account for that?" his voice snaps accusingly, as now he thinks he's on to something at last.

Now it's my turn to look nonchalant. "Boys will be boys, Officer. The truck's a write-off, the gas all burned up. Putting in some target practice, that's all."

He doesn't believe me and sneers. "Your boys must need it if they have to use a target as fucking big as that."

"There's nothing to see here, Sheriff." Devil uses his most commanding voice.

The officer doesn't want to give up. "I'd like to come up to the compound."

"Not unless you've got a warrant." I deny him permission, but pleasantly.

He shakes his head, water cascading off his raincoat as he

does so. He's got nothing to go on and he knows it. He might be suspicious, but there's nothing to back up his doubts.

"Lightning strike, eh?" He turns to Snake's man, masquerading as the truck driver. "Seems you're a lucky man."

With a wide grin spreading across his face, and brushing water off his face, the Californian replies, "That I am, officer. That I am."

With one last disbelieving look, the lawmen get back in the cars, and thank fuck, drive away.

I turn to the good actor, and at last, have a chance to ask his name. "Marvel?" I question once he's enlightened me.

He chuckles. "Can't help that I like comics."

I don't give a fuck why he got his handle and shake his hand firmly. "Thanks, man, we owe you one."

He throws back his head and laughs. "Most fun I've had in years. If this is what it's like here in Tucson, perhaps I'll put in to transfer."

"Can't guarantee we'll always have this much excitement, but if you're serious, I reckon we'd be lucky to have you."

CHAPTER THIRTY-FIVE

*S*am...

I'd tried to hide my worry from Drummer, not wanting to burden him with my concerns on top of everything else he's got on his plate today. I've no idea what he's got planned, but it's likely it will be dangerous. It's easier to shake off the thought that more harm could come to me than the idea of him getting hurt, or worse, if I never see him alive again. I was right to send him off with a clear mind so he can do what he has to do without being worried about me.

But it's hard to pretend and, as I make my way up to the house where the women are staying, difficult to get myself into the mindset where I'm going to be able to conceal my anxiety from everyone else.

Focusing on what I'm going to do when I get there, I try to rehearse in my head exactly what to say. Do I just walk in there and announce that I'm now Drummer's old lady, like that makes me the queen or something? Not for the first time, I wish I had more experience of dealing with women. Now, if they could discuss how to rebuild an engine, I'd be on much firmer ground. I run through the groups I'll be facing, the dozen rescued women and the old ladies for starters. How's Sophie going to feel?

Wraith's woman? I'll be treading right on her toes. She was top woman up to now. And the sweet butts? I don't even want to think about them.

The house comes into sight, I straighten my back and invoke my inner mom, or memories of her when she was goading the guys in the shop back home into line. Oh, she could be fierce when she wanted to be! Carefully schooling my features, and as confidently as I can, I open the door and immediately duck as something comes flying across at me. Looking down, I see it was a scrunched-up paper cup.

"You cretins! You wankers! What the bloody hell made you say that?"

Cautiously I take a step forward and see Sophie, her hands on her hips, shouting at Beef and Joker. Joker's holding his hands out in supplication. "She asked me how big I was—"

"She meant how bloody tall you were, you tosser! She didn't want you to offer to show her your dick!"

I look around, expecting to see a traumatised woman quivering in expectation of further abuse, but what I find is a pretty twenty-something with auburn hair with her hand over her mouth trying to smother her laughter. The other women range from a slight quirking of their lips to outright grins. Noticing my entrance, Sophie looks across at me and winks, immediately making me understand she's got a good handle on the situation. Despite the very English insults thrown his way, Joker doesn't look at all put out. And neither does he look contrite.

"Look, I can show you the goods and prove it." His hands go to the zip of his jeans.

Cries of 'no, put it away' and 'oh God, not that' come from the women, and a few more give an actual laugh. He's putting on a show for them, and at the very least taking their minds off their predicament.

I decide it's time for my input. "If, in the unlikely event I'd like to see your cock, Joker, I think Drum would cut it off if he knew you'd been waving it around."

"Fuck, Sam. Didn't see you there." He pretends to do up the zip he never took down and removes his hands smartly. "Prez would have my balls."

Amongst the laughter, a couple of strange looks are thrown at me by the sweet butts. Jill, Allie, and Pussy are huddled together with a couple of the new women, who seem to be taking their lead in not joining in with the general air of amusement. Their slight air of detachment presumably aimed at putting them above the rest.

Jill smirks as if letting on she knows precisely what size Joker's cock is. And she probably does, probably had it in every orifice a time or two, even in the short time he's been at the club. But I'm not here to judge. In the hierarchy of the club, the whores have their place, and it's time they know mine.

As I swallow, trying to summon up the right words, it's Sophie who comes to my rescue. Making her way cautiously through the bodies taking up all seats available and some spilling onto the floor, she comes over to me and puts her arm around my shoulders. "Hey, everyone. We've got a new queen. Drum's claimed Sam as his old lady."

Hoots and whistles from the men, looks of disgust from the whores, and various glances of surprise from the other old ladies. Sandy is first to react, coming over and hugging me tight.

"So this means you're staying here. For good."

Pulling her in close, I nod my head. "Reckon it does, Sandy."

She's beaming at me. "Viper's going to be so pleased."

"Welcome to the family." Crystal's the next to come over, taking Sandy's place and planting a kiss to my cheek. "Never thought Drum would settle down." Stepping back, she holds me at arm's length, as though assessing if I've got what it takes to be the club's first lady. What she sees must satisfy her, as she nods, then moves away, scooping up Amy in her arms. She stage-whispers to the little girl, "Maybe more friends for you to play with in time."

I note Sophie's blush, but not for long, as Sandy screams, "Grandbabies! Yeah!"

Now it's my turn to go red. "Bit too early for that," I respond while wondering whether there's one already in the making. With all this support around me, it occurs to me that I really wouldn't mind.

"Now you're going to have to let me have a go at your hair sometime." Carmen's input makes me laugh; she's mentioned my hair before. Never having been a girly girl, I don't bother much with it, keeping it long as it's easy to tie back out of the way.

"Not sure about that," I tell her in reply, as she too comes up, holding me close for a moment.

"Congratulations, Sam. Drum's been waiting for someone like you. You'll centre him."

I thank Bullet's old lady.

Now that that's out of the way, it's time for me to take charge. Recognising my new elevated position in the club, some of the captured women are looking at me in anticipation, while others are continuing their own conversations. The club whores are sniggering amongst themselves, two of the newcomers listening to them attentively. Motioning to Sophie to stand beside me, and pulling myself up to my full, not very impressive height, I clap my hands. A few fall silent, but not all.

Beef puts his hands to his mouth and lets out a loud whistle. As eyes are drawn to him, he points at me.

"Ladies…" I circle my hands to show I'm addressing myself primarily to the women who were taken captive. "I've got some good news. Today is the last day you'll need to stay here." I might be crossing my fingers behind my back, but they're not going to know that. "The FBI will want to talk to you, and presumably give you the support you need to help you get home." I break off to let that sink in, examining the expressions on the faces surrounding me, which range from hope and elation to despair.

The woman I'd become friendly with, Monica, puts up her hand. "None of us have any money and only the clothes you've provided to us. What will the FBI do about that?"

I nod, well aware they possess only the borrowed clothes they're standing in. "As you heard from Agent Haughton yesterday, there's a special task force that deals with human trafficking. They know full well you need clothing and possibly even housing. If back home, wherever home is, you've got bank accounts, jobs, family, or friends, they'll help you get there safe and sound. If not, they'll help you start afresh."

A few of them nod. I think rapidly. From what Drummer had said, the FBI had left us in the lurch, so in my view, the Satan's Devils owe them nothing. "If you don't want to go with the feds, the club will help you get home."

"They'll want to interrogate us, won't they? But is there anything we could say that would help them?" Monica seems to be their mouthpiece.

I sincerely hope not. By the time I see Drummer again, I hope all the ringleaders will be dead. "To be honest, I think they know all they need to know."

"I'd rather go straight home," a young girl with a cute round face pipes up. "I don't have family, but I've got friends who'll help me until I get my life back on track."

A couple of others agree.

"Why don't you all take some time to decide what you want to do? While we," I indicate the old ladies and point at the sweet butts, "get this place tidied up and start some lunch? After we've eaten you can let me know what you've decided, and we'll make it work for you."

There's general murmuring of agreement, except from the five women sitting at the back.

Noticing, Sophie steps forward and points at club whores. "You lot, you can start gathering up the rubbish and taking it out."

"Hey, Sophie, darlin', how many times do we need to tell you it's garbage?" Beef's cracking up, and I appreciate Soph's done it on purpose to lighten the mood.

"You're a bunch of heathens." Her grin taking the sting out of her words. "You can't even speak the queen's bloody English."

"We dispensed with your *queen* a long time ago." In comparison, Jill's tone could cut glass, and her glare tossed toward me makes me feel cold. It sounds like she wants to get rid of this one, too. *Hmm, one I'll need to watch.*

The door opens and Roadrunner comes inside. Looking over in surprise as I didn't think he should be out of bed, I can't remember a man ever looking so white and pale. I rush over. "For goodness' sake, sit down, Road. Before you fall over."

"I'm fine." He waves me off, but nevertheless crashes down on the seat Carmen vacates for him. He looks across to Beef and tilts his head. Beef nods, and without alerting the woman, goes out to take up station outside. Jill gets up and goes over to Roadrunner, but he waves her away, looking pointedly at the black sack Sophie had shoved into her hand.

I leave them to sort themselves out. The old ladies follow me into the kitchen, where Crystal leans her butt against the counter and folds her arms. "Spill."

I don't pretend to misunderstand her. Motioning for the others to come close, I lower my voice. "The slavery gang are coming to try to take the women back. The club's obviously not going to take that lying down."

"They're fighting." Crystal puts her hand over her heart, her eyes open wide. I can see a pulse beating in her temple.

"Drum's got this," I assure her, fiercely. "It won't be anything they can't handle."

"That's why Joker and Beef are here?" Sandy's shaking her head. "In case they get through?"

I pat her hand. "A precautionary measure, but there's no way into the back of the compound, and the boys have taken all their toys. We'll all be fine, Sandy."

Carmen's fingers go to her mouth. "But will *they*? Shit, it's what I hate about this life. The waiting, the not knowing what's going on."

As she speaks, I realise this life's going to be mine. *Can I live with it?* I'll have to if I want to be with Drum.

"Doesn't mean we have to like it."

I nod at Crystal. "But it's the biker we fell in love with. Which means we have to accept everything that goes along with it."

"*You* brought them here." Jill's voice makes me swing around; she's carrying a bag full of trash. "If it wasn't for you, our men would never have gotten involved," she continues, scathingly.

Carmen rounds on her. "They're not your fucking men. They're *ours*. And don't you forget it."

"Not all of them," she continues, and then points at me. "And if you think you're enough to satisfy the prez, you're going to be very disappointed, hon." She looks me over from top to bottom. "You don't got enough to hold his attention for long. And he isn't gonna be satisfied with just one. Me and Allie, we know how to keep him going all night... Ouch!" She rubs her cheek where I've just slapped her. Hard.

I'm not a violent person, but I know that to not literally slap her down at this point would be a sign of weakness. I follow my action up with words. "I'd be very careful if I were you, *hon*. Reckon Drum would have you out on your ass if he knew what you've been saying to me."

She's got no comeback; she knows I've only stated the truth. I might not know much about biker life, but I know enough to understand you don't insult or threaten the president's old lady—not if you're a lowly sweet butt. As she realises she could lose the place where she lives, and the biker cock she so loves, she takes a step away, physically stepping down. I indicate the door behind me, and she disappears with the trash.

She reappears a moment later with empty hands. "Storm's brewing," she says, merrily, as she goes back into the main room.

I glance at Sandy, who's stifling a laugh. "Message received and understood there I think, Sam."

Now we're all grinning and turn to the task at hand, getting lunch ready. It's what they do, get on with business as usual while trying not to worry about their men. It's what I now have to learn to do too.

It's when we're circulating with trays of food that the storm hits in earnest, God's fireworks in an impressive display while rain pelts down, drumming on the roof of the building we're in. Some of the women jump with the thunder, the flash of lightning almost synchronised with the sound showing the storm's right overhead. One crash so loud most of us jump a little nervously.

"Is it always like this?" I ask Beef who's come back inside, maintaining his vigilance at the window.

"Only in summer," he replies.

CHAPTER THIRTY-SIX

*D*rummer...

We might almost be getting washed away, but at least it's helping to disperse the blood the police had luckily missed—along with any other evidence should they come back and investigate further. Dart and Blade have been scouting around picking up all the spent shells they can find. We know how to leave a scene clean.

Slick gets the last truck loaded, and we make our very wet way up to the compound, deciding to go on foot and come back for the bikes when it's drier. I never thought I'd be grateful to the extremes of the Arizona weather, but it's certainly been on our side today. The threat of being caught out in a flood may have added to the police officers' decision to believe our story and head back to the city.

Reaching the clubhouse, it's already full of men cheering and clinking bottles of beer together. With the prospects up with Sam, Dart's behind the bar. A sense of satisfaction washes over me. We're all alive, and we've eliminated our enemy. I feel empathy with my brothers' desire to party. But there's more work to do before we can relax.

Seeing Doc standing waiting, I throw him a nod, indicating

my arm. Quickly, he confirms what I already knew, the bullet had just clipped me and already the bleeding has stopped. It still stings but isn't incapacitating. He applies a bandage, then goes back to checking out the others.

A slap on my back almost has me reeling. "Peg," I greet my sergeant-at-arms.

The frown on his face shows he's not ready to start celebrating, and that like me, he's well aware our work is far from done. He gets straight to the point. "Got twenty bodies to dispose of, Prez. That's a fuckin' lot for us to handle."

Like him, I'm worried about that. It's got to be done quick, before the police department comes calling again, this time with a warrant. Or the feds. I give a loud whistle. "Red, Snake, Wraith, and Blade, with me!" Having caught their attention, I wave to show they should make their way into the meeting room.

Devil approaches. "You need me to sit in on this?"

"Nah, man. Best you're not involved now."

As he nods in agreement, I guess I don't have to spell out to him what we're going to be discussing. "Okay then. I've contacted the feds. They'll be coming to collect the women early tomorrow morning. They're making arrangements to get them into their protection programme or whatever. I've finished here now, so I'll be on my way, Drummer. You've got my number should you need anything."

I clasp his hand in mine, and reaching around him with the other, pull him to me in a hug. He's fought beside me and my brothers today. In my world, that counts for a lot. When we pull apart, he lifts his chin, then makes his way out of the clubhouse, receiving slaps on his back from the rest of my brothers when they realise he's taking his leave. As the scarred man disappears out of the door, I wonder whether our paths will ever cross again.

But now it's time to join the others. Entering the meeting room, I wave them to seats around the table. When they're settled, I start on a high. "Good fuckin' work today. Especially your man, Marvel, Snake."

The president of the San Diego chapter's face splits into a grin. "Seems he likes the excitement here. He's a good brother. Yours if you want him. Make up for that fucker Buster."

Wraith swears when he hears the name, it left him with a bad taste in his mouth about brothers from the Southern California chapter. "You sure about him, Snake?"

Snake is well aware why Wraith's challenging him and doesn't take umbrage. "Yeah, I'll be sorry to lose him, but you seem to need all the men you can get here." He looks at me and smirks. "Mother chapter sees more than its fair share of fuckin' action."

I shrug. Lately, he's not wrong about that. And we are on a recruitment drive. "Thanks for the offer, Snake, we may very well take you up on it. And I'm grateful to both you and Red having our six today."

"No worries, Brother." The two presidents speak in unison.

I drum my fingers against the table. "As you said, we're not unused to problems here, but this one's left a residue that's a lot bigger than we normally handle." I pause, and my gaze takes in the men seated around me, so they're left in no doubt about the seriousness of the situation. "We've got twenty dead bodies need disposing of. And before the law comes knocking."

"Any undertakers in your pocket?"

Snake's suggesting cremation. "Couldn't handle the volume," I reply, shaking my head, already having dismissed that option. We might pay a bribe and get one or two into the incinerator, but no amount of money would get anyone to agree to look the other way with the volume we've got on our hands.

Blade's tapping his teeth with his knife. "Drain the swimming pool, fill it with sodium hydroxide or potassium hydroxide—"

"Ew, fuck that, man. I like swimming in there." Peg's looking disgusted.

Well, at least the enforcer's thinking,

"It would take too long, I think. Don't you have to heat it up to the right temperature? Would need to boil a fuckload of kettles." Wraith's taking the suggestion seriously.

I wipe my hands over my face, thinking this is one of the most bizarre conversations I've ever had.

"Any pig farms around here?" Snake's rubbing his hands with glee as if he's enjoying himself. He would; it's not his problem.

Peg sneers. "I think the farmers might notice if we dumped that amount in their pens."

"Not if you chopped them up first."

I wince, thinking of amount of body parts that would entail.

"What about a wood chipper?"

"Pieces would fly everywhere! We'd never clear them up." Wraith raises his eyebrows at Peg.

"We could wrap them up and deliver them to the feds. They brought them to our door in the first place."

I roll my eyes at Blade. Yeah, that sounds great. The feds are just looking for a reason to shut us down. Mass murder would work.

My brothers are tossing ideas around, but in my mind, there's only one option. We need to bury them. Up in the forest above the compound. And, very carefully.

I bang the gavel. "What I need is men."

"You thinking the old route, Prez?"

"Yeah, Wraith. Need to bury 'em deep though."

"We can provide manpower. You got enough shovels? At least the earth will be damp with all this rain." Red's pulling at his fingers as if getting ready to get his hands dirty. He nods at Snake, who gives him a jerk of his chin in return.

Now it's my turn to grin. "Don't need shovels," I tell them. "We work construction out of the compound. Got a digger on the site. Just need men to cover the tracks, and to go out hunting."

"Hunting?" Red frowns.

"Yeah, get a few wild animals to bury on top."

Wraith nods. "Not foolproof but it does help fool the cadaver dogs."

"Just got to make sure no one goes looking." And it's down to me to be convincing enough to prevent that. Somehow.

"We don't cover our tracks. We make more."

My eyebrows rise as I look at Peg, wondering if he's gone mad. "What the fuck you talking about?"

A smile slowly spreads across the sergeant-at-arms' face. "I don't want to lose my patch over this, but I'm thinking about having a ride on that rice rocket of the prospect's."

I'm still not certain where he's going with this. Wraith, too, is looking bemused.

Seeing we're still not with him, Peg explains, "We dig the trench, make it narrow, the width of the digger. Cover the bodies, then continue moving the earth around the forest, making a track. I'll take the dirt bike around a few times—hell, anyone who's up for it can have a go. Cover our tracks, literally."

"Road's bike's here, in the shop. Sam was working on it with him. It's ready to roll as he was going to race on Sunday." Instead, he got shot.

Thanking Blade for his information, I consider the idea. My apoplectic fit of averted when I understood Peg had not lost his mind. I now find myself giving a cautiously optimistic grin. "Peg, fuck it. It could work! Anyone else got a better idea? No?" Looking around the table, I see Peg's plans has caught everyone's interest. Picking up the gavel, I bang it down hard. "Okay, let's fuckin' get to it."

As I get to my feet, Blade and Wraith are both telling Peg they'll take a few turns with the bike. They even seem to be enthusiastic about helping it look like the track's been well used. Fuck me, getting down in the dirt isn't for me, but it might be interesting to watch for a laugh. I start looking forward to a bit of entertainment—once the bodies are buried, of course.

"Wraith?"

My VP turns.

"I'm going up to see Sam. Wanna come with? Viper, Heart, and Bullet might as well come before the ol' ladies go crazy. Then we can go up to the forest."

Peg waves us away. "Go see to your women. Give us a couple of hours, Prez. With the digger and the brothers we've got to help, it won't take long. Once the bodies are underground, we can have us some fun."

"Good idea, Peg!" Now it's my turn to slap his back, and I make sure he can feel it.

I lead our merry band of pussy-whipped men—nah, I'm not afraid to admit it, Sam's about got me tied up in knots—up to the house where the women are. I don't know or care how the others greet their old ladies, as soon as mine notices me, she runs over and leaps into my arms, her legs going up and around my waist. Bracing myself so I don't stagger and fall under the impact, I look into the beautiful eyes that just a few short hours ago, I feared I'd never see again, and lower my mouth to hers in a punishing kiss.

She opens for me immediately, our tongues probe and meet, our teeth clashing together in such a violent coupling as though joining that part of our body we reaffirm the bond between us. My hands squeeze her ass, my cock hardening of its own accord and I know that I need her. Now.

Groaning, I release my hold, letting her slip down my body, knowing by her gasp she feels how hard I am. Her eyes widen, her mouth loosens against mine as she pulls back just enough to tell me, "I need you, Drum. Now."

Thank fuck she's on the same wavelength. I keep one arm tight around her and draw her away from the other women, taking her out of the house and over to mine. Opening the door, I push her inside, her body is pliant and willing. As soon as we enter, she turns, her hands going to the bottom of her t-shirt and pulling it over her head. Then she's removing her bra, shorts, and her panties until she's naked before me.

My hand shakes, the pent-up emotion, the *relief* that we're both alive and the danger behind us makes my touch almost reverent. As I trace the healing scars marring her beautiful breasts, and then the blue-black bruising on her side, my gut clenches at what she had to suffer.

"No one is ever going to hurt you a-fuckin'-gain." My vow is as serious as any made in a church.

She smiles as she cups my face. "You can't promise that, Drum. Much as I'd like to believe it, if I'm your old lady, it comes with risks. Just as I can't promise to keep you safe either."

"I'll do everything I can to protect you."

"You've got too many clothes on." Her voice is husky as she pushes my cut from my shoulders, taking it off and folding it neatly before putting it on a chair. Then she returns and treats my shirt with far less devotion. I bend so she can pull it off, and she discards it on the floor. She pauses, her eyes seeing the bandage on my arm.

"Drum... This..." Her hands reach out gingerly.

I'm not letting anything get in the way of what I want. "It's nothing. It's a scratch. Not even bleeding." I flex my arm to show it's not going to stop me.

She examines my face and then gives a nod, accepting my words.

Her fingers toy with the button on my waistband, a twinkling in her eyes as she makes me wait. And then she's unfastening it, carefully undoing the zip and pushing my jeans around my hips. As my turgid cock springs free she reaches forward, first placing a kiss on the tip, then flicking out her tongue to lick the pre-cum from my slit. My hand goes to the wall behind me as I feel my legs weaken.

With a small satisfied smile, she falls to her knees, and with a gentle tap silently asks me to lift my legs so she can remove one boot, and then the other. Now she's removing my pants. Women have stripped me before, fuck, I've done everything and had everything done to me that it's possible for a man to experience, but never have I felt such sensations as this woman summons forth from me. An arousal that's almost painful in its intensity, an emotion that makes me want to fall to my knees and worship her. Her hands, so much smaller than mine, unusually calloused for a woman, affect me more than any other's smooth manicured touch has ever done.

My cock throbs, twitching all by itself, as I wait in agonizing expectation for what she'll do next.

Her fingers start to rise, gently trailing up my legs. When she reaches my thighs, she looks up. I gaze at her face, her pupils dilated, her breathing coming quickly. Her lips curve, one side more than the other. "Use me, Drum."

I don't waste a moment taking advantage of the gift she's giving to me, my hands going to her head and taking hold of her hair. "Open your mouth." My voice is gruff as I tug her toward me, and she takes me inside. I push in, hard. "Relax your throat, breathe through your nose," I instruct, as I start to fuck her mouth wildly, almost out of control. I push in; she gags, I pull quickly out.

"Don't stop," she gasps. "Make me feel alive, Drum."

"I don't want to hurt you." Fuck, but she's tempting me.

"Do it, Drum!" Her fingernails of one hand dig into my ass, holding me tight to her, the other hand palms my balls. *She wants this. She needs this.* I start thrusting again, not holding back. She gags again, but I ignore her, I'm not holding her tight enough to force her, if she couldn't handle this she'd pull away.

She swallows as I push in, I tighten my hold around her ponytail. My head falls back on my shoulders, my eyes rolling back until I'm staring at the ceiling, incapable of any rational thought as the pressure grows unbearably in my balls and I feel my dick swelling. As I thrust again, she pushes against me, so I'm deep in her mouth, almost all of me inside. Her throat muscles massage me, and I know I'm constricting her airways as I come. And come. Draining myself in her mouth, again and again as she swallows it all down. As soon as I'm sated, I pull myself free, and drop down beside her, taking her into my arms.

Her eyes are watering, and she's heaving to get much-needed breath into her lungs.

"Fuck, darlin', I lost control. I shouldn't have done that."

Leaning, so her forehead touches mine, she takes a couple more breaths. "I wanted it. I needed it. I love you, Drum."

"Babe, I fuckin' love you too." How could I not love a woman who knows exactly what I need to get rid of the tension, the fear, the worry that had haunted me today? "You've given me that, now let me return the favour."

Standing, I pull her up and drag her behind me into the bedroom, feeling like a caveman who has to possess his woman. Blood is surging south, my cock's rising again. Lifting her into my arms, I drop her onto the bed and come down over her, the weight of my body pressing her down into the covers. One hand behind her head, I press my lips to hers. As we kiss, I taste myself and know I'd prefer to be sampling her essence.

Moving down her body, my hands pull up her legs so her knees are bent, feet flat on the bed. I push them open and gaze at the feast laid out for me, already glistening with her arousal. She's so fucking turned on and ready for me, it's all I can do not to plunge straight inside her. Taking a strong hold of my baser desires, I lower my mouth and swipe my tongue over her slit, lapping at her cream, unable to stifle a groan at the taste that's all her. This woman, my old lady.

She's writhing beneath me, and I know it won't take much to make her come. I go to work, sucking her clit, biting it, breathing on it. My fingers work inside her. Just her flavour and her perfume make my balls tighten.

Taking hold of her hand, I place it on her mound. "Make yourself come."

She looks confused, so I cover her fingers with mine, trailing them down until she's covering her clit. "Do it, babe. I want to watch."

Her face, already red from exertion, burns brighter, but she does what I've asked, and starts strumming her clit. A moan escapes her lips.

"Don't hold back, sweetheart. Fuck, that's it. That's what I want to see. Good girl, go for it."

Rocking back on my heels, I take myself in hand. As I tug at my cock, I see the sight excites her. Her fingers work harder; my strokes speed up. Her body starts bowing off the bed; my whole spine goes rigid. Her body is trembling; my muscles are taut. And then she comes with a scream at the same time as long white streams of cum shoot from my dick to cover her stomach and chest.

Gazing down at my mark on her, I swallow to keep back the moisture threatening to leak from my eyes. Unable to help myself, my palms go down, rubbing my cum into her skin, covering the marks on her breasts, and the bruises on her body. Marking her as mine, in the way only a man can do.

As I worship her body, my cock twinges again. Christ, I'm a never-emptying cum-well where this woman's concerned. Now her breathing's returned to normal, her eyes sparkle when she looks down at my cock already erect and ready, her very gaze feeling like a caress.

"I'll never get enough of you, Sam."

"Good," she encourages me on. "Fuck me like a biker, Drum. Give me all of your love."

"You sure you're ready for that, darlin'?"

The jerk of her chin is all the permission I need. I hoist her hips onto my thighs, positioning my cock at her entrance. "Up for this?"

Again, that half smile. "I'm game."

I thrust inside, holding nothing back, my balls banging against her ass. She gasps, but she asked for it. I start hammering in and out, my legs working like pistons pounding forward and back, almost brutalising her body.

Her head rolls back. "Drum, yes, Drum." Her cries only encourage me.

I'm striking that sweet spot, over and over again. Banging into her in the way that got me my name, and this woman's taking everything I've got. Her screams and sobs are egging me on as I pulverise her sweet pussy in a punishing rhythm.

"Drum, Drum..." she whimpers, as her fingers tighten, her fists grabbing the sheets beneath us.

Then her body contracts around me, her muscles choking my cock and I start thrashing, feeling yet more cum rising through my dick.

We scream our completions together. I pump and pump, wave after wave, an impossible amount of cum which just keeps on coming, as if I've an innate desire to flood her with my seed, uncaring I've come twice already.

She drains me completely; my arms shake with the effort to hold myself up. With a loud groan, I throw myself down beside her, pulling her to me and holding her tight. "Sam, oh, Sam."

"Drum," she replies, breathily. It's as though neither of us can find other words.

Closing my eyes, I will air into my tortured lungs.

Tersely I ask, "Did I hurt you?"

"No." She pants out her denial. "Drum, I can't think of words to use which could describe that."

Neither can I. It was out of this world, far out of reach of my humble vocabulary. "I've claimed you and marked you. And," I place my hand on her stomach, considering the amount of semen I've just injected inside her anything else seems impossible, "perhaps given you my child. You're mine, Sam."

Her head turns to face me, her hand caresses my cheek. "And you're *mine*, Drum. Mine. No one fucking else's."

We steal a moment to just think about the implications of

that. Air being sucked into starved lungs, our chests heaving in unison.

After a while she breaks the silence. "Drum," her voice is quiet, my name stretched out.

The tone of her voice strikes me. "Got something you need to say, babe?"

She raises herself on one elbow. She's looking down at the sheets, her hand picking at a loose thread. She looks contrite as she tells me, "I'm not a violent person, Drummer. Really I'm not."

I wonder where this is going. "You saying you want to fight me?" For some reason the thought of our bodies wrestling together makes me grin.

She offers a half smile. "No, not you, Drum. But I've got to tell you, I slapped that whore, Jill."

That's out of character. "Why?" I growl, waiting to hear the worst, knowing it had to be bad for Sam to act that way.

"She said I wouldn't be enough for you. Not that she put it quite so nicely. I said you'd have her out on her ass if she insulted me again."

I snarl, as red heat blazes through me at the thought of anyone hurting my woman, with words if not with their hands. "Too fuckin' right I will."

She nods, a small smile of satisfaction coming to her lips. That subject dropped, she gets onto another topic. "Some of the women don't want to be questioned by the FBI. I told them they didn't have to deal with them. That the club would help them get home."

Fucking hell, this woman. She puts the club whores in their place and deals with club problems. She's going to make a fucking great old lady. And... it might not be the right time or place, but that's not going to stop me asking.

"Sam, you've totally drained me, don't think I could get on my fuckin' knees right now. But I want to sew this up in every fuckin' way I can. Want you to be my wife, darlin'. Make it official."

I've stunned her. Her mouth drops open. Then she laughs, her belly shaking as the chuckles roar from her.

But she hasn't said yes.

"Sam?" It wasn't quite the reaction I'd expected.

She pushes me onto my back and throws her body over me, her body still wracked with giggles. Smoothing her hand over my forehead and tunnelling her fingers into my hair, she at last gives me a response. "I suppose that's a biker's proposal." Another chuckle. "You do know what that means, don't you? That Viper would be your father-in-law?"

"Christ, I hadn't thought about that." I mock pout.

"And Sandy, your stepmother-in-law."

I make my face fall, as though I'm reconsidering my offer. But she sees right through me, her little hand forming a fist and thumping my chest. Then her body stills, and her face grows serious. "I'd like that. I'd like to be your wife, Drummer."

CHAPTER THIRTY-SEVEN

*S*am…

I came to the Satan's Devils' compound to find my father as a way to make the loss of my mother easier. I never expected to stay, never thought I'd find love and a soon-to-be husband, and never dreamed I'd become an old lady, and the president's old lady at that. I wouldn't have considered it in my wildest dreams. But that's what's happened, and something tells me I've found my place. That this is where I'm meant to be.

Drummer's now sleeping, his face relaxed in repose. More than one person has told me I'm good for him, and I have to agree, I make him laugh, and the rusty tones when he does suggest he didn't do much of that before. I make him smile. And God, can I make him come.

If I'm not pregnant now, I know I soon will be. He seems intent to make it that way, and though the notion takes me by surprise, I don't mind at all. The thought of creating something between us, the start of a new generation fills a hole inside I didn't even know I had. *Perhaps a biker president is not exactly what you'd have wanted for me, Mom, but I know you wanted me to be happy.*

Drummer's cum is still on my body, tightening my skin as it

dries. A physical sign he's left on me, but nothing to the mark he's left on my soul. I couldn't leave him now. To do so would be to leave behind an essential part of me.

I'm still deep in thought as Drummer stirs, he stretches and yawns, and bestows such a beatific smile on me, I lose a little bit more of my heart.

He watches me for a few seconds, then his hand comes around and slaps my backside. "Time to get your lazy ass out of bed. We're needed somewhere."

"Where?"

"Up, get dressed and then you'll see."

We shower together. Still both too sated to take advantage of his large and surprising well-appointed shower, built to his specifications he tells me. He's a big man and might be a burly biker, but he does like some luxuries and the good things in life. Underneath our idle chitchat I know he's keeping something secret, something that amuses him. My intrigue makes me towel off fast, throwing on my clothes even as drops of water bead on my skin. But it won't matter, the storm has passed, heat will have returned, and I'll dry fast in the warm air.

We leave his house, taking the ATV he had stored in his garage, which I hadn't noticed before. We leave the compound via a discreet back gateway and head up into the hills. We drive for about half an hour, leaving the desert below us, and going into the forest made up of pine, fir, and spruce. Soon we're following a muddy track. It's not long before I hear voices and Drum comes to a halt.

All the brothers are here as well as the old ladies and sweet butts. Even some of the less traumatised women have made their way up. Now I can see a smaller, single file track snaking around through the trees, then I hear the commotion.

"You're not riding my fuckin' bike!"

"Come on, Prospect. I've got this. I'm not gonna be ripping it up!"

"If anyone's gonna, I'll do it."

"Fuck, man, you can barely stand."

Hearing Roadrunner and Peg arguing, I step forward to see what's going on. Drum close behind me.

"Prospect!"

"Prez?"

"Get over here."

I watch as Road slowly makes his way across, his face whiter than white, his tan almost invisible.

"Drum, he shouldn't be here." I can't help but be concerned for the man who got injured, pitting himself up against impossible odds while trying to save me.

"I know, darlin', I'm not blind. But we need his bike."

At first confused, I take a good look around and then it hits me. "You've built a dirt track?" It seems an odd thing to have done. It's recent and new, and I can't fathom why.

He answers with a simple nod.

But why do it so soon after their fight today? At first, my brow creases. Ah. Now, my momma didn't raise no dummy; I catch on fast. "You buried bodies?"

Drummer goes still, and then he barks a laugh. "Fuck, woman! Can you read my fuckin' mind? Hell, it took us hours to come up with the idea." He adds, hissing, "No one else is to know."

"I'm not stupid, Drum."

"I'm fuckin' aware of that, babe." His hands come to rest on my arms, giving me an appreciative look. He places a quick kiss on my cheek, then turns his attention to Road, who's now reached us, every step looking like it's causing him pain. "We need your bike, Prospect. You can't ride it. Be sensible."

As Road's face drops, I know exactly he feels. He's put as much love and energy into that dual sport bike as I've done with my Vincent, and part of his livelihood is earned from his winnings. But Drum obviously needs his help. A Harley's not going to be able to get around a muddy track. I make him a promise. "Hey, Road. If anything happens to it, I'll make it as good as new for you, okay?"

Road stares at me, glances up at his prez, and at last gives a slow nod. "Knowing you, Wrench, you'd make it better than good. Okay, if you personally handle the repairs..."

"At fuckin' last!" Peg pumps his fist in the air, and without further ado, steps astride the tall bike. "Fuck, this feels like a toy."

"You'll need a bit of throttle as the ground's wet, Peg, but go easy. Too much and you'll lose the front end." Road's brow creases as he gives his advice.

"I know how to ride, boy." It comes out as a growl.

Road looks at me, I shrug. We both grin.

"Here, Prospect, sit on the ATV before you fall over. You can watch the fun from here." Wraith takes his arm and helps him across.

Peg takes the dirt bike off the stand. Standing astride, he fumbles as he looks for the ignition switch, then, just as I'm about to shout out, he realises with a rueful grin and thrusts his foot down on the kick-start, a quirk of competition dirt bikes. Unused to starting his ride that way, he hasn't used enough pressure and it recoils. "Fuck, nearly lost my other fuckin' leg!" He rubs at his ankle.

As I grimace, feeling his pain, a roar of laughter bursts out—modern Harleys all have push button ignitions. I suspect if someone else tried they'd have had the same problem. Mind you, they're not trying to ride with an artificial leg.

He isn't going to give up and lifts his foot for another go.

"Give it some welly!" Sophie yells out. I think we all get what she means.

This time the engine starts with a roar. Kicking it into first, he tries to pull away. The ground is covered with a carpet of sweet smelling pine needles made even softer by the rain. Peg applies a bit more throttle and still doesn't move. He twists his hand hard, the front wheel coming off the ground, but he recovers fast, controlling the wheelie and then he's off.

The track winds up and down through the trees. At first, we can watch him, then he disappears out of sight before reappearing again. There's a drop coming down, hell, I thought he was going to come off then, but he's taking it cautiously. Now he's got to go up a steep bank; the bike topples to the side, he's got his feet down, increasing the power, loses ground then is moving again. He's made it to the top. Even over the engine noise I hear a triumphant roar. Now he's back, having completed the circuit, his eyes sparkling with delight.

"Fuck, Prospect! That was fun! I'm starting to see the fuckin' attraction."

Turning, I see Road's been covering his eyes, but seeing his bike safely back, grins at the sergeant-at-arms. "Why d'ya think I do it?"

"I'm going again." Peg seems reluctant to get off.

"I'll time you," Drum suggests. "Then I'll take a turn." As I turn to stare at him, he gives a rueful shrug.

"Oh, fuck no," Road groans behind me.

Peg takes off; we can see he's slightly faster this time. When he's in sight, Drum's watching him carefully, noting what he's doing to stay shiny side up.

"Two minutes forty," Drum yells as he comes back to the start. "My turn."

He gives his phone to me, I wait for him to be ready. Having learned from watching Peg, and of course, being used to his old vintage bikes, he uses sufficient force as he kicks down to get it to turn over. As he moves off, I click the timer. He wastes seconds getting moving, but then gets his speed up. He comes down the hill too fast, and the bike slips on its side. Drum eases himself out from underneath, brushing pine needles off and waves to show the forgiving ground had cushioned his fall. He's fine. Once we see he's alright, there's good-natured laughter at the mud-splattered president.

"Peg had two goes. I'm going again." It seems his fall hasn't deterred him.

And he's off. This time he's learned his lesson but takes the uphill faster having watched Peg's struggles. Back safe and sound, I give him his time.

"Two minutes twenty."

Flipping his finger at Peg, Drum yells, "Put that in your fuckin' pipe!"

Dart puts his hand on the bike. "I'm fuckin' trying this." They swap places. Like Peg, he has a bit of trouble with the unfamiliar kick-start.

Drum comes over to me and picks me up, swinging me up and around him. "Now that's how it's fuckin' done!"

As he plants a smacker on my lips, I laugh and push him away. "Get off me, I'm supposed to be timing Dart."

"Babe, he hasn't fuckin' figured out how to get it running yet!"

But just as he finishes speaking, Dart gets off to a flying start, but his attempts at the hill have everyone cracking up. His time, on his second run, is two minutes twenty-five.

Drum starts to boast, saying no one will beat him. It's Viper's turn next. When he comes in the last place so far, Sandy commiserates with him, his booby prize a big smacker on the lips.

"Getting slow, old man!" Drum calls out.

"Hush, Drum, that's your future father-in-law you're insulting." I hit him gently on the arm.

As he turns and his eyes blaze into me, I know it's not the race he's thinking off, but the commitment we'd just made to each other. A shout brings me back to my senses and I remember at the last second to time the next man.

One by one the bikers take their chance, both from the Tucson chapter and Snake and Red's men. Poor Road looks like he's having a fit, hardly daring to watch as his bike's receiving a hammering. Leathers are getting covered in mud, and if the idea was to make this look like a well-used dirt track, it's certainly succeeding. The bike has picked up a couple of dents, but it's alright, I'll get them out. I continue my role as timekeeper, keeping note of the scores.

Sophie hugs Wraith when he beats his prez's score by a couple of seconds, and Drum playfully punches him in the chest, enough to make him fall back.

"Sore loser, Drum?" Wraith's not hurt, he's laughing.

"Fuck off!"

Bullet starts off as though thinking he's going to prove his name, but going faster than a bullet has its pitfalls on this uneven ground. He's out of the race when he comes off and twists his ankle.

"Fucking bike." He kicks it as he walks away. "Plastic piece of Japanese crap." He shrugs off Carmen's arm and stomps off alone.

Drum raises his eyebrow, Carmen's grinning. "I'll go after him. He'll come around."

Heart's run is good. When he beats Wraith, Crystal leaps on him, circling her legs around his waist and kissing him as if he's won a major competition. She's so pumped up she yells loudly, "My man. Did you see my man fuckin' go? Did y'all fuckin' see *that?*"

"Fuckin' go, Mommy," a little voice repeats in a singsong voice.

"Oh shit, pet, I, oh." Crystal realises she better stop talking with Amy picking up her every word.

"And you blame me for teaching her wrong." Heart's laughing out loud, then chuckles even harder as both Drum and Wraith flip the bird at him and he returns the gesture.

The rest take their turns, Joker's ahead now by nearly ten seconds. Then it's almost neck and neck between him and Lady, with the latter only a second behind. Of course, the ex-Vegas boys are slapping their backs and saying how they've shown the Tucson guys how it's done. Red's beaming with pride.

Marvel steps forward. "San Diego's gonna trump both your

asses," he tells them confidently. His starting smile wiped off his face when he completes in a poor two minutes forty-five. Snake commiserates with his man.

Our lot try hard, but nobody beats Joker. His ex-prez, Red, slapping him harder on the back when each other brother fails. When the final man has completed his run, I step forward. "My turn now."

Drum looks at me in consternation. "Sam…"

"Drum?"

He shakes his head.

"Drum, I can do this." Throwing a look over my shoulder, I see Road giving me a wink.

Joker steps forward as though expecting to receive a trophy.

"Not so fast, Joker." I narrow my eyes.

"Anyone got a brain bucket? My ol' lady's going to have a go."

At the roar of laughter, I swing around to Drum, thumping his arm. "Drummer! For goodness' sake!" With one final glare at him, I go to the bike, mounting it easily and taking it off the stand. It's taller than the bikes I'm used to, but I'll be able to handle it okay. Means standing on tiptoes, though. I get it balanced and using the technique I'm well practised in with the Vincent, kick down to start the engine first time.

"Gears are on the left, Sam!"

Ignoring him and the chuckling his comment causes, I give Drum the finger and take off.

The track's been well used now, so I need to avoid the worst of the ruts. The going's quite easy in the early stages, and then there's the downhill—I take it at just the right speed, skidding a bit toward the bottom, but still well in control. Then it's the uphill, applying a bit more throttle and without falter, I'm at the top. Mud's spitting up around me, but I don't give a damn. In my element, feeling free at last, the nightmares of the last few days fading into my rearview, I twist the throttle a bit more and fly over the finish line.

Drum's staring at his phone, his eyes wide. He's shaking his head.

"Drum, my time?" It seems I need to prompt him.

But still he stays silent.

"Yeah, Prez, what was her time?"

At last, he looks up to meet my impatient gaze, another shake of his head, and then his lips curl. "One fuckin' minute fifty-eight," he calls out and then repeats it as though nobody's heard, "One fuckin' minute and fifty-eight fuckin' seconds." Now he's racing toward me; I'm still sitting on the bike. He grabs hold of my hand and raises it into the air. "The fuckin' winner is my fuckin' ol' lady!"

"You cheat, Sam? You done this before?" Peg's stomping toward me, his nostrils flaring.

"Nah, Peg. Never done this before." I pat the bike's engine. "Might do it again, though. Hey, Drum. Might get myself a dirt bike." I grin at the expression on his face.

"Think the track's gonna become a permanent fixture," Wraith observes as he steps forward to take the weight of the bike from me. "That was fun." Then his eyes narrow. "And now we've got a target to beat. How the fuck did you manage that, Wrench?"

Shrugging I tell him, "I speak engine, remember."

As Wraith steadies the bike, Drum swings me up and off and into his arms. "Fuck, Sam." Then he whispers into my ear, "You might have won the fuckin' race, Sam, you might have beaten me, but I feel like the fuckin' winner here. I won you. You're gonna be one hell of a president's ol' lady."

Yeah, I beat you Drum, but I won you, too. More important than any race.

READING ORDER

Turning Wheels
Drummer's Beat
Slick Running
Targeting Dart
Heart Broken
Peg's Stand
Rock Bottom
Joker's Fool
Mouse Trapped

Paladin's Hell (Colorado Chapter #1)

Blade's Edge

Demon's Angel (Colorado Chapter #2)
Devil's Due (Colorado Chapter #3)

Truck Stopped

Devil's Dilemma (Colorado Chapter #4)
Amy's Santa (Next Generation #1)

Ink's Devil (Colorado Chapter #5)
Devil's Spawn (Colorado Chapter #6)
Coming Soon
Being Lost (San Diego Chapter #1)
Hawk's Cry (Next Generation #2)

Note 1:

Each book can be read as a standalone, but to get the best reading experience for the Satan's Devils, read the books in the order above.

Note 2:
While the Blood Brothers series is completely separate to the Satan's Devils series, there is some crossover. Turning Wheels continues the story of a minor character who appears in Second Changes, and some characters appear in both series.

OTHER WORKS BY MANDA MELLETT

Blood Brothers – A series about sexy dominant sheikhs and their bodyguards

Stolen Lives (#1) Nijad and Cara

Close Protection (#2) Jon and Mia

Second Chances (#3) Kadar and Zoe

Identity Crisis (#4) Sean and Vanessa

Dark Horses (#5) Jasim and Janna

Hard Choices (#6) Aiza

Satan's Devils MC - Arizona Chapter

Turning Wheels (Blood Brothers #3.5, Satan's Devils #1) Wraith and Sophie

Drummer's Beat (#2) Drummer and Sam

Slick Running (#3) Slick and Ella

Targeting Dart (#4) Dart and Alex

Heart Broken (#5) Heart and Marc

Peg's Stand (#6) Peg and Darcy

Rock Bottom (#7) Rock and Becca

Joker's Fool (#8) Joker and Lady

Mouse Trapped (#9) Mouse and Mariana

Blade's Edge (#10) Blade and Tash

Truck Stopped (#11) Truck & Allie

Satan's Devils MC - Colorado Chapter

Paladin's Hell (#1) Paladin and Jayden

Demon's Angel (#2) Demon and Violet

Devil's Due (#3) Beef and Steph

Devil's Dilemma (#4) Pyro and Mel

Ink's Devil (#5) Ink and Beth

Satan's Devils MC - Next Generation

Amy's Santa (#1) Wizard and Amy

GLOSSARY

Motorcycle Club – An official motorcycle club in the U.S. is one which is sanctioned by the American Motorcyclist Association (AMA). The AMA has a set of rules its members must abide by. It is said that ninety-nine percent of motorcyclists in America belong to the AMA

Outlaw Motorcycle Club (MC) – The remaining one percent of motorcycling clubs are historically considered outlaws as they do not wish to be constrained by the rules of the AMA and have their own bylaws. There is no one formula followed by such clubs, but some not only reject the rulings of the AMA, but also that of society, forming tightly knit groups who fiercely protect their chosen ways of life. Outlaw MCs have a reputation for having a criminal element and supporting themselves by less than legal activities, dealing in drugs, gun running or prostitution. The one-percenter clubs are usually run under a strict hierarchy.

Brother – Typically members of the MC refer to themselves as brothers and regard the closely knit MC as their family.

Cage – The name bikers give to cars as they prefer riding their bikes.

Chapter – Some MCs have only one club based in one location. Other MCs have a number of clubs who follow the same bylaws and wear the same patch. Each club is known as a chapter and will normally carry the name of the area where they are based on their patch.

Church – Traditionally the name of the meeting where club business is discussed, either with all members present or with just those holding officer status.

Colours – When a member is wearing (or flying) his colours he will be wearing his cut proudly displaying his patch showing which club he is affiliated with.

Cut – The name given to the jacket or vest which has patches denoting the club that member belongs to.

Enforcer – The member who enforces the rules of the club.

Hang-around – This can apply to men wishing to join the club and who hang-around hoping to be become prospects. It is also used to women who are attracted by bikers and who are happy to make themselves available for sex at biker parties.

Mother Chapter – The founding chapter when a club has more than one chapter.

Nomad – In an outlaw MC a **nomad** is typically a member who's been given permission/instruction by the national president to enforce the laws of the club at other chapters.

Patch – The patch or patches on a cut will show the club that member belongs to and other information such as the particular chapter and any role that may be held in the club. There can be a number of other patches with various meanings, including a one-percenter patch. Prospects will not be allowed to wear the club patch until they have been patched-in, instead they will have patches which denote their probationary status.

Patched-in/Patching-in – The term used when a prospect completes his probationary status and becomes a full club member.

President (Prez) – The officer in charge of that particular club or chapter.

Prospect – Anyone wishing to join a club must serve time as a probationer. During this period they have to prove their loyalty to the club. A probationary period can last a year or more. At the end of this period, if they've proved themselves a prospect will be patched-in.

Old Lady – The term given to a woman who enters into a permanent relationship with a biker.

RICO – The Racketeer Influenced and Corrupt Organisations Act primarily deals with organised crime. Under this Act the officers of a club could be held responsible for activities they order members to do and a conviction carries a potential jail service of twenty years as well as a large fine and the seizure of assets.

Road Captain – The road captain is responsible for the safety of the club on a run. He will organise routes and normally ride at the end of the column.

Ronin – A biker who travels alone, sometimes wearing a patch denoting he's Ronin. Not affiliated to any club, but often bearing a token which will help ensure safe passage through territories of different clubs.

Secretary – MCs are run like businesses and this officer will perform the secretarial duties such as recording decisions at meetings.

Sergeant-at-Arms – The sergeant-at-arms is responsible for the safety of the club as a whole and for keeping order.

Sweet Butt – A woman who makes her sexual services available to any member at any time. She may well live on the club premises and be fully supported by the club.

Treasurer – The officer responsible for keeping an eye on the club's money.

Vice President (VP) – The vice president will support the president, stepping into his role in his absence. He may be responsible for making sure the club runs smoothly, overseeing prospects etc.

SATAN'S DEVILS MC
Brothers protecting their own

ACKNOWLEDGMENTS

Acknowledgements for Drummer's Beat

A massive 'Thank You' to my beta readers Colleen and Brandy. You guys are amazing giving up your time to read the draft. Your encouragement and support is invaluable.

Cover design and formatting by Freeyourwords.com Lia, you excelled yourself this time! I absolutely love the cover design you came up with!

Editing by Phil Henderson – thanks for helping to knock this book into shape, Phil.

Proofreading by Brian Tedesco (Pubsolvers.com). Very much enjoyed working with you.

I can't thank my husband enough for his support and encouragement. His encyclopaedic knowledge of bikes proved invaluable in writing this book.

A big thank you also goes to Maggie Kern who's re-edited this book and helped eradicate some of the errors which crept into the original.

I'm grateful to everyone who's taken the time to read Drummer's Beat. If you enjoyed it, please leave a review – writers write in a vacuum, locked away in their lonely towers. We love to know what you think of our books.

STAY IN TOUCH

Email: manda@mandamellet.com

Website: www.mandamellet.com

Sign up for my newsletter to hear about new releases in the Satan's Devils and Blood Brothers series.

Facebook reader group: https://www.facebook.com/groups/mandasbadboys/

 facebook.com/mandamellet

twitter.com/manda_mellett

ABOUT THE AUTHOR

Manda's life's always seemed a bit weird, starting with a childhood that even today she's still trying to make sense of, then losing her parents in the late teens. Going from the tragic to the bizarre, who else could be unlucky enough to have had two car accidents, neither her fault, one involving a nun, and another involving a police woman?

There isn't enough space to list everything that's happened to Manda, or what she's learned from it. But by using the rich fabric of her personal life, psychology degree, varied work experiences, and amazing characters she's met, Manda is able to populate her books with believable in-depth characters and enjoys pitting them against situations which challenge them. Her books are full of suspense, twists and turns and the unexpected.

Manda lives in the beautiful countryside of Essex in the UK, the area's claim to fame being the Wilkin's Jam Factory at nearby Tiptree. She can usually find jars of jam which remind her of home wherever she goes. As well as writing books and reading, Manda loves walking her dogs and keeping fit. She lives with her husband of over 30 years, who, along with her son, is her greatest fan and supporter.

Manda is thankful that one of the more unusual, and at the time unpleasant, turns her life took, now enables her to spend her time writing. Confirming, in her view, every cloud has a silver lining.

Photo by Carmel Jane Photography

Made in the USA
Columbia, SC
07 July 2023

20145898R00205